CELESTIAL
INVENTORIES

STEVE RASNIC TEM

ChiZine Publications

FIRST EDITION

Celestial Inventories © 2013 by Steve Rasnic Tem
Cover artwork © 2013 by Erik Mohr
Cover design © 2013 by Samantha Beiko
Interior design © 2013 by Danny Evarts

Distributed in Canada by
HarperCollins Canada Ltd.
1995 Markham Road
Scarborough, ON M1B 5M8
Toll Free: 1-800-387-0117
e-mail: hcorder@harpercollins.com

Distributed in the U.S. by
Diamond Book Distributors
1966 Greenspring Drive
Timonium, MD 21093
Phone: 1-410-560-7100 x826
e-mail: books@diamondbookdistributors.com

Library and Archives Canada Cataloguing in Publication

Tem, Steve Rasnic, 1950-
Celestial Inventories/ Steve Rasnic Tem.

Short Stories. Also issued in electronic format.
ISBN 978-1-77148-165-6

I. Title.

PS3570.E53C44 2013   C813'.54   C2013-900791-1

CHIZINE PUBLICATIONS
Toronto, Canada
www.chizinepub.com
info@chizinepub.com

Edited by Kelsi Morris
Proofread by Samantha Beiko

Canada Council   Conseil des arts
for the Arts   du Canada

We acknowledge the support of the Canada Council for the Arts which last year invested $20.1 million in writing and publishing throughout Canada.

ONTARIO ARTS COUNCIL
CONSEIL DES ARTS DE L'ONTARIO

50 YEARS OF ONTARIO GOVERNMENT SUPPORT OF THE ARTS
50 ANS DE SOUTIEN DU GOUVERNEMENT DE L'ONTARIO AUX ARTS

Published with the generous assistance of the Ontario Arts Council.

Printed in Canada

CELESTIAL
INVENTORIES

CONTENTS

THE
WORLD
RECALLED

BED SLIDE

When Frank awakened, suddenly an old man, he discovered that the words no longer came easily. Objects had lost some of their definition as their names slipped away.

He remembered the word *aphasia*, but thought it was a peculiar sexual act.

The bed was narrow, yet he couldn't find the edge of it. He could not move his arms, although he could flutter his hands like broken birds. If he twisted his head around as far as it would go, he could see another bed behind his, and another bed behind that one, rising layer after layer into an unending night. He was traveling the bottom edge of a great bed slide, the force of it pushing all sleep aside, creating ripples up and down the dream continuum, where vacationers flew without airplanes and family members refused to wear their own faces.

As a child he had never felt truly safe in bed. Beds had seemed too rich with possibility for comfort. Blankets, sheets, pillows— inside their cases were the debris left behind after centuries of nightmare erosion.

But during late adolescence his attitude changed. He made love in these beds, never comfortable anywhere else. People were born in beds and with luck they died there and surely no important decision should be made outside the confines of a bed.

In middle age he had slept much of many days away in these beds. He supposed that had been diagnostic of some grave personal crisis, but he had slept too much to figure it out.

Now he sleeps very little, and the bed is picking up speed, nudged and rocked by the countless beds pouring down the mountain of night behind him, the bed slide roaring out of the darkness with a sound like worlds collapsing, scooping him up like the arms of a mother, the arms of a lover, as he is swept away into the final sleep.

CHEESE PILLOW

Live long enough and smells go away, but the memory of them lasts forever. Live long enough and the memory of your strongest taste lingers without dissipation. His pillow was a pillow of memories. His pillow was ripe as yesterday's banquet, and had been for years. Sometimes he thought there was no reason to eat some prepared dinner when he could kiss his pillow open-mouthed like a sleep-contented child dreaming of its mother. It had dairy texture, his pillow, and was at its peak of tastiness. Visitors to his convalescent bed envied the feast which greeted him each day: luncheon sheets, milk blankets, and a cheese pillow, their tastes recalling the daily meals of living that had brought him here, a worn out gourmet.

Won't you be my cheese pillow? It was the last thing he had said to his wife on her deathbed. She had smiled and kissed him with lips of bread.

When she died she smelled like starched shirts hanging outside on a stretched cotton rope, and the rain is coming just over the apple orchard, there.

NOSE CUP

He had been asking for his nose cup all day, but the nurse paid no attention. She went on with her knitting, letter writing, peculiar sexual acts with interns and insurance agents, breast feeding of the dead while he was in desperate need of his nose cup.

"Nose cup! Nose cup!" he would cry, but she paid no attention. And virtually immobile as he was, there was nothing he could do about it, not even drink at her breast unless *she* insisted upon it. "Nose cup! Nose cup!" he would cry, as if that were the name of the horse he was betting on.

He wasn't sure which nose cup it was he had these days—he was sure his daughter had packed one for him when he left for the hospital, but that had been years ago, and by now some envious soul might have stolen his nose cup. He had no clear memory of which nose cup it could have been: the tall one with the bright red lips around the opening, the short squat one with the lime-green edge, the sharp one that left his nose bruised and bloody. It could have been any of them, and right now any of them would do, but the damned nurse would not answer his call.

The damned nurse would not answer most of his calls, as a matter of fact, preferring to attend to her own average affairs. That's what happened when you got old, he supposed, but in fact it had been happening all his life. People refused to answer his calls. Whenever his wife had been cross with him, his voice might as well have been the ambient breeze for all the attention she paid to it. His bosses had ignored his suggestions without exception, making him wonder why they bothered to keep him on at all. His son the archplumber (and what was that?—he could not remember) had always turned the other way when he was talking. His daughter drove him and carried him and nursed him those last few years at home, but it had been his body she had responded to so dutifully, not his voice.

"Nose cup! Nose cup!" he cried again, thinking of how its mere presence would soothe him. How it would contain and preserve the smells of the day. How it would bottle up his sickness and keep it from spreading. How it would take him back to an earlier time, when his mother did all the nursing, and the only things invading his body were those *he* had put there, and the smell of his own life was the most intoxicating spirit of the world.

CLOSET WEATHER

He kept telling his nurse to keep the closet door closed: inclement weather was hiding among his old coats and pants, and he certainly didn't want any of that slipping unnoticed into his room. Closet weather was the worst possible sort, even when it was sunny closet weather. Because of being forced indoors, he supposed, and crammed into such a small space. It turned upon itself, festering its intemperate wounds with squalls and tornadoes. If let out into his room it might very well do a great deal of damage. Closet weather had no sense of boundaries. Closet weather had no sense of embarrassment.

He could hear it now behind the closet door: gnashing, weeping, filling his shoes with tears and hail.

KEY TREE

He asked the doctor to order a key tree for his room. He supposed hospital administration made the final decision, but perhaps if they thought it was of medical benefit the doctor's recommendation would influence them. His doctor was the self absorbed sort, however, always nodding and smiling at him, so he really had to speak up and use his best salesmanship to convince the man of the benefits of a key tree.

"We had one in our house in New Jersey," he explained. "My wife was skeptical at first. 'What do we need all those keys for?' she asked. She was a woman. She didn't understand. The keys would drop to the floor and make these little shiny piles on the carpet. If you didn't pick them up and use them right away they would tarnish, lose some of their definition. And of course if they lost too much definition they wouldn't fit anything. I tried to tell her, but she would just complain about the clutter. 'Clanky, clinky clutter!' she called it.

"After awhile she came around, though. She began to see the benefits of having a key for everything. I'd known I'd wanted such a thing since childhood. The bigger the better. I didn't care that it made the living room floor sag. First thing in the morning I would pick the freshest key, the one that grew near the top, and use it to unlock the first wonders of the morning. A series of keys got the toaster and the stove to work. And after much thought I'd choose a key to unlock a smile, or a grimace of determination, whatever was required.

"After a time my wife learned to use the keys quite well. She had keys for all manner of small satisfactions. She stayed content.

"I could never find the key for money, however, or the one for courage. I used to stay up nights worrying that I had missed them, that they had fallen off and rotted before I'd had the sense to pick them up."

The doctor had seemed unimpressed, even when the old man presented the key to his constipation, and an enema proved no longer necessary.

WINDOW LAMP

"Turn it off!" he cried out in the middle of the night. But no one would come to help him. So he had to stare at the window floating in the middle of his hospital room, the one that illuminated his life as it had been, when there had been friends to visit, when there had been friends alive to visit.

"Turn it off!" he cried, but the window continued to burn brightly, an endless vista of the past stretching within its narrow frame, until he thought he would go blind from it all.

The next morning they found him asleep on the floor by his bed, his arm stretched overhead, his hand clutching an invisible cord. A nurse went to the window by his bed and opened it, and the old man woke up in the light.

ARMCHAIR BRUSH

This is what had gotten him into the nursing home in the first place. This armchair brush which now lay in the bottom drawer of his bureau, underneath the socks and underwear he no longer wore. He'd gotten it for his favourite armchair, the one his wife had bought him: "You're always standing around, bothering me. You need a place to sit. A good, comfortable place to sit so maybe you'll stay there awhile and leave me alone."

A heavy brown chair with plush seat, back, and unusually high sides so that he might nestle in for the day. So heavy the chair was that there was no thought of ever moving it: the delivery people brought it into the middle of the parlour, set it there on the Persian rug with its shades of multicoloured effluent, and there it would stay. And there he would sit, day after day hour after hour, moving so seldom he began to think his wife had plotted some sort of premature atrophy for him by getting him this chair. He sat through her cooking and cleaning and her secret activities which she'd been freed to do now that he was trapped by the chair. He got up once, he remembered, to go to her deathbed, speaking of cheese pillows, but then he sat through her death which he didn't discover for hours as he was trapped in the chair. His daughter tried to get rid of it after his wife's funeral but he stopped her. He was used to it by now and besides, it was the last thing his dear wife had ever bought him.

But it was only a few months after her death that the brown pile of the comfortable armchair began to grow, grow like a woman's hair in the fullness of her youth. Then grow as quickly as in a dream, several inches per nap, a foot or more overnight. In no time it covered the floor, crept out into the hall, strangled two of the cats who'd wandered in after his wife's death because he couldn't get to them in time. He tried cutting the armchair's luscious long hair, but it grew faster than his arthritic fingers could snip.

So it was that he came to purchase the armchair brush, sensing a need which he could, if he remembered well enough, fulfill. Just as he had brushed his wife's long hair when they were first married and so much in love, he brushed the long hair of his armchair, singing to it and talking of the days gone by.

Until they found him, and took it all away.

FORK FILE

He had constructed the fork file a few years before his wife's death, thinking that the old age which appeared to be threatening them both might be delayed, even circumvented, if they could insert some better organization into their lives. But the fork file was dangerous, or so his wife had complained when she was jabbed by some naughty fork while rifling the file for a spoon or a clean pair of socks.

"No wonder!" he'd protested. "It's a goddamn fork file, Elaine! No spoons, no socks, forks only!" And she'd stared at him with the disdain of someone whose patience has packed its bags and run away with a bible salesman.

So the fork file had become his project, and he'd spent hours each day on it, polishing row after row of tines, organizing the forks smallest to largest, most broad to most narrow. He wouldn't permit Elaine to set the table with any of them, since he couldn't bear to have them soiled, so they'd had to do without forks at mealtimes, which made the consumption of meats and baked potatoes a far more difficult proposition, but somehow they managed, and he had something nicely organized and impressive to show off on those increasingly rare occasions when company came to call.

KITCHEN TABLE CLOCK

The kitchen table had always kept good time, even though Elaine wasn't always interested in the times it had to tell. Really, it was simply a matter of sitting at the table long enough, and staring at its shiny surface at just the right angle, and then everything might be revealed.

"Time to mow the lawn! The kitchen table says so."

"It's the middle of winter," Elaine would grumble. "There's a foot of snow on the ground."

"Then we'll just shovel off the goddamn snow! The kitchen table doesn't lie about these things. Time's a wastin'! The kitchen table says so."

So Elaine would finally relent and give him the key to the garage where he might find the snow shovel and the mower.

"Time to buy us some fly swatters. Kitchen table says so."

"How many fly swatters?" Elaine would ask wearily. He hoped the kitchen table would tell him it was time for her to go to bed soon. The poor woman looked completely worn out. But the kitchen table rarely clocked the events of his wife's life. It was obviously far more interested in him. He hoped his wife didn't feel too badly about that.

"About thirty. No thirty-two. Thirty-two flyswatters, that's what the kitchen table says."

"Expecting a massive fly infestation, are we?" He didn't always care for the tone of Elaine's voice, but she had her problems. The kitchen table refused to give her the right time.

"No, Elaine. Potato bugs. The kitchen table says it's potato bugs this time. Thousands of them."

NEWSPAPER LADLE

Every morning he would take out his newspaper ladle and stir the barrel full of newspapers by their front door. That morning's paper would always be on top, so he had to stir the papers well to get the news mixed thoroughly. When news was mixed improperly he could not achieve a good perspective on the events of the day. When news was mixed improperly bad days tended to cling together, making for bad weeks.

He'd always read his news randomly, just as likely perusing some article about a conference of police chiefs from last month as today's piece about a summit of super powers. He didn't see this as particularly eccentric. Viewed over a length of time, news events were fairly predictable. Good and bad events, even surprising events, were distributed in the expected ways. To the young, virtually everything was a surprise. Old people knew better. But reading the papers day by day one could lose sight of the even distribution of fates. Some days a succession of truly terrible events might occur. Enough such days and a person might forget anything good ever happened.

Over time moisture and dirt would get into the newspaper barrel and the newsprint would begin to crumble, disintegrate, clump together into doughy balls of word fragments and abstract black and white photographs. The newspaper ladle proved exceptionally effective at this point, mixing these ingredients until entirely new events, more hopeful and interesting events, appeared in the bowl of the ladle. "Flowers rocket presidency!" he would read gleefully. "Old landfills achieve Dow Jones!"

Sometimes he would announce these new and improved news events to the neighbourhood, but the only response he ever received was the closing of curtains, the dropping of shades. "Well, just kill the messenger!" he'd shout at their suppressed houses, and return to his stirring.

MIRROR BOOK

It was the only artefact he had from his father. Heavy pages of polished metal welded to a series of brass hinges: if you weren't careful turning its pages you might cut yourself grievously. In fact he did just that once when he did not like what he read on a particular page.

"The most important thing," his father used to tell him, "is the face you show the world." To find that face, all he had to do was look it up in the book.

The surprising thing was how that face changed from page to page, as if turning the pages of this mirror book moved him forward and backward through time. He couldn't always be sure in which direction he was going: his face was alternately wrinkled and smooth, but seemingly in no particular pattern. A young man, he had the creased brow of a man decades older. An old man, he had a baby's full and rosy cheeks.

He had known little of his father all those years—the man had had no hand in raising him. All he'd imagined was a distant figure with an outrageous sense of humour.

In fact he had completely forgotten what his father had looked like in pictures until now, when he finally turned to the last page in his mirror book. There the old man smiled at him, winking, no doubt wondering why it had taken him so long just to turn the page and say hello.

COLANDER HAT

He could not remember where he might have gotten the thing—perhaps he had been required to wear it during one of his many hospital stays—but what struck him most about it now was its terrible impracticality. The metal of it was much too rigid for true comfort, and its numerous holes permitted the weather to moisten or even freeze what little hair he had left. It had never been a comfortable or stylish hat from what he could remember, and people stared at him rudely when he wore it outside the house.

But however he might have obtained this odd piece of apparel, he didn't want to waste it, so he took to wearing it inside the house while watching TV, at the dinner table, a few times even in bed. His wife complained half-heartedly, but he was convinced that secretly she envied him his colander hat. After all, she was always borrowing it to drain the spaghetti noodles.

Sometimes at night the most intense of his thoughts from that day would gather just under the surface of his hat before escaping through the holes. They would rise to the ceiling then and chase each other playfully until the endless cream of the ceiling might absorb them so that he could go to sleep. During those quiet, relaxing times he could say to himself, "Thank God! Thank God for my colander hat!"

DRAIN SHOES

His wife had told him that they would make his feet much more comfortable. She had taken to picking out all his clothes for him and he was ready to accept that she always seemed to know best. If left to his own wits he might choose something totally inappropriate to wear upon his feet.

Healthy feet depended on good drainage. He believed he'd actually read that in a magazine somewhere. If sweat was permitted to accumulate around the pores of the feet, a good deal of rotting might occur.

But one day the drain shoes clogged and his feet began to swell. His wife was out of the house, so he went shoe shopping without her. A small, timid clerk was dusting ladies' pumps. Frank grabbed him by the collar and pulled him close. "I need new shoes," he growled. "My wife bought these shoes here and now they're killing me."

A shadow of alarm crossed the shoe clerk's face. "I'll . . . I'll see what I can do." He fell to his knees and as he fiddled with the drain shoes Frank felt a series of strong emotions, culminating in an almost sexual relaxation which started in the balls of his feet and spread throughout his body. He could hear the clerk weeping as he frantically made adjustments, but the man's tears did not make him at all nervous. Whatever the man was doing, it felt wonderful.

"These drain shoes are just terrific," he told his wife that night over dinner.

"Sure, Frank," she replied, and finished eating her carrots.

DUST TIME

Until that day he had never thought of dust, never felt the dust, had never even seen dust as far as he could remember. But when he awakened that morning dust was all he could think about.

On the ceiling were great continents of dust. Dust lined the insides of lampshades. Dust baked on the hot bulbs. Dust lay over his sheets and pillows in shapes vaguely reminiscent of crime scene body outlines.

Dust powdered his hair, plugged his ears, coated the soft inside of his mouth.

Trails of dust led him from room to room, outside to the car and back again. He took off his shoes. A silt of fine dust covered his bare soles and he was alarmed to discover that layer by layer his skin was crumbling into powder.

He slipped on the thickest pair of woolen socks he could find and went in search of other deposits of dust. There were many more: dust in the kitchen cabinets, dust painting the worn seats of his chairs, dust coating his books and photograph albums, dust filling his wife's eyes when she looked at him.

She always said he didn't listen to her, he didn't focus. This time he really tried, but the dust swallowing her tongue made her impossible to understand.

Every other month or so an old friend of his would die. Could this be their dust, their way of making sure he remembered them?

Not that he blamed them—he desperately wanted to be remembered himself. He would not settle for mere dust.

If he avoided mirrors and clock faces maybe the dust wouldn't be noticeable, would blend in with all the petty little deteriorations of the day. So he sat down in a chair in the middle of the living room, eyes and head straightforward, and committed himself to be oblivious to time.

Dust slowly filled his eyes until he saw through a permanent grey haze. Then he knew that his own personal dust time had arrived.

NEWSPAPER CURTAIN

During the latter part of middle age he became much more concerned with matters of efficiency. Everything in life took up entirely too much time, and he wasn't sure he had the time to waste. He also became almost obsessed with the wasting of our natural resources, which seemed to him to be an extension of his concerns about wasting time. Time itself, surely, was not only the most valuable resource, but also the most personal.

He began carrying around a stopwatch so that he might time meals, trips to the bathroom, the time spent making love to his wife. All might be trimmed of excess seconds, minutes, even a whopping half-hour here and there. It was simply a matter of discipline, and certainly great discipline would be required if he hoped to make it into old age.

This was all fine with his wife, even the curtailed love making ("It's nothing like it used to be, anyway.") Surprisingly it was the newspaper curtain which became a source of friction between them.

He'd erected the newspaper curtain in order to make the most of the time he spent sitting at meals or simply walking about the house, travelling from one room to the next. The frame of it he fashioned from coat hangers. The bottom of the frame followed the contour of his shoulders. With the central gutter of the paper firmly clamped between a series of wires, other wires could be used to turn the pages. In this way he might study a particular column of news for hours if he so desired, or turn the pages so rapidly they tore, if that was how he felt about the day.

"Get your head out of the paper!" she'd shout. Then, "Get the paper out of your head!"

She never understood. How an event forgotten is an event wasted. How sad it was when the ecology of personal tragedy was ignored.

PLANT COMPUTER

It was no good at counting or tracking his investments, but it always seemed to know if the sun was shining or if he might expect rain that day. His plant computer had grown on the windowsill since both his children had been little. His daughter bought it for him one Father's Day, with money saved from three bake sales (Play Doh cookies) and the proceeds from one weekend's lemonade stand.

"You always tell us plants know more than they're telling," Marti said, handing over the pot. "Maybe this one will whisper its secrets to you! I already talked to it. I told it you were a good Daddy and it should tell you *everything* it knows!"

So the plant computer sat on his bedroom windowsill and he watered it religiously. It stayed healthy but did not grow—in fact he had no clear idea how to take care of it since he didn't know what kind it was. It didn't show up in any of the plant books from the library and Marti couldn't remember where she'd purchased the thing.

Good Daddy or no, he never really adequately thanked her for the plant. He never adequately told her how much he loved her. Nor did he even understand how much he loved her. She was his daughter. She was female. And he'd never had any understanding of women. She grew up, and except for occasional phone calls and letters home, he had very little contact with her after that.

"What has happened to my daughter?" he asked the plant computer.

In answer it grew and grew, quickly doubling its size.

"How much does she love me?" was his second question. In reply the plant computer doubled its size again.

"She's *mine*!" he shouted at the plant. "Where is she?"

And the plant uprooted itself, casting itself out through the window, where it joined the endless greenery below, becoming indistinguishable from the mass.

TYPEWRITER BLOOD

He used to type everything, afraid his handwriting might reveal secrets. Not that he believed he had any secrets—the really scary thing was that someone might be able to uncover secrets he did not have. But to type without revealing things unintentionally required focus and determination. It required that he hit the keys evenly and firmly in order to force away innuendo, to drown out surprise by means of the elevated key clatter.

So he took lessons and constantly refined his techniques, retyping meaningless lists into the night. But occasionally something would appear in the typescripts to disturb him—the name of a lover long dead, a bluntly-stated opinion he hadn't even realized he had, a recipe for murder—and he would have to begin his typing all over again to eliminate all possibility of errors intended or implied.

These exercises made his fingers strong and supple. The typewriters, the sleek black or grey machines, fared far worse. Typing instructors eventually refunded his tuition, barring him from their classes due to destruction of class equipment. Keys snapped off, typeface arms bent and jammed.

"But typing is in my blood!" he would declare outside the locked classroom doors. Inside, his instructors knew better. Inside, they had the ruined machines which proved the blood was in his typing.

BOOK SCREW

By the time he'd entered his thirties he'd pretty much stopped reading for pleasure, concluding that most people—professional writers most of all—inevitably lied when they put words down on paper. Perhaps they had no intention of lying, but it always happened just the same. The lies might be exciting or placating, but they were still lies, and they annoyed him. Not that he was completely immune to falsehoods himself—to have thought so would have been the most arrogant of lies.

Then a friend who worked in a library introduced him to the adjustments made possible by the book screw. "I feel sorry for you," the friend had said one night, teary-eyed. They'd been drinking together for hours, journeying from bar to bar across the west side of town. "So I'm going to tell you about this one thing, but you have to promise to keep it to yourself. Big, big secret. I'd lose my job."

Out of his jacket pocket he'd pulled a small hardcover book and demonstrated the book screw. Most commonly found on the spine of the book, obscured by the publishing company's logo, the book screw could be tightened or loosened to fit a wide variety of settings and calibrations.

Frank took the book home with him. He bought more books— he located their adjusting screws.

He soon discovered that if he wanted more action, more sex, more violence, dirty words, there were settings for all those things. If he wanted more truth, there was a proper setting for that as well.

Not that he ever used it.

MAILBOX TREE

At the end of his street grew a mailbox tree.

It hadn't always been so. When he and his wife had first moved in, certainly, there had been no such vegetation. Someone had to have planted it. At one time he had assumed the mailbox tree had some sort of official status with the post office department. Occasionally people went to the tree and came away with things in their hands. He'd always wondered what determined who did or did not receive their mail there.

So one day he intercepted his local carrier at the door and asked, "Why do some people get their mail at the mailbox tree and others do not?" Now that he was actually asking the question, putting the mystery into words, he felt somewhat slighted that they did not get their mail at the mailbox tree. He felt discriminated against.

"What? What tree is that, sir?"

"The one on the corner, with all the mailboxes attached to it."

The mail carrier shrugged. "Never noticed it. Maybe some kids put it together, I mean playing around, you know? Maybe those are birdhouses on the tree, or, hey, houses for their dolls. Like a doll tree house?"

That day he walked down to the corner to examine the mailbox tree. They weren't birdhouses or dollhouses—they were mailboxes, and each had someone's name on it. He was startled to find a mailbox with his name on it.

He looked around to see if anyone was watching, then pulled down the front lid of the box and peeked inside. A dusty letter lay on the bottom. He reached in cautiously, fearful of a nasty paper cut, and pulled out the letter.

According to the return address it was from himself. Addressed to himself. He looked at the postmark: many years into the future.

He opened the letter and read it. It was one sentence, scribbled, barely legible:

Beware the bed slide!

COFFEE TABLE AQUARIUM

His wife had bought it at a yard sale: a large mahogany coffee table with an aquarium built in. Back then she was always finding bargains to fill their sparsely furnished apartment. She said the coffee table aquarium made a great conversation piece, but they soon discovered it mostly stopped conversation.

Frank would look down through the glass top of the table with its scattered air holes (a removable lid permitted feeding) and the fish would stare up at him with expressions of disgust. He became convinced they didn't like the magazines he subscribed to, or the coffee table books he had purchased on "Great Clocks of the World." When it came time to feed them his wife took over, as the fish refused to respond to any food he personally sprinkled into the tank.

Eventually the fish died, of course, and he talked his wife into replacing them with a bed of sand, cacti, and scattered colourful stones. Now and then he would open the lid and pour a few ounces of water inside: a god bringing rain to the desert.

There came times, however, when he'd be reading a magazine or one of his coffee table books on the glass top, and he'd peer into the glass and see one of those old fish staring up at him with a scowl on its face. Sometimes there would be several of them, floating in the hot desert air, their skin dry and flaking away, waiting for the rain only he could bring.

WHISTLE UNDERWEAR

They'd been married only a few years when his wife gave him the whistle underwear for Christmas. It had been a joke on her part, of course, and she was quite alarmed when it became plain that he liked wearing the underwear. Some nights he would rush down to the basement washer himself—and he'd never done his own laundry before—anxious to launder the shorts so that he might wear them again the next day.

The whistle underwear played various tunes, apparently in random order. He became particularly fond of its Rogers and Hammerstein selection.

Eventually the underwear wore out, as such things do, but for ever after he would whistle merrily when changing his clothes.

FRUIT PICTURE

When he was a teenager he'd beg his mother for a television, but she would direct him to the fruit picture instead. On their dining table she always kept a huge bowl of fruit, and this bowl always had at least two or three fresh pieces, and two or three old pieces, souring pieces, pieces that were starting to get bugs on them. And that was a necessary combination. Because if you had all fresh fruit, or all spoiled fruit, you didn't get the same tensions, you didn't get the transitions. And those were the qualities that put the pictures into your head.

Probably most teenagers wouldn't have put up with such craziness from their moms, but he wasn't like most teenagers. He would sit at the table and watch the fruit picture for hours: a few tiny bugs leaving a recent rupture in the dark brown area of the pear, corruption spreading almost undetectably across the surface of the apple, darkness rising through the plump flesh of the banana.

The changes were just that subtle, but when you reached the end, when he was left staring at a desiccated, rotted bowl of fruit, a cascade of memory was triggered, and suddenly he was weeping over all that he had ever lost, or due to lack of imagination, had never attempted to grasp.

CELLAR SOCKS

They were the only socks he ever wore as a child. Although his mother insisted on doing his laundry, she never touched his cellar socks: he kept them hidden, in the cellar, down in the dark where they belonged.

Cellar socks were cool on the feet, a little too large, in order to accommodate the atmosphere that always tagged along with them: mushrooms, disgraced underwear, dreams not to be spoken aloud. He put his cellar socks on just before leaving for school each morning, always wearing long pants, even in hot weather, to conceal the grey of cellar that wrapped his ankles.

"Why are children your age so stubborn about bathing?" his mother would ask, and he just smiled as if she had no chance of understanding. Adults had outgrown the need for odour, had lost a child's fine-tuned appreciation of it. For a child pungent smells were like candy: sharp and specific on the tongue.

BATH TUB KNIFE

He bought the knife from a friend after a week of watching old mystery movies. The victims in these movies were usually young women caught in bathtubs behind white doors that had been carelessly left unsecured, but it might be difficult for a near-sighted deviant to tell a young man with long hair from a young woman from behind, so he thought it best that he buy the knife just in case. It came in an attractive waterproof sheath which he hid under the sudsy water like some sort of deadly water snake. Every time he heard a creaking of the floorboards outside the bathroom door he'd put his hand down on it and make himself ready.

Not once did anyone ever open the door, except for his mother who berated him for leaving it unlocked. He threw the knife away after an incident in which he'd been playing German submarine and accidentally nicked his special place, which would forever seem a bit less special after that.

SPIT MAP

When he was eight years old his mother took his crayons away for drawing on the walls, so he made himself a spit map showing all his secret hiding places. He'd put some lemon juice in his mouth then tried to spit it out onto white paper and draw with his fingers to show the landmarks and directions required. Then once it dried he could read the map by holding it over a light bulb.

What he liked best about his spit map were the splotches and lines he didn't make on purpose—they were just the accidental things that happened when he spat. He believed there were great and wonderful things marked by these accidental sprays, if he could just figure out how to read them.

FECES PANTRY

Mommy had a feces pantry where she kept every poo poo he'd ever made, each one weighed and wrapped in pretty paper, and then she wrote the date on the paper, and the number, and weight. The feces pantry was like a big refrigerator that kept all the packages nice and cold. The feces pantry stood right next to the avocado refrigerator in the kitchen.

"Look look!" Mommy cried, showing him a teeny little package. "It's your number one number two!"

TREE KNOB

The trees in their back yard were old and all covered with big bumps. Mommy said that the trees were sick, that trees got diseases just like people did.

But Frank knew the big bumps were knobs, and when he got bigger he would pull and pull until the trees opened so that he could go inside and play. And maybe that's where his daddy had gone and if he went there he would see his daddy again.

But he wouldn't tell Mommy.

FLOOR VEGETABLES

There were all kinds of good things on the floor he could eat. There were jelly babies and broken crackers and dust bunnies and marbles and pennies and paper. He decided the marbles were too big and hard.

Paper was the best vegetable he ever ate. It tasted just like paper!

BELLY CHIME

Everybody had a belly chime, but Mommy had the very best belly chime. If he put his ear right on her belly and listened real hard he could hear her heart laughing!

OVEN TONGUE

The oven tongue was big and white and hot like the sun. Mommy put water and flowers in and the oven rolled out bread on its hot hot tongue!

WINDOW EYES

Every new day the windows looked at him until they got tired of looking at him and they closed and Mommy told them all a story and Frankie and the windows all went to sleep. Until the very next day when everything was bright and warm again and the windows looked so hard at him they hurt his eyes.

WHISTLE LIGHT

The whistle came from a place a long long way away and it got louder and louder until it made everything so white, so bright, and then there was Frankie just like he'd always been there, and nobody could quite believe he wouldn't be there forever.

THE DISEASE ARTIST

"[B]ecause I couldn't find the food I liked."
—Franz Kafka, "A Hunger Artist"

The hardest thing is finding the right way to end. You are weak and in pain, the degree of weakness and pain dependent upon how many of the modern amelioratives you've decided to apply to whatever ancient or largely extinct illness you've selected for the core of your performance. Too many and your act fails to convince, too few and you are so distracted by discomfort and imminent mortality you lose the perspective necessary to make the performance an art.

He could feel Mickey, his lover of two decades, hovering in the wings off-camera. This *was* a broadcast performance, was it not? For the moment he could not remember, and there was too much sweat in his eyes for him to see clearly. He coughed up a glob of blood and felt it trickle down his chin. The hemorrhagic symptoms had always been the most difficult for Mickey to witness—somewhat strange in a medical professional, but maybe, with modern fluid control, lower level attendants encountered minimal blood outside its proper vessel. Mickey hovered, ready to end the performance prematurely, to apply more neural blockers, to end the mess. Mickey had always hated mess. It made them an odd couple.

Spread-eagled on the see-through bed, tilted steeply as if to launch into the crowd—the position was designed to display the plague tumours in the groin and armpits, a balanced selection of egg- and apple-sized, a variety of buboes, boils, knobs, kernels, biles, blisters, blains, pimples, and wheals.

The lower portion of the bed would be thoroughly smeared with blood and diarrhea by now. The stench would be terrible, but some paid extra for an olfactory broadcast. People in the Dark Ages had believed they were being killed by a magical change in the very composition of the air. Back then everything had smelled, everything had been a mess. Here, all the stage techs would be wearing filters in their nasal passages, Mickey's the most powerful. Jerome wore the most porous filter possible, to experience his condition thoroughly, but not be overwhelmed by it.

"It's time to end this one." Mickey in his ear like the voice of the medieval god.

"Not yet," he sub vocalized. "I haven't reached the moment yet."

"Death isn't a moment, Jerome. Death is forever."

Jerome knew his smile would look like either a grimace or delirium. "Not that moment. That peaceful moment when you understand what it means to be mortal."

"Save the bullshit for the interviews, okay? Let's get out of here—your vitals are looking a bit less artful."

Jerome blinked rapidly until his vision cleared. "I want to see some of the audience first."

God sighed dramatically in his ear. "It's your show."

The air in front of him was suddenly layered with images of crowds, small groups, individuals lounging in comfortable chairs, just a selection of those who permitted, or demanded, a two-way feed. Jerome recognized a number of the regulars: a wizened old man in antique lounging pyjamas, the middle-aged French couple with their three teenagers, a small group of adolescents, several people with the image of The Disease Artist as the biblical Job emblazoned on the front of their robes along with the inscription *He destroys both the blameless and the wicked. JOB 9:22.*

Despite his convictions about the importance of his performances, he believed there were things children did not need to see, but he'd had little luck controlling their access. An increasing portion of his following consisted of children and teens, with particular interest from The Filthies. Having decided to forego contemporary personal hygiene technologies in favour of an unwashed look, the Filthies professed a belief in the "natural realities" of dirt and odour, and claimed that the bulk of contemporary society had removed itself from the "real" world.

"You put this stuff out there," Mickey would say, "and you have to live with the fact that people are going to make of it what they will."

Normally he would end a performance simply by closing his eyes for thirty seconds or so. Often at that point, the transformation of his body would appear to accelerate, skin turning colour and erupting, sometimes showing actual decay faked within the transmission in order to show the eventual progress of the disease.

Sometimes a private client would request a demonstration of old fashioned embalming techniques after the disease had completed its work. Such demonstrations were completely canned, differing from each other only in the diseased appearance of the apparently dead body. He'd never told anyone that these embalming shows were essentially reruns, but then no one had ever asked.

The children's stares were attentive, questioning. This time he just started crying. Somewhere in his head God cried "Cut!"

From *The Disease Artist: A Performance Chronicle*:

His first performances were in prisons, for the population at large, or sometimes for an individual inmate whose crime was particularly heinous. In perfect safety, of course, his act broadcast from a studio to protect him from the inmates and the inmates from the disease he had chosen to nurse along and bring to some spectacular and dramatic conclusion.

These performances, not surprisingly, were somewhat controversial. It seemed now that there were as many prisons in the world as universities, with a commensurate number of advocates and activists. Everyone had at least one friend or relative in such an institution, and the common belief was that the performances of the Disease Artist constituted cruel and unusual punishment.

The warden who had ordered the performances claimed they cheered the inmates by demonstrating how much worse their conditions could be, and by putting them in touch with the "absolute value" of life itself.

The Disease Artist had his doubts—he could see the look on the faces of his captive audience when Ebola made him cry tears of blood. But at least he was performing, and that was what mattered. He appeared in a black-barred cage, pleased with how the backdrop showed off his poses.

The Disease Artist always made his talents accessible to members of the scientific community. But he insisted that they pay like any other customer.

As he passed through the restaurant Jerome could hear the intermittent whoosh of air jets: scent and disinfectant, so prevalent anymore that people rarely noticed them. Jerome noticed them. With each of his steps a push of air followed. He'd stop, and the jets in his immediate vicinity would stop. He had long believed that this daily orchestra of nozzle and pump paid him particular attention, tracking his progress through the world. When he'd start walking again, the hissing breath of dozens of hidden vents pursued him.

Intent on his lunch of steam, Mickey appeared not to notice his arrival. Mouth open over the wide nozzle, careful to avoid accidentally grazing his straining lips against the spout, he inhaled deeply. No mess, no worry, nothing to mar the teeth or stain the mouth.

"Have you ever thought," Jerome said, "about what it takes to turn a cow into steam? I mean the mechanics of it, what they have to *do* to that cow?"

Mickey glanced up, closed the spout. "Jerome, don't start." He wiped his lips carefully with a disposable disinfect, although there was nothing to wipe. "This is beef now. Beef, Jerome. I can't remember the last time I saw a cow."

Jerome glanced at the menu, as usual couldn't find anything he liked, put it down again. "I'm doing cholera next week," he said. "Symptoms show up in 12-48 hours so you'll need to infect me at the last minute. I'll spend the next few days preparing mentally."

"Cholera's old news. You've done it half a dozen times already."

"It was important," Jerome said. "It was the world's first global disease. India to Russia to Europe. It was a full partner with the Industrial Revolution."

"People didn't know how to handle their excrement. It made its way into everything, including the drinking water." Mickey inserted his fingertips into his front pocket, which buzzed as sonics scrubbed the fingernails and tips. When he removed them they looked as transparent as glass. "I'll get everything ready. But don't let this one go on too long. You're doing too many performances. Your resistance is down.

"It's what I do." He wrapped his arms around Mickey, felt him shrinking away in aversion. Jerome could not remember the last time he had really held Mickey. As if Mickey's very flesh feared that some of him might rub off.

Mickey modified the cholera strain so that the illness would last a week and a half rather than the usual two days, giving him more time to ease into the role, and time for more people to attend. This tampering was well documented, of course, but no one seemed to mind. Ticket sales, especially for the live seating, were way up. Several entertainments concerning the early nineteenth century had been popular recently, and the kids, especially the Filthies, liked the clothes from that period. Whole troops of them climbed into the cramped seats. Jerome didn't believe anyone should be too comfortable at one of his performances, so he controlled the seating where he could. He also didn't like to see the same people in the audience for extended periods of time, but he gave discounts for repeat tickets.

Some people wanted to see The Disease Artist for a short visit each day, to note the subtle progress of the disease and form their own appreciation of its changes. Some liked to sit in the audience for an eight-hour stretch, content to listen to The Disease Artist's own chronicle of symptoms and perceptions. Many appreciated most his careful attention to details and set design. For the cholera epidemic he had replicated a Paris of costume balls and mass graves.

And for a small additional charge they could touch the bare flesh of The Disease Artist himself. All inoculations included.

"It chose its victims erratically and suddenly," he announced, gesturing toward his legs and rib cage. "See how the skin becomes black and blue, how the hands and feet shrink within their gloves of skin." Suddenly he collapsed under the pain of extreme muscular cramps. The audience gasped and pressed closer.

Jerome felt his mind slip in and out of dementia much like a change of clothes. Long ago he'd recognized that first putting on a new disease was like putting on a new suit, being acutely aware of where it fit and where it didn't, in general feeling a little uncomfortable, and not quite yourself. But eventually the suit becomes you, and you gradually become something other: a lizard or a bird or a dragon. You become the body trying to find its kinship with the world. Through disease he had become the universe temporarily made conscious, so that the universe might know its own suffering.

He opened his eyes. People were rushing around. A small girl had crawled forward, trying to kiss him. "No!" he screamed. Trying to push himself away from the child, he had a sudden vision of filth leaving the body, of oils and hair and a variety of blood products pulled skyward in a silent exodus of fluids and skin flakes and white cells and sweat and this dew of urine and fecal fractions rising out of the mass of humanity and smearing the lens of God's eye.

He blinked. Blinked again. God's lips to his ears. "I'm getting you out of here," Mickey whispered.

"The problem, the problem is . . ." He felt himself choking.

"Jerome, calm down!"

"The problem is people have forgotten how to honour their mortality."

Jerome's sister had died five years ago, just before the height of his popularity. One of Mickey's colleagues at the hospital had called to say she was failing, but by the time Jerome reached the hospital his sister had already passed, to use the old word now back in common parlance. He almost didn't recognize her, wrapped in that thick, bluish, so called "life blanket" the hospitals always used. The blanket appeared to have its own respiratory and circulatory systems, breathing in and out with groaning sighs and subtly changing shade like a living thing. It supplied oxygen and some medication, but more importantly absorbed the mess: the fluids, the odour.

Of course a death blanket was what it actually was—it was the clothing the contemporary dead person was expected to wear. But Jerome thought his sister looked better than she had in years. And that there was something terribly wrong with that.

He stepped up and kissed her on the lips. She seemed dry as a mummy, liable to flake away at any moment, that the blanket had taken something out of her.

He was struck by how thick the blanket was, how organic—it looked like some great flat fish or manta ray. Tentatively he reached down and touched the thing. It felt vaguely fish-like. He could feel something like scales. It seemed to push toward him slightly, gradually gripping his finger, then letting go, as if realizing he wasn't on the day's menu. *Sorry,* he thought, *some day you'll get your chance. But you already know that, don't you?*

He lifted the blanket away from her. He picked her up gently and carried her to the window, an astonishing thing to do. Her body in his arms was lighter than his memories of her.

The Disease Artist watched as images of himself washed across the bedroom wall, having followed him there from every other wall in the apartment. Mickey had always insisted that they must keep informed. The coverage was of the panic at last night's *Cholera!* performance. Suddenly the images focused in on an old interview: he marvelled at how young he looked. Since then he'd accumulated a number of scars he had chosen not to repair.

The caption along the bottom read *Interview excerpt, The Bulletin:*

Q: Do you feel pain when you take on the full symptomology of a disease?

A: We now have extremely effective painkillers, of course, so theoretically I wouldn't have to feel any pain at all. But the look of a disease depends as much on the physical constraints that pain imposes as it does on the smell, colour, and distortion of flesh. Pain also imposes certain attitudes which are necessary to a good performance. So part of the art comes from inviting pain into the performance, but regulating it so that the artist's perceptions remain clear.

Q: What about your audience? Are you causing them pain?

A: People have been genetically engineered to resist disease and limit infection. That pretty much limits their pain repertoire. Disease is an expression of how we view our internal mortalities, and eventually of course, our impending deaths. What I choose to do to the outside of my body is only an expression of the audience's internal fears concerning their own death and destruction. The closer the pageantry of my performance reflects some intangible unease the more powerful the performance is going to be.

Q: But to what purpose? Shouldn't society's goal be to eradicate disease?

A: I've never suggested that anyone but myself should be infecting themselves. But disease used to be as much a part of our lives as eating, drinking, sleeping. Of course it still is, but its effects have become so muted, so distanced from our consciousness that we usually aren't even aware that we are ill. I believe that our appreciation of our frailties in a world that will travel on without us has been stolen from us.

"The philosophers and religious toastmasters speak of a paradise which was, or will be, free of disease. Disease has been our punishment for disobedience, they tell us, for following the unapproved ways. It is as if these diseases were administered by demons—in the old days they often had the names of mythological creatures—and can be alleviated through prayer and obedience. So we pray to modern medicine and we do what the professionals tell us to do. I'm not sure that's always a good thing."

"You shouldn't grant so many interviews, you know. If you keep yourself a bit of a mystery we'll make more money. And spouting off about the medical profession isn't to our benefit—they're still responsible for about a third of our income. Besides, in case you've forgotten, *I'm* a medical professional."

Mickey spoke to him from the shower. Mickey was always
speaking to him from the shower. Most citizens who could afford

it had a full communication system in the shower. A layered shower of sound, heat, water, and air was about the most relaxing thing a person could do in the modern world.

"Answering questions isn't what you do best," Mickey said, sliding into bed next to him. He put his hand on Jerome's chest, feeling the scar tissue there, pretending to be slightly repulsed, but his gentleness betrayed him. "Are you ever going to get your nipples back?"

Jerome glanced down at the two little patches of scar where his nipples should have been, a left over symptom from his six months as a victim of Hutchinson-Gilford progeria, the rapid aging disease. In many ways it had been one of the most rewarding—as well as difficult and dangerous—of his transformations, involving surgeries, bone reduction, and genetic tampering. The result was not a perfect emulation of progeria by any means, but close enough for this world.

Most rewarding of all had been when the three remaining victims of progeria came to visit him and share the stage. "The bird people," Mickey had said of the four of them together, and thought it inexpressibly cute. Jerome had found them ineffably sad. During their limited time together they'd felt like the brothers he'd never had. Those with progeria resembled each other far more than they resembled the members of their own families. His recovery from progeria had been long, two years in the making, a process of countless surgeries and painful genetic experimentation, and costing far more than he'd made from the performances. But it had been an emotionally full time for him, and he'd retained the scars in lieu of nipples as a monument to the journey.

"No," he said finally. "I think this is the way they're going to be from here on out."

Mickey pursed his lips but said nothing. He slowly began touching Jerome's torso, checking out each scar, each monument to a past performance.

"Cut it out, Mickey. Please, not tonight."

"We haven't checked your skin thoroughly in awhile. That's my job, remember? Looking for hot spots, places where one of your little escapades is attempting a comeback?"

"I know, just leave it tonight, okay?"

"Hold on." Mickey reached over and grabbed a cleanser off the bedside table. "You got a little pustule coming back. That could mean serious stuff. Gross . . . why can't you just have the measles sometime?"

"Dammit, Mickey." Jerome pulled himself out of bed and hobbled to the chair. Something in his leg was bothering him, but he wasn't about to tell Mickey that. "I'm just never *clean* enough for you, am I? That's what this is about."

"What this is *about* is that you're getting careless. You're supposed to run through one of the hospitals at least once a week, remember? Get checked out? That was the deal we made with the Health Services in order for you to practice this 'art' of yours. You haven't had a thorough check in three months."

"I've always passed. There's never been a problem." He'd stumbled over the word "passed," hoped Mickey didn't notice.

"So what are you afraid of? Why not get checked out?"

Jerome looked at him: his perfect nails, his perfect skin. His perfect hair: Jerome used to watch Mickey when he cleaned it, each hair pulled individually into a nozzle of the vacuum head, stripped and scented, then a scalp scrub and scrape. When, to please Mickey, Jerome had tried the same thing, and the derma shaves, the full body wipes, he'd been injured or had had to stop because of the extreme discomfort.

"I've never been clean enough for you. I've never been tidy. I leave things scattered around, I carry things around with me, I can't let them go. I can't forget, I don't want to forget. I crave contact, Mickey. And contact is always messy."

Mickey responded by getting dressed again. As if in defiance he slipped on the shiny stiff clothes of his profession, clothing which would not crease and therefore trap dirt. His translucent nails glittered against the red material like jewels. Even from this distance Jerome could smell the particularly acidic aroma of the cleansing mouthwashes Mickey used to clean his teeth and gums and kill anything—even taste—that food might leave behind.

Jerome knew that Mickey sometimes swallowed the scouring wash even though there were strong warnings against it. "I'm a professional—I know just how much my body will tolerate." Once every two years Mickey, like half the population, submitted to a painful and dangerous blood cleansing.

Jerome's face suddenly blazed into existence on the mottled white bedroom wall. "Disease Artist may face charges in recent

Cholera! mishap," the high-toned announcer said. There followed a collage of interview segments:

> "Tuberculosis was the disease of the Industrial Revolution, syphilis of the Renaissance, and melancholy of the baroque period. The message then was the same as now: disease is a sin, disease is not normal."

> "In ancient times epilepsy was considered a holy disease."

He sounded ridiculous, and trapped within the rough wall texture, he looked quite ill.

From *The Disease Artist: A Performance Chronicle*:

> During the last year of his career, following the disruption at his *Cholera!* engagement, The Disease Artist enacted a number of manifestations in a relatively short period of time:
>
> His scrofula was remarkable in the brilliance of its "neck collar" rash, a bright red which awed the spectators. The accompanying suppurations were plentiful and some said spelled out intriguing messages if you understood the language.
>
> His short-lived sleeping sickness performance disturbed some of its audience when The Disease Artist manifested a morbid craving for meat, devouring a number of dead animal parts and then attempting to bite his partner of ten years, Mickey Johnson.
>
> His portrayal of a memorable yellow fever victim, attempting to explain the breeding habits of mosquitoes while vomiting up large quantities of blood made greasy and black from gastric juices.
>
> His leprosy and his yaws were cancelled in mid-performance. There are no existing eyewitness accounts.

With Mickey gone and the government threatening to close down his career, The Disease Artist found that his recuperation times had lengthened and the side effects of his various recovery regimens were increasing. He had been experiencing severe shortness of breath for several days before he decided to return to his local hospital. But once the day's attendant recognized him, he ordered a battery of screening tests to check for any lingering issues.

Jerome waited over two hours for the attendant to return. He wondered how sick you had to be to actually see a full-fledged doctor anymore. Worm food. Mickey used to say that his art was coarsening him.

The hospital was as slow and quiet as most of the city's restaurants. And every bit as concerned with disinfection. The spray from the nozzles was a constant background music.

He did not know when hospitals had become places of such quiet. Now you could walk inside a hospital and be almost oblivious to pain and blood and the mess of illness. Of course this did not mean that the patients no longer felt the pain, no longer spilled the blood. There must be a higher survival rate in these new hospitals, but in their hush and tidiness they felt more like old fashioned funeral homes.

A sudden rush in the corridor, figures passing, a whoosh of pressure, sharp perfume scent. Curious, he climbed off the gurney and walked into the hall.

In the next room activity was manic. Attendants rushed around a small figure in the narrow bed. Blood everywhere. The significance of this did not occur to him immediately. Blood everywhere. He stepped closer. A young woman lay beneath one of the blue life blankets, but something had malfunctioned, things had gone messy, and the girl was bleeding out through nose and mouth and from wounds invisible.

Suddenly Jerome realized he was alone in the room with the bleeding girl. There was so much blood, more blood than most had seen in decades, more blood than any small human had the right to contain.

Mickey thought he would retrieve the rest of his belongings while Jerome was out. He watched the apartment for days, and seeing no activity during that period he used his handprint to get in, both saddened and pleased that it had not been erased from the building's memory.

He found Jerome wandering from room to room, followed by jets of disinfectant and his own image from the day's newsreels. The stench was as bad as from any of Jerome's performances. He thought about checking the supplies of masking and cleansing compounds for the apartment, then remembered he didn't live there anymore.

"If I'm doing my job correctly, if I'm taking the particular malady far enough, some permanent physical damage always occurs: even after the course of the disease has been reversed, scars are invariably left behind. As far as mental scars, well, how can I even answer that?"

"They're saying I've retired," Jerome said, still walking, now swinging his arms in agitation, now scratching at visible sores. He did not look at Mickey directly. "This is some sort of documentary retrospective on my work. They say no one has seen me in months."

". . . constant treatment for tissue repair and scar removal. It leaves a mottled, textured appearance to my skin (He shows the camera his arm.) Mickey says it's like touching an enlarged fingerprint: you find yourself trying to identify and interpret the ridges and whorls. Mickey? He's my assistant, no, more than that: my partner."

"I heard about the incident at the hospital," Mickey said. "That must have been awful. Those blankets . . ." He paused. "Well those blankets *never* fail."

Jerome stared at him as if unsure who he was.

". . . molecular computers and various antibiotic vehicles handling most of the repairs. But their work is never one hundred percent complete."

"It really wasn't that bad," Jerome finally replied. "I mean, that's the way it used to be, right?"

"Relics and ruins get left behind: a discolouration in the skin, a twist in the joint, an internal pattern which persists. I am a relic and a ruin. I believe we all are."

"It used to be injury, pain, and dying, right? Used to be it was always messy."

"Mickey says that one of these relics is going to kill me eventually, and Mickey is probably right, but so what?"

"That's what my art's about, reminding people of all that."

"But so what?"

Mickey stopped and looked at him. "That's really what you think?"

"Well, of course. That's why the people come."

"It's just the human condition."

"Oh, Jerome. They already know about the likelihood of injury, of death. All that mess. But you still keep it tidy for them. Watching you is like looking at a painting or watching one of those old films. You keep the mess out of their living rooms."

"I should know. I've been doing this, *we've* been doing this, such a long time."

"No one cares, Jerome. No one even remembers. You ask those Filthies kids, or those Job characters, why those people used to die, why it happened, what it meant, especially what it means about them and being human, they're not going to know. They're just going to point to that picture of you on their cloaks, and sound out whatever slogan they have written there. That's all they know how to do."

Mickey thought Jerome might have stopped after that, but he was wrong.

From *The Disease Artist: A Performance Chronicle:*

The only film remaining of The Disease Artist's last performance is of rather poor quality, shaky and a bit out-of-focus, obviously taken with an antique film camera. Under normal circumstances this film would have been enhanced and brought up to contemporary standards, but a clause in the will of the original owner, The Disease Artist's long time partner Mr. Mickey Johnson, forbids any form of alteration and/ or augmentation. Few first-hand accounts of this performance have survived, most of those merely relating that The Disease Artist appeared to be in a state of advanced mental deterioration due to his disease, and babbled incoherently throughout the final days of the performance on any and all subjects which passed at random through his mind. This lack of specifics as to his final commentaries is particularly troubling in that the sound was turned off for most of Mr. Johnson's less-than-adequate filmed record.

Also puzzling is the choice of The Disease Artist's final ailment[128]: a rather undramatic assemblage of symptoms—weight loss, a barely visible swelling of the lymph glands, dry cough, fatigue and fever— symptoms indicative of a number of conditions. Only the white blemishes on the tongue, the red, brown, and purple marks on the nose and eyelids, and the various skin rashes are of any particular aesthetic appeal.

Only at the end of the Johnson film do we hear any clear statements from The Disease Artist. At one point he is heard to say, "It is our need to be remembered, to let other people know that we once walked this world." And at another, "To tell them how it was, how it used to be, how it felt to be there."

---

128 The AIDS epidemic ran its course some fifty years ago. With the exception of The Disease Artist's final performance, there have been no reported cases since that time.

Clearly, we must take this as an artist's statement about what it must mean to be an artist in a world that does not always appreciate one's chosen art form. It is unfortunate that like the fictional Hunger Artist before him, who never found his defining food, our own Disease Artist passed from us without ever discovering his defining disease.

HALLOWEEN
STREET

Halloween Street. No one could remember who had first given it that name. It had no other. There was no street sign, had never been a street sign.

Halloween Street bordered the creek, and there was only one way to get in: over a rickety bridge of rotting wood. Grey timbers had worn partway through the vague red stain. The city had declared it safe only for foot or bike traffic.

The street had only eight houses, and no one could remember more than three of those being occupied at any one time. Renters never lasted long.

It was a perfect place to take other kids—the smaller ones, or the ones a little more nervous than yourself on Halloween night. Just to give them a little scare. Just to get them to wet their pants.

Most of the time all the houses just stayed empty. An old lady had supposedly lived in one of the houses for years, but no one knew anything more about her, except that they thought she'd died there several years before. Elderly twin brothers had once owned the two centre houses, each with twin high peaked gables on the second story like skeptical eyebrows, narrow front doors, and small windows that froze over every winter. The brothers had lived there only six months, fighting loudly with each other the entire time.

The houses at the ends of the street were in the worst shape, missing most of their roof shingles and sloughing off paint chips the way a tree sheds leaves. Both houses leaned toward the centre of the block, as if two great hands had attempted to squeeze the block from either side. Another three houses had suffered outside fire damage. The blackened boards looked like permanent, and arbitrary, shadows.

But it was perhaps the eighth house that bothered the kids the most. There was nothing wrong with it.

It was the kind of house any of them would have liked to live in. Painted bright white like a dairy so that it glowed even at night, with wide friendly windows and a bright blue roof.

And flowers that grew naturally and a lawn seemingly immune to weeds.

Who took care of it? It just didn't make any sense. Even when the kids guided newcomers over to Halloween Street they stayed away from the white house.

The little girl's name was Laura, and she lived across the creek from Halloween Street. From her bedroom window she could see all the houses. She could see who went there and she could see everything they did. She didn't stop to analyze, or pass judgments. She merely witnessed, and now and then spoke an almost inaudible "Hi" to her window and to those visiting on the other side. An occasional "Hi" to the houses of Halloween Street.

Laura should have been pretty. She had wispy blonde hair so pale it appeared white in most light, worn long down her back. She had small lips and hands that were like gauges to her health: soft and pink when she was feeling good, pale and dry when she was doing poorly.

But Laura was not pretty. There was nothing really wrong about her face: it was just vague. A cruel aunt with a drinking problem used to say that "it lacked character." Her mother once took her to a lady who cut silhouette portraits out of crisp black paper at a shopping mall. Her mother paid the lady five dollars to do one of Laura. The lady had finally given up in exasperation, exclaiming "The child has no profile!"

Laura overheard her mother and father talking about it one time. "I see things in her face," her mother had said.

"What do you mean?" Her father always sounded impatient with her mother.

"I don't *know* what I mean! I see things in her face and I can never remember exactly what I saw! Shadows and . . . white, something so white I feel like she's going to disappear into it. Like clouds . . . or a snow bank."

Her father had laughed in astonishment. "You're crazy!"

"You know what I mean!" her mother shouted back. "You don't even look at her directly anymore because you *know* what I mean! It's not exactly sadness in her face, not exactly. Just something born with her, something out of place. She was born out of place. My God! She's *eleven* years old! She's been like this since she was a baby!"

"She's a pretty little girl." Laura could tell her father didn't really mean that.

"What about her eyes? Tell me about her eyes, Dick!"

"What *about* her eyes? She has nice eyes . . ."

"Describe them for me, then! Can you *describe* them? What colour are they? What shape?"

Her father didn't say anything. Soon after the argument he'd stomped out of the house. Laura knew he couldn't describe her eyes. Nobody could.

Laura didn't make judgments when other people talked about her. She just listened. And watched with eyes no one could describe. Eyes no one could remember.

No, it wasn't that she was sad, Laura thought. It wasn't that her parents were mean to her or that she had a terrible life. Her parents weren't ever mean to her and although she didn't know exactly what kind of life she had, she knew it wasn't terrible.

Yes, she was born out of place. That was a big part of it. She didn't enjoy things like other kids did. She didn't enjoy playing or watching television or talking to the other kids. She didn't *enjoy*, really. She had quiet thoughts, instead. She had quiet thoughts when she pretended to be asleep but was really listening to all her parents' conversations, all their arguments. She had quiet thoughts when she watched people. She had quiet thoughts when people could not describe her eyes. She had quiet thoughts while gazing at Halloween Street, the glowing white house, and all the things that happened there.

She had quiet thoughts pretending that she hadn't been born out of place, that she hadn't been born anyplace at all.

Laura could have been popular, living so close to Halloween street, seeing it out of her bedroom window. No other kid lived so close or had such a good view. But of course she wasn't popular. She didn't share Halloween Street. She sat at her desk at school all day and didn't talk about Halloween Street at all.

That last Halloween Laura got dressed to go out. That made her mother real happy. Laura had never gone trick-or-treating before. Her mother had always encouraged her to go, had made or bought her costumes, taken her to parties at church or school, parties the other kids dressed up for: ghosts and vampires and princesses, giggling and running around with their masks looking like grotesquely swollen heads. But Laura wouldn't wear a costume. She'd sit solemn faced, unmoving, until her mother finally gave up and took her home. And she'd never go trick-or- treating, never wear a costume.

Once she'd told her mother that she wanted to go out that night her mother had driven her around town desperately trying to find a costume for her. Laura sat impassively on the passenger side, dutifully got out at each store her mother took her to, and each time shook her head when asked if she liked each of the few remaining costumes.

"I don't know where else we can try, Laura," her mother said, sorting through a pile of mismatched costume pieces at a drugstore in a mall. "It'll be dark in a couple of hours, and so far you haven't liked a thing I've shown you."

Laura reached into the pile and pulled out a cheap face mask. The face was that of a middle-aged woman, or a young man, cheeks and lips rouged a bright red, eye shadow dark as a bruise, eyebrows a heavy and coarse dark line.

"But, honey. Isn't that a little . . ." Laura shoved the mask into her mother's hand. "Well, all right." She picked up a bundle of bright blue cloth from the table. "How about this pretty robe to complete it?" Laura didn't look at the robe. She just nodded and headed for the door, her face already a mask itself.

Laura left the house that night after most of the other trick-or-treaters had come and gone. Her interest in Halloween actually seemed less than ever this year; she stayed in her bedroom as goblins and witches and all manner of stunted, warped creatures came to the front door singly and in groups, giggling and dancing and playing tricks on each other. She could see a few of them over on Halloween Street, not going up to any of the houses but rather running up and down the short street close to the houses in *Idareyou* races. But not near as many as in years past.

Now and then her mother would come up and open her door. "Honey, don't you want to leave yet? I swear everybody'll be all out of the goodies if you don't go soon." And each time Laura shook her head, still staring out the window, still watching Halloween Street.

Finally, after most of the other kids had returned to their homes, Laura came down the stairs wearing her best dress and the cheap mask her mother had bought for her. Her father and mother were in the living room, her mother having retrieved the blue robe from the hall closet.

"She's wearing her best dress, Ann. Besides, it's damned late for her to be going out now."

Her mother eyed her nervously. "I could drive you, honey." Laura shook her head.

"Well OK, just let me cover your nice dress with the robe. Don't want to get it dirty."

"She's just a kid, for chrissake! We can't let her decide!" Her father had dropped his newspaper on the floor. He turned his back on Laura so she wouldn't see his face, wouldn't know how angry he was with both of them. But Laura knew. "And that *mask*! Looks like a whore's face! Hell, how can she even see? Can't even see her eyes under that." But Laura could see his. All red and sad-looking.

"She's doing something normal for a change," her mother whispered harshly. "Can't you see that? That's more important."

Without a word Laura walked over and pulled the robe out of her mother's arms. After some hesitation, after Laura's father had stomped out of the room, her mother helped her get it on. It was much too large, but her mother gasped "How beautiful!" in exaggerated fashion. Laura walked toward the door. Her mother ran to the door and opened it ahead of her. "Have a good time!" she said in a mock cheery voice. But Laura could see the near panic in the eyes above the distorted grin. Laura left without saying goodbye.

A few houses down the sidewalk she pulled the robe off and threw it behind a hedge. She walked on, her head held stiff and erect, the mask's rouge shining bright red in the streetlights, her best dress a soft cream colour in the dimness, stirred lightly by the breeze. She walked on to Halloween Street.

She stopped on the bridge and looked down into the creek. A young man's face, a middle-aged woman's face gazed back at her out of dark water and yellow reflections. The mouth seemed to be bleeding.

She walked on to Halloween Street. She was the only one there. The only one to see.

She walked on in her best dress and her shiny mask with eyes no one could see.

The houses on Halloween street looked the way they always did, empty and dark. Except for the one, the one that glowed the colour of clouds, or snow.

The houses on Halloween street looked their own way, sounded their own way, moved their own way. Lost in their own quiet thoughts. Born out of place.

You could not see their eyes.

Laura went up to the white house with the neatly trimmed yard and the flowers that grew without care. Its colour like blowing snow. Its colour like heaven. She went inside.

The old woman gazed out her window as goblins and spooks, pirates and ballerinas crossed the bridge to enter Halloween Street. She bit her lip to make it redder. She rubbed at her ancient, blind eyes, rubbing the dark eye shadow up into the coarse line of brow. She was not beautiful, but she was not hideous either. Not yet. No one ever remembered her face, in any case.

Her snow-white hair was beautiful, and long down her back.

She had the most wonderful house on the street, the only one with flowers, the only one that glowed. It was her home, the place where she belonged. All the children, or at least all the children who dared, came to her house every Halloween for treats.

"Come along," she said to the window, staring out at Halloween Street. "Come along," she said, as the treat bags rustled and shifted around her. "You don't remember, do you?" as the first of the giggling goblins knocked at her door. "You've quite forgotten," as the door began to shake from eager goblin fists, eager goblin laughs. "Now scratch your swollen little head, scratch your head. You forgot that first and last, Halloween is for the dead."

WHEN WE MOVED ON

We tried to prepare the kids a year or so ahead. They might be adults to the rest of the world, but to us they were still a blur of squeals that smelled like candy.

"What do you mean *move*? You've lived here *forever*!" Our oldest daughter's face mapped her dismay. Elaine was now older than we had been when we found our place off the beaten path of the world, but if she had started to cry I'm sure I would have caved. I hoped she had forgotten that when she was a little girl I'd told her we'd stay in this house until the end.

"Forever ends, child," her mother said. "It's one of the last things we learn. These walls are quickly growing thin—it's time to go."

"What do you *mean*? I don't see anything wrong—"

I reached over, patted her knee and pointed. "That's because the house is so full there's little wall to be seen. But look there, between that sparkling tapestry of spider eggs and my hat collection. That's about a square foot of unadorned wall. Look *there*."

She did, and as I had so many times before, I joined her in the looking. I was pleased, at least, that this semi-transparent spot worn into our membrane of home provided clear evidence: through layers of wall board like greenish glass, through diaphanous plaster and thinnest lathe, we could see several local children walking to school, and one Billie Perkins honoured us with a full-faced grin and a finger mining his nose for hidden treasure.

"Is that Cheryl Perkins' boy?" she asked. "I haven't seen her in years." She sounded wistful. It always bruised me a bit to hear her sounding wistful. I've always been a sloppy mess where my children are concerned.

"You should call her, honey," her mother said, on her way into the kitchen for our bowls of soup. My wife never tells you what's in the soups she serves—she doesn't want to spoil the surprise. Some days it's like dipping into a liquid Crackerjack box.

Elaine had gone to the thin patch and was now poking it with her finger. "Can they see us from out there?" Her finger went in part way and stuck. She made a small embarrassed cry and pulled it out. A sigh of shimmering green light puffed out in front of her, then fell like rain on the floor.

I handed her a cloth napkin and she busily wiped at the slowly spreading stain. "They just see a slight variation in colour," I replied. "It's more obvious at night, when a haze of light from the house leaks through."

She smiled. "I've noticed that on visits. I just thought it was the house sparkling. It's always been . . ." She stopped.

"A jewel?"

"Yes. That's not silly of me? I always thought of it as the 'jewel on the hill,' so when it seemed to sparkle lately, to look even more beautiful than ever, I thought nothing of it."

Of course she has been using this phrase since she was a little girl, but I said "What an interesting comparison! I'd never thought of it that way before. But I like that, 'The Jewel on the Hill.' We could paint a sign, put it up on the wall."

"Oh, Daddy! Where would you find the room?"

This was, of course, the point of the conversation, the fulcrum about which our future lives were to turn. A painting can become too crowded in its composition, a brain too full of trivia, and a house can certainly accumulate too many plans, follies, acquisitions, vocations, avocations, heart-felt avowals, and memories so fervently gripped they lose their binding thread.

All about us floated a constellation of materials dreamed and lived, attached to walls and door and window frames, layered onto shelves and flooding glass-fronted cabinets, suspended from or glued to the ceilings, protruding here and there into the room as if eager for a snag. There were my collections, of course: the hats, the ties, the jars of curiosities, monstrosities, and mere unreliabilities, the magazines barely read then saved for later, and later, all the volumes of fact and fiction, and the photographs of fictive relatives gathered from stores thrift and antique or as part of the purchase of a brand new frame, bells and belts and pistols and thimbles, children's drawings and drawings of children drawing the drawings, coloured candles and coloured bottles and colours inexplicably attached to nothing at all, my wife's favourite recipes pasted on the walls at levels relative to their deliciousness (the best ones so high up she couldn't read them clearly enough to make those wonderful dishes anymore), and everywhere, and I mean everywhere, the notes of a lifetime reminding our children to eat that lunchtime sandwich as well as the cookie, don't forget piano practice, remember we love you, and please take out the trash. Our notes to each other were simpler and less directive: thinking of you, thinking of you, have a great day.

In one corner of the living room you could see where I had sat reading a year of my sister's unmailed letters found in a shoebox after her death, each one spiked to the wall after reading, feeling like nails tearing through my own flesh. And near the windows kites and paper birds poised for escape through sashes left carelessly ajar. An historical collection of our children's toys lay piled against the baseboards, ready for the sorting and elimination we'd never quite managed, and floating above, tied to strings were particularly prized bits of homework, particularly cherished letters from camp, gliding and tangling with the varied progress of the day. And the authors of those works, our precious children, preserved in photos at nearly every age, arranged around the ceiling light fixtures like jittering moths, filling with their own illumination as the ceilings thinned to allow the daylight in. Gathered together I thought each child's history in photos could have been portraits of a single family whose resemblances were uncanny and disturbing.

There were trophies mounted or settled onto shelves for bowling, swimming, and spelling, most candy bars sold and fewest absent days. And the countless numbers of awards for participation, for happy or complaining our children always did participate.

Some of the collections, such as the spider eggs or selected, desiccated moth wings I couldn't remember for sure if their preservation had been intentional. Others, like the gatherings of cracks in corners or those scattered arrays of torn fabrics were no doubt accidental, but possessed of beauty in any case and so needed to stay.

These were the moments of a lifetime, the celebrations and the missteps, and I wondered now if our children ever had any idea what they both stepped in and out of on their average day in our home.

"What's going to become of it all?" our daughter exclaimed. She moved through the downstairs rooms unconsciously pirouetting, glancing around. She'd seen it all before, lived with all but the most recent of it, but blindness comes easy. I could see her eyes trying to remember. "You can't just throw it away!" she cried, when a rain of doll's heads from a decayed net overhead set off her squeals and giggles.

"You kids can have whatever you like," my wife replied from the passage to the kitchen. "But thrown out, left behind, or simply forgotten, things do have a way of becoming *gone*. Which is what is about to happen to your lunches, if the two of you don't come with me right now!"

Within the sea of salt and pepper shakers (armies of cartoon characters and national caricatures with holes in their heads) that covered our kitchen table my wife had created tiny islands for our soup bowls and milk glasses. I had the urge to sweep that collection of shakers off onto the floor, just to show how done with this never ending tide of *things* I'd become, but I knew that wasn't what Elaine needed to see at that moment. She stared at the red surface of her soup as if waiting for some mystery to emerge.

"Sweetheart, we just don't need all this anymore."

"You seemed to need it before," she said to all the staring shaker heads.

"It's hard to explain such a change," I said, "but you collect and you collect and then one day you say to yourself 'this is all too much.' You can't let anything else in, so you don't have much choice but to try to clear the decks."

"I just don't want things to change," she said softly.

"Oh, yes, you do," her mother said, patting her hand. "You most certainly do. Everything has an expiration date. It just isn't always a precise date, or printed on the package. And you would hate the alternative."

I'd been distracted by all the calendars on the kitchen walls, each displaying a different month and year, and for just that moment not sure which one was the current one, the one with the little box reserved for *right now*.

Elaine looked at her mother with an expression that wasn't exactly anger, but something very close. "Then why bother, Mom? When it all just has to be gotten rid of, in the end?"

"Who can know?" My wife smiled, dipping into her soup, then frowned suddenly as if she'd discovered something unfortunate. "To fill the time, I suppose. To exercise—" She turned suddenly to me. "Or is it 'exorcise'?" Without waiting for an answer she turned again to her soup, lifted the bowl, and sipped. Done, she smiled shyly at our daughter with a pink mustache and continued, "our creativity. To fill the space, to put our mark down, and then to erase it. That's what we human beings do. That's all we know how to do."

"Human beings?" Elaine laughed. "You know, I always thought you two were wizards, superheroes, magical beings, something like that. Not like anybody else's parents. Not like anybody else at all. All of us kids did."

My wife closed her eyes and sighed. "I think we did, too."

Over the next few weeks we had the rest of our children over to reveal something of our intentions, although I'm quite sure a number of unintentions were exposed as well. They brought along numerous grandchildren, some who had so transformed since their last visits it was as if a brand new person had entered the room, fresh creatures whose habits and behaviors we had yet to learn about. The older children stood around awkwardly, as if they were reluctant guests at some high school dance, snickering at the old folks' sense of décor, and sense of what was important, but every now and then you would see them touch something on the wall and gasp, or read a letter pasted there and stand transfixed.

The younger grandchildren were content to straddle our laps, constructing tiny bird's nests in my wife's grey hair, warrens for invisible rabbits in the multidimensional tangles of my beard. They seemed completely oblivious to their parents' discomfort with the conversation.

"So where will you go?" asked oldest son Jack, whom we'd named after the fairy tale, although we'd never told him so.

"We're still looking at places," his mother said. "Our needs will be pretty simple. As simple as you could imagine, really."

I looked out at the crowd of them. Did we really have all these children? When had it happened? I suspected a few strangers had sneaked in.

"Won't you need some help with the moving, and afterwards?" Wilhelmina asked.

"Help should always be appreciated, remember that children," I said. A few of them laughed, which was the response I had wanted. But then very few of our children have understood my sense of humour.

"What your father meant to say was that moving help won't be necessary," my wife said, interrupting. "As we said, we're taking very little with us, so please grab anything you'd care to have. As for us, we think a simple life will be a nice change."

Annie, always our politest child, raised her hand.

"Annie, honey, you're thirty years old. You don't need to raise your hand anymore," I told her.

"So what are you really telling us? Are we going to see you again?"

"Well, of course you are," I said. "Maybe not as often, or precisely when you want to, but you *will* see us. We'll still be around, and just as before, just as now, you'll *always* be our children."

We didn't set a day, because rarely do you know when the right day will come along. We'd been looking for little signs for years, it seemed, but you never really know what little signs to look for.

Then one day I was awakened early, sat up straight with eyes wide open, which I almost never do, looking around, listening intently for whatever might have awakened me.

The first thing I noticed was the oddness of the light in the room. It had a vaguely autumnal feel even though it was the end of winter, which wasn't as surprising as it might normally have been, what with the unusually warm temperatures we'd been having for this time of year.

The second thing was the smell: orangeish or lemonish, but gone a little too far, like when the rot begins to set in.

The third thing was the absence of my wife from our bed. Even though she always woke up before me, she always stayed in bed in order to ease my own transition from my always complicated dreams to standing up, attempting to move around.

I dressed quickly and found her downstairs in the dining room. "Look," she said. And I did.

Every bit of our lives along the walls, hanging from the ceiling, spilt out onto the floors, had turned the exact same golden sepia shade, as if it had all been sprayed with some kind of preservative. "Look," she repeated. "You can see it all beginning to wrinkle."

I'd actually thought that effect to be some distortion in my vision, for I had noticed it, too.

"You know what you want to take?" she asked.

"It's all been ready for months," I said. "I'll be at the door in less than a minute."

I ran up the stairs, hearing the rapidly drying wooden steps crack and pop beneath my shoes. When I jerked open the closet door it seemed as if I was opening the door to the outside, on a crisp Fall day, Mr. Hopkins down the street is burning his leaves, and you can smell apples cooking from some anonymous kitchen. I brushed the fallen leaves from the small canvas bag I had filled with a notebook, a pencil, some crackers (which are the best food for any occasion), and extra socks. I looked up at the clothes rod, the rusted metal, and nothing left hanging there but a tangle of brittle vines and the old baseball jacket I wore in high school. It hardly fit, but I pulled it on anyway, picked up the bag, and ran.

She stood by the front door smiling, wrapped in an old knit sweater coat with multicoloured squares on a chocolate-coloured background. "My mother knitted it for me in high school. It was all I could find intact, but I've always wanted to wear it again."

"Something to drink?" I asked.

"Two bottles of water. Did you get what you needed?"

"*Everything* I need," I replied. And we left that house where we'd lived almost forty years, raised children and more or less kept our peace, for the final time. Out on the street we felt the wind coming up, and turned back around.

What began as a few scattered bits leaving the roof, caught by the wind and drifting over the neighbour's trees, gathered into a tide that reduced the roof to nothing, leaving the chimney exposed, until the chimney fell into itself, leaving a chimney-shaped hole in the sky. We held onto each other, then, as the walls appeared to detach themselves at the corners, flap like birds in pain, then twist and flutter, shaking, as the dry house chaff scattered, making a cloud so thick we couldn't really see what was going on inside it, including what was happening to all our possessions, and then the cloud thinned, and the tiny bits drifted down, disappearing into the shrubbery which once hugged the sides of our home, and now hugged nothing.

We held hands for miles and for some parts of days thereafter, until our arthritic hands cramped, and we couldn't hold on any more no matter how hard we tried. We drank the water and ate the crackers and I wrote nothing down, and after weeks of writing nothing I simply tore the sheets out of the notebook one by one and started pressing them against ground, and stone, the rough bark on trees, the back of a dog's head, the unanchored sky one rainy afternoon. Some of that caused a mark to be made, much did not, but to me that was a satisfactory record of where we had been, and who we had been.

Eventually, our fingers no longer touched, and we lost the eyes we'd used to gaze at one another, and the tongues for telling each other, and the lips for tasting each other.

But we are not nothing. She is that faint smell in the air, that nonsensical whisper. I am the dust that settles into your clothes, that keeps your footprints as you wander across the world.

THE WOODCARVER'S SON

The knock was soft, but the fine wood Alejandro's father had selected for their front door carried it well, so that the sound still had a fullness when it reached the back of the house where Alejandro had laid down to rest, like the sound a wooden bell might make, or like the now-and-again beating sound of the wooden heart of the house itself.

He padded the long way through the house, avoiding the room where his father wept. All day his father slept, or his father wept, but he would not speak. Not to Alejandro. Not to anyone.

The man at the front door was Señor Echevarría. He had a face of split timber. "Is there work today?" he asked.

Alejandro shook his head sadly. "I am sorry. Not today. My father . . . my father says not any day. But perhaps someday. But not today."

Señor Echevarría nodded but did not leave. Alejandro was ashamed, thinking that Señor Echevarría must recognize his lie. Alejandro did not know why he lied, except that his father's crying and sleeping embarrassed him. Sleep eased his father's pain but did not cure it, even after all these months. And as the only one his age in the village, Alejandro felt neither *hombre* nor *chico*. He had no one to tell the truth to. He was alone.

"*De verdad*," Señor Echevarría said. "After my brother's wife died, he could not live, and yet he could not die." He rested his hand against the smooth wood of the door, his thumb caressing the grain one could see but not feel, the grain of a dream. Alejandro did not believe Señor Echevarría could have taken his hand away from the door and walked away then, even if he had wanted to, even if he had been paid. "The village . . ." His brown eyes drifted to the side, to the narrow dirt road. "They all need the work. But they all still wish him better."

Alejandro stared up at the man, trying to remember how long he had worked for his father in the woodcarving business, and knew it had been longer than Alejandro had been alive. His mother had told him. His mother had known Señor Echevarría when all who were now old in the village had been young. "But it will happen someday they will not wish him better, they will not wish him well," Alejandro said.

Señor Echevarría nodded solemnly. "The old ones will tell you that even a fly may have a temper. And the fish that sleeps is soon carried away by the current." Then the man closed his eyes and leaned forward and kissed the beautiful wood of the door, the most beautiful thing his father had ever carved ("for it is the door to our hearts") and then he left. And then Alejandro closed this beautiful door and it was all dark inside once again.

Since Alejandro's mother died his father had carved no wood. Sometimes Alejandro would see him in his bedroom walking around, making strange motions with his hands, twisting his face into strange faces, and other idiotic things which might be substitutes for dreaming, and for carving. Perhaps being a fool eased his pain.

But it still angered Alejandro that his father had not spoken to him since the day of his mother's death. And it shamed him that he had not spoken to his father because he did not know what to say.

"It will be dry again today," Alejandro said to the wood of the house: the beams, the mantel, the smooth trim, the tightly-knitted flooring. "It has not rained for months. Your beautiful fathers and mothers in the forest must be parched and dying, leaning one against the other with bare, brittle limbs."

But the wooden heart of the house did not reply to Alejandro, no matter how sweetly he talked. Perhaps it was aware how the boy had stopped oiling its wooden extremities, because they could not afford the oil. Perhaps it knew that it too would die like its relatives in the forest, die from the outside in, the dryness creeping from roof and timber to door to mantel and trim, drying into the heart where it would flake and disintegrate and disperse its memories of the lives it had sheltered up and down the dusty street.

Perhaps it was aware of how little the boy knew of the world beyond this dying village. For Alejandro, the son of the greatest woodcarver in the village, had never seen the forest.

In any case Alejandro decided the house need not worry about the drought, for in the other bedroom his father wept, and the house drank from his sorrow.

Alejandro spoke to the house and his father spoke to no one. The house drank his father's tears and held its wooden tongue.

Alejandro's mother had been the most beautiful woman to ever live in that village. There were some women in the village who dressed up more, who spent money on cheap jewelry, but a burro is a burro, even if he wears a silver collar. And all the old women said she had been the best mother as well. Alejandro did not understand how this could be, since she had died and left him—her only child—in this silent wooden house.

But she had been beautiful, this he had known to be true. And even as a small child he remembered how everyone—men and women both—had talked to her, how their voices had become softer when she was around, how they had pleaded so softly, how they had wanted. *Felicia*, they would call. *Come sit with us! Felicia, come talk with us a while!*

And she always had time. For the old ones, especially. Alejandro remembered being angry they took up so much of her life.

The other men his father's age had still laughed about how the beautiful Felicia had hooked him all those years ago. How he had been such a *poor* fish, but a happy fish for all that.

Every Monday then his father would drive his truck out of the village and across the plain into the forest to choose the wood that he and his workers would turn into furniture and carvings for the shops in cities far away. And Alejandro's mother, Felicia, had always gone with him. It was the only time she ever left the village. Alejandro never left.

Then one day there were no more trips. There were no more workers in the big workshop snug to the back of the house, on the other side of the wall from Alejandro's room so that he could always hear the nick and the scrape and the tick and the saw as the beautiful carvings were made.

There were no more carvings, no more words or time for anyone from either of Alejandro's parents. For that was the day his father had had the accident, and the day the splintered bit of wood had miraculously passed through glass and passed through metal and passed through the heart of the beautiful Felicia.

He had heard the old women of the village say how this bit of wood had been like a giant thorn, a thorn that had pierced the heart of Felicia. It was these same old women who had brought all the food to their house the day after his mother had died. They had come in their long black dresses and shawls, their faces barely showing, like large black birds, flock after flock, so many and all of them dressed alike. Alejandro had wondered who they were, where they had all come from. He had not believed there were so many old women in their small village. He saw some come from houses he had not known contained old women before that day.

They brought deep into the darkness of that hollow wooden house great bowls of steaming beans, tortillas, platters of meat, plates of silvery, staring fish, offerings of potatoes, cheeses, breads, and desserts of all kinds. Alejandro had never seen such a feast.

On their table top of tree slabs sanded and joined into a glass-like perfection, the feast had sat a day and then another day, untouched. Sometimes his father would come to the table at the usual time, sit and stare at the soft and gentle spread of food with tears in his eyes, his fingers rubbing the smooth edges of the table endlessly. But he would not eat. Alejandro, too, had sat solemnly, not touching the food the old women had brought, because perhaps this feast was for watching and not for eating.

Instead he had stolen fruit and bread from the local merchants to keep himself alive, nibbling on the small bits as he sat back in the dark and empty woodcarver's shop.

After a few weeks the stretch of feast softened and ran like yellow wax in the heat. The nuts fell out of the cakes and breads. The fruit rinds blackened, the meat turned greasy and sour, and flies speckled the collapsed mounds like dark garnish. The fish grew thinner, their eyes larger and clouded. Sometimes he witnessed his father staring at the remains, whispering silently to himself. Sometimes he had to fight off the urge to cover the decay with a sheet, thinking it somehow obscene but afraid of how his father might react.

Eventually the flies spread beyond the dining room, gathering in neighbourly groups and filling the house with the first conversation Alejandro had heard in weeks. A sweet stench flavoured the young boy's dreams. Alejandro expected the beautiful wood of the house to begin to show at least some small signs of this decay, but this did not happen.

Again he woke late in the night to the sounds of weeping. He wondered if his father was drinking his own tears, if that was what was keeping the master woodcarver alive. Alejandro missed even the nervous talk of the flies.

But then the weeping suddenly stopped, and he sat up in bed, trying to control his breathing. A rustling came from the dining room, and he immediately thought of rats though he'd never seen one in their house. He crawled out of bed and walked slowly down the dark hall, clouds of flies separating on either side of his face like a lively and murmurous beaded curtain. He clamped his mouth shut. Flies don't enter a shut mouth.

His father sat slumped over the ruins of the table (Alejandro had to remind himself that it was the feast in decay, and not the beautiful table itself). His father stared off into the distance, as if waiting. The ragged shadows atop the table shifted, then moved with a scrape of claw and a slide of tail, slowly trundling off into the deeper black like props being moved about between scenes of a play. Occasionally some of the odd baggage revealed itself in a sliver of moonlight from the windows high in the wall: pale and mossy things, red-encrusted pink softnesses, sharp-edged, exposed bone, congealed liquid splatters, all kinds of obscene things Alejandro thought best buried, best all forgotten.

But to all this there was a strange quiet, a seriousness, unlike anything he'd witnessed outside a church. And then Alejandro wondered if he was in a kind of church here, watching the processional. The ushers were guiding the people to their seats. The props were being moved about. Someone hushed a talker in the back pew. Someone was weeping.

His father jerked out a hand desperately and tried to stuff some of the moving food into his mouth, the great black backs of shiny insects drifting over his face like crude widow's lace. Kissing the food, spreading it over his mouth and cheeks for comfort. For communion. "Felicia . . . Felicia . . ." He mouthed the name over and over, but would not release it.

On the other side of the room someone moved in and out of shadow.

The woman in the grey dress carrying the large splinter of dripping wood might have been his mother as she had been at a younger age. The old women said that a man sometimes saw a woman like that—not as she was but as she used to be. Certainly the woman in the grey dress was beautiful in the same way that his mother had been beautiful. This he was sure of.

His father opened his mouth but would not speak. Alejandro wanted to ask him if he saw the same things as he, but could not bring himself to do this. His father had caused all this—the rotting feast, the woman carrying the great, bleeding splinter—just as he had caused the death of Alejandro's beautiful mother. It was a hard thought. Once he had admitted this in his head he felt tension melting away from his face and chest, as if it were food rotting and falling into bits, even though he knew he could never say such a thing aloud. His father's fantasies, his father's grief, embarrassed Alejandro, and he could not make himself speak to him.

A hand appeared out of the darkness and set a plain wooden cup of smooth, white milk on the table by Alejandro's hand. He looked at his father's face, the lips struggling for sound, the lips pale, dry, dead-looking.

He needed to speak the truth, but he could not. He needed to talk to his father of his grief, but he could not. The milk sat in its cup unused, souring, until after the woman had left the room and the remains of the feast were gone.

Still his father could not speak, and Alejandro could not bring himself to speak to his father. Alejandro would brood over this failure, he knew, the rest of his life. But he could not help himself. And he could not change things now.

When the old people in the village had a problem they went to find a *bruja*. His father was sick, he could not speak, and he was seeing things. A *mestizo* woman who lived in an old shack a half-day's hike outside their village was said to know of such things. Some said she was a witch and some said she just had friends who were witches. All the old men in the village were suspicious of the old woman and some said they should go to her shack, drag her out to the arroyo and kill her there. The old women said the men were just jealous of a woman's warmth, a woman's strength. They laughed about the old men's complaints and pointed out that the men never did anything about them. The old men blamed everything on this old woman: when the crops failed, when business was bad. Alejandro thought that soon they would blame these things on his father.

First Alejandro gathered together what little money had been left in the house: old coins from the sooty can above the wood stove and newer pesos and centavos from the small mahogany box with the carving of a pig on its lid. Alejandro had never had any use for money before and knew very little about what was the proper amount for things, and besides that he felt strange about taking his father's money, even though his father would never miss it and even though it was to help his father. Witches always wanted money for what they did—he had heard the old men and women say this many times.

Then for something extra he caught the scrawny yellow cat with the red eyes who always stayed behind their house and howled. He had heard that those who deal with magic like to keep such odd-looking cats around, for companionship, or perhaps for ingredients. He tried to keep the cat in a bag but it kept clawing its way out and crawling up Alejandro's back to perch on his shoulder, its claws dug in until they stabbed through the thin cloth of the boy's jacket and into his brief coating of skin. This was very painful but the cat did not attempt to escape from here so Alejandro left him on his perch.

Finally Alejandro went to his room and retrieved the staff he had carved under his father's supervision. It wasn't a very good staff and the carvings were amateurish but it was large and it was thick. He had shaped one end into the crude form of a snake's head. A narrow, crooked tail turned slowly on the other end when Alejandro rolled the staff in his palms. Out on the plains near the forest he had heard that wolves and great cats lived. His staff would not be much help, but it was all that he had to protect himself.

And it seemed right that he should have a decorated staff with him when he met the *bruja*.

He started out early in the morning with a fog sour and milky still filling the dirt lanes. They had terrible fogs here, the old people said, because the village was by a brackish, shallow river that had turned bad because it passed through the dirty cities far away. He did not recognize his village at first. Since his mother had died, he had hidden from his neighbours, a boy without a mother.

Then he wondered if the village looked so different because of the fog. It drifted high and low, aimless and wild as the drought-plagued villagers' dream of fresh water. It collected in the sinkholes like milky pools waiting to be drunk from. The scrawny cat leapt from his back as if to oblige, but then scampered back when it crept close enough to the pools to smell.

The pale brick and wooden houses floated out of the fog like great sea creatures coming up for air. He had never seen a sea creature, but he had learned enough from the old people's stories that he knew this must be how they would be.

No one was in the streets. The cat dug its claws into him until he cried out. The houses were in poor repair, the roofs torn and many windows shattered. Bushes and flowering plants were brown, or grey as ash. Winds had painted the walls with shadowy faces of dust. But there were no human faces in the windows or at the doors to serve as models for these portraits. There had been a time when the people of his village would be out and working by now. A giant hand of fog drifted by him and the faces disappeared from the walls nearest him.

But then he recognized the Lucero house, and the Echevarría house, and he knew this surely was his village. He moved down the dusty lane holding his staff tightly, the scrawny cat stiff on his shoulder like one of his father's carvings of cats that were so popular with the American tourists.

Sometimes the walls of the houses seemed to melt down into the fog, thickening its pale colour. Sometimes the walls seemed not to be there at all, as if the house had rotted away a long time ago. The dark windows watched stupidly. The roofs sagged in despair. No chickens squawked at him. No cows bellowed. No dogs sniffed at his heels. The villagers had eaten all of their animals.

Once he left the village the world became a noisier place. This made no sense to him because the village was full of people, and no one lived out here on the plains. But he had not realized how very silent the world of the village had become until he was on the road out on the plain, where gravel crunched beneath his soles and the wind crackled the few dry trees and insects and birds were waking to begin their daily labour of survival.

Several hours outside the village he met his first wolf. It didn't seem as big as he had imagined a wolf to be—more like a medium-sized dog that had been poorly loved—and by walking a good distance out of his way he was able to avoid the creature entirely.

The next wolf to come into the road was another matter, however. It stood crouched and heaving, large enough to satisfy even Alejandro's generous imagination. Alejandro approached it slowly, wiggling his snake stick back and forth near the wolf's head. The wolf's huge grey eyes followed the wiggling stick with interest. Then the great beast leapt and turned somersaults in the air like some circus animal before lying down to sleep in the middle of the road.

Beyond the wolf, immediately past a bend in the road, Alejandro found the shack of the *bruja*.

There was no answer to his knock. He was amazed at how grey and worn the door to this shack was—his father would have been dismayed, if he had senses back, to see such a thing. If this were the door to the old woman's heart, she was an ill old woman indeed.

There was no reaction when he rattled the windows in their loose frames. "*Hola!*" he cried, but there was no response. He went around to the back of the shack, where he found a huge cow standing in a pitiful patch of grass. The cow, fat rolling down its sides and with an udder as large as a soup kettle, gazed at him with blue, unblinking eyes.

You miss your mother, muchacho. The cow spoke inside Alejandro's head. Alejandro stared at the cow. *But you miss your father more.*

Alejandro had heard that in the old days the witches had more power. Back then a witch could turn herself into a cow. *Verdad!* the old people would say. "What do you know about me? What do you know about my father?" Alejandro asked with a trembling voice.

The cow lowered her head and dropped open her mouth. She bit into the dirt around a clump of poor-looking grass and pulled it in with her tongue, roots and all. Alejandro saw the scrawny cat approaching her udder with great slowness. He had not realized it had even left his back. The cat went to one of the cow's great teats and began to nurse. The cow sighed contentedly.

I know you have lost your mother, the cow began. *And your father has lost his wife. Which is like losing your mother, since even old men are like boys. Your father misses the same things you miss, muchacho. He misses holding her. He misses nursing at her breast.*

Alejandro blushed and looked down, dropping his staff. The staff shook and wiggled, becoming a long black snake that rippled like a narrow shadow across the ground to where the cow stood. Then it raised its head and grabbed a nipple beside the cat, and it too began to nurse. The cow closed its eyes and chewed. It moved its great hooves back and forth, finally stepping on the snake which snapped into two rigid pieces of staff.

All living things require such healing. All living things must drink at the place of their beginnings, a drink that takes them back to the times before their beginnings.

Without thinking, Alejandro had gone to the side of the cow, and now knelt there, where he touched the full roundness of the udder. The cat stopped nursing a moment and opened its mouth. Alejandro could see blood dripping from the nipple.

And they must believe they will live forever, even though they know they will not.

"What can you do for my father, you old witch?" The boy had begun to cry.

I can do nothing for your father. He has become a ghost. Your mother has passed on, but into the realm of transformation. What changes, lives. It is your father who has died, for your father is frozen, and refuses to change.

"But what do I do?"

Take him some of my milk. Make him drink. Speak to him of your mother. Shake him from his dream.

"But you're a witch! You could bring my mother back! Let me lead you into the forest where she is buried, and bring our mother back to us!"

Stay out of the forest, niño. It is a perilous place.

Then the cow disappeared, leaving a bucket full of milk, the cat mewling around its rusty sides, and the staff broken in half on the ground.

Alejandro fully intended to do what the *bruja* said. He had the two pieces of staff wedged under his belt, the bucket of milk in his hand, the cat following closely behind to lap up any spills. But then he caught a glimpse of the tall trees at the edge of the distant forest, and their trunks gleaming despite the drought, and all that they promised. This was the source of all the wood in the village. This was the place where the legendary Black Walnut and Spanish Cedar grew, the raw materials of his father's dreams. This was where the thorn that ended his mother's life came from, and where his mother now lay buried.

Alejandro walked away from the road and toward the distant line of trees, hoping that the witch cow would not see him. The milk bucket suddenly felt heavier in his hand. He wondered how much of it his mother's corpse would have to drink before she would consent to come back to them.

He had of course never seen where his mother was buried; the old woman who stayed behind while the others were at the funeral had told him simply that she was buried behind the chapel at the edge of the forest. Happily, the chapel proved easy to find.

He approached the chapel slowly, as there was much weeping and wailing inside. It was a simple structure of mud bricks and boards, but with no roof: the wreckage of this lay to one side, as if torn off by the wind. Tall trees surrounded it, their lower branches knit together and hanging over the bare walls. A small goat cart with digging tools inside was parked by the open front door. A gravedigger's cart. The goat stared at Alejandro with eyes like a woman's. A beautiful wooden cross had been planted in the ground near the door. Buds had sprouted from one arm of the cross; two pale green leaves had opened. The sound of weeping from inside the chapel was tremendous, and frightening.

But when Alejandro entered the chapel the weeping stopped. There was no one there. A woman lay on the altar, but evaporated into the shadows when Alejandro reached to pull aside her veil. Behind the altar Alejandro could see there was no wall: he could see the forest there, endless and cool and a green so dark it might have been a shade of black. He walked past the empty altar and into the dark green.

The ground between the trees was littered with broken headstones and splintered wooden crosses. But one remained standing and whole, and unmistakable in the excellence of its sad,

sad carvings. The empty eyes and the empty arms and the long and intricate flow of his mother's hair. Two feet from this cross a giant tree reached toward the distant dim light of sky. Alejandro turned, and the goat cart was there beside him, the goat smiling, winking at him, pursing its lips. Alejandro reached into the back of the cart and pulled out the ancient pick and shovel.

The work was hard, the roots of the tree growing through the grave tough and massive. Alejandro pulled the axe out of the cart and worked on the roots, which sighed and trembled with each new loss of sap. He chewed the ground without mercy, creating a wide hole around the tree and descending well below its roots. Soon he was covered with the thick, black dirt. He could hardly breathe, but he persisted in his descent.

Alejandro dug and hacked his way through brush and soil, roots and finally the long wooden box of walnut, finely detailed with scenes of his father and mother embracing, the village so busy he barely recognized it, the shallow faces of the villagers so serene. But eventually the well-made box fell apart under his hands, and then there was his mother's beautiful dark hair, her limbs thin, skin clinging stubbornly, and her steady look, as if chastising him for what he had done.

The base of the tree pierced her chest. It was the thorn; in her endless sleep she had dreamed it into a tree.

But Alejandro hacked and hacked until he had his mother free. He reached down under and between the roots and embraced her, pulling her out of the ground. Dirt filled his eyes and his mouth until he could no longer feel himself; he was a worm filled with dirt and wiggling up out of the darkness. A splinter of wood still grew from Felicia's chest, but she was up into the light now, his mother once again.

He laid her on the ground. He fed her some of the witch's milk. He was amazed at how light she was when he lifted her into the cart. The goat smiled, seeming to laugh at Alejandro, but willingly followed the boy's tug.

For hours they travelled the dusty road back toward the village: Alejandro and the goat, his mother leaned up straight and stiff in the cart, and the thirsty cat following behind. Now and then he would stop and give his mother another drink, and sometimes he could almost see her smile.

Just as he had the village in sight his mother fell over in the cart. Alejandro scrambled around to the rear and climbed inside with her, the bucket still in his hands, the milk slopping out and washing his clothes, turning the plank floors of the cart into healthy, green wood.

She stared up at him with wormwood eyes. He gave her more and more of the witch's milk. Her pale white tongue lapped greedily, but still her wooden eyes would not move, no matter how much he cried for her, how much he screamed he still needed her, or how much he confessed to her about the anger he felt at her leaving. Her body lay stiff and unmoving, with only her wet white worm of a tongue wiggling obscenely in the dark bore of her mouth. Finally he poured the remaining milk over her, but this brought no further changes.

He knew he could bring her like this to his father, this creature so like a wooden carving, and his father would have been satisfied. His father would dress her and hold her and keep her forever, and no one would be able to dissuade him. Nothing would ever change. Alejandro had ignored the witch, and wasted her milk.

He retrieved the two halves of the crude staff from his belt. He wrapped the pieces together with twine, binding them tightly. He hefted the mended staff and tested it for strength. Then Alejandro stood over his wooden mother and brought the staff down again and again, the snake biting her into more chips and splinters than he could count.

Through the back door Alejandro let himself into the house of the woodcarvers, and into the empty shop. He examined the hollowed out blocks of wood his father had arranged on a dusty shelf. As he took down each one he tried to remember the things his father had taught him about these samples:

The cypress . . .it doesn't wear well. The willow . . . your mother, she likes the willow tree—but it has a tendency to split.

Now the Spanish cedar, it is easy to cut. But when his father pushed the sample up to Alejandro's nose he had shaken his head. He did not like the smell at all. He remembered how hard his father had laughed then.

Some like the finished look of poplar. But for the woodcarver . . . His father shook his head doubtfully. *It bruises too easily, and it grabs the tool like a cat with the cheese, and will not let go of it. It refuses your cuts, so why should you fight with it? Life is too short, muchacho.*

So Alejandro chose the Black Walnut, his father's favourite wood. *See the fine, tough grain, Alejandro? This wood will accept more detail and undercuts than the rest . . . it will welcome the hand guided by a dream. It finishes beautifully, and has the darkness one expects in a dream . . .*

He worked carefully with his father's tools, including the ones his father had not taught him yet, the ones whose names alone he knew from his father's working sing-songs. *The carbon knife . . . take the carbon knife, make the stroke but don't bump against the tang. The tang. Use the mallet well, but use the mallet care . . . fully. Take the needle rasp, take the rasp riffler, and the fishtail, the fishtail, shank . . .*

Alejandro adopted his father's techniques to his own dream, making of the skew chisel a knife for carving all the faces of his mother he could remember, all the postures of his father's hands during a day spent carving, paring and drawing the fine lines of their marriage, using chamfer cuts, hollow cuts, and rocking cuts to shape the designs on his black walnut bowl, using the scrapers to smooth out his mother's undying cheeks, the rifflers to define the delicate contours of his father's fingertips as they caressed his mother's face, Alejandro's head, and the sides of this bowl itself.

Until he finished, and took the bowl with its offering of plain water to wet his father's silent throat.

Make him drink. Speak to him of your mother. Shake him from his dream. The witch cow had said these things and many more. He had spoken with a cow and he had spoken with their wooden house and he had spoken with his dead mother. Now it was time to speak with his father who lay weeping in the other room. *He misses holding her.*

Silently he entered his father's bedroom, stepping in exaggerated fashion like a young fool, gesturing in mute pantomime. He showed his father what he had made with his hands.

He told his father how unhappy he had been, and how much he missed his mother, what he remembered of her, some things she had done and said to him, how much he missed the carving and the talk of the workers in the shop, and how much he missed his father's own talk. He told him how angry he was sometimes.

He told him of the cat and the cow, his snake broken into two halves of staff, of the goat with a woman's eyes, and the great tree that his mother had dreamed out of her grave.

And then they shared their drink of sadness. *All living things must drink at the place of their beginnings.*

And later the old men and old women would tell how there had been so much weeping in that house, and yet how now and then, could be heard the healing laughter.

For what changes, lives.

INVISIBLE

Over the past few months something painful and awkward had come into the light. Ray was never quite able to define it, and of course did not feel he could check out this perception with anyone else. It would be an odd thing to say, and he knew he had a reputation for saying odd things, although no one had actually told him so.

There were days he could barely stand to open his eyes. Something in the atmosphere, perhaps, that stung the cornea. Every object he looked at was outlined in bright white light. A brilliance he was not supposed to see, a visibility not meant for him. These haloing strokes appeared hesitant, as if part of an unsure painting.

It was the kind of light he imagined you would see at the end of the world: a sad, quiet fading of form and colour, as if all earthly materials were dissolving from a mass failure of conviction.

Although he did not expect confirmation of his anxieties, or really want one, Ray listened to the hourly radio weather reports, noting the announcer's tone when he spoke words such as "overcast," "upper atmosphere," and "visibility." There was anxiety in the slight, random trembling of the otherwise smooth voice. Did the weatherman hold something back? The answers were all there, he suspected, floating through the air, hiding in the aftertaste of water, momentarily visible in the bright, painful regions of reflected sun, if one only knew the right way to see, to taste, to hear.

He called his wife two or three times during the day to see how she was feeling, thinking she might be sensing something similar, but he was unable to ask her directly. At some point they'd stopped authenticating each other's sadder perceptions about their places in the universe.

At least in the office there were few windows, and the predictable lines of the cubicles were comfortably familiar. Weather ceased to be a factor once he arrived at work.

Anyone up for lunch? Ray had waited an hour or so for someone to make the invitation. He normally timed his work so he could be available any time between noon and one.

He stood up in his cubicle. Several other heads popped up out of the maze of short, upholstered partitions, like prairie dogs out of their holes. The others waved to the speaker—Marty, a lead programmer—and grabbed their coats. After an awkward pause with Marty staring straight at him, Ray tentatively raised a hand and waved as well. Marty's expression didn't change. He couldn't have missed Ray's intention.

Ray saved his work, jotted down some notes, stood and slipped on his coat. He got to the elevators just as the doors were closing. His coworkers stared out at him without recognition. No one tried to stop the doors. He waved again, said, "Hey!" He ran down four flights to the lobby. He almost ran over a woman on the second floor landing. He stopped to apologize but could see the distaste in her eyes (or was it pity?). Out of breath, he reached the outside doors. He watched as they pulled away, all of them jammed into Marty's green Ford. How did they get out there so quickly? Again he waved as the car swung past the entrance and out the driveway. A woman from another office scooted by him and out the door. It suddenly embarrassed him that she'd seen him with his hand up, waving to no one, greeting nothing as if nothing might wave back, and he lowered it.

He went back upstairs to his cubicle, hoping no one had seen him return. He went back to work on the day's projects, not thinking to remove his coat. From time to time hunger pains stroked his belly like nervous fingers. He had a lunch in the office refrigerator—he always had a lunch in the office refrigerator—but he didn't bother to go get it.

The sky outside went from a misty white to a deep blue, then to greys and oranges, as if painted on an enormous turning disk. He did not learn this from looking out the window but saw it reflected in his computer screen. Days passed in this awkwardly glimpsed view of the world. He could feel his hands on the keyboard begin the painful petrifaction that must surely lead to transparency. At some point Marty and the others wandered past as they returned from lunch, louder than usual. Marty eventually brought some papers by for Ray to look at. There was no mention of the missed lunch. Ray thought perhaps his intentions had been misunderstood. They were all well-meaning people here. The world was full of well-meaning people. It wasn't their fault he didn't know how to conduct himself.

At the end of the day he took the stairs down to the parking lot, leaving fifteen minutes early. He did this every day. It was unlikely he'd be fired for such an offense, but he somewhat enjoyed imagining the possibility. Perhaps an announcement would be made. Perhaps he would be forced to exit through the reception area carrying his box of meagre belongings as other employees stood and watched. Would any of them wish him well in his future endeavours?

Outside the air shimmered with possibility. He did his best to ignore it.

Traffic was again heavy and slow, the cars unable to maneuver beyond the occasional lane change. There was a quality of anger in the way people sped up and slowed down, changed lanes, slipped into the breakdown lane in order to make an illegal pass on the left. The anger made Ray feel as if some explosion was imminent, some volcanic eruption of blame he might drown in.

But he didn't mind the traffic per se—it gave him the opportunity to gaze into the interiors of the other cars, to see what the people were doing when they thought no one was looking, observe the little things (singing, grooming, picking their noses) they did to divert tedium, follow the chase of expressions across their faces, all of them no doubt feeling safe and assured of their invisibility.

His was simply one more can awash in a sea of metal. He was content to wait until the tide brought him home.

Janice didn't turn around when Ray walked into the kitchen. "It's almost ready," she said. "We have to be there by six-thirty. We can't be late."

"If we're late, she might think we're not coming. We can't let that happen."

"No, we can't." She dealt slices of tomato rapidly into the stew. "So, what did you do for lunch today? Did you go out with anybody?"

She always tried to sound casual about it. She always failed.

"No." He started to make up a satisfactory reason, then gave up. "I worked through." He looked over her shoulder into the bubbling liquid, always fascinated by the way carrots and meat, potatoes, peas, and corn blended simply through constant collision. He pulled back when he remembered how much she hated him looking over her shoulder when she cooked. "How did you do today?"

She dropped a handful of peas into the pot. She filled a pan with water, slid it onto the burner, took two eggs from the fridge. "No one noticed my new hair. A hundred and twenty dollars. If it had been anybody else, they'd say something. Even if they didn't like it."

She stood there with her back still turned, eggs in hand. Ray reached to touch her arm but stopped an inch or so away. "I'm sorry, honey. I don't know why that happens."

"It's always the same conversation, isn't it?" she said. "It's like talking about the weather for us."

"It shouldn't happen that way," he said, not knowing what else to say. When she didn't respond, he started to go upstairs to change.

"But what I hate most is that it's all just too damn silly!"

He paused in the doorway. "It's not silly if it's hurting you." She was crying, still with her back to him. The right thing to do would be to put his arms around her. But he couldn't bring himself to do it. He didn't want to talk about this. He didn't want to say that he, too, felt it was silly and stupid and he felt small and petty every time his own feelings were similarly hurt. And he didn't want to say that he was angry with her for not being better at this than he was. She'd always been the more socially adept of the two of them—if she couldn't solve this, what hope did he have?

"There are people without homes," she said, "people who have lost everything. There are people whose every day is a desperate gesture, and here I am crying because some silly women at the office where I work didn't notice my new hairdo!"

"I know. But it's more than that."

"It's more than that. It's the lunches. It's the conversations. It's all the moments you're not invited in."

"It's feeling like whatever you say, they're not hearing you. That no matter how much you wave your arms and jump up and down, they're not seeing you. You feel stupid and crazy and paranoid, because you know it doesn't make much sense—it has to be something you're doing, but you never can find a good enough reason in the things you're doing to explain it."

"And when you . . . when we die, no one but our daughter is going to remember we were ever here."

"I just can't believe that," he said.

"Really? You don't believe that?"

"I can't accept it," he said.

The high school parking lot was full and then some. It was all senior kids in the show, and for many of these parents it would be their final opportunity to see their children as children, even though so few of them looked like children anymore.

"I never imagined her this way," he said.

"What way?"

"Grown up. It's ridiculous, but I never imagined this day would actually come."

"Wouldn't it be sad if it never came, Ray?"

"Oh, of course. But still, it feels as if she just went out to play one day, and never came back."

They ended up in the overflow parking by a rundown grocery. They crossed the street nervously, watching the traffic. Visibility was poor. Wet streets and black, shiny pavement, multicoloured lights drifting in the wind.

Ray kept glancing at the front entrance as he pushed forward. Around them the headlights and car reflections floated randomly, like glowing insects looking for somewhere solid to land.

The lobby was packed with parents and their children, leaving little room for movement. Molly would already be on stage, waiting nervously behind the curtain. Janice wanted to rush into the auditorium, always afraid they'd be left without a seat, but Ray held back. Like Janice he hated crowds, but he needed to take in this part of it one final time. He would never experience this again. No more opportunities to act like other parents, in front of other parents.

These were families he had seen at dozens of events over the years, not that he really knew any of them. Some looked so pleased they actually glowed. But most had the anxious look of someone who has forgotten, and forgotten what they have forgotten.

He couldn't focus on any single group or conversation for more than a few seconds. He closed his eyes against the growing insect buzz, opened them again to clusters of coloured dots vibrating asynchronously. If he were only a little smarter, he might understand what was going on here.

A man a few feet away exclaimed "Hey there!" and started toward him. Ray recognized him as a neighbour from a few blocks away—the daughter had been in Molly's classes for years. Ray felt his face grow warm as the neighbour—Tom? Was his name Tom?—held out his hand. Deep in his pants pocket Ray's hand itched, sweaty, as he began to pull it out.

"Quite the special evening, don't you think?" said Tom, if that was his name.

Ray had his hand out and managed a smile. Tom looked somewhat startled, nodded curtly, then brushed past to shake the hand of a man behind Ray. Ray wiggled his fingers as if stretching them, then stuck his hand back into his pocket.

Janice tugged at his sleeve. "Let's just go inside," she said, strain in her voice. But Ray didn't think he could move.

The lights blinked twice, and he was thinking there might be a power outage when he realized, of course, they were signalling the curtain. The crowd pushed forward and he felt himself dragged along, Janice's hand clutched in his.

When the curtain rose and the music started—an impressive storm of violins and horns—they craned their necks looking for Molly. The bandleader tended to move her for almost every performance. Ray always had the fear that she would be left out, that she'd be depressed that evening and hide out in the bathroom (she could be surprisingly dramatic for an offspring of such parents), or that she'd be miscued, misplaced. He was always prepared to defend her with his anger, for it was one thing to ignore him, or to ignore Janice, but it was beyond bearing for the daughter they both adored to be ignored, to have her feelings hurt.

But there she was! Second row back, close to the end, her black bangs whipping as she vigourously sawed with the bow. He could feel Janice settle back with relief. He sighed and started to lean back himself when he heard the high cry of a violin and looked up, already knowing it was Molly, playing the first solo part of the night, her eyes streaming. Leaning so far forward he could breathe the warmth of the woman's head in front of him, Ray felt himself beginning to cry and buried his face in his hands as his daughter's violin made that sweet, lonely sound floating high into the rafters and beyond.

He barely heard the rest of the concert, but it sounded impressively professional. Not that he was qualified to judge, but it had none of the rough, slightly off-key flavour he had expected. Nothing to impress the way Molly's moment in the spotlight had, but quite good, surely, none the less. He and Janice decided to sit through the break, not wanting to wade into that crowd scene again. He watched the audience: some still on the edges of their seats, some leaning back in bored, awkward semblances of relaxation. A few with heads bowed, touching each other, as if praying.

Did any of these people realize they were being watched? In their private moments did they imagine they, too, were invisible?

He glanced back up at the stage. Molly was staring at him. He felt a rush of embarrassment, hoping she didn't think he had been ignoring her performance. She looked smaller, younger, and it made him think of when it seemed she had been mostly his and not this almost-adult travelling at the speed of light out of his world. Claire didn't invite me to her sleepover and I'm, like, her third-best friend! The way she had looked up at him that night, surrounded and embraced by toys she'd soon find babyish, he had thought she was demanding some explanation. It was as if she'd suddenly discovered she'd inherited his leprosy—why hadn't he told her before?

"These things happen, sweetheart." Of course they do, especially in this family. "I'm sure she didn't mean to hurt your feelings." Because she wasn't aware of you or your feelings. "Sometimes you just have to be the organizer, the party-thrower, and invite her." It had been good advice, but he had prayed she wouldn't follow it. What would he say to her when they ignored her invitations?

In fact, Molly did not follow his advice, and he never heard

another word from her on the subject. Perhaps she understood better than her parents. A child prodigy in the realm of invisibility. If she had friends after that, if she was invited places, she didn't share that information.

After the concert they made their way backstage to congratulate her, even though the seeming aggressiveness of the crowd agitated him. Janice pressed herself as close to the walls as possible, her cheekbone practically rubbing the brick. Finally they stood huddled together backstage as rivers of people flowed around them, spinning off into laughing, celebratory groups. Ray scanned the room for Molly, thinking that of course none of this should be any cause for anxiety, but he felt a rising tide of nervousness, beginning with an itchiness in the bottoms of his feet, tightening his calves and creating small but intense shooting pains in his knees. He held his head up stiffly and gulped for air. The room grew suddenly grey, the people moving around him outlined in ice and silver. He held one hand out, the skin ragged around the outlines, fading.

"Daddy?"

Molly stepped out of the bright light and into his reach. She carried her violin folded into her arms like a baby. Her eyes were wide, frightened, but they did not blink, did not avert from him even for a second as she looked at him, looked at him.

He pulled her to him and the three stood close together, not hugging—none of them good about hugging in public—but making sure they maintained contact as the world spun and jerked and solidified in its slow return to the real.

Molly hardly spoke on the way home, turning away their compliments with uninviting syllables, grunts, and nods, even refusing her father's proposition of hot dogs and sundaes at a neighbourhood shop. She retired early, but they could hear her playing her romantic classical CDs softly, rearranging furniture, "doing her inventory" as Janice called it, packing for college and the life to come. She'd been packing for more than a month, trying to decide what bits of her old life to bring forward. The plan was she would leave in three weeks for a summer job at a music camp in upstate New York, and from there to school in the city. They had argued for months over whether they would drive her—it felt wrong not to be there with her for the big transition. It seemed all terribly too grown up and recklessly premature to Ray, who already missed her to the point of physical pain. But something about Molly's determination that she do this alone finally persuaded him, and Janice reluctantly went along. Now Janice refused to speak about it.

The most difficult part of it all was that he was almost thrilled she was leaving. He imagined her going north, being absorbed into the life of the city and coming out of it a success, a famous person who had escaped the sick anonymity passed down from her unfortunate parents. In his imagination she became a fabulous, soaring star, and even as his heart was breaking in anticipation of her absence, his lost, invisible voice inside was saying go, go, go, don't look back.

Even with that sense of hope, however, they could not escape what their lives had become. An hour later Ray and Janice were ready for bed. They lay down together in loose-fitting pyjamas, pushing off the bedclothes lest they bind and constrict. They both could feel the pain approaching, as if from a long distance gathering speed, its mouth open and the night wind whistling through the narrow gaps between its needle-like teeth.

They clasped hands as their spasms began, Janice's rocking her body almost off the bed. She clutched his hand until he cried out, which triggered even worse convulsions in the both of them, bodies snapping at the ends of whipping arms, mouths pulled back in fish-expression grimaces, tears and sweat burning across their faces and softening the roots of their hair. He willed his body to stay together, to remain solid, begged it to stop its flow across the bed and onto the floor, as every skin cell fought against transparency and his mind battled evaporation.

They bit their lips until they bled, clamping their mouths to prevent the escape of their cries. They had decided long ago that Molly must not know, that if she weren't told she might even escape this. And if she were to overhear, what could they say to her? For how do you explain the terrible pain of invisibility?

A month later Molly was gone as planned. Another week and she'd still not called to check in. It bothered them both, but perhaps Janice the most. Now and then he would catch her visiting in Molly's room, but she would not speak of any of it.

Eventually Janice quit her job without notice. She'd been there fifteen years, but she said she'd "never felt welcome."

"Never? Not even in the beginning?" Ray couldn't quite believe it. He was a little angry with her—they needed the money, and she hardly seemed ready for job hunting.

"In the beginning I pretended. I don't know why, but now I can't pretend anymore. I go in and I shut my office door and I cry all day."

"All day?" He wanted to be sympathetic, but he was too shocked. He'd believed she'd been happy until the last few years. She hadn't been like him—she'd seemed to have friends, she talked as if there'd been a camaraderie at work, her opinions were respected. He'd always suspected that the invisibility she'd felt these few years had been something she'd contracted from him. "I'm so sorry . . . I had no idea."

She collapsed in his arms. He wanted to tell her he understood, that he knew how she felt.

Finally, a few days later, Ray decided to call the place Molly worked. At first the person on the other end claimed never to have heard of her. Ray sat down on the edge of the couch, holding the phone to his chest. Then someone else came on who knew her, then finally it was her voice, distant yet energetic, interested in a way he'd never heard in her before, and yes she was all right, she'd just been busy, yes she would write, but she was just so busy.

Ray didn't tell her that her mother had quit her job. He said they were doing wonderfully; they had so many things to do they couldn't fit them all in. He went so far as to make up the name of a couple they'd recently met, with similar interests, and the events they had attended together.

Molly responded with a few stories of social events of her own. He had no idea if she was telling the truth, but he decided to believe her, and she did sound convincing. She sounded as if her parents had no further place in her life. Although this brought a note of genuine sadness into everything he said to her after that, he still cheered her on, and actually hoped, God help him, that she stayed as far away from them as possible, for her sake.

He told Janice about the call, making it seem that he and Molly had talked far longer than they actually had. She nodded as if disinterested, but he could see the wetness of her eyes, the stiffness in her features. She wouldn't talk about it.

That night the spasms were more violent and painful than ever before. Janice's sweeping arms broke a bedside lamp, and he spent half the night comforting her and bandaging her wounds.

At work Ray made himself say hello to everyone in his office every morning. It was part of a plan to make himself present. Never mind that he had tried similar tactics before. He used to keep a journal of such attempts: times he'd said hello with no response, times he had been ignored in conversations, obviously excluded from invitations. Stores where he had been unable to get sales assistance, restaurants where the waiters ignored him even when he waved menus in their faces, times cars had almost struck him in pedestrian crosswalks, days in which he'd had absolutely no human contact before the daily escape home to Janice and Molly.

Now he pulled this journal out of his desk and threw it into the trash, determined once again that these things wouldn't happen to him again or, if they did, he would ignore them. He would be his own company, if need be. The best of companions.

That afternoon the building had a fire drill. He walked out with the other employees, offering up his own jokes to match theirs. He couldn't be sure whose jokes were being laughed at, and whose ignored. Too much noise and confusion. But he at least felt like part of the group.

Out in the parking lot the group of employees separated into two groups, one on either side of him. He looked around: he was at the exact centre, the point of separation, standing with neither group. He turned to the group on his left, listening to the general conversation, seeking an opening. Finally he offered up some comment about the hot pavement. He could almost see his words slide by their faces, catching on nothing, drifting beyond the group. He turned to the group on his right, wondering aloud how long the drill was supposed to last. The group appeared to stare up into the hot sun, preferring to blind themselves rather than to acknowledge him. When the all clear sounded, the other employees returned to work upstairs. But Ray climbed into his car and went home.

Another month passed and he noticed Janice seemed to have less and less to say to him when he called home. Then there was a period of days in which she didn't answer the phone at all. After work he would walk into the house to confront her, and her excuse would be she must not have heard the phone ringing, she'd been out working in the yard (their yard, layered as it was with gravel and wood chips, seemed to have little to work on), or she'd been out shopping (but what did she buy?).

Then there came the morning Ray called home every ten minutes with no response.

A few minutes after his last call he found himself loitering outside his boss's office door, coughing, trying to look as ill as possible. He felt like a kid. He winced dramatically as he walked through the door, then looked up to see his boss hadn't noticed. Of course.

Ray cleared his throat. No answer. "Excuse me, Jim?" Jim appeared to be hypnotized by whatever he had up on the screen. "I'm feeling really ill. I have to leave!" He practically shouted it.

His boss looked up in surprise, said, "Sure, do what you have to do," and turned back to his computer.

At first he couldn't find Janice. She wasn't in the kitchen, and the living room TV was cold. He called her name from the bottom of the stairs, but there was no answer. He went outside and walked around the yard looking for signs of her supposed gardening activities. The yard looked as sad and neglected as he'd expected. He felt compelled to look into the shrubs, pull back weeds and search the ground for her body. He found some of Molly's old toys: a yellowing Barbie and a toy ice cream truck. They must have been hiding out there at least a decade. He looked up at the house. It appeared abandoned. The roof was badly in need of repair. How long had it been deteriorating? He looked at his hands, half expecting them to be an old man's hands. Had he been asleep? How many years had he lost?

Finally, in their bedroom, he found her.

She writhed in pain, an insect pinned alive to the bed. Her arms and legs wriggled, her mouth opened and closed silently. He'd never imagined she did this alone—this was something they'd always shared.

He looked more closely. Some distortion of the body. Then he realized she had no hands, no feet.

Ray called in sick the rest of the week and stayed home with Janice. The week after, with her no better, he applied for two weeks of sick leave. On the phone his boss again seemed nonchalant. Do what you have to do. As if Ray really had a choice. Did his boss even know Ray was married? Ray didn't think the man had ever asked. Ray wore a ring, but it was pale yellow, blending into his skin. Invisible if you weren't really looking.

He saw no evidence, however, that his remaining home did her any good. During her better times she would lie there, staring at the ceiling, her skin glowing with the grey of fish in shimmering pools. Now and then one piece or another of her would fade into shadow, or bleach to the colour of the surrounding sheet, making of her body an archipelago as she slept. These bits would fade back into visibility as she awakened, and sometimes she would be reinvigorated, getting up and walking around, fixing herself something to eat.

At her worst she shuddered and convulsed, gripping the sides of the bed with hands that weren't there, the skin on her arms and legs flickering in and out of existence like quick bursts of lightning. Despite his growing horror at touching her, he would lie down next to her and embrace her, hold her tightly as if to anchor her to the world. The irony was that he rarely convulsed himself during this period and had not been aware of his own painful invisibility for some time.

"I'm taking you to the doctor," he said one morning. "It's ridiculous that we've waited this long."

"You can't," she said from under the covers. She'd pulled them up over her head, so that all he could sense of her was her frail voice, a few rounded shapes, stick-figure limbs beneath the quilt. If he went over and pulled the covers back, would he see anything?

"Why can't we try?"

"He won't believe you."

"Maybe there have been other cases, and they're not letting on because it would cause a panic. Besides, he'll see the spasms, he'll see what happens to your body, your skin."

"Do you really think he'll see anything? Do you think he'll notice anything at all?"

Of course not. But he would not say it. "We have to do something. I have to do something."

"Stay with me. That's doing something."

And he did.

One night he awakened to her coughing. He lay watching her, her naked back glowing, pulsing with each cough. There was a pearly

84

green aura he thought strangely beautiful, and he felt guilty that he could think it beautiful. She sighed. The coughs grew softer, the colour shifts more subtle, a gauzy, greenish cream. She seemed to recede from him into the other side of the bed. Cough. Into the wall.

And then he was looking at the bare wall, the empty plain of bed beneath it. He held perfectly still. And waited. He gave it time, gave her time to come back to him. Waited an hour. Then waited two hours. And then began to cry. And then began to sob.

He did not leave the house for several weeks. This was a conscious decision. Not out of grief. He wasn't even sure he was grieving. His reasons were investigative. Experimental. Since she had vanished so suddenly, couldn't she reappear suddenly as well? He could be sitting at breakfast, and she might suddenly be sitting in the chair across from him, sipping her coffee and reading the morning paper. Or perhaps she'd show up at the front door, knocking, since she hadn't had her keys when she disappeared. Or perhaps he'd wake up one morning and she'd be lying in bed beside him, her face nuzzled against his arm, because their bed was the last place he'd seen her.

Ray worried that if he wasn't in the house when she arrived, Janice might panic. It made perfect sense to him that she would arrive back in this world in a state of some confusion. He couldn't let her go through that alone.

He didn't bother to call work. It certainly didn't surprise him that they didn't call him. He imagined going to work as usual, then disappearing out of his cubicle leaving a half-eaten sandwich behind. How long would it take them to realize something was amiss?

But it seemed less funny after four weeks with no one calling. The automatic deposit of his paycheques continued uninterrupted.

Each day he spent an hour or so sitting in different chairs in different rooms. He saw things he had never noticed before: a small truck in the background of a painting, a birthmark on the ear of an anonymous relative in one of the photographs in the living room, a paperback book he'd thought lost under one side of the couch. He developed a new appreciation for the pleasant home he and Janice had created together.

After that first month he considered whether he should come up with a story to explain her absence to the curious. For the first time he realized how suspicious the circumstances of her disappearance might look to the police. He thought it fortunate that Janice had quit her job. She had no living relatives that he was aware of, and no friends out of her past (had there even been any?) ever bothered to call. Wouldn't the neighbours be a bit curious, wouldn't they notice that now he lived alone? Of course not.

Molly had to be told eventually. The next time she called he would offer some sort of explanation. He owed her that. But what if she never called? Should he track her down, introduce this sad twist of physics into the life of the one human being he still held dear?

Ray could not bear the idea that his daughter might never look into his face again, making him feel, at last, recognized. But it seemed as inevitable as his wife's fade from the world.

Four years later Ray was walking past a church a few blocks from home. It had become his habit each night to walk the nearby neighbourhoods, not returning home until sometime after midnight. Each house window was like a dimly-lit television, the people inside moving about with unexplained purpose behind partially drawn shades and curtains. The noises could just as easily be sobs or laughter, and he had no responsibility for knowing which was which.

Sometimes he attended nighttime lectures at this church, sitting near the back to observe. The lectures were usually nonreligious or at least nondenominational. Usually on a social issue "Of Concern To Us All," or a recounting of some overseas trip or expedition. Never anything he hadn't heard a hundred times before.

"Spontaneous Human Invisibility," it said on the church activities sign. "8 PM Wednesday." It was five after the hour. The lights inside appeared dim, and he thought for a moment the lecture must have been cancelled. A woman his age, greying hair pulled back, a pale brown, unflattering knee length dress, appeared suddenly out of the shadows and turned into the church, disappearing through the doors. Without thinking he hurried after her.

"In every case the person was physically present, but according to reliable witnesses of good reputation and standing in the community, the person could not be seen or heard."

The man at the podium wore a stiff white shirt, striped tie, black pants. Black shoes that gleamed with a high gloss, plastic-like finish. He reminded Ray of a Jehovah's Witness who had once come to his door, except the fellow at the altar wasn't smiling.

Perhaps eight or nine people sat in the front rows and an equal number on the sides. He could see movement in the unlit overflow seating sections off to either side behind rows of pillars: a fluttering as of birds trapped in shadow, a jerky nod, a gleam of cuff link or teeth. It seemed odd that people would sit in the dark, unless they were embarrassed or didn't want their attendance noted.

Then there was the lady he'd followed in here, sitting a few rows ahead of him. Particularly noticeable in that she was the only person in the room smiling.

"Besides these third party witnesses, we have limited testimony from the victims themselves, limited apparently because of embarrassment, or because they could not believe anyone would listen to their stories."

Ray felt movement nearby, saw three men sitting a few feet away, listening intently. They must have arrived after him, but he hadn't seen them come in.

"We have the story of Martha, who stopped going into grocery stores because not once in six years had a clerk answered any of her questions."

A nodding to Ray's immediate left. More late arrivals, but he hadn't felt or heard them sit down.

"And what are we to make of Lisa, a gorgeous woman from all accounts, who hasn't been asked out on a date since she was sixteen?"

A stirring in seats all around him, as if the air was charging with emotion.

"These are active, living people, who through no fault of their own have found themselves sadly, spontaneously invisible, often at the very moment they needed to be seen the most. Missed by their children, ignored by their spouses, underappreciated in the arenas of commerce, I contend these are members of the most persecuted of minorities, in part because it is a minority whose existence has gone for the most part unperceived."

These remarks were greeted with thunderous applause. Ray glanced around: every pew, every seat was filled. He stared at some of the faces and saw nothing remarkable about any of them.

Nondescript. Forgettable. The lady who'd led him here got up and headed briskly toward the door. He scrambled to follow her.

He passed close to one of the dark overflow areas. The faces staring out at him were grey, with even greyer eyes. They filled every inch of space, a wallpaper of monotone swatches.

When Ray got outside he discovered to his dismay that the woman was already more than a block ahead of him. Her shadow hinged like a stick insect as she made the corner.

"Hey!" he shouted. "Hey!" And ran after her.

He followed her for several blocks, never making much progress. He shouted and screamed until his lungs were on fire, at first thinking the local residents would be disturbed. Infuriated, they would call the police.

No, he thought. No, they won't.

And so he shouted and screamed some more. He yelled at the top of his lungs. There were no words in what he was screaming, only fragmented syllables his anguished mouth abused.

At the end of the street the sky had lightened, yellow rays spreading through lines of perspective, stringing the distant houses together with trails of fire. He could see the woman had stopped: a charred spot in his retina, the edges of his vision in flames.

He arrived breathless and on the verge of fainting, awed by the observation that the sun had arrived with him. All around him the world lightened, then bleached, became day, and then became something beyond. White and borderless and a pain in his heart. He was amazed to find she was looking directly into his face.

"You see me," he whispered. Then, "But am I still alone?"

It seemed as if he'd never seen pity until he'd seen it in her face. Looking at him, looking at him, she nodded sadly for him and everyone else waking up in solitary beds at the edge of nonexistence.

And the world was silver. Then pewter as it cooled. He waited, and waited, then, finding enough shadow to make a road, he followed it to his house and the rest of his days there. Alone.

And to any eyes that might pry on that place, occasionally, and only occasionally, visible.

HEAD EXPLOSIONS

Last week a downtown gallery paid twenty of us five hundred dollars each to sit quietly in chairs while high paying customers walked among us and stared. The customers weren't supposed to touch, there was plenty of security on hand, but there are always a few idiots in any fair-sized crowd. While most are appalled or awed enough by the transformation in our appearance to keep a respectful distance, there are always a few who cannot resist putting their hands in, feeling the surfaces, interfering with the equipment. For us it can mean varying degrees of traumatic sensory confusion, an outrageous violation of our person. But I suspect it's somehow worse for the curious few who dare.

After the show was over I went back to my apartment to eat. I don't eat in public anymore—I don't know any of us who does. I cook entirely with a microwave and a blender. Sauces, juice blends, and smoothies mostly, but my appetite's pretty much the way it's always been—I crave good, solid food. Nothing else will fill me. So sometimes I chop a little cooked fish and meat up separately to add to the liquid diet.

I was exhausted, but I still forced myself to examine each piece of meat, prodding with my finger, taking the measure of it, trying to decide if it was small enough. It's a delicate balance—you want the pieces big enough that you feel as if you're eating a filling amount, but small enough that you won't choke on them. Few of us have teeth, you see. I have one, displaced to the outside of the base of what's left of my neck, like a broach or a miniature Christmas tree ornament. So every bite is like teasing asphyxiation.

Our bodies have compensated by creating a great deal more stomach acid. Every one of us suffers from nightmarish heartburn, which requires a constant wiping down of tender exterior anatomy to avoid deterioration.

When I finally got a mixture that seemed the proper balance between risk and reward, I pulled back the sore flap of skin covering the stubby opening that leads down into my stomach and poured it in, splashing it into the fleshy filaments surrounding my throat stalk. I hate that—they're so difficult to clean.

There are rumours that a few of us have videotaped our meals and sold the tapes. Apparently for some there is a sexual appeal in this act. We live in interesting times, but I'm willing to concede that perhaps we've always lived in interesting times.

I wouldn't care to watch such a thing—I've finally permitted myself to look into a mirror but I certainly wouldn't eat near one. I'm not going to judge those who want to make money off their own eating habits, however. Most of us have trouble holding down a regular job.

All over the country the terrorists are blowing up heads. The explosive is a liquid or gel, consumed in the form of a fast food drink, a popular brand of shampoo rubbed into the hair, a flavoured toothpaste brushed across the teeth. The fuse, according to our government, is a "dangerous thought."

My memories of the moment of my own transformation are somewhat vague, full of colour and thunder, and I suspect mostly fantasized. My life before this was no one's fantasy. I loved my wife and children, but without much passion. I thought work was okay, a way to put food on the table, but a thousand other jobs would have served just as well. I can't honestly say I was interested much in anything, and I can't honestly say that realizing that bothered me in the least. But I was content. I was content just to breathe and taste and see whatever it was that passed before my eyes.

I believe it was a Saturday. As I did most weekends I watched TV a few hours, took a nap, then stared out our bedroom window at the sprinkler, and the way the falling beads of water made the car on the other side break apart into distorted little bits of shape and colour. I had some conversation with my wife and daughter. I don't

believe my son and I spoke, but I'm not sure. It was an ordinary day, just like the days of most people in the world. Most people have ordinary days I think, nothing remotely special. Later I went into the bathroom to wash. I have always liked washing my hair—call me strange, I don't care. Then I was shampooing my hair from a new container I'd bought that very afternoon on sale. The day-glow-orange containers filled several shelves. Additional shampoo was available in the dumps at the front of the store. Pictures of happy-go-lucky shampooers hung from the ceiling. I bought four bottles and rushed home, unaccountably eager to clean my hair.

I was standing in front of the bathroom mirror. I remember that image of myself: smiling goofily. I lathered my head vigourously, with what seemed manic desperation, my hands a blur. The flash was so bright—I remember thinking it was the late afternoon sun through the window, reflecting. But such a memory is impossible, I think now, for my head was already gone. I have no memory of having had dangerous thoughts. I'm not sure I could even identify a dangerous thought from among all its less dangerous brethren.

The government will not reveal the brand names of the products involved, fearing the effect such information would have on the economy. (Actually, the exact expression the President used in his speech was "our economy," but how many people truly feel that kind of ownership? Instead they have bills to pay, families with needs, and paycheques which will not stretch. Even the names of the retail outlets which sold the booby-trapped liquids and gels are suppressed.

As a result, very few brush their teeth or shampoo their hair anymore, and they consume their fast food meals (for to give them up entirely would be out of the question) without anything to wash them down. In consequence, approximately point-oh!-five percent of the population died last year choking on said meals. Most of those incidents occurred during lunchtime rush hour, drivers eating in their cars as they hurried back to work following the mandated truncation of lunch breaks passed during the last session of Congress. Another point-oh!-oh!-eight percent of the populace died in traffic accidents caused by drivers in the throes of asphyxiation. The government is looking into the problem; corrective legislation is being contemplated.

Personally, I do not drive anymore. My very presence in an automobile would be a distraction, a potential cause of more accidents. I try to imagine that I am lucky just to be alive.

Among those whose heads have exploded, fatalities, in fact, are rare. And most of these have been due to the inevitable distractions—it is hard to drive one's car safely, for example, when one's head is in mid-explosion.

The actual explosion of the head, while disturbing, shocking, and/or disruptive, is completely survivable when it's a result of this kind of terrorism, as we now know.

I allowed myself to watch an internet broadcast of one such incident. I don't believe I could watch it again, but the one time was instructive, and it illuminated a great deal about my own situation. In this surveillance film a man in a department store dressing room is brushing his hair. He takes a small bottle out of a shopping bag, opens it, and proceeds to rub the yellow cream into his hair. Suddenly a bright white light fills the screen. When the image clears, the man is holding his arms up to the sides of his head, fluttering his hands. There is no head, really. The parts of his head, at least we must assume these are parts of his head, are floating in the air above his slightly burnt, truncated neck, apparently in a kind of stasis imposed by agents and methods unknown. After a couple of minutes the bits of floating head and bone, flesh, blood, and grey matter settle down, arranging themselves into an aesthetically-pleasing *object* resembling an exotic plant or abstract sculpture. After this event, we are told, the brain and sensory apparati, although profoundly altered, continue to function, albeit differently.

Personally, I have no useful recollection of the moment of explosion. It doesn't really hurt. As I said before: colour and thunder. This has led to a certain amount of paranoia which I've done my best to control. How do I know there was an explosion at all? Perhaps I was drugged, anesthetized, taken to some clinic where highly experimental plastic surgery was performed. If there was an explosion, even with their advanced methods of putting Humpty Dumpty back together again (incorrectly, of course, but I suppose that was their intent), why didn't I die from the shock? None of the doctors the media have interviewed has provided a decent answer. There are too many unanswered questions.

But then, there have always been too many unanswered questions.

And do my "apparati" function much the same as they did
before? I'm not sure exactly how to answer this. I forget people's

names, but I was starting to forget people's names before the incident. It's a natural part of aging, I'm told. I've retained most, although certainly not all, of my previous memories. But I'm hardly the same person. I certainly live a different life. Ask my wife and children, if you can find them. I live in a small apartment, I work only sporadically, I have no friends. It's all been blown away.

As one commentator has explained, "If you sculpt chicken-flavoured cat food into the shape of a rose, it's still chicken-flavoured cat food."

There are huge problems with such a metaphor. I would hope that for most of us, our brains function entirely differently than cat food.

On the other hand, the rose metaphor is an apt one in that the brains in these redesigns-by-explosion appear to be peeled away into a variety of layers and swirls reminiscent of petals, sepals, stamen, stigma, and filaments. And each flower is different. Each "head" is of its own, individual species. They resemble no earthly flower, but perhaps flowers native to some other world.

I had not seen many of my fellow victims together in one place, just two or three at the specialist's office many of us now go to. Of course I've seen them on the news, but never a great many of us together. I never even thought much about it—it was a natural reluctance. Then I walked into that gallery last week, and encountered nineteen of my own. I have to say, it was one of the few times I've ever felt a part of anything.

I was late. The others were already seated in chairs arranged throughout the gallery. But I took the time to go around and shake the hand of each one. Although I could not tell where most of them were looking, I got the distinct impression they were paying as much attention to me as I was to them.

They tended to wear unisex clothing, making it difficult in some cases to tell the women from the men. Did this experience make you feel sexless somehow? I suddenly realized that I hadn't thought about sex, at least in any personal way, since my change. And I was wearing a baggy shirt and pants, so loose in fact they might have been used to drape furniture.

In several of them the eyes remained intact, but with altered attachment. One eye might perch on a stalk, while its partner lurked on the underside of a faux leaf. For the majority (myself included) no eyes were evident at all. But we aren't blind; our visual functionality has shifted to other elements of the reconfigured head. I have no actual eyes that I can see in the mirror, yet sight does occur. As far as I can tell, vision comes from six or eight overlapping points of view, and somehow this is coordinated into more or less a single image in the perceptual frame.

More or less. Sometimes I see behind people. Sometimes I see the secondary facial expressions they attempt to hide, which contradict the emotions they're presented to the world.

But no one tells the truth, not completely. Hasn't that always been so?

I'm told that the hearing functionality in these cases shifts from the ears to any available orifice. In the weeks following my change I tried to pinpoint the sense of hearing in my own equipment, playing music then touching, holding, covering various bits to see if there was some diminution of sound. My findings were inconclusive—the point of perception appeared to change each time, as if running away from my attempts to suppress it. Finally last week I was carefully washing down the various stems, shafts, flutings, and fibres now making up my countenance—a toilet I must do almost daily—when my forefinger strayed upon a series of tiny flute-like holes along the central shaft rising out of one side of what used to be my esophagus. As I closed each one the ambient sounds of my apartment diminished a little more, until with my fingers splayed all along the shaft the voice of the world silenced completely. I had found my new ears.

Noses are apparently considered superfluous by the terrorists and in all reported cases of head explosion the victims lose their sense of smell. I would miss the aroma of freshly baked Dutch apple pie if pie weren't so difficult to eat.

Mouths are recreated depending on the needs of the new configuration: sometimes they reside at the junction of two flapping "leaves," sometimes they are placed at the centre of a neck stem, and sometimes they appear to take over every part of the exploded head, a voice issuing when all parts vibrate in unison to form a word.

I would not care much for the latter. Something feels a bit too supernatural about its methodology. In my case the eating functionality and the vocal functionality have separated. Nourishment is taken through that inarticulate, sewer-like ruin my throat has become. But I've traced my voice to a freshly sprouted bulb near the top of a tall, gently waving structure approximately where my right ear used to be.

Sometimes the exploded heads are remarkably beautiful and sometimes the exploded heads resemble, as would be expected, exploded heads. The terrorists face the same problems as the aesthetic pioneers of any era—at first no one knows exactly how to interpret what it is they have produced. But over time theories evolve, academics in need of some specialized area for their vitae become self-appointed experts, a few books and papers are written, a conference is called, and a new movement is born.

The phone is ringing again. Although I have no more friends and no more family the calls pour in every day. The idea of holding that plastic appliance up to my delicate new parts fills me with revulsion. I walk to the phone and rip the cord out of the wall, tossing the phone itself behind the couch. If it isn't the government's remarkably unhelpful doctors, it's the hordes of desperate academics.

There is no real comfort for the victims. I try not to let it get me down, but I wish they'd just leave us to the air and sunlight. I do appreciate the sunlight now, far beyond anything I felt before.

As the darkness rises out of the streets I steel myself. I sense the vermin rise with the dark, the roaches and the rats still trying to figure out what they can do with me and my altered head. Am I now more edible? I do not wish to know.

Our government has condemned these acts of terrorism, pledged to use troops as needed, and curtailed the rights of all its citizens for their own protection.

I see that one of my kind is on the television screen. I keep the television on all the time now, not because I'm anxious about the terrorists (what more could they do to me?), but for moments like this, when one of us appears before the cameras. I'm amused by the way the networks have placed their microphones, hanging at all angles around him? her? I turn up the volume.

"Why, there's no question the government itself is behind these attacks. Open your eyes, unclog your ears! Do you need your heads exploded before your senses will perceive the truth? Only the government has the resources to come up with such an advanced technological terrorism! This is surely the first of many experiments in surreal crowd manipulation!"

He's obviously insane. Wouldn't you be, undergoing such a traumatic change? It's simply an absurd response to an absurd world. But these are the times we live in. People are willing to believe any damn thing, because people feel, perhaps rightly, that nothing and no one can be trusted. Particularly the government which is supposed to serve at our will.

A few months ago a team consisting of a doctor, a social worker, and two police officers showed up at my door. They were ready to take me directly to a support group, they said. "It's for your own good," the doctor reassured me. "I understand how you feel. I've recently received special training in your problem."

Countless public service announcements have been made concerning my special "problem." Talk shows and news specials have covered the topic ad nauseum. Books have been written. Movies have been rushed into production. A twenty-four-hour hotline has been established to report, and support, new victims.

No one knows anything, really. The terrorists, if they do exist, have made no demands. There are ten thousand suspects, someone said. Someone else said a million, maybe more. A few people have been arrested, but for "informational purposes only." Whatever that means. The complete lack of information has become its own nihilistic art form.

No one likes looking into our new "faces." They don't know where to look.

Now they have that stupid political science professor on the screen. Why do they keep interviewing him? If anyone could use a healthy head explosion it would be him. "Perhaps these victims deserved their fate. Anyone who is a passive supporter of a corrupt government is hardly innocent of blame." People have demanded his firing or resignation. A minority group has gathered a defense, preaching academic freedom. The ACLU is involved.

I don't think I deserve this, at least no more than anyone else. But when I think about how I was as a father, how I was as a husband, I can't really say that I deserve better. In a sense, I suppose, I'm lucky. And I don't mean just because I'm alive, or that without an artistic bone in my body I became art. Even though that *is* a helluva thing.

I'm lucky because something finally happened to me. Something life-shattering finally has occurred.

I fall asleep in front of the TV as I do almost every night. I wake up with the sun coming through the window again, warming my leaves. There is a comfort in the sameness of this routine—it reminds me of the days before my head exploded, when I was a father, a husband.

This morning I think about what I want to do for my next step. I start by cleaning the apartment, paying particular attention to the bathroom where this change occurred. I find bits of blasted tooth in one corner by the sink. I stick them inside a padded envelope in a bottom drawer beneath my old jeans.

I spend most of the morning gazing at myself in the mirror. I believe that wide, convoluted blossom on the left-hand side, the one that resembles a bit of cauliflower, was once my cerebellum. The cerebrum, I think, forms the four leaf-like clumps around it. My medulla oblongata stands flush and proud near the centre of the new structure. And bits of spinal cord curl like snails around a pale stalk of esophagus.

This afternoon I sit at the open window, letting the sun warm my narrow spiral of temporal lobe, a passing breeze setting these other delicate parts into gentle, humming vibration. I, what's the word, *vegetate*? My life has changed, I think, but ultimately it has changed very little.

CHAIN REACTION

Friday, 10 AM

For you the world has always been shaky and hand-held. Focus, more often than not, is problematic. You've never understood how people can pick the most important thing out of a selection of too many.

Everything begs for your attention. Every object contains its own mating call. That peculiar rock, shaped like a bell. That half-dead tree miming its final fall. The sun, always present and hurtful, and always too low. The severe network of rips up and down the hillside, erosion from the recent torrential rains. Unidentifiable twists of rusted metal lying alongside the cracked and weathered road. And just ahead of you, in the back of that brown 1974 Buick Estate station wagon, the longest and heaviest station wagon ever made, sit the three children from Hell, illegally without seat belts, the Devil's own hounds, who have poked fun and made faces at you throughout the past thirty miles. But because the trucking company that owns you and your Peterbilt insists on a highly unlikely level of courtesy, their corporate phone number emblazoned all over your vehicle, demanding that they be contacted regarding any lapse in said please-let-me-kiss-your-ass civility, you have smiled at these brats until your lips have started cracking.

You have grown to hate the driver of that monstrosity, not only because of his ineffectiveness as a parent, but because he is irresponsible enough to own and drive such a vehicle, a dinosaur which should have been outlawed years ago. Everything in life has become so crowded, but the highways most of all. You can feel your throat, your chest, tighten. *How does he keep that thing even alive?* you wonder, convinced there must be blood and human body parts involved.

You cannot believe things were always this bad. You're convinced that once upon a time cars were built better, roads were built better, people were built better. What you see today are networks of stupidity. You are forced to take your big rig over narrow mountain roads not much better than cattle trails. The state doesn't know how to take care of the roads anymore. Up on the embankment above you can see the bright yellow graders and bulldozers making repairs that should have been done years ago. And the way they're being driven, their wild swings sending gravel and stones tumbling onto the road below, you expect to see one of those huge steel beasties somersault down the slope any second now.

No wonder you're shaky. "Jittery!" you shout, punching the roof of the cab. As in *jitterbug*, as in your nerves dancing, wrapping around your throat until you can hardly breathe. "Jitter jitter jitter!" you shout, punctuating each word with a roof punch. As if in response the world takes a quick turn to the left, and you overcompensate, your right wheels throwing gravel into a row of windshields behind you. A scream of horns and you give a barking horn right back at them. Not your fault, you did nothing wrong. Guys like that Buick, they have no right to be on the road.

Red highlights are a razor blade across the eyeball. You scream louder than the pain warrants, but you've found that sometimes it feels good just to scream. You reach into the passenger seat for your pills, the cab jerks after hitting god-knows-what, and your hand hits your iPod, knocking it loose of its cord. The player hits the floorboard and you fear the worst. You barely notice the abrupt stop of music—lately everything is just so much noise.

"Dammit!" you slap the horn just for emphasis. Somewhere back in the line of cars someone answers with an annoyed horn of their own, and you seriously consider slamming on the brakes just to see who back there is paying attention.

You fumble with the pill bottle and snap the cap, get a green one, a yellow, and a red. The yellow is for wimps and cowards, but you swallow it anyway, thinking the red and green will cancel it out. You don't remember, exactly, what any of these pills do, but you know they do the trick, and tricks are what you need right now with so many assholes out on the road.

"They just level things out," is what you told Gena. "Like taking a plane to a rough board. *Smooth*." Which is as much poetry as you can stand. Gena always wants poetry, which means she likes being lied to.

"Smooth!" you shout, punching roof, punching windshield, and seeing with a smile that you made a little crack. You'll tell them back at the office that you spit up a rock.

Then the Buick wagon slows down and you have to slam those brakes after all. "Goddammit!" You know he did it just to get to you, thinking that he owns the road. Horns all around you screaming like it was the end of the world. Red light stabbing your eyes again. So you just jerk the wheel hard right to make them all stop, front end going right into that eroded embankment. But the back end gets away from you, swings wide across the road, jerking the cab out of the bank, turning you around with it, dragging you, so that now you're looking back down the highway behind you, the windshields bright and staring like a feast of insects, and your truck keeps spinning, so that you can hear the crunch and grind and smash of it all, but you can't see anything that you're hitting. And that's when you see the entire embankment give way, and the cars disappearing all around you as if they had been hallucinations, and now at last you're waking up.

Friday, 10:20 AM

Yellow blast of light and sound. Skies of dirt and stone. Random, brightly-painted metal, glass, bits and parts passing impossibly one through another. The backwards screaming thunder of the world's pain.

Friday, 1 PM

At last you climb over the edge of the world. The torn rim of it digs into your abdomen as you pull yourself onto the scattered roadbed. You hear crying, a release of steam, and overhead: voices, equipment.

You pull yourself to your feet. The vehicles in front of you lie half-buried in rock spill that extends in ridges up over the edge of the slopes.

"It's going to take some time!" you hear above your head. A voice electrically amplified. "Everything's too unstable! We'll cut a new path going down, shoring as we go, and pull you up that!" You fight the sun in order to raise your eyes high. Against the glare, leaning over the edge, stands a man in a construction helmet, a shadow growth from his face as if his mouth exploded: an electric megaphone. "I said it's *too windy* to bring a helicopter up here! Stay away from the edges! You, sir!" You think maybe he is pointing at you. "Stay away from the edge!"

Angry, stubborn, but you try to do what he says. Your legs don't seem to be working too well. But nothing ahead of you except a bunch of old wrecks. You turn back around, walk closer to where you climbed up from. The man's electric shouting is a bee in your ear and you wave it away. You look out over the edge. The road is gone. You keep looking, out to where the road wrapped around the bend in the mountain, and there is the bend, or at least the jittered margins of it. But there is no road. There is nothing between here and there but sky.

You try to look down into the hole, but you can't make yourself. You start walking toward all those old wrecks covered in broken stone and great arms of sand. The man's voice stops buzzing your ear.

Maybe you'll just walk back down the road. You'll walk back down this road all the way to Denver. If you see anybody else, you'll suggest that they do the same. You wonder why the man with the electric megaphone didn't suggest something like that. He didn't know what he was talking about. He was just trying to cover his ass. These stupid people. They didn't even know enough to walk away, to walk on down the road.

Then you see it: the jagged edge on the other side. The big empty. And between the two big nothings this flimsy shelf you're standing on, with these old wrecks, and with whoever is inside these old wrecks.

Friday, 1:15 PM
1985 Mk V Mini, Dark Blue (restored)

The front end is squeezed like a giant juice box for its last drops. Large stones, a couple of boulders, gather there. You can't stop staring at them. One looks like a dog. Another looks like a giant grey bird, landed and now feeding on the car.

The torn metal prevents you from getting all the way into the passenger seat, but by standing on the shoulders of the boulder dog you can lean through one of the windows.

You shove your jittery hands inside to check the female driver's pulse. Your palsied fingers flail inexpertly at her wrist.

"I'm sorry. Did that hurt? I'm so sorry. I'm just stupid about this."

Finally you detect a beat, unless it's some other vibration, the ground shifting under the roadbed. Beside your feet the gravel moves. You hold your breath.

"I guess it's holding my feet," she says. You jump, pull your hands back. She groans. Her head rotates against the rest, staring at you, small pupils swimming in twin pools of milk. "It's like a tight embrace, a hug, you know? If my ex-husband had held me like this we'd still be together."

She grins, then, her upper lip split, starting to bleed again.

"Try to stay calm," you say, automatically, even though she is perfectly calm.

"I won't be a problem," she says, "I promise. I know you don't want a hysterical woman on your hands, right? Well, despite all the things Frank used to say about me, I'm not hysterical."

She grins again, bloody drool slipping down her chin.

"You're okay. Help will be here soon. Did you hear the announcement? I can hear them up there working. They know what they're doing—they'll be here soon."

"Oh yeah, I'm sure. A lot of people hurt?"

"A few," you say, although you have no idea.

"Anyone dead?"

You shrug. But it embarrasses you, makes you feel stupid. You don't know if she can even see you shrug. "A couple that I'm sure of," you lie.

"But a few more you're kind of sure of?"

You look at her head, the blood caked there. "I don't really know."

"Right. You never can tell."

She sighs, closes her eyes, but her chest continues to rise and fall in ragged rhythm. You keep one hand on her arm, but you can no longer look at her. Instead you look out beyond the car: mist floating above the vehicles, and above that the rescuers up on the ridge, doing nothing as far as you can tell.

Your attention swings back. She sits perfectly still. Your fingers probe her wrist, shaking. You lean over with your left ear just above her nostrils. You let go of her wrist. You back out of the car.

A man's voice, yelling. You can't tell if it's pain, anger, or urgency.

Panic fills yours throat. You quickly glance over the wrecked vehicles in a desperate, manic inventory, searching for the big brown Buick station wagon with the three kids in the back. The heaviest, longest station wagon ever made. It is impossible to miss. It really stands out in a crowd.

You can find no sign of it.

Friday, 1:40 PM
Honda C100 Cub Motorcycle (year unknown)

The yelling continues, animal-like growls, punctuated by barks and quite human curses. Turning in that direction—a distant form, a highly animated stick figure, throwing its arms up and around with each shout, as if exercising, exorcising demons, but the legs are strangely still, fixed in place, glued to its display stand.

Closer, passing dented, colourful metal, the voice screaming, scattered, shattered rock on each side, faster, spurred on by the increasing volume of the scream, the torn world passing, passing, until at last face-to-face with this noisy animal, upright, his backside wedged against the unhappy front grille of the green pickup. Face filling your eyes, mouth stretched, spitting anger.

"Dammit it to Hell get me outta here ain't no sonovabitch gonna lend a feller a hand, damn!" the face caterwaulers on. Following the torso, the bloodied leg, down into the rock, the broken world, surrounding the legs, and here and there bits of the shattered motorcycle, the yellow frame swallowed up, pulled under, when the world exploded and the sky came down. "Damn! Ain't you gonna *do* something?! This goddamn mountain done half swallered my leg! Why don't you do something you goddamn stupid son of a bitch!"

Arms raised to the heavens now, screaming a prayer of rage. Somewhere back in the line of broken vehicles a horn sounds in agreement or complaint, so hard to tell in this nervous jumble of metal and stone discards, and then another, and another, punctuated by the repetitive phrase "Shut up! Can't you shut up?" making their meaning clear.

The exposed, broken figure, though still compelled to stay upright, lapses into silence then, tears streaming down his face, "Ain't nobody care for a feller in pain, a feller what got its leg caught like a rabbit in a steel trap, feeling bad enough he'd cut his own leg off if he . . ." He looks up, the brilliant whites of his eyes blazing through dirt and black grease. "Say, you ain't got a saw, now, do you? Hacksaw'll do. Hell, even a knife. Slide took me right off my bike, ate the bike and left me standin' here, tight against this old truck, now every time some body or some thing moves, anywhere on this god-blessed *earth*, that fallen mountain chews a little more into that leg, like now it's got its last meal, and it's gonna hang on to it for awhile, chew on it, you know? But I've got a knack for doing what needs doing, so you get me that saw, and I'll get to doing. We gotta deal? Oh, I'll do it, you betcher. Ask the folks in the truck, they know me, they're neighbours a mine. We're all up here together, for the grannie's birthday picnic."

You climb over the hood of the green truck to get to the inside, leaving behind the desperate figure punching the air with its screams and curses. He makes you embarrassed for yourself.

Friday, 1:50 PM
1980 Ford F-100 Army Green Pickup Truck

The old woman behind the steering wheel lies slumped against the driver's side window, a dark brown smear gluing her dirty grey hair to the glass. Her tongue protrudes slightly between almost nonexistent lips.

Three women in their early twenties lie in the truck bed, covered with blankets and propped up on pillows. They murmur to one another constantly, adding emphasis to their monologues with slightly louder, clearer statements. They appear dazed, confused, but largely unhurt. Scattered rock debris covers the blankets, with a few larger stones piled up behind the tail gate.

"Something wrong with Granny. She's asleep—she won't wake up! She is *rude*."

"*She* drove. We don't drive. What can we do?"

"You drive? Sure, you can drive. Say you can drive! Drive us away from here!"

"I don't know what happened. Do you? The mountain fell up, the mountain fell down, I don't know what happened! Can you drive?"

"I have a new outfit. Do you think it's yellow? I won't tell, unless you ask me. I think it's pink, yeah, I think it's pink."

"I'm hungry. We can go now, I'm ready to go! Dinner time! Say it after me, dinner time!"

"Are we going, soon? Can we take Granny? Do you have to stay here?"

"I don't want to leave Granny here!"

"The ground's all broke. I didn't do it. It was an accident. Accidents happen and somebody gets hurt. We had an accident today!"

"I need the bathroom. Where's the bathroom, John?"

"His name isn't John."

"Where's the bathroom, John?"

"His name isn't *John*!"

"Where's the John, John?"

They all laugh. The one on the left starts coughing, and can't stop coughing.

"No, I mean it. I need the bathroom *now*!"

"Are you crying? I'm not crying."

"That man is yelling! Why is that man yelling so loud? He hurts my ears."

"He hurts my heart."

"He's hurt! He's mad! He's mad that he's hurt!"

"What happened? Don't cry!"

"That man is crying! I'm not crying!"

"Why does stuff keep happening? I didn't do anything wrong. Stuff keeps happening!"

"Why does that man scream? I want to scream."

"See, I know how to scream."

"Stop screaming!"

"We don't know what happened. Is it a secret?"

"What happened? I don't want to be here! I don't want to scream!"

"Get us out of here! Help! We don't want to be here! I don't want Granny dead!"

"Are we going to die?"

The three sit quietly, blinking. They look at each other. The man in front of the truck keeps screaming, gradually going hoarse. He stares at you, then starts screaming again with sharp, staccato, raspy screams.

"It happens and happens and happens and happens."

"And then there's just nothing."

"Nothing but rocks and dirt and dirt."

"And nothing. Just nothing."

"But maybe some cake. I _like_ cake!"

They all laugh.

"Okay, okay. We'll just sleep now."

The three close their eyes tightly, lids creased from the effort. They are quiet.

The sun has begun its drop. It's going to be a cold one tonight. It's always ten to fifteen degrees colder up here than in Denver. You're not wearing your jacket. It's in the truck. But the truck, of course, is gone. As far as you are concerned, the truck never existed. This is the first day of the world, and survival is always the first chore on the first day.

Friday, 2:30 PM

1968 Light Green International Harvester Travelall

It looks like a giant metal lunchbox with wheels, pushed to the side and severely tipped, out of line with the others. But no more out of line than when it was driven on the highway, part van part truck part station wagon part SUV, poor cousin to them all. It looks undriveable, but it probably always has. Dirty brown rust creeps up the sides in long, meandering fingers. The tires are smoke-grey and cracked. The yellow dust from the morning sticks to the windows like a coat of mustard.

From inside the car music squeals and bellows, getting louder when the driver's window eases down to expel another cloud of smoke.

Sharp highlights in the metal fenders scraping the eye the closer you get. You almost expect quills to come flying, or some evil scent cast out of the exhaust pipe. But the clouds are starting to come in, and you know it won't be that long before the sun drops behind the last distant ridge.

As if the machines up top are waking from their naps their noises suddenly sound more aggravated. Progress, some might say, is being made. You wonder if they'll be able to work after dark. If they will dare.

The Travelall's window grates coming down again, and you think of all that grit fallen into the mechanism, scratching it into ruin. "Stop right there!" from inside a cloud of smoke. "Tell me what you want!"

You try to speak but the words aren't there. Neither are any sounds further evolved than a rasp. You wave your hands helplessly, as if falling over backwards.

Your mime almost causes a real fall. Your ankle tips and you overcompensate to escape the pain.

Smoky laughter from inside the Travelall. You wonder, briefly, if there's anyone actually inside. Maybe the car itself has a voice.

"Okay. Get in. You look harmless enough. But I warn you—I ain't."

You creep to the passenger side, the ground here feeling the most unstable of all. You think you hear the world cracking under your boots. The passenger door pops open just as you get there. Smoke pushes out like a trapped storm cloud. You close your eyes and make yourself sit down. A gorilla's arm brushes past you and strong-arms the door, shutting you inside with hot smoke and animal stink.

"The name's Rake. And you?"

You discover you can't open your mouth. You try to speak with your eyes but you know that you have no talent for it.

"Oh, I forgot. Avalanche got your tongue. *Snick snick.*" Like scissors, but it's the sound he makes when he laughs.

His face has too much hair. Hair fills the planes of his cheekbones, spills down his chin and neck. There's even hair, though not quite as thick, just below both eyes. You don't think you've ever seen that before, outside a comic book.

"I'll only warn you once. Don't look like you're gonna try anything. Then follow that up, by not trying anything. Look at the glove compartment. Don't open it! Just *look* at it. I'm not going to show you what's inside. I can't show you what's inside. I'm going to let you imagine that, and while you're at it, imagine what will happen if you do anything wrong, and I have to open that glove compartment."

You stare at your hands. You tell them not to move.

"Meet the wife and dog," he says.

Trash on the floor: Reese's Cup wrappers, a Pepsi can, a letter or two, covered in chocolaty shoe prints. The rusty glove compartment door.

"Behind you, halfwit!"

A twist in perspective: shaky car hood, interior light with no lens, stained upholstery peeling off the metal interior frame and hanging down. Then so close that he could bite off your face: a huge black Lab, directly behind you the whole time. Stink a little less than that on the man.

A twist to the other side: there, back in the far corner near the double doors, a woman ten years the man's junior, at least, her knees pulled up to her chin, dirty straw hair scratched down over her forehead.

It's then you realize the seats have been taken out, the interior filled by a striped mattress, flowered with brown rust stains.

You turn back around. The man is stroking the black ball fixed to the top of the long, crooked gearshift. "You get on outta here," he says. "If you ever find your voice, you tell the others what you seen. And what you didn't. I just wanted you to see the glove compartment. I just wanted you to think about what might be in there."

Friday, 3 PM
1974 Honda Accord, Green

Both headlights and front grille missing, the Accord sits back on its rear tires like some bloodied circus animal, front tires shredded in the effort to stop the inevitable, fluids dripping out of the engine, a spreading pool on the chewed pavement.

Once you're inside, the car bobs from wind or your own weight. Dark grey upholstered ceiling. Dirty black rubber mat jeweled with broken windshield. Torn soft grey seats, stuffing erupted in white tufts from multiple rips. But no driver.

A glimpse through the missing windshield: searching the surrounding grass, pavement, for an ejected body.

A small moan.

A hurried gaze back into the rear of the car, behind the driver's seat, the body thrown there, a man about thirty, maybe a little older: compressed from the collapsing rear-end of the car, squarish, his shoulders squeezed up into a confused shrug: the man has been reshaped into a suitcase.

Suitcase Man opens his eyes suddenly. The left eye socket is full of blood. Both eyes gaze forward, determinedly focused.

Suitcase Man opens his mouth, or maybe it's just the light changing. You can't tell. There's so much blood.

"I couldn't stop. The car just, jumped. I could feel myself, floating. I must have, blacked out. I woke up sitting here. I couldn't remember if I'd been driving. I was in the back seat! How could that happen? I kept thinking how lucky I was that my little girl wasn't with me. My wife died a year ago, and I have to work a lot out of town. My sister takes care of her. I'm supposed to see her this weekend. I hope this doesn't get in the way."

Your own hand suddenly appears, rising in the space between you like an apparition, a magic trick. The arm it is attached to is so caked with dark blood and grime it virtually disappears in the dimness, so that the hand appears severed, moving separate from the body.

Suitcase Man's mouth is open, and he is crying without sound. The hand floats toward Suitcase Man's shoulder, and touches it ever so lightly, as if to comfort, and Suitcase Man's mouth suddenly finds its sound as it fills with a scream.

The face of Suitcase Man darkens, recedes into the shadows, and closes.

A shaky glimpse through the open car door: dark-stained gravel, tennis shoes scuffling past. Somewhere a child cries. The light becomes painful as you get out.

―――――――――――――――

Friday, 3:20 PM
2007 Chevrolet HHR Panel Truck, Brown with Yellow Trim/Lettering
No visible damage except for a shattered front left headlight. Debris has slid beneath the front tires, filling the space under the axle, raising the front end almost a foot above the roadbed. A rich, caramel brown colour, the side panels are heavily ornamented with

yellow scroll work and the elaborately lettered "Johnson's Furs" and "Repair, Cold Storage, Delivery" and "Denver's Finest."

The panel truck is still running. Its sound is a soft and musical hum, in contrast to the construction equipment up on the hill.

The right turn signal blinks steady yellow. Where does it plan to go? There is nothing on this side but a couple of feet of torn road, followed by air.

The passenger door opens a few inches. The speaker is hidden: "Can you make it up those rocks? Climb in—I have bottled water. Hurry now—I've got the humidifier running. I can't leave the door open for long."

You glance off the side, then step, step, the sharp clink of useless keys in the right front pocket. The sky waves you on, back and forth. The caramel panel truck appears to rock in an attempt to free itself, and leap off the side, but you know it's an illusion caused by your run.

Feet slide sideways on the small incline of gravel and sand. The right front wheel dips suddenly, spitting a fist-sized rock past your thigh. You hesitate, then with a single stride reach the door and jerk it open, slamming it shut behind you as you tumble inside.

"Thanks for being quick about it," the speaker says, offering up a small bottle of Aquafina in your direction. You take it—he's already loosened the cap. You finish the job and take two long swigs, cap it.

It doesn't taste like water. If anything, it tastes like stale air.

The speaker nods. His uniform is a darker brown than the outside of the panel truck, but with the same yellow designs and lettering. His hair is a shade lighter brown, a pleasing complement. "My boss is crazy for the stuff. He keeps a cooler behind the seats, full for the mountain runs." He turns his head, staring into the side mirror. "Everybody okay back there? I have to keep the vehicle running to keep the humidifier going. So I'm not just wasting gas. In this climate the furs dry out quickly. My boss says the clients pay good money to keep that from happening. They store them cold, then they deliver them cool and humid." He looks out the windshield, his hands sliding up and down the steering wheel. "Coats, jackets, purses, hats, mini-vests, boleros—that's a kind of vest, but with sleeves. Fox and mink mostly, all kinds of colours. Expensive. You can only open the doors from up here—it's all electronic."

In the distance the clatter of equipment changes tone, as if it's running down. He looks at the gas gauge.

"But I don't want to run out of gas, either. Any ideas?" He looks at you directly. The shaking isn't the panel truck, or the ground, you remind yourself. It is your own head, signalling a negative.

The whites of his eyes become more prominent, their centres blacker. "You're thinking I won't need the fuel, right? We may get out of here, but our vehicles certainly aren't."

He stares at the wheel, the gauge. "My boss is gonna die. We've got some real expensive furs in here. But he probably has insurance, right? Not such a disaster, but the customers, they're rich people up in the ski towns, and they get steamed when everything isn't perfect. That's where I was headed. They want their furs in time for ski season, all fresh and clean. My boss calls it *rested*. 'They like their furs rested,' he says. But they'd probably stop using him, even when it's an act of God." He pauses. "I mean, that's what it was, right? An act of God?"

He abruptly turns the switch. The humming stops. And with it a subtle vibration you hadn't even realized was there. He stares at you, eyes wide. "I make this drive a couple of times a year. Nothing's ever happened before. If they stop using him he'll be ruined."

He turns the ignition, and if not for the sudden change of atmosphere in the cab you'd not know the vehicle was running again. A rivulet of sweat rolls off the man's cheekbone. "It gets pretty hot in here. See, it's set up with a humidifier in the back, and an air conditioner up here, because the air conditioner dries them out. But the air conditioner doesn't work that well when the humidifier is on."

He stares, then grins. "So I guess I'm screwed." Serious again, he says, "That's why I didn't get out and distribute water to everybody. I mean, not just that I need it myself. But because I can't leave the truck. All these expensive furs, you see, they're my responsibility.

"But you take a few bottles, okay? Give them to the ones what really need them."

When you're a few yards away you realize you forgot the offered bottles of water. But you do not go back.

Friday, 4 PM
2006 Chrysler Sebring, silver convertible
No signs of a driver or passengers, but a few bloody handprints on the dusty upholstery. The front seat is full of stones, 3 to 6

inches across, scattered clumps of dirt, and a small tree complete with root ball, upright in the passenger seat, the leafy head peering over the windshield, on the lookout for perils.

Friday, 4:15 PM
2005 Toyota Yaris, red

The driver has a cut on his forehead. The seepage has turned his blonde locks red in front, so it looks like he has dyed just the tips, or perhaps he is a redhead who has bleached most of his hair, but interrupted, he was unable to complete the job.

"Please don't bother me now," he says. "I'm fine—I trust everyone else is as well. I just want to finish my book before help arrives. See, I'm almost done."

He holds up a worn, dog-eared copy of AZTEC, by Gary Jennings. He grabs the last few pages—thirty or so—between thumb and forefinger and gives the book a shake.

Friday, 4:45 PM
2005 Dodge Caliber, silver

The woman, half-asleep, has her eyes covered by a glove. She peers up from beneath an empty thumb. She waves you away.

Where is everybody? You can hear the rescuers talking up on the ridge overhead. Occasional, inappropriate laughter. You imagine that's the way angels sound when God isn't watching.

Friday, 5:30 PM
2004 BMW Z4, grey

Within a dozen feet of the vehicle you can hear the argument: the woman's voice and the man's voice filtered through the closed windows into something more formal, more musical than was no doubt typical for them. You can't make out the words, but the gestures seem all too familiar, the face contorting with a raised fist, the head-shaking sneer when something beyond belief has been said. But watching closely you can see a private etiquette:

they are taking turns with their outbursts, each waiting patiently as their partner finishes. They don't even know you're there, and before they have a chance to see you, you slip away, like a spirit on the road from here, to there.

Friday, 6 PM
1999 Daihatsu Charade, orange

You know there is a car here, *was* a car here, only because of the orangeish bits of metal, which match none of the other vehicles you have seen. The largest bit has the Daihatsu symbol still affixed. A river of stone has erased most of what rested here. Wedged between two stones you find a single, shiny word in more or less permanent script: *Charade*.

Friday, 6:30 PM
1978 Lincoln Continental Town Car, black

It sits with all windows rolled up. Sleek, huge, an older kind of luxury. The engine isn't completely silent—there is a subtle whine, an intermittent tick, in its steady bass—but that only magnifies its perfection. You've seen no one leave, or enter, this vehicle since the disaster. Now and then a window has rolled down an inch, maybe two. Now you approach, anxious, short of breath. You can hear yourself, and you're surprised by what you hear.

A back door opens. You're surprised when the cold air hits you. A man with white hair slides his head into view within the interior. "Welcome," he says. "We were wondering when your travels would bring you to our little neighbourhood."

You hesitate, but the cool air makes this invitation irresistible. As you step within the angle of the open door the gentleman slides over to make room. However unlikely it seems, you feel important.

The door clicks shut behind you, smooth as a well-greased vault door.

"Care for some wine, some champagne?" He hands you a glass. He gestures toward a small bar mounted to the back of the front seats. A line of bottles await. You are suddenly incredibly thirsty.

But then you remember all the pills you consumed earlier, and you shake your head.

"We have fruit!" An eager, youngish voice from the other end of the back seat. The gentleman leans back, and the young woman juts her chin forward, and in her outstretched hand, six sections of bright, glossy orange. "These oranges, well, they're to *die* for." She emits a distinctly unladylike snort.

You accept, and with the first bite you are in complete agreement.

"Our rescue is proceeding smoothly, I assume?" An older woman in the front, peering around the edge of her seat, showing one eye.

You nod dumbly.

"Very good. Clarisse will put together a bag of oranges for you."

When you leave the cool air you have the bag clutched in your fist. You hold it slightly behind your back, hoping no one else will see.

Up on the ridge the rescuers are arguing. It's too dark to see, but there are no more sounds of machinery and you assume that is not a good sign. There appear to be many more people up there now. Vans. Emergency vehicles. The squawking of two way radios.

You have only one more vehicle to check. You do not know what you will do with yourself after that. You have been going over every inch of ground, counting the ejected bodies, erecting a pile of stones beside each body. You hadn't realized there were so many. They had been disguised by the rocks and the other debris. And you had been focusing on the vehicles.

It's going to be very cold tonight. You feel very bad about leaving the bodies out here in the open, but of course you know they are past feeling anything.

Friday, 7 PM
1999 Subaru Outback Wagon, white

The car is on its right side. Approaching from the undercarriage side you hear the music, something soft and folksy, and dim. As you're climbing you see dark red and purple sky, the dead car, sky again, the silhouettes of abandoned construction equipment up on the ridge. Dark sky. Your feet slipping, finding purchase again. The dead car, with its driver's side window open. But where's the driver?

You can look down through the driver's window now into the interior of the car. The overhead dome light is on, and that's enough to allow you to see his legs, the side of his hip, but his head is somewhere below. He's still strapped into his seatbelt, and he's twisted around, hanging there.

"Hello? I'm caught," he says. "Hello, I'm caught. My leg's hung up. I don't know, something went into my leg."

You move around, get a better view. Then you see the piece of metal, where it enters, just above the knee. The pants are soaked a dark colour, the wound still dripping, running down the metal, pooling over the scattered magazines down below the head you can't see, a dozen or more magazines—issues of *People, Us, Entertainment Weekly*—covering the glass at the bottom of the car, what used to be the passenger side window, now cracked, sections missing, the holes plugged with the blood-soaked magazines.

"Can you see? Can you see? No, don't tell me. I think I'd rather not know the details. I know it's bad—that's enough."

You want him to turn off that music, but you restrain yourself.

"I wasn't even supposed to be up here. These contracts needed to be delivered up in Aspen. Nobody wanted to do it. I didn't want to do it. It's my daughter's sixteenth birthday today, and I didn't want to do it. So why did I volunteer? I'm always doing stupid things like that. Always have."

Everything is quiet now. You look away, across to the other vehicles. Almost dark. A man stands by one of the cars, gazing your way. No other movement.

"My point is I didn't have to be here." You can't see his head, so you gaze at the magazines, slowly darkening with blood. Pictures of starlets, singers. Britney Spears. Anna Nicole. "But I came. I delivered the contracts. Then I realized I'd forgotten to pick up my daughter's birthday present back in Denver. I can get it tomorrow, but that's not the same is it? She loves magazines, she loves reading about the stars, you know? She knows as much about their lives as, well, her own. And she worries about them. She reads about the troubles they're having, and she goes on the internet everyday, searching, reading, until she finds out that those troubles are over, or that they've changed into some other kind of trouble. So I stopped at a drugstore and picked up all these magazines. She'll love them. And then I can pick up her real present tomorrow. Wasn't that a great idea?"

He falls silent. The dark is close—they've turned on work lights up on the ridge, but they're not doing any work, and very little of that light spills over onto the wrecks below. But here you still have the dome light, and what little it can illuminate inside the car.

"If I hadn't come up here. If I'd remembered her present. If I hadn't stopped for these magazines. I wouldn't even be here. Isn't that crazy? And now I'm going to be late. Anyway."

You've curled up beside the Subaru. The driver stopped talking hours ago. The dome light burned out. You can hear someone moving out among the vehicles, but you can't see them.

You were never very good at waiting. You were always too jittery. It's so very cold out here.

"Here." A voice out of the darkness. Suddenly his face appears above you, hovering like an angel's. It's the fellow from the fur van. He is handing you a small, dead animal.

"It's a bolero," he corrects you. "Red fox and mink. Reversible, not that that matters a damn. It'll help with the cold."

He sits down beside you. He is wearing a full length coat. Sable, you think. You think he's been crying, but you say nothing.

Saturday, 6 AM

When you wake up you believe you are being eaten by a small animal. You scream aloud and try to tear it off you, then remember it's the fur thing the delivery man gave you the night before. You look around. The delivery man is nowhere to be seen. The day is warming up, so you take the bolero off and toss it aside. All around you the bodies are adorned with fox and mink, red, black, brown, and white furs. It looks as if a hunting massacre has occurred here overnight.

You walk down the line of wrecked cars. The man from the Travelall is standing beside his vehicle, hiding his right arm behind him. He waves with his left and grins. A stylish fur stole is wrapped smartly around his neck.

There are a great many people up on the ridge, silently watching you. Camera lens flash. Soft spoken narration. There is no other movement. No signs of progress on the rescue road.

All around you the world groans. A buzz of excitement. A sudden rush of movement up on the ridge.

You walk by the green pickup. The young women wave gaily from the back, looking beautiful in their new fur clothes.

You pause at the torn edge of the world. You get down on all fours. There is a sharp barking from the distant electric megaphone, but you cannot understand the words.

You crawl over the edge and begin your descent.

You hear yourself groaning, and an answering groaning from the broken heart of the world.

Yellow blast of light and sound. Skies of dirt and stone. Random, brightly-painted metal, glass, bits and parts passing impossibly one through another. The backwards screaming thunder of the world's pain.

THE
SECRET
FLESH

The stimtech moved her wand slowly over his son's quiescent body. The tubes that ran into Mark's neck and chest were well-hidden. Jim could detect them only when the boy's chest had risen to its full extension, and there were slight linear shadows beneath the skin where the tubes pulled against the flesh.

She was a small woman: narrow hips, flat waist; he thought of Tinkerbell. She held the bar motionless above the bridge of his son's nose. Mark's left eyelid opened slightly, exposing a narrow crescent of bluish white. Jim's stomach tightened as he stared at the small sliver of eyeball. He tried to swallow away the bitterness rising into his throat. But the bad taste was the only thing preventing him from screaming at her.

As she moved the thin edge of the bar down from the eye, the left cheek drew in slightly, causing a vague, lopsided smile to crease Mark's little boy face.

"He is left-handed. Am I correct?" she asked.

Was, he thought. Jim nodded, then realized she was concentrating too closely on his son to notice. "Yes. He wanted to be right-handed like his friends, so that last year he practiced switching off. I don't think he managed the trick though. He never could get his shoes tied right." Jim almost smiled, and caught himself in horror.

She didn't say anything at first, and once again he felt like a fool with these people. He wanted to talk about his son, at least about some of the small things that maybe wouldn't cut too close to the nerve (although it wasn't always easy predicting what those things were going to be), and after Alicia ran away there'd been no one left to say those things to. But these people were the consummate professionals. They said as little as possible, and he always said too much.

"I am not detecting as much strength on his right side," she said. As if to confirm the statement, she rotated the flat of the bar over Mark's nose, paused, then carried the edge up and down above his right cheek. Her hand was long and slender, slightly cupping the bar as she gripped it. A perfect finger glided slowly up and down the upper edge as if to guide and encourage. There was a subtle tightening of the skin covering Mark's cheek, and a slight nervous pulse in the eyelid, but no other signs of life.

Jim felt his own face tighten. "He's brain dead," he made himself say, and could feel the skin around his eyes loosening. "I don't know why you people keep doing this."

She held the bar steady above Mark's mouth, and looked up. "That is a rather old fashioned term, Mr. Melville. In this era it means almost nothing. We know little. In some ways far less than before. Certainly far less than we thought."

Her eyes were slightly oblong, with no corners. They were able to stare, to hold with a look, better than any other eyes he'd ever seen. "You're one of them," he said simply. It amazed him that he hadn't noticed before. She stared at him, unblinking, because she had no lids. The slightly bluish fluid that periodically glistened over her eyes made her look as if she had been crying, but Jim didn't know for sure if the aliens ever cried or not. He wondered what it must be like, not being able to cry, no matter what happened to you. Then with a jolt, he knew. Because he'd always known.

Her unblinking stare was beginning to unnerve him, her eyes shining with the blue tears she would not release. He'd heard that the thick fluid also protected their eyes from the pollution in Earth's atmosphere. "That is true," she said. "If that disturbs you perhaps I can find someone else to continue your son's treatment."

"No, no, of course not. Your people brought us the treatments, so who better? I was just . . . startled. I never met an alien close up before . . . that's all."

She executed a barely detectable nod, as if in assent, or acknowledgement that she saw through his small awkwardness.

Her eyes appeared to widen even further, as if reception were opening up. Like a flower. Her eyes took him in and made a reading. It was frightening.

For a moment he wondered what happened when an alien died, and there were no lids to close. Would the eyes change colour? Harden? What happened when the fluid supply stopped? He imagined alien blue eyes hardening to stone, a permanent stare into the secrets of the universe. His morbid speculations embarrassed him.

She turned and guided the bar down Mark's legs. There was no movement at all.

"When do you decide a person's dead?" he asked her.

"I do not decide. A committee decides. Sometimes they ask my opinion."

"And your opinion here? Is Mark dead or isn't he?" He wanted to rip the bar out of her calm, controlled, perfect hands. He wanted to stare into those perfect eyes, far bluer than any human's eyes, bluer than any eyes had a right to be, until she had to turn away.

Her eyes seemed to grow larger. The movement of the fluid seemed more pronounced. He imagined ocean waves in the whites of her eyes. "You must miss your son very much," she said.

Mark's flesh appeared to breed shadows: vague, embryonic shadows just beginning to push their way out through the inner layers of skin. Each day there were more.

That night Jim dreamed he was kissed by a beautiful stranger.

He often thought of the last time he had kissed anyone. He and Alicia had spent eight hours at Mark's bedside that day, during which time they feigned hope and optimism. There hadn't been that much holding them together in the first place. Whatever they had originally felt they'd had in common had proved to be short term. Now Jim had a problem understanding how any two people could have anything in common.

There had been Mark. And there had been the sex.

"You don't have to go back tomorrow," he'd told her. "I'll go. I'll take care of it." Little did he know. She lay on her stomach with all her clothes on. He'd started rubbing her shoulders.

"That feels good," she'd said, but not as if she meant it.

He leaned over and kissed her on the back of the neck. He moved his lips slowly up to the back of her left ear. "I'm so sorry," he whispered.

He could feel her tense beneath him. "Why are you sorry? You didn't do anything wrong. Do you think I did anything wrong?"

"No, of course not." He stopped and laid his cheek against her back. He could hear a roughness in her lungs. He could see Mark's face darkening, Alicia frantically trying to pull the small plastic piece out of his throat, Mark's eyelids dropping shut, showing the blue white crescents. They'd always been good parents, everyone said they were good parents. But Jim couldn't fit that picture of Mark into any possible meaning of 'good parents.' "I'm just so sorry it happened. That's all." He felt his voice growing tight with an anger he'd never quite understood.

"Of course." He could hear the same kind of aimless anger in her own voice. "Of course, we're all sorry it happened. Being sorry doesn't help. I just want him back."

I want him back, too, he thought, but for some reason could not say that to her. "We don't know that he's . . ."

"He is. I would know."

"But if he's not, if he's just out of it somewhere. We have to be here when he gets back."

Alicia turned her face into the bed. Jim rubbed her neck, her shoulders. He opened his hands and ran them up and down her back and thighs, testing her strength, looking for any response. He made his hands receptive: for warmth, for life. He searched for the secret flesh where hope might be hidden.

He slipped his hand into the loose neck of her blouse, slid it over to cup her shoulder. He moved his hand in circles there, feeling where bone and ligaments joined together. He let his fingers glide to the other side of the shoulder joint, then pulled until Alicia was lying on her side.

Jim rolled over in front of her and tried to look into her eyes. She kept them closed, but relaxed as if she were asleep, showing those pale and hard to interpret crescents along the bottom edge. Her breathing was strained and shallow, as if she were forcing herself to sleep. Her mouth slackened like a child in sweet, never ending sleep.

The top button of her blouse had come undone. He rested two fingers there, spread them, moved them down to the next button, touched the hard plastic lightly with the tips of those fingers, as if it might cut or burn, as if his fingertips contained raw, exposed nerve endings. He slipped the button loose, and then the next, and the next.

Alicia's arms rose up around him, as if she were floating away in her dreams. Her breasts floated out of her blouse. He whispered nonsense, and cloth evaporated into their breath. He closed his eyes and tried to dream his way into the places where she had hidden herself. His mouth and hands found folds and rises, hollows, dry and wet places. He probed with fingers and tongue for the secret place that would fill him, for the one flesh that would last, for the one depth or contour of the body that would not be a gravestone. And, once again, he could not find it. He could not be satisfied. He had never been able to be satisfied.

He allowed his lips to slip over her flesh, tasting her. He discovered spider patterns of broken blood vessels and could smell the coppery blood just beneath the top layer of skin. In the pewter moonlight, her body grew shadows.

"It's not enough to be hungry," she whispered in her dreams.

A few hours before dawn he awakened for a few minutes. He sat up in bed as if he had heard something, as if his body had said things to him in his sleep. He stared down at her sleeping form: moonlight had turned her face blue and silver, breathless. Her skin seemed to be slowly turning transparent, as if a memory. Where is she? He leaned over and kissed her as if he were kissing a beautiful stranger.

The next morning he was not surprised to find Alicia gone.

"It is like . . . mining," the stimtech said. "Your people's term, I believe. Sometimes you discover something."

The stimtech moved the rod a little more quickly, as if carving the dead air over Mark's body. Jim wondered, crazily, if maybe the dreams stayed close to you when you died, invisible yet fast to the body like a sack you cannot escape. He imagined some anonymous gland or duct in the body storing the immortal dreams.

She raised and lowered the bar, working it down the length of Mark's body. Jim thought of divining rods, well diggers, séances.

The beautiful alien angled the bar and sliced it upward through the air. Mark's right hand jerked slightly, fingers rising, hand pulled upward and hinged at the wrist, the lower arm still as if sewn to the mattress. Mark's head rolled slightly toward Jim as if in reaction to that hand, but his features remained slack.

Jim thought of a marionette, his son dancing off the bed and hitting the floor with a crash of broken parts, his head lolling on a loose-jointed neck. "Stop!" She turned and her eyes took him in. The blue wash in her eyes was so heavy her pupils were almost obscured. "Please. Stop," he said.

"Very well," she said. "This need not be done just now."

"What's the point?" Jim found he had to look away from the terrible, wonderful blueness of her eyes.

"Perhaps you should not watch."

"If it's going to be done, I need to watch." Jim stared at Mark's body. Once she had removed the bar, it held no more life than the mattress.

"Something may come of this," she said. She had moved closer. Jim looked down into the ever open eyes. They looked into him as no other eyes could. He found himself searching their surfaces.

"What's going to come of this?" he whispered.

She found his hand. The sensation of her fingers wrapped around his own, guiding, controlling, was strange, but he could not look away from her face. She took him to her room.

"What is it you are looking for?" she asked softly.

He didn't know what to say. It was a true question; he was looking for something. But he had no words for it. As if to mine for the word, to draw it out of him, she reached up and wrapped her narrow arms around his neck, pulled herself up to him, and placed her mouth over his. It wasn't a kiss exactly, at least not like any kiss he had ever had. She simply held her lips against his, as if to allow breath and saliva to be exchanged, to become acclimated one to the other, to become chemically compatible.

He tried to move his lips against hers, to rub and work his way into some sort of kiss he was accustomed to, but her lips would not budge. Then he tried to close his mouth, but her lips prevented that as well. Her lips had muscle, were capable of more tension than human lips, and when she began moving them up his face toward his eyes he was finally able to pull his head away from her. He could see that the dark lipstick she wore was simply human camouflage, obscuring the additional lines demarking the various muscles of her lips. Then she pulled him back to her lips, and he could not free himself from their strength again.

When she reached his eyes it was as if her lips extended to gain better purchase, as she sucked and tasted his eyes, so vigorously he thought she might draw them completely out of their sockets, but somewhere short of pain, where an exquisite pleasure still hides. In the grip of her lips his vision was of liquid landscapes, his flesh melting to join her flesh, Alicia's flesh, the last decaying vestiges of his son's flesh.

"Noooo . . ." he tried to speak, but it came out a moan of pleasure. He could feel his body becoming alien, with its need to flow.

She ran her strong, smooth fingers down his chest, finding the soft strips between the ribs, the pockets lower down where fat had gathered to shield the pains in his belly. He could feel places opening up all along her surface, mouths opening up to taste him, smell him, to test his flesh with minute amounts of glandular secretions, heat sweat, tears. Inside his skull the closed flower of the brain stem began to bloom.

His thighs spread and peeled apart. Wounds gathered over his intestines and multiplied, revealing the pockets beneath his rib cage. His mouth tasted of melons, then of melted steel.

He saw the blue white crescents smiling under Mark's eyes, and imagined his own eyes the same. He saw Mark's arms flopping like something wounded, Mark's body falling, separating into meat. His tears seemed to run backwards, etching trails as they made their way down his throat.

"What is it you are looking for?" she asked again, insisting.

"I want the flesh," he said, crying, "the flesh he would have been. The flesh that lasts forever."

And then she opened up around him, and in so doing pulled him apart. And he lost the last vestiges of his control. And the secret flesh within him began to whisper in Mark's voice, filling the emptiness of his body.

When Jim arrived at the hospital the next morning a different technician was in charge. A young man, short dark hair, very professional. A human. The young man Mark might have been. A sheet covered Mark's body.

The technician frowned slightly. "You are?"

"His father." Always.

The young man's composure slipped a fraction. "Oh, I'm sorry. The committee . . . made a decision. We . . ." He gestured toward the body.

"That's okay," Jim said. "There's no need to apologize."

The young man's movements suddenly became quick and slightly awkward. He touched the bed bearing Mark's body, and twisted back to look at Jim. There seemed to be a vague sort of panic in his eyes. "You can view the body, if you wish. Would you like that?"

"I already have," Jim said, and turned away.

The flesh that would have been Mark's. A flesh that would last beyond the small details of a life. What he had always needed. What anyone needs. Jim could feel the gift of their lovemaking opening up inside him, new sensory apparatus for interpreting and dreaming the world.

Somewhere below Jim's rib cage, hidden among pancreas, kidneys, and intestines, the organ of his secret flesh took nourishment from longings and dreams, and with a steady supply of blood began, at last, to function.

ORIGAMI
BIRD

Almost at once it became habit. During long days in the file room
with no one to talk to, his hands normally unoccupied would snag
some scrap of paper or trash and speak what he was unable to find
words for. Staring at the scenery his eyes invented out of textured
ceiling, out the window where gorgeous creatures reclined in cloud,
he would catch his hands pulling and twisting at a candy wrapper,
a hen-scratched Post It, a sheet of lost and yellowing stationery,
until at last the first glimmer of bird came through.

He had no inkling of the long traditions of paper folding. He
knew far less than his hands knew: of bending, pressing, worrying
free the shape poised for flight out of garbage. And when he ran
out of garbage he made birds out of the grim chronicles of neglect,
disease, and grief salvaged from these long-dead patients' files.

That first paper bird had been a strange thing: wings with the
shattered angles of lightning, beak a twisted black tear. Over the
years the shapes refined: at times almost delicate in the ways the
multiple-creased necks reached up to support the complicated
heads, at times unsoundly fantastic as paper stub wings evolved
into great wavering flyleaves of actuarial data ready to take the
sad facts of a life and journey south over some dark and troubled
continent to the nesting grounds along the far edge of where we all
came from.

There was no money in what his hands made, of course, but
then he had no talent for money, or much else, working only to

clothe and feed his small family. Freedom was something fine and good in the antique gold-tooled novels his grandfather had passed his way, which he had sold after a single reading. And he knew he was lucky to live in a country that had so much of it, although he'd never quite been able to grasp the details.

Years later when they cleaned out the old hospital records, decades of paper and film and what no longer matters, carried the lot to bins and incinerators, they discovered the waste of his hands and heart: birds put away neatly in every folder, birds tucked into envelopes and nested in the gaps of the unused alphabet, birds secreted into record books, birth records, treatment plans, and autopsy reports, birds by the thousands spilling from the boxes the workers carried outside, caught by the wind funneled between the tall buildings, rising with the orderly progress of the flames, set free into air and light, and they all, all of them stopped their lives that day to watch.

IN
THESE
FINAL DAYS
OF SALES

Main thing is, you're selling something those folks need, something they can't live without.

"It's not the bang in your buck, it's the buck in your bang." At the end of the commercial the words blaze a brilliant white across the black screen, then fade. Emil remembers a time when clarity was of the utmost importance in sales, conventional wisdom being that people would not buy an unknown quantity. Of course, what they thought they were getting might not bear much resemblance to the object eventually delivered wrapped in brown paper C.O.D., but at least the transaction began with that image in mind, clear if erroneous.

Now, a certain degree of clairvoyance is required to discern what goods are actually being advertised. Emil, himself in the sales business, watches commercials in the hotel rooms along his route, trying to map out exactly what the rules are now. What troubles him most is that they seem to be not just about new sales techniques, but about a change in the human psyche itself. We have become the creatures in our dreams, he thinks, poured into pleasing and biodegradable packaging.

People want something—that has been the message behind the message in every ad or commercial. *You want something*, they remind us. The ads advertise want. They advertise need. No wonder the actual product remains in the background. At some level the advertisers have finally realized their products are merely symbolic, almost irrelevant.

Much of the mysterious advertising, Emil has finally concluded, is for various brands of pants.

After a few years, all the towns, all the countless burgs and villes line up like endless doors opening one by one, and seem like the same town, the same Main Street with the same row of worn brick or white-washed wood on each side, the same people of pink or yellow or brown in their denims, corduroys, cottons, or polyesters, waving or not waving depending on how friendly toward strangers they are feeling on this particular day. And yet Emil, the professional salesman, has never really thought of himself as a stranger.

That was the first thing he learned in sales: you cannot act like or think of yourself as a stranger. Not if they are going to trust you. Not if they are going to *buy*. And how is buying any different from shaking a hand, giving a good how-do-you-do, getting married, kissing the kids good night? Not much, when you really think about it. Just another form of social exchange, value for value, you rub my back and I'll rub yours. You don't want to be left back on the shelf when everybody's buying. That's the very worst thing. You don't want to remain unsold all your life.

Sometimes Emil is so intent he is on the eventual accounting that he forgets sales is more than that. It is a matter of wishes and dreams, of planning and foresight, of frustration and expectation. After years on the road, each town is exactly what he'd expected it to be. The streets are exactly what he'd imagined; the people are perfectly familiar because they've already walked these streets in one of his countless motel daydreams.

It is as if, every day, the citizens of these tiny communities rebuild their town according to his expectations, anticipating his particular arrival. Given how self centred human beings are, this is no doubt a common misperception. It is one of the first things you learn as a salesman, and if you are good at your job, you use it to your advantage.

Emil is not good at his job. In fact, if there is a worse salesman out there on the road Emil has not yet met him. The man with the off-kilter eyes fills the screen with a loopy grin. A dolly back to reveal the rest of the family: the wife rubbing up against him in her new red dress, barely able to contain herself, the kids jumpy. Emil thinks the boy may have peed his pants.

They are all holding up great wads of fake cash to the camera: the portrait on one of the bills resembles Clark Gable more than any president Emil can think of. And yet these people are so thrilled to have it in their hands—they jump around as if affected by some nervous disease.

Having little tolerance anymore for the manic patter of commercials he keeps the volume down as he watches the television family pantomime surprise, joy, delirium. They've gotten what they've always wanted, or at least now they can afford to buy what they've always wanted. Failing that, perhaps they can rent it. If it's still available. If they can ever figure out what it is.

He really shouldn't make fun, he thinks. If people didn't behave this way, if they stopped looking for something to make them happy, they wouldn't buy.

Of course, people seldom buy from him in any case. In fact, Emil has come to think of himself as the Anti-salesman, like some super villain with a huge grey cape and unpleasant teeth.

Emil has in his pocket a letter from an old salesman he used to meet out on the road a couple of times a year. Their paths might cross in Goodland, or in Hugo, perhaps even in Kansas City. Supposedly Walt had been quite successful in his time, but Emil knows him only as this tired-looking fellow who might have been a retired teacher or someone recently recovered from a lengthy illness.

"Emil, This is a job offer of sorts. Not for a specific job really but it is the promise of a job, a good job with regular hours and good benefits. And there's *no* travel involved. My friends and I have had this dream we've developed over years on the road, a dream built a stick at a time in hotel rooms and all night diners, of someday having our own town, a factory outlet town where customers would come to *you* to buy the things they really needed to buy. So no sales pitches or how-many-should-I-put-you-down-fors. Why, any pressure high or low would simply be out of the question! We need salesmen to run the stores of this new town, trained salesmen who have become more interested in helping people than they are in earning high commissions . . ."

Emil has taken this letter out and unfolded it and reread it so many times it threatens to fragment into a dozen or so worn paper squares held together by a few commas and dashes.

He has never visited this new town. It just makes him feel good knowing that it is there.

Sometimes Emil fantasizes that he will find a way to sneak back and catch the residents of a town unawares. Then he will find out exactly what each of these places is really like. Perhaps at last he will discover what people really think about him. The thought is both exciting, and dreadful.

Emil's career in sales hasn't always been like this. In the beginning he never knew what to expect when he arrived in a new town. It had been interesting. It had made him anxious. He never knew if he'd find hell or a paradise. Most of the time it had been neither, of course, a necklace of grey towns and grey people, but at least that heady anticipation had always been there.

"The *main* thing is . . ." Jack looked around for a place to spit. Emil moved his feet out of the way. Finally the old man looked over his shoulder and spat behind him. "Main thing is, you're selling something those folks *need*, something they can't live without."

"I don't want to lie to anybody," Emil had said.

"Lie? Who said anything about lying, boy? I don't want you to *lie*, for chrissake! Who knows what anybody needs? I don't know what you need. Are you arrogant enough to tell me you know what *I* need? Do you really know what *you* need? I doubt it. Even occasional self knowledge is a rare thing, boy. It's luck, pure and simple. So don't talk to me about lies. Guesses, would be more accurate."

"I don't even know what I'm selling," Emil said.

"That's because I haven't told you yet, boy." Jack pulled an oft-creased, yellowing square of paper out of his back pants pocket. Ignoring the tiny paper slivers that flaked off and littered the floor, he unfolded it, unfolded it again. When it was about a yard square he stopped and pressed his nose against it. The paper was so worn and discoloured it made Emil think of a thin layer of old skin. He could practically read Jack's expression through the huge square:

the wrinkled forehead, the pursed lips, the mushy dark grey eyes like a baby's. But Emil couldn't make out any of the writing, or even if there was any writing.

"There's some difference of opinion on this." Jack's voice raised and lifted the paper as if it were a floating tissue. "But encyclopaedias best for a beginner, I suspect. You're offering them the world of knowledge, the flying carpet to distant lands, all of that for just a few bucks a month. Just gotta remember that with encyclopaedias you only call on people who have kids."

"Because most adults think their learning days are over," Emil added helpfully.

"Somethin' like that. Tell me, are *you* willing to learn, or do you just want to put your own two cents in?"

"Oh, yes, I want to learn. Really." It was just to be a short term job following graduation, something to put food in his mouth and a roof over his head until something better came along.

"OK, then. The thing about selling encyclopaedias is you can convince them they need to buy a set for their kids' futures. Everybody wants to do things for the future of their kids—in this country we spoil them rotten."

Emil's own parents had begrudged him every penny. You would have thought they might have found the cure for cancer if only they hadn't had to worry about their only son.

If he ever had children, if he ever could convince a woman he was worth raising a family with, he'd surely buy them a set of encyclopaedias. A whole damn library. You could not do enough for your kids.

"You'd buy your own kids encyclopaedias, wouldn't you? I mean if you had any?" It was as if the old man read his mind. A good salesman, according to that first training manual, could tell when interest had peaked, when the customer was growing bored, as well as determine the particular magic phrase that might turn sales, and lives, around.

"Oh, well, of course. If I had the money . . ."

"Even if you didn't have the money you'd do it! You'd find a way somehow. Now don't tell me that you wouldn't!"

"Well, you're right . . ."

"See now, *that's* what I'm talking about. In this country we buy our kids things, especially if we have even the vaguest notion it'll give them a better life than what we've had. Something bright and shiny, and fluttering with colour and motion. That's pretty much the American way."

Jack somehow found an opportunity to drop the word American into practically every conversation, his particular style of sales patter. Emil wasn't sure he himself had his own style, even after all these years, except that it involved a great deal of sitting, of daydreaming through visits in old fashioned parlours and newly-decorated living rooms, waiting for a change in the air or the light, or the order of the universe.

"You know, I've never sold anything before," Emil said.

"Sure you have. Like everybody else you've been selling all your life. The question is whether you've been giving the people good value."

Sales had been as unlikely an occupation for someone of Emil's temperament as anything he might imagine. He'd gone on very few dates, unable to sell himself to women. He'd been passed over for the simplest jobs, because he'd been unable to sell himself to employers. Whatever friends he had acquired seemed largely accidental.

He had no aptitude for closing the deal, shaking the hand, laughing at the obligatory jokes. It was the world's sense of humour that had brought him into sales after graduation—you understood that sort of thing if you were a salesman.

So it had all come down to the day he'd picked up his sample set at the warehouse, along with the brochures and studies proving how kids raised on encyclopaedias had increased IQ, appetite and stamina, and set out his first time on the road using the route map the old man had given him. Instead of the usual dots or squares to represent towns and cities, there were little drawings of houses, all of them the same size, crude yet childishly cheerful, pastel yellows and blues and pinks. When he examined those tiny houses with his magnifying glass he spied children's faces in the windows of several, here and there a smiling mother or father out on the lawn, baby brother in a stroller, the shirtless neighbour watering his lawn. A tiny blotch of ink that might have been a dog, or a cat.

A company-owned car was provided for his first trip out. Imagine, a company car! But he was alarmed to discover a broad scrape along the length of the passenger side, and cracks in the windows. "They want you to keep that passenger side parked away from your customers' houses at all times," the chief dispatcher informed him.

The brown dashboard had enough cracks in it to fill a dried-out riverbed. The clock was missing an hour hand (if he scrunched sideways against the steering wheel he could just see that missing hand reclining in the bottom scoop of the dial). The seat and back had even more cracks, futilely repaired with a variety of tapes that caught and pulled at his neatly pressed suit.

Out on the road he realized that major cities—New York, St. Louis, Philadelphia, Chicago—weren't even depicted on the map. "We like to leave the big places for the veterans," Jack had told him.

Now and then over the years he would come to a town that felt far more familiar than most. With a "B" name like Bennett or Bailey or Baxter, it would be a town with ambition: the main street in the process of restoration, new motels and restaurants at the outskirts, and at least one new mall. A construction sign just outside town limits advertises a multiplex. Overpriced town homes are being erected along the distant foothills.

Emil has met the desk clerk at the cheapest hotel and asks about the health of his youngest daughter. The clerk does not act surprised. At the bake sale outside the post office, the woman in the bright yellow dress sells him a small bag of ginger snaps for the eighth time this year.

In the windows of the hardware store are pictures of missing children. It is an epidemic; he wonders about the strangers who steal children out of the Baileys and Baxters and Bennetts of the world. Perhaps the kidnapper is an airline pilot, he thinks. Perhaps he is the representative of some obscure government regulatory agency. Perhaps he is a travelling salesman who is lost in the identical towns and quiet streets of America.

It never occurs to him, that anyone might suspect him, anymore than it would occur to him to commit such a crime.

The automobile on the flickering screen is unlike any Emil has ever seen: so sleek, so modern, it appears to drive itself, passing without damage through tornadoes, mudslides, nuclear attacks. The message of the commercial is that a person could not die in such a vehicle. Death has always been the big mistake, the nasty trick, the unacceptable penalty. Emil believes if he just didn't have to die he might someday become a successful human being.

Now, in these final days of salesmanship, Emil is on his twenty-sixth company car. He knows this from the files of paperwork in a cardboard box in the back seat. He wonders if bad driving is one of the by-products of salesmanship, this pushing through the highways and byways of the assigned route, whatever the weather or road conditions, this nervous and careless passing, this incessant hurry to get nowhere. If it all came down to driving habits, he'd have been declared the perfect salesperson a long time ago.

But he has no talent for sales. He sometimes wonders what kind of man he must be, to spend his life dedicated to something he is so poor at. But if he has learned anything at all in his wanderings it is that life itself, for most of humanity, is this constant doing and undoing, doing poorly at what we attempt, undoing the better efforts of those who have come before us.

Still, survival requires food for the mouth, a pillow for the head, motion of the eye and a new day's list of prospects for the brain to process.

In these last few days of salesmanship his lack of aptitude cannot be helped. In these last few days of salesmanship there are many more towns to investigate, hotel rooms to rent, long hours to spend waiting on the couches and good chairs in the living rooms of America, meditating through the afternoons in quiet contemplation of the people who need everything and nothing. He means no criticism in this, it is simply the life we live in these last days of sales, trying not to think too much about the small tragedies or joys.

The sound at the door is more a rubbing or a scraping than a knocking. He hesitates to open it—no one knows he is here except the clerk.

A small old lady of grey flesh peers up at him beyond the dire weight of her glasses. "I just wanted to thank you for that new Bible you sold me," she tells him, and lifts her head to kiss him on the cheek, exposing the ragged hole in her throat.

He tries to close the door on her, but she shoves the shiny red leather Bible between the door and the jamb. He turns to escape and trips over his sample case. She drapes herself over him, whispering, *I just want you to sell me again*, and he is appalled to discover the erection growing like an impending purchase beneath his belt.

Remember that there's a pit waiting for you in self pity, so put that I in try and get back on your feet and run!

The cheers, the applause, the feet stampings are so loud Emil is compelled to fiddle with the volume control. It takes some time for him to figure out that the dark-haired man on the screen is not a preacher, but a salesman like himself. Or not like himself, for this man is wildly successful the world over.

The man sells tapes and books, and a correspondence course of some sort, but even more clever than that, Emil suddenly realizes, the man is *selling people back to themselves*. An incredible idea—an endless supply of product with so little overhead.

There is a sadness about it all, he thinks, but who is he to say? Who is he to even have an opinion on such matters?

That A in ambition is as high as any mountain, but climb it anyway! Don't eat the pear in despair. Remember there's no hope in dope! Take that H out of whining and you'll be winning!

Emil cannot understand why the company has never fired him. In all his years on the road he has never once met his quota. And yet he has been allowed to continue making contacts, meeting prospects, conversing for long, leisurely days in the living rooms and on the front porches of America.

Periodically the home office sends out trainers (usually men) whose job is to sharpen the skills of the sales force. He isn't sure what their real job is—half the time they make no pretense of training.

Just as he suspects, their courtships of his customers are for the most part rewarded. It is amazing, sometimes frightening, to watch as the salesman nods, and the customers nod in return, as smile echoes smile, and laughter echoes laughter, as the customers slowly transform into salesman doppelgängers, and a good time is had by all, except for Emil, who stands by the door and attempts to shake off his anxiety.

Many of the salesmen appear to achieve their success by means of sheer animal dominance. These are the alpha males, and although the herd of customers may mimic the salesman's gestures to the point of slavishness, they can never hope to match the salesman in strength or confidence.

Other salesmen at first glance appear to be no more impressive than Emil, but they are persistent almost to the point of their, and Emil's, humiliation. He spends one appalling afternoon camped out on a front porch, the fox-like salesman with the wired eyes refusing to leave until the elderly couple has purchased something. The husband gives in with shaking hands and cornered eyes.

A few of the men the company sends are interrogators, and they grill many of his prospects as to their needs and dreams, why they were at all hesitant to buy such a fine product. They use the customers' own hesitations and rationalizations against them.

And there are those for whom Emil can think of no better word than crazed, the ones who affect a certain delirium—dancing a jig, forcing facial spasms, singing spontaneously and inappropriately— that so troubles the customers they buy what they can in order to get rid of them.

Emil, of course, is unlike any of these salespeople. There is no good reason for the company to retain him, and yet he remains year after year, hoping for the blessed dismissal which will free him, which he cannot ask for himself, and which never comes.

And here he is again, the wife on the couch making polite conversation, the husband puttering around in the next room, pretending to make repairs, but whose real business is to listen in on the wife's dealings and make sure she does not spend too much of their rapidly disappearing funds. The wife has no real desire to buy except out of politeness or pity. Her real need is to have someone to talk to about the children, share her memories of the sister's dead baby, her own medical troubles, her thinly disguised fears that her world is a precarious thing about to end, and her husband will not listen, has not really listened in years.

Outside it is a kind of Kansas, although they are miles and years from that state: sun burning the distant edges of crops, the horse moving slowly across the hill, the small boy on his bicycle struggling through mud ruts deep enough to swallow his wheels.

Soon the wife will offer her final apologies, so many unexpected expenses of late, folks hereabouts having pretty hard times, such a good product it's really too bad we don't have the money to spare, I'm afraid we can't see our way and it's not your fault at all . . .

And he will happily be free once again to step outside and stride to his car, relieved that he will not have to fill out all the paperwork that an actual sale entails.

"So my husband agrees we should take one, at that discount rate you said you were offering today, one time only and not to be repeated and who could pass up such a bargain, I mean, *really*."

Emil stares at the young wife as if she has suddenly gone crazy, as if she's been spitting and drooling and speaking in tongues. But in fact she is an older woman, greying at the temples and wearing an old fashioned housecoat fading into transparency around the hem. He cannot understand—it is as if he's nodded off with the unending familiarity of his own sales spiel, and the woman's mother has replaced her in the chair. He gazes around the vaguely familiar room and sees her elderly husband slumped forward in his overstuffed chair, sleeping or dead.

"Just a minute," he finally manages to say through a rising panic, "Just a goddamn minute!" Has he really cursed a customer? "I've got my order book here somewhere. We'll get you fixed right up. Yes, indeed, you won't be sorry about *this* purchase, nomaam! It's the gift that keeps on giving, the key to a lifetime of success, the satisfaction of knowing you're doing . . . you're doing, well, what you're doing, it's the cap . . . on the toothpaste, the bridge . . ."

Emil's hand flops about in the worn out leather satchel like a broken sparrow. He's not sure what he's seeking, in fact cannot remember the last time he'd reached into his sales valise, when his fingers seize the tattered edges of the sales book and retrieve it carefully as if it were some moth losing wing scales in frightening amounts. He spreads it open on his lap, carefully positioning the disintegrating slip of carbon paper, writes "1" as the quantity, then stops.

What is he selling this woman? He looks up at her expectantly. "You wanted one . . ." His dry tongue adheres to his bottom lip.

She smiles so broadly he thinks her mind is, in fact, gone, and he will not have to complete the order form after all. But then she nods slowly, happily, as if perfectly aware that she is doing the right thing for herself and the generations to come.

For the briefest of seconds he is unable to pull his tongue from his lip, and when finally he does it is so painful he feels a tear balanced dangerously in the corner of one eye. "One . . ." he repeats, and looks around for the sample he has been showing her, but it is nowhere to be seen.

"Deluxe edition," she finally replies, so he knows it isn't the Sports Weathervane, or the Speedo pocket groomer, or five of the twelve handy household helpers he sells, or used to sell. If he could only remember what it was he was selling this trip out, what he had put into his sample case, but there is nothing there, and nothing anywhere to be seen but this giant book bound in red leather she grasps so lovingly in her two, trembling hands.

"I only wish our son Johnny would read this with us. So long he has been away from the Lord . . ."

"One Deluxe Bible, Red Leather, with the special painted map inserts tracing Jesus' path through our mortal world," Emil says confidently, writing *1 RB* onto the pad.

He settles back, calmed, as the elderly woman (but he recognizes her now, remembering how he had stopped here when she *was* a young bride, and realizes how much she must regret not having bought that Bible the first time he came by, when her baby was still a magical creature of hope and possibility) drones on about the sorry affairs of her son, the all too familiar litany of failures and small betrayals.

Gazing out the window Emil sees a small blond boy on a backyard swing, perhaps this woman's grandchild, or impossibly, her son at a better age, conjured up by her sad monologue. Emil rises from the chair—the woman does not seem to care, or notice, while the husband continues his uninterrupted rehearsal for death—and climbs out the window, strides across the bright lawn bordered in corn and sits in the child's other swing, the one reserved for playmates yet to arrive.

"It's too nice a day to be indoors," he says, both an explanation and an introduction.

"Who are you?" the little boy asks, staring up at Emil's face.

Emil gazes out over the endless and precisely aligned rows of corn. The sun glazes the leaves a green-gold, and he feels a smile travel unbidden across his face. "I'm nobody, really," he finally replies. "Just a salesman, calling on your parents with my promises and offers, my bag full of hope and secrets."

Suddenly stern, the boy says in an old man's querulous voice, "Are you going to try and sell me something?"

Emil is startled. He has been asked the question before, and it never fails to upset him. "No, no," the salesman in him lies. "I'm not selling anything today."

"Then what are you doing here?"

"I'm spending time here in this swing. I'm the customer this afternoon, buying myself a piece of this beautiful day."

The boy stares intently over the corn as if seeing a body hanging from the line of the horizon. When he looks back at Emil, his expression is eager. "So you've been to a lot of different places, not just here?"

"More places than I can count, son. I hope you don't mind the familiar."

"And the people in these places, they're all different in these places?"

"Well, you know it's funny that you should ask that, young man. It's been my experience that people are the same the world over, subject to the same wants and needs, accessible by the same techniques."

"No, you're lying!" the boy shouts. "Tell me that they're *different*! They *have* to be different from here!"

"Well . . ." Emil scrambles for the right words that will calm the boy, that will sell him some peaceful behavior. "We wouldn't understand each other too well, now would we, if we were all that different from each other."

"Get off my swing!" Alarmed, Emil trips getting out of the swing and sprawls on the ground. He heads back toward the open window, dusting off his pants as he goes. Behind him the boy sobs, but Emil will not let himself turn around. Customers don't like it when you watch them cry.

He climbs back through the window and slips into the chair. Spying a strand of burry weed stuck to one dress sock, he leans forward to remove it. The woman continues narrating her list of sadnesses. But it is not the same woman. This woman is younger, a brunette, and although the room is of the same style as the previous one, there are differences.

This husband is livelier than the other one. He rushes back and forth, a gun in his hand. "You hear that?"

After some delay Emil realizes the question is addressed to him. And then he *does* hear something coming from outside: gunshots and shouting, the alarmed cries of animals.

"What . . ."

"It's that Wilkins boy—Johnny! He shot his ma and pa, and now he's killing all the livestock in sight!"

Emil can hear a rumbling engine between the shotgun blasts. "But he's just a boy . . ."

"Sixteen if he's a day! Old enough to blow a stranger's head off if he's dumb enough to stick his head outside! Guess he didn't read those encyclopaedias you sold them ten years ago."

Crazily, Emil wonders if the Wilkinses had purchased their easy annual update volume subscription plan. It has been designed to keep your youngster apprised of all the latest developments not only in the sciences but in the arts as well.

An hour later it is all over. Emil cannot remember if this family has placed an order or not. But there is such a relief in leaving a customer's house he could care less. It is the best he ever feels.

Emil comes out of the house feeling that now would be a good time to take a walk, a relaxed stroll through a friendly neighbourhood where he has lived all his married life. Their kids know his kids— they don't always get along but they play together every day— and he sees the parents at the grocery, in church, and every other Wednesday night for bowling. They aren't exactly friends, but there is a kind of comfort in these small, recurrent encounters. It is a good life, if you avoid looking too many steps ahead.

When he sees his battered black Buick parked at the curb, he recalls that he is a salesman, has never been married, and has very few friends to speak of. His key sticks and hangs, as if the lock mechanism has not been used in some time. He is careful not to strain the key too far as he manipulates it against the roughness of the internal workings, and finally there is a giving, and a surprised suction as he jerks open the door.

Inside, the air is as thick and cloying as the air trapped in a dead grandmother's old trunk, and the fast food wrappers layering the floor appear to have been there for years. He sits in a bed of dust as soft and thick as another layer of upholstery.

He has no hope of starting this vehicle. This is a dead machine, designed for the transportation of the dead. He puts his key into the ignition and turns it anyway. There are no signs of electrical activity. He gets out of the car and looks under the hood. The engine appears to have been ripped out ages ago.

When he calls the main office he is too embarrassed to tell them that the car is an ancient piece of junk which has not been driven in years, because of course this would make no sense. He simply reports that his career in sales has outlived another vehicle, and that he will need a replacement. They authorize a budget and he picks a used car dealer at random from the phone book, his only criterion that it is within walking distance.

He waits at a safe distance from the car lot and watches as people drive in, are greeted in rapid succession by eager, excited salespeople, are spirited away to the cars that will change their lives, the cars that were made for them and them alone, with bucket seats, SRS brakes, extras and more than extras, the cars that will strain their marriages and bankrupt them. Many of these customers already know the possible end result of their reasonable time payment purchases, are perhaps even determined that it not happen to them again, and yet they will be so excited, so agitated by the experience and all the grand possibilities they will be absolutely thrilled to pay more and more for less and less.

Emil has an advantage. For so many of these people, a new car means a new life, transportation out of bad decisions and past mistakes. For him it is simply a continuation of the long, sad trip he has been on all of his life.

He waits until the right couple comes in driving the roughest, most battered vehicle he has seen in years. But it does not smoke, and there is no obvious wobble as it pulls in front of the dealership. An hour later they drive away in a bright blue teardrop of promise, and he walks across the street and into the sales office.

"What do you mean that doesn't include floor mats?" speaks a surprised voice out of a tiny office to his left.

"I want to buy that car, there," Emil says to the first salesman to approach him.

"Excuse me, sir?" Emil might have asked to buy a tombstone in a shoe shop.

"That car, there."

The salesman glances over Emil's shoulder without much interest. "Must be a trade-in. It hasn't been worked up yet."

Emil struggles to look the man directly in the eyes. "That's the one I want."

The salesman attempts to stare him down in the friendliest possible way. "What if I told you I could get you into a better car for less money?"

"You and I both know how much it's worth," Emil says a little shakily. "Take that figure and add fifteen percent." He forces himself to pause, and looks even more directly at the man. He isn't sure if he's pulled off a smile. "I'm a salesman, too. Since college— it's the only job I've ever had."

The car salesman nods, unimpressed, and Emil decides this has been a failure. "I'll have to take this to my manager," the salesman says, and for an unreal moment Emil thinks he is about to be arrested. Emil gazes after the man as he enters another office, waits anxiously as the salesman confers unemotionally with his boss who glances up at Emil only once, then down at a notepad. The boss gives the salesman a piece of paper, who carries it out to Emil and puts it into his hand. He almost expects the car to stall out as he drives it out of the lot, which would be embarrassing but survivable.

Studying the violent screen flickers of these motel room TVs, Emil has developed a theory that these sporadic discharges of light are part of an attempt to hypnotize the viewer into buying whatever product is being discussed. This sales maneuver is doubly clever because these residents are generally poor travelers who cannot afford to leave their rooms. They watch these commercials in a state of desperate exhaustion.

A collage of images impresses onto the tired and ill-used tissue of his brain: children, small tidy houses, walks in the park with the family dog, vacations at the beach. *Be A Man* floats eerily across the screen in colours muted to suggest a whisper. *What are they selling?* There is no way to determine. Whatever it is, it is certainly something he does not have.

ARE YOU READY? in bolder than bold type shouts at him from the screen. He waits for the kicker, the product revelation, the final sales pitch before he is returned to their regularly scheduled program. But there is no return. There is no change. The words remain frozen, oppressive, unforgiving, even when he unplugs the television in frustration.

Emil is travelling I-70 just outside Salinas when he sees the billboard "The City of Commerce" with a huge red arrow perched on top. The sign is somewhat worn, but he thinks maybe this is from the road construction he's seen in the area over the past year. He thinks of the letter folded up in his pocket, and he turns onto the access road: all black and shiny with promise.

He might quit his job this very day, call the company office and have them pick up the car and his samples if they care to bother.

He passes no cars on the road and considers the afternoon heat and thinks this must be a slow time for shopping traffic. He spies the gleaming steel tower from a couple of miles away, a variety of buildings spread about its base like flowers planted around an airport control tower. In the afternoon sun everything gleams like a nest of needles. Just before he turns onto the main street, another large sign appears. *Welcome to the City of Commerce*, with a picture of a happy little girl gesturing to the wonders behind her. *Alice in Wonderland*, he thinks, and the artist's vision of the shopping centre confirms the notion—it might easily grace the cover of some edition of something by Carroll or Baum.

Emil is bewildered by the cold tears he feels leaking from his eyes. What is happening to him? He should just turn around. "City of Commerce" indeed. It almost makes him laugh.

Then he sees the bullet holes above the little girl's head almost making a halo, the torn passages through the faded backdrop of city.

A turn onto the main street of the City of Commerce confirms that the place has been abandoned for some time. The finished buildings appear empty and the unfinished buildings ready to collapse beneath their architecturally unsound frameworks. He has nothing better to do—never did have—so he continues his leisurely drive past the vast fields of asphalt.

The streets appear to have been laid out with remarkable care: a perfect grid of block after block of abandoned buildings, partially finished constructions, lots full of dried up landscaping, mounds of mysterious concrete, in one place a huge outdoor skating rink (*Remarkable! Ice skating in Kansas!* The signs scream.) Now it looks like a large, shallow swimming pool with no water, much less ice. Remarkable, indeed.

The abandoned construction sites in particular draw Emil's eye. Much of the time he cannot tell what the building was intended to be. Multiple girders jut out sideways in parallel like huge claws taking a swipe at the sky. Rooflines twist and turn like the skeletons of roller coasters. Giant square passages where walls might have been form windows for watching the world change colour. Enormous Mondrian sculptures line up like a fleet of cubist spaceships.

He parks along one street of gravel and sand and peers through the great transparent teeth of a clownish building with round window eyes. The swirling pink and orange paint job within makes him think of an ill child after a day's overeating at the circus.

What might they sell in such places?

The fact that the buildings are relatively new, unlike those in the Western ghost towns of old, fills him with a peculiar dissonance, as if he is hearing dozens of ill tuned chimes playing nearby.

He turns the corner and is face-to-knee with a silver metal beaver at least a dozen feet tall. Beside it, and still gigantic at half the beaver's size is a brilliant white fibreglass baseball. The beaver's eyes are wide and staring, as if it is as surprised to see this baseball as Emil is.

He can find no specific business these statues might be attached to and therefore assumes this must be some sort of installation of public art. He wonders about what the customers must have thought of these two objects, forever how long this place had customers.

As he walks past the rows of storefronts it occurs to him how insubstantial everything seems—the empty stores like huge display boxes having no value without their goods. The wind thunders against the expanse of glass and shiny metal. There are no indications of residences, of schools, or any other structure where the day-in and day-out of life might take place. But of course, this is the City of Commerce, a container for commercials and impulsive retail exchange. Now even the signs indicating what might have gone on here are gone.

One door is slightly ajar. Emil tugs it lightly and slips inside. This one has been occupied at one time—the outlines of counters and shelving decorate the floor. Dead electrical cables dangle where light fixtures have been removed. Here and there lie a candy wrapper or a bit of a magazine, grey tracks in the dust where small creatures have roamed. There has been surprisingly little vandalism.

"You don't belong here." The dry voice speaks from behind.

Emil turns to see a man with one hand poised over a holster. "Hey, easy now," Emil says softly. "I . . . I have an invitation, I guess, to work here." He slides one finger into his front pants pocket, fishing for the paper, careful to let the guard see the rest of the hand. He retrieves the letter and extends it.

The guard shakes his head. "Not necessary—I didn't think you were the stealing type anyway. You're the salesman type. I've seen a lot of you around here, sniffing around. All of them had letters like yours."

Emil puts the paper back into his pocket. "What's to steal around here anyway?"

The guard looks around the vast room as if for the first time. "Fixtures," he says, with a hint of sadness.

Emil walks past the guard and out the door. Then he pauses. "How long?"

"Oh, about three years."

"What happened?"

The guard smiles a little. "They had a huge supply of what people didn't want."

On the otherwise unnaturally quiet walk back to his car, Emil finds himself chuckling aloud.

In these last few days of sales, generous discounts can be offered, bonus gifts pulled out of the dusty trunk and placed into hesitant buyers' hands. In these last few days of sales, he is full of compliments and important news for everyone's family. In these last few days of sales, he represents the church, the school, and a benevolent government. In these last few days of sales, he cannot remember what he is selling, nor does he recognize the odd objects in his sample case. In these last few days of sales, he cannot bring himself to ask *Which do you like best?* and *How many should I put you down for?* In these last few days of sales, he knows that sometimes a customer just wants a warm body to talk to. In these last few days of sales, he sees all the lonely people on his list, all the sad people for whom his brief visit is a major event.

He has been travelling for quite a long time. *Of course*, he thinks. *You're a career salesman—you've been travelling forever.* Towns have died during the time he has been a salesman. Local economies have been disrupted. Great masses of people have lost their definition, reduced to reading self help volumes and watching far too many movies. Everyone he meets is desperate to sell, but so many are reluctant to buy, having been disappointed so many times, having been cheated and lied to, having been murdered for their dreams and ambitions.

The towns he passes through are painted in FOR SALE signs. People have moved on ahead of him. Those left behind in the streets walk aimlessly with eyes like dull pennies.

In these last few days of sales, he yearns to complete one last transaction. Coming upon the white-haired man out on the street thrills him as nothing has in years. He lets the man have one last swig from his bottle, then props him against the wall. The old man resembles Jack, the fellow who trained him years ago, but he resembles the guard at the City of Commerce as well. He may resemble the salesmen who built the City of Commerce, but Emil doesn't know how they might have aged. He resembles most old men Emil has ever known. Perhaps he resembles Emil himself, who has not looked at his own face for a long time.

"You only want the best for them," he begins. "Your children. Your grandchildren. And if you don't have children it's the children of others you want to thrive—is this not so? Because then you can believe that something of this life will go on, and do well, and make of itself a thing of beauty against the failing of the light. For what else is there, but the spark of us carried by children into the lands where we will never travel?

"And so you buy them things, grand things your own parents could never afford. And you hand these things to them, as if you were handing down sacrifices and offerings to some fierce and unstoppable god. 'Take these things I have given you and do well,' you say. 'Make my dreams into something capable of movement and breath. And do not damage me, make no attempt to rob me of my last remaining dignities because I swear, I only wish you well.'

"And that's the best you can do. That's the best any of us can do, in these final days of sales."

Placing his sample case on the concrete in front of the old man, he goes into the trunk of his car and hauls out box after box of Bibles and encyclopaedias, grand dictionaries full of ideas he has never been able to express, baskets of outdated kitchen accessories which have lost both their utility and their names, perfumes and cleansers, small gifts for every occasion. The old man stares drunkenly at the salesman, unable to manage even a thank you.

The salesman walks away empty handed, leaving all the voices, all the give and take and the I've-got-something-special-for-yous behind, knowing full well that he will not have to sell himself to the rain, or the wind, or the ground with its daily increase in gravity. And there is a peace in knowing that not all deals have to be closed.

From the outside, his home looks no different from all the others. This is the way he wants it—there is a comfort in the cloning of every house he has ever seen on television, the slavish duplication of columns and brickwork, the same angled roofs repeated again and again across the horizon to become a geometry of reassurance.

Emil has no reason to leave his house. The company pension provides for him quite comfortably. Why he should be receiving a pension, why they should reward decades of poor salesmanship, he has no idea. But then reward and punishment has always been a puzzle he is unable to solve.

Groceries can be delivered relatively cheaply from the smaller stores. Items may be ordered over the phone even without a catalogue: he will work from lists of merchandise but pictures of anything are forbidden in his house. He receives a daily newspaper, but pays the man next door a handsome sum to censor it for him, until the paper is like lace in his hands, beautiful in its way as shreds of celebrities and the dire news of the world allow the morning sunlight to pass through, making intricate shadowscapes on his Formica kitchen table.

He spends much of his day walking around naked. He has grown increasingly uncomfortable with clothing: even the plainest garment seems to evoke one style or another, and then he feels he is wearing packaging, and cannot breathe until it is shed.

Without clothes he can clearly see the damage that wraps him. There are cracks in his lower face and left arm from hours driving directly into the sun. There is dry and flaky skin across a chest and abdomen which no one has touched in years. There is an arthritic right hand which burns and freezes in the position of one asking for money. Several of his toes are missing. He does not remember what he did with them.

He has lost the full range of motion in his left arm. His left leg twists awkwardly inward, making it painful to maneuver up and down steps. *I didn't even sell these things,* he thinks. *I was never that good. My arms, my legs, my hands, my heart pulled and squeezed: I just gave them all away.*

His front doorbell rings. He peers out a nearby window. A small boy, staggering under the weight of a large box, looking up at Emil's closed door forlornly, as if behind it lies the only safety the boy has ever known, and yet the door must seem hundreds of miles away. Emil wraps a towel around himself and goes to greet his visitor.

The boy's eyes grow huge when he sees Emil. But he musters his courage. "Sir, I'm trying to earn extra money this summer selling these fine candies . . ."

"Son." Emil crouches next to the boy, careful not to expose himself. People are scared, they're scared everywhere he's ever been, and he doesn't want them to get the wrong idea. "Son, listen. You've got to get my *attention* first. Then you've got to pique my *interest*."

"Peek, sir?"

"Then you have to show me some *conviction*. Then you have to kindle my *desire*. And finally you have to *close* the deal. Nothing really happened here today if you can't manage that last part. It was all just a dream, one big fantasy if there's no closing. AICDC, son. Attention, interest, conviction, desire, close. Remember that."

Emil realizes the boy is staring at his belly. Poor salesmanship, drawing the prospect's attention to his own faults. "So are you gonna buy a candy bar, Mister?"

"Say I do buy a candy bar from you. What are you going to do with the money? Are you going to save that money, son?"

"I'm gonna go to the movies with it, if you buy a box of 'em. Six to a box. Ten dollars."

"OK, then. I'll buy two boxes."

"Do you have a wallet, sir?" the boy asks skeptically.

"I own a wallet, even a pocket in a pair of pants to keep it in. I probably even sold myself that pair of pants. I don't always walk around naked, you know?" The boy continues to stare at him. Emil stares back. Finally Emil asks, "Do I give you the money first, or do you give me the candy bars first? Anymore I'm not so good . . . at this commerce thing."

When they find him a week later only half the candy bars have been consumed. The property is on the market for several years before it finally sells, longer than any listing the local realtors can remember. In fact, the poorly painted "For Sale" sign becomes a familiar landmark that the neighbours actually miss when it is gone.

LITTLE
POUCET

Little Poucet was born small as his father's middle finger, smaller than a mouse, smaller by far than his six brothers who had all come out normal sized. Although he would eventually grow a bit larger than this, inside he would always feel that same size. His parents ignored him, expecting him to die, because he was so small, and because he was mute.

Because he was mute he had never found much use in words. Words were walls and boxes enormous adults built: the caves and castles and impassable mountains that made lies and broken promises out of each new day. Words could not be trusted. The adults in his life used words with an emphatic pounding of fist against table and a broad, fleshy palm across the face as they told you who you were, what was to become of you, and what you must believe. Little Poucet vowed that when he eventually used words, as he knew he would someday, they would be practical words. They would *mean* something.

But in the beginning Little Poucet relied on dream, and memory, and for as long as he might remain a child, he knew these would be very much the same.

Little Poucet's most important dream was the lush memory of his mother's bedroom, where he would spend every minute of his life until departing on the journeys that would make him so famous later on. He supposed it was his father's bedroom as well, although this faceless mountain of flesh (except for the whale's eye of him which would stare at Little Poucet even in sleep) visited the bedroom rarely. When his father did visit, the children were kept asleep with warm, oily drinks before bedtime. This was so that the mountain that was his mother and the mountain that was his father could crash into each other with a great moaning and quaking of the bed, without the children disturbing them. But Little Poucet never drank the drink. Little Poucet never slept, waiting up all night to hear the words his parents used with each other.

He had no experience of other bedrooms so he could not know whether the world of his mother's bed was grand: for someone of his small size it was preeminent. He had come into the world into the pale soft folds and dark-haired shadows of this bedroom, as had all his six brothers, and if his parents had so decided he would have left the world by way of this same room. He remembered lying on his mother's immense white breast, her billowy flesh extending in all directions across the bed and toward the dark walls of night beyond.

Always a small lamp glowed in this room, but it served only to intensify the darkness of those distant walls until Little Poucet was compelled to give them the name Terror. The lamp spotlighted his mother's oily flesh, the pink nipple, the heavy wet smell of her as she breathed in and out like waves pushing the raft of him to another side of his contained world.

His mother was always the central event of this world, her size at times making her indistinguishable from the bed, her creams and perfumes and powders and foods ranked on the tables beside her head and the forest spread of her thick black hair, her sighs and moans and gaseous eruptions providing a background music to his day, her silvery flickering black box a gate to one side of the darkness beyond the world of the bed, a gate full of noise and words and dancing dreams, which Little Poucet would not gaze at for long for fear he'd be struck blind as well as mute.

And beyond this the cracked rectangle of yellow-brown shade that covered the window, made to glow half the day with loud noises from other giants and hard smells close to, but not as pleasant as, the smells his mother created.

So central in fact to this world was his mother that on those rare occasions she gathered her heaving flesh and left to get something from the Kitchen or to Go Potty, Little Poucet would huddle to himself with his eyes closed, desperate to find in his dreams some comforting memory of her.

When time for Little Poucet to Go Potty it was small and insignificant (later he would understand this to be from the rarity of food), and collected into a can his mother kept in the nighttime beyond the bed. Sometimes he would see her smelling the can before she put it away, smiling and nodding so that her great black tresses fell all over flesh and bed, covering his own scarce flesh like a web that caught and thrilled him.

Sometimes she'd pull him up to her huge blue eyes (the whites slightly yellow, the entire eye long and fish-shaped) and watch his nose. A smell sour enough or sharp enough would make his nose wiggle, and she would know to put more powder on, or more perfume, or she would rub herself with a wet cloth, moving him like a divining rod over every bit and crack of her. What he did not think she understood was that his nose wiggled out of pleasure, because as much as he enjoyed the perfumes and powders which hung in a cloud over the great bed, it was the slightly corrupt fragrances underneath which really thrilled him.

Sometimes she would pull from behind her tables a large book smelling of insects and dirty linen, and she would read to Little Poucet written-down dreams of giants and trolls and nightmare castles, and missing princesses and ravenous wolves and even solitary elves, such as himself, who lived out their lives in lands no bigger than this, his mother's bed.

Besides his mother and the smells and the murmuring gate and his own small presence and the occasional mounds of his six larger brothers (although usually they slept on the Rug in the dark outside the bed), there were always the pillows, of various sizes— each one bigger than he, and ranging from four to eight in number. The pillows were marvellous because although not as soft as her skin they always smelled of his mother and remained accessible to him when his mother was out of the room or quaking with the powerful presence of his father. Sometimes they surrounded him like her own breasts and legs, and sometimes he mounted them where they carried him off to dream. In his head he made up songs about the pillows, about their softness and firmness, about their sizes and shapes, about how they sometimes resembled his sleeping brothers, and about his occasional fear that they might be used by his mother to smother him.

Then into this world of his mother's bed his father might loom, a towering cliff as dark as the walls. He was more a voice than anything else, and sometimes a pair of huge rough hands. His father always picked up Little Poucet and moved him to some distant valley of pillow when the giant came and entered her bed, there to roll and rumble and laugh, and to backhand Little Poucet off into unkempt shadows if the baby ventured too close to the adults' play. But they were never very careful about what they had to say to each other, thinking Little Poucet's mind to be small as well, and no threat to the slap and tickle that went on each night.

Sometimes his father smelled of distant rooms and other giants, however, and at those times Little Poucet's presence was welcome in the family bed, as was that of his brothers, and they all played naked in the family caverns and on the mountain ranges the adult bodies made and remade throughout the evening, their motion so constant, fluid, and restless that Little Poucet could not tell where his own self ended and these ancient forms of creation began.

As grand as these reunions were, Little Poucet most loved the secret times when he was shoved to a corner of the bed and wrapped in pillows. His father the giant uncovered the thing Little Poucet understood to be Brother Eight, who seemed every bit Little Poucet's size when he stretched his muscle, who had dark hair gathered about his feet leaving his glistening head bald, and who had been born with no face at all, which explained why his father kept him hidden.

During these frightening, exciting secret times, his father would plunge Brother Eight back into the dark original folds of his mother as if desperate to allow the distant ancient seas of her to effect a change, and at last to provide Brother Eight with a face. These attempts never worked the necessary magic, however, and so Little Poucet vowed never to tell the other six brothers of the secret of Brother Eight. Instead Little Poucet contented himself to lie beside the still, soft form of the only brother who was even more an embarrassment than he himself. Sometimes his mother's hand came down during these times to stroke Little Poucet, in a way to suggest that she might be confusing Little Poucet with the almost identical Brother Eight. In his dreams they were two damp, slim little pixies, secretly smarter than their brothers, and by far the favourites of their monstrous parents.

"Can't feed them no more. Nothing left, Sadie."

Little Poucet almost missed the significance of his father's statement in his wonder at the sound of his mother's name, which he was sure he had never heard before. But having heard something once, of course Little Poucet never lost it, and going back over his father's words he felt a growing alarm.

"Enough food for me and you. As little as they eat, still too much."

His father spoke softly, deeply, as he did when he was trying to make Brother Eight a face. His mother's face had grown soft and blurry, as if her flesh were melting.

"Hush now. You'll wake the others," his father said, looking at him with that great whale eye the way he might look at Brother Eight, something without sense and with only one purpose, and in Little Poucet's case, a purpose his father obviously valued very little.

"Tonight, couple hours after dark. You dress 'em, I'll take 'em out into the city. Stop your blubberin' now. Here, I'll give you somethin' for the pain of it." Adult words, all of them.

And the rolling and heaving of the bed put Little Poucet back to sleep.

He woke sometime later from dreams of a giant troll beneath the bridge of his bed. The whale eye was closed, and his mother smelled of night. Carefully Little Poucet crawled over the dark coverlet of her hair and reached for the bag of black cookies with the dazzling white fillings, brighter than the bed sheets, that were his mother's favourites. He hid the bag beneath one of the pillows, thinking of whose clothes might hide them best tonight when his mother dressed him and his brothers for their journey outside the world. He closed his eyes and pretended to sleep, searching his head for the words he might use for the first time to persuade his brothers of the value of his plan.

When he opened his eyes again it seemed as if he had indeed slept, and were still in the midst of a dream. Six of his brothers (Brother Eight, as expected, was off with his father somewhere) stood groggily upon the expanse of bed, his mother slipping over their heads rags she referred to as Their Clothes. Little Poucet had never seen these clothes before. As his brothers gradually woke up they smiled and winked at each other, as if on the verge of a great adventure.

"Pierre, Maurice, Charles . . ." She counted and recounted, stroking their sweaty heads. Then when she turned, Little Poucet slipped the bag of cookies into the back of Pierre's trousers, which were much too big for him anyway.

Pierre turned in surprise as Little Poucet whispered behind him, "Be still until I relate my plan to the others," keeping his mouth shut in obvious shock at his mute brother's use of words.

Their father came in then, Brother Eight hid behind heavy coat and pants (*He's to stay behind because he's mother's favourite*, Little Poucet thought). "Come along," his father boomed. "It's time you boys helped your father earn his living." And so Little Poucet was forced to leave the world of his mother's bed for the first time in his life.

Little Poucet was surprised to find that the world of the City was not unfamiliar. It was the world of the dark night walls in his dreams. The City was all buildings (this Little Poucet knew from the flickering gate) and what were buildings but walls that went on forever, filled with night and the stink of garbage and sour flesh and sheets? His father pushed the seven of them in front of him, prodding them along with a thick stick as if they were dirty, ill-fed geese. Now and then he would stop to retrieve a wallet from some drunk or addict sleeping it off in an alley, or he would gaze at the unbarred windows of stores and warehouses with a look of intense concentration on his great face, as if he were considering matters of stress, strength, approach. It was only then that Little Poucet understood how it was their father made his living.

Every few yards, hiding them with care and a small, swift prayer, Little Poucet scattered the dark cookies with their creamy fillings. He was careful not to let the others see him, for he knew they were so hungry now they would have gobbled them up instantly. It was hard enough for Little Poucet to handle them without risking a surreptitious lick.

Once they were deep into the tallest walls of the cool, smelly city, Little Poucet realized he had not felt his father's sharp prod or heard his heavy footsteps for some time. He turned around and looked behind him. His father was nowhere to be seen.

"So, the old man's taken off and left us little fools here all by ourselves," Little Poucet said.

His brothers turned and looked at him in amazement. "He talks!" Maurice exclaimed.

Jean Paul stepped forward and examined Little Poucet's mouth. "Maybe it was someone else," he said. "A ventriloquist." Little Poucet bit down sharply on his brother's finger. Jean Paul did not cry out, but examined his bloody finger in the streetlight's dim grey. "He bites as well," he said.

"I will try to control my hunger," Little Poucet said, but found himself gazing at his brother's finger as if it were his mother's huge and wonderful tit. He forced himself to look away. "I've left a trail. We must hurry and find the bits of it before someone eats it."

They found each and every one of the cookies, passing them back and forth between them for nibbles, Pierre licking the fillings and Little Poucet taking the smallest bite for himself each time.

By dawn they had arrived back at the dark and greasy brick wall beyond which lay the apartment of their mother and father. Upstairs and outside the door they could barely hear their mother's sobbing above the chatter of the flickering gate.

"With that score you made on the way home we might have kept them!" she cried.

"We can always make more where those came from," the father shouted, and again the great bed began to rock and their mother's cries to subside.

Little Poucet had neglected to plan what they all should do when they arrived back at their parents' apartment, and before he could make a suggestion his brothers had beaten down the door and poured into the grand bedroom shouting, "Here we are! Here we are!"

Little Poucet ran in behind his brothers, and was not surprised to see that Brother Eight had taken his place in their mother's bed and now nestled his quivering form at his mother's pale breasts. The giant father stared at Little Poucet then left the bed. His mother opened her arms then and he and his brothers stripped off their travelling clothes and disappeared into her embrace.

Only two nights had passed before Little Poucet's father had exhausted his recent earnings and there was no food again. During those two nights their father and Brother Eight were gone from the apartment, returning fatter on the third. As his mother and father crashed together that night with even greater clamour than before, Little Poucet again overheard their conversation:

"No food no room no peace no food no good good good . . ." his father chanted in a low growl. After his parents were asleep Little Poucet again slipped up to his mother's bed table and stole more of the black cookies with the dazzling white centres.

On the next night their mother dressed them again, kissing each of them goodbye with tears on her fat cheeks as their father took them out exploring. Little Poucet planted a bag of cookies each on Jean Paul and Maurice, but this time letting those two—the oldest of his brothers—in on the details of his plan.

This night their father took them even deeper into the dark valley that was at the city's centre, where there was no air for the stench, and no lights at all other than the shining whites of their small eyes. Half the time they couldn't see their father at all—so dull and oily was his outfit, his skin—so it came as no surprise at all to suddenly find him gone.

They stared at each other: at the whites of their eyes, at the bright fillings of the two remaining cookies Little Poucet held in his hands. "Don't worry, my brothers. I've been making a trail as I did last time."

But then Pierre opened his mouth to laugh, and his tongue and teeth were dazzlingly white with the thick, gooey fillings from the cookies Little Poucet had planted all along the way.

"Hmmmm . . ." Pierre sighed.

Little Poucet shook his head. "You've killed us, my brother."

Little Poucet led his brothers on a snaky trip through the cold night of stone and damp asphalt, but nothing was familiar. Everywhere the walls towered above them, stinking of garbage and the press of generations of sweating, dying bodies, so dark they blended and became indistinguishable from the night sky around and above. Now and then they would stumble over some form or other, sleeping or dead on the greasy pavement. Hands with long, slick fingers clutched at their ankles and trousers, slipped inside their cuffs to creep toward their thighs and groins. Maurice tittered and Little Poucet told him to hush. Some of the bodies in the dark leaked fluids and they gave these a wide berth.

When the others complained of hunger Little Poucet warned them not to stray from the path he was reimagining for them, so they kissed Pierre's sticky teeth and lips with their open mouths and tongues, sharing in the last bits of the sweet white goo, filling their bellies with the dazzling light that permitted them to continue through such darkness.

Muffled cries and howls floated just as slowly down from the dim windows high above, fixed there like distant, complaining stars. When they shuffled past the darker mouths of night, they could hear teeth rubbing, tongues lapping at the gritty stones.

At some point in the night it rained, but the night air had grown so thick they barely felt the drops.

"Where are you taking us?" Pierre whined.

"Home," Little Poucet replied, less and less sure of himself. "Wait here." He climbed a scarred and deadened lamp post and twisted his body round and round its head searching for distant signs of life. Once upon a time he would have been able to fit his entire body on the head of such a lamp. He was surprised at how much larger he had grown. And how much his skin now smelled of adult garbage.

Down a distant corridor walled by two different shades of black, he saw a distant glimmer of light low to the horizon like a ground floor window. Thinking of warm kitchens and broad beds and small boxes flickering he slid down and led his brothers off in that direction. They complained that they could see nothing in that direction, but they had become used to following him so they did.

Often he lost all sense of direction and led them down into holes and wet places where invisible, spongy flesh rubbed against them. But eventually they came to the glowing window set beside a rough grey door in the back recesses of an alley stacked high with soggy cardboard cases of rotting meat.

Little Poucet reached as high as he could and pounded his fist against the door. After a few minutes a frail, worried looking woman with stringy yellow hair answered.

"What do you children want at this time of night?" she demanded. "If it's stealing you're thinking about I warn you my husband is not a forgiving man."

"Food, ma'am," Pierre spoke up. "We're *so* hungry!"

She jittered her eyes from one face to the next, finally resting on Little Poucet's diminutive form. "Looks like someone has already eaten the best part of this one." She paused, considering. "Very well.

Come in then and I'll toss you an old fruit or two before sending you back to your parents, if you should have any."

Inside the dusty building Little Poucet tugged on her skirt. "We're lost, ma'am. Perhaps you could call the authorities?"

"Authorities?"

"The police? Social services?"

The withered little woman began laughing. "The *police*? Oh, my husband would dearly love that!" Then she laughed some more and Little Poucet could see that when she laughed she looked even thinner, her skinny arms flapping and beating her narrow torso, the loose material of her dress lifting away from her tight skin and pressing against it again, so that he found himself thinking of his mother, because this woman was the complete reverse of his enormous mother and in that was a kind of a negative twin, a sister to her.

"Perhaps just a bit of food, then," Little Poucet said softly, and the woman started laughing even louder than before. Little Poucet was embarrassed, and gazed down at his feet.

Just then the scrawny woman's head shot up, her neck stretching like a startled chicken's. "You hear? It's him, my man come home! You hear? Oh, you poor children—he'll be murdering you for sure! Here . . . here . . ." She stretched out her arms and legs and gathered the seven brothers to her, and despite her resemblance to a gigantic praying mantis then, Little Poucet allowed himself to be gathered with the others. "Here, here . . . let Auntie hide you. Auntie won't let bad old Otto get to you!"

She rushed them into the back of the building with desperate pattings and *shoo*ings of her long-fingered hands, pushing them past greasy piles of old clothing, dusty collections of children's shoes, children's toys, through passageways littered with dirt and what appeared to be yellowed animal bones, dried chicken skin, and a scattering of tiny teeth—Little Poucet figured dog, cat, badger. Pierre was sniveling, but there was no time to comfort him as she practically lifted them up to the first landing of the back stairs whispering hoarsely: "First room on the left. Get under the bed there. But don't wake my daughters if you know what's good for you! Get under the bed there. I can't think of a better place to hide you."

Little Poucet waited until his brothers were all safely tucked away under the bed before joining them there. As he rolled under the bed he looked at the bed on the opposite side of the room, and one great bloodshot eye peering over.

His brothers huddled together silently, staring at him. He could hear the sound of a bearlike voice downstairs, much like his father's. He heard a slap, then crying. His eyes now adjusted to the dim light under the bed, he looked around him and his brothers: several small skulls, a rib cage that might have housed the tiniest of birds, leg bones and arm bones, a tiny skeletal hand with a small child's ring on one of the fingers. Tiny teeth marks on all the bones, aimlessly crisscrossing the tops of the skulls, like the tracks of some small animal, like a tattoo. Downstairs more bellowing, and a breaking of furniture.

"But I can *smell* them, dammit!" And suddenly Little Poucet heard the thunder move to the stairs. Another eye joined the first atop the bed across the way, equally bloodshot, then the long dirty blonde hair, the high cheeks, the sharp nose and thin lips and teeth filed to points like knitting needles. The chin stained dark.

The thunder was right outside the door now. Little Poucet could hear the lightning strike, the torrents of rain as Auntie wailed for the seven brothers to run, but Little Poucet knew of nowhere to run. Six more identical heads joined the first on the other bed. The heads leaned over the edge and smiled down at him, their long tongues slipping over their chins. They leaned forward some more and he could see that they had no clothes on. They rubbed their tiny breasts (in two or three only one had begun its development) and made a sound like swarming moths.

Otto burst through the door, and at first Little Poucet thought indeed that it was their father who had followed them here. He had the size (like a wall, a dark and heavy wall) and the voice, and the way of wrinkling his nose as if he were always smelling a bad smell. And the large, broken teeth.

Otto strode over to the bed and lifted it to uncover the seven frightened brothers. "Such pretty boys . . ." he cooed. He turned to his wife. "Get them ready for bed! I'll want them rested in the morning. No challenge otherwise." Otto looked back down at Little Poucet. "Sweet little thing," he said, and patted Little Poucet's head, stroked his shoulders, felt for muscles in his arms and legs. Then Otto gently spread his great hand until it covered the whole of Little Poucet's chest. He leaned over him, his breath sour with beer. "I can feel your heart beating," he whispered. "I can almost taste it, too. Wait until the morning." He massaged the boy's rear, circled the boy's groin with a huge, blunt forefinger. "You'll see."

After Otto left (Little Poucet could hear him drinking and singing downstairs), Auntie gave them a quick dinner of cold noodles and helped the seven brothers strip off their clothes. She shook her head at each naked little boy. "Oh, you're all much too soft and tender. He likes them soft and tender." She handed each of them a ragged, dark-stained nightshirt, then turned to leave. Her daughters began to giggle. "Hush up now!" she told them. "There'll be time enough tomorrow for what you're wanting. Go to sleep now!" And she left the room.

The seven little girls looked over at the seven naked little boys and whispered excitedly to each other. Then they all laughed one last time and pulled the covers over their heads.

Pierre started pulling on his nightshirt. "Stop that!" Little Poucet cried. "Can't you see the stains, the torn places? It's like butcher's wrap!" He looked back over at the other bed, the seven sisters starting to snore and snarl under their covers. He pulled his brothers close to him. They snickered at his cold touch on their bare skin. "Hush up now . . . once he's got enough drink in him to bring out the beast he'll be back up here quickly, I think. I have an idea. Do you remember how our father trained us not to wet the bed?"

The other six nodded solemnly, their eyes pale and tight in their tiny faces.

First he gathered seven leftover noodles from the cracked plastic bowls Auntie had provided them (Pierre's bowl, of course, had been wiped clean). A bit of thick, flour-based sauce had settled into the bottom of each one. He dipped each noodle until it was heavy in the sauce, then with great stealth crept over to the girls' bed, pulled back the covers, and gently stuck a noodle to the sex of each one. They snarled and snapped in their sleep, but did not move off their backs. Soon, he knew, the sauce would become a paste, the paste would dry, and their disguise would be perfected. His brothers' hair was just long enough that in the dark Otto might not suspect.

After a quiet search of the room Little Poucet found enough string to take care of all seven of them. Each brother tied one end of the string to the tip of his penis, passed the remaining string back between his legs, and gave the other end to Little Poucet (who also held the end of his own string). Little Poucet became the puppeteer: all he had to do to turn him and his seven brothers into instant females was to pull on the string and thereby tuck each of their penises back under their asses. With their soft bodies and bad teeth, and by pressing their arms close to their sides to accentuate their breasts, they became wonderful, matchless little girls. Lying there together on the bed Little Poucet really found them quite irresistible.

To no one's surprise Otto did come up later that night, stumbling drunk, and went straight to the boys' bed. Little Poucet jerked hard on the string causing Jean Paul and Maurice to gasp, but they drew their gasps out quickly into yawns.

Otto reached under the covers and felt for their groins. "What's this? My daughters? I could have made a terrible mistake." He paused for a time, smiling, gazing off into space. Finally stirring himself he said, "But no time for this," stood up suddenly, and walked to the other bed.

He reached under the covers there and laughed. "Tiny they are, but unmistakable! Here's one seems a little stale." He pulled out a sharp knife and rapidly cut off the heads of his seven daughters and dropped them into a large bucket by the bed. He then proceeded to flay the bodies, making miniature vests and tiny leggings. He pulled out one of the heads and removed the skin of the face, turning it into a small mask. "This'll be a good mask for the dog to wear when he watches TV with me," he said, holding it up to the light coming through the window. He stared at it a time, then dropping it as if it were something truly disgusting he cried out, "Imogene!" and spun around to the other bed.

But the seven brothers were already out the door and on the staircase, their strings trailing along behind them. Otto leapt up and ran after them, bellowing. He stepped on one, then another of the trailing strings. Pierre and Maurice screamed and tumbled down the stairs. Otto lost his balance and followed hard upon them. Auntie suddenly appeared at the bottom of the stairs, and, startled by the naked, bleeding children tumbling down her staircase, she went up after them, only to watch helplessly as they wheeled past her, and her husband Otto, Otto the Butcher, Otto the Cannibal, crashed into her.

The seven brothers gathered what they could find in the litter and rot of the house: mostly jewelry and clothing from Otto's past victims, and all manner of cutting instruments and devices of torture. They dressed in the cleanest rags they could find, and when daylight finally came, Little Poucet led them home with all their loot.

Their parents were of course overjoyed to see them, especially with all the items they had taken from Otto and Auntie's house. They were puzzled by the fact that both Pierre and Maurice had become girls while away on the journey, but this fact was of very little importance to them. "After all," their father would say, "children are children."

But the world of his mother's bed was never the same for Little Poucet again. He stayed awake nights. He listened for voices in the distant, dark walls. And sometimes when his parents were unusually noisy, when their cursings and crashings and complaints about how many mouths they had to feed became almost too much to bear, he would reach into his pillow and take comfort in the knife and the hook, the club and the razor, and dream of their readiness.

THE BEREAVEMENT PHOTOGRAPHER

"So, have you been doing this a while now?"

"A few years."

"Sorry for asking, and tell me if I'm out of line, but you can't possibly be making a full time living doing this can you?"

I actually almost say, "It's a hobby," which would be disastrous. But I don't. I look at the fellow: sandy-haired, a beard whose final length appears to be forever undecided. He looks terrible in the suit—either long outgrown or borrowed for the occasion. And it is an occasion—a grim occasion but an occasion none the less. He watches me as I set up, without a glance for his child. The young wife fusses with her to make ready for this picture, this family portrait.

I'm used to this. Who could blame him.

"I'm a volunteer. They reimburse me for film and lab costs. It's a way . . . of being of service."

He glances down, gazes at his wife rearranging the baby in her arms, glances away again, with no place to look.

Me, I have only one place to look. I peer through the lens, musing on composition issues, the light, the shadows, the angles of their arms. "Could you move her a little to the left?" The husband and father stares at me, puzzled, then bends to move his wife's chair. She blushes.

"No, sorry. You, ma'am." I straighten up behind the camera. "Could you move the baby a little to the left?" Notice how I said "the" baby, not "your." I try to avoid upsetting words. These are family portraits, after all. Just like all families have. Most parents don't want to be crying. I have folders full of photographs of mothers and fathers wailing, faces split in the middle. Believe me, they don't want to keep those. Sometimes I have taken roll after roll until there is sufficient calm for me to make the picture that will go into some leather bound matte, slipped into some nondescript manila folder, or, if they're so inclined, up on the living room mantel in a place of honour, there, oh so much *there*, for the whole world to see.

I've been doing this for years. But still I find that hard to imagine.

I feel bad that I haven't found the right words for this father, the words that will soothe, or at least minimize his discomfort and embarrassment. But sometimes there are just no right words. At least I can't always find them.

"I'll be taking the shot in a few minutes," I say. "Just make yourself comfortable. This isn't going to be flash flash flash and me telling you to smile each time. The most important thing is to try to make yourselves comfortable. Try to relax and ease into this shared moment."

This shared moment. Whatever words I say to my subjects, I always include these. Even though I've never been sure they were accurate, or fair. The moment is shared in that it happens to both of them. But most of the time, I think, the experience is so personal and large it will soon split the marriage apart if they're not careful.

I've seen it happen so much. I've seen so much.

"Okay, then," I say in warning and again I move behind the camera, almost as if I expect it to protect me from what is to come. As I peer into the electronic viewfinder, so like a small computer screen, so distancing in that same way, I see the mother's smile, and it is miraculous in its authenticity. I've seen it before in my portraits, this miraculous mother's smile, and it never fails to surprise me.

And I see the father at last look down upon his dead baby girl and reach out two fingers, so large against the plump, pale arm, and he lets them linger, a brief time but longer than I would have expected, and I realize this touch is for the first, and last, time.

I again shift my focus to the light, to the shadows and the play of shadows, and ready myself to shoot. The father attempts a dignified smile, but of course goes too broadly with it. The mother holds the child a bit too tightly. And I trigger the camera once, then twice, the baby looking as if she were merely sleeping. The baby looking. Then I take a shot for the photographer, a shot I will never show the parents, an image to add to the growing collection I keep hidden in a file drawer at home, the one in which the baby opens its eyes and fixes its gaze upon me.

I should explain, I suppose, that I've never had much talent for photography. I have the interest, sometimes I've had the enthusiasm, but I've never had the eye. I got this volunteer position because my next door neighbour is a nurse, and she used to see me in my back yard with camera and tripod shooting birds, trash, leaves, whatever happened to land in front of me. Inconsequential subjects, but I was afraid I'd screw up a more significant one, which would have broken my heart, maybe even have prevented me from ever taking another photograph. I didn't want to risk that.

Not that I wanted to risk taking such an important photograph in a family's life, either. But Liz had talked about how temporary this was, how they just needed someone to man the camera now, and every time I tried to tell her I really wasn't that good at it, she said I didn't have to be—the families just wanted the photograph—having it was the idea and they wouldn't care how good it was, technically.

But I told her no anyway. Even unpaid, I would have felt like an imposter. Not only was I not that good as a photographer, but I wasn't that good with kids.

Maybe that sounds terrible under the circumstances. It seemed to me at the time that the appropriate person for this kind of sensitive task would be someone with a strong empathy and dedication to and involvement with children. And I didn't have that. Of course I used to be a child, and my sister Janice and I had pretty good parents, but I don't remember childhood as being a particularly happy time. I could hardly wait for it to be over so I could be out on my own. And I can't say that I've ever *enjoyed* children. I've never particularly liked spending time with them. My nephews are okay—I've taken them to ball games and movies and such and I think they're great kids now that they're older. When they were little I didn't know what to say to them and, frankly, they scared me a little. They seemed so needy and fragile and that was pretty much the extent of their personalities.

As far as other kids go, I'd have to say I've basically ignored them. Their concerns are not my concerns. Most of the time I haven't even been aware they were there.

That weekend I was in the city park taking bad pictures. I tried shooting couples, failing—everything looked fuzzy and poorly-framed. Composition was eccentric at best, whatever I tried. A number of families were barbecuing. I noticed one small group in particular: really young parents, kids themselves, with a huge, dish-shaped barbecue looking hundreds of years old.

Suddenly there was an explosion of shouts, barking, shapes racing through the crowd. Then several large dogs burst from the wall of people to my right, followed by a half dozen teenage boys, red-faced, barking like hyenas, and all of them converging on that young family.

I shouted a warning, but too late. One of the dogs knocked the unwieldy barbecue over, and several others a few feet away. The little kids started screaming, the mother and father running toward them, but the air was full of thick, white, choking smoke. The mother grabbed up two of their kids and folded them into her. But the little one, "Jose!" the young father screamed. "Jose!"

I could not breathe in the smoke, but I could not close my eyes. And almost as if to protect my eyes I raised my camera in front of my face and started taking pictures of the turmoil and the panic, the father gesturing as if mad, and I'm wondering how could this be, all this over some kids and their pets, but these poor people, their lives changing forever. And then the little boy appears out of the smoke like some apparition from the mists, some ghost back to rejoin his family because the taking of him had been a mistake, arms reaching up for his daddy, crying and sobbing and the father sobbing as well.

It was at that moment I decided to say yes to my neighbour, and became the hospital's bereavement photographer. Even before I saw the photographs I had taken: the looks on the young couple's faces on their rapid descent into despair, and that small boy appearing out of the clouds like a tragedy retrieved from the fierce and unforgiving eddies of time.

"Oh, Johnny, those poor people!" Janice is my older sister, my confessor, and, I'm a little embarrassed to say, my barometer as to what's normal or abnormal, what's okay and what's not okay.

The day after I'd made that decision to volunteer my photographic services (Would I have changed my mind if she'd responded negatively? I still don't know.) she had a barbecue of her own. I was invited, of course. With no family or even regular girlfriend, I usually ate at her house three, four times a week. Tom didn't seem to mind, but of course you never really know when you visit married couples. They might have been fighting for hours before you got there, but when they open the front door they're like a glossy advertisement for the connubial life.

"Sounds like pretty sad work to me," Tom said morosely.

"Tom!"

"I'm not criticizing him, Janice. It just sounds like it'd be pretty grim stuff, and he's not even being paid to do it."

"Well, I wouldn't be doing it every day," I said, somewhat off the point. I just wanted them both to believe that, contrary to appearances, I lead a pretty balanced life. Despite the fact that I had no girlfriend, spent most of my spare time at their house, and obsessively took photographs even I didn't think were very good.

Janice snorted. "Don't listen to him, Johnny. It's a noble way to spend your time. We should *all* do at least one activity like that."

The subject mercifully disappeared into a conversational salad of new movies, music, old friends recently seen, what my twin nephews were doing (now fifteen, athletic, and a deadly combination with an alarmingly broad age range of females), and, of course, the pregnancy.

"You should have one of your own, sometime," Janice said, smiling and rubbing her belly as if it were silk.

"Wrong equipment, sis."

"I meant with a *girl*."

"Oh, duh, I didn't understand."

"You guys." Tom, an only child, didn't get it.

"Actually I think I would, even have it myself, if it made me half as happy as you look every time you're pregnant."

"Every time? Two times, little brother."

"Could be more," Tom said, and ducked when she tossed the ketchup squeeze-bottle at his head.

I looked around. The angle of the light had changed, deepening some colours, brightening others. There had always been an intensity and vividness about my sister's life. It was almost unnatural the way the environment shifted its spectrum to suit her. The bright blue stucco house, the grass green as Astroturf, the red- and white-checkered cloth over the redwood table, laden with matching yellow plates and cups and a rainbow of food. A few feet away the tanned blond boys passing the football through the jeweled spray from the sprinkler. Unexpectedly, the sight made me hold my breath. My beautiful nephews. I could have been a better uncle. But perhaps for the first time, their connection to me seemed sharp and undeniable, and it didn't seem to matter that I didn't understand them most of the time.

All of it like one of those Kodachrome photographs from the sixties: colours so intensely unrealistic, so vividly assaultive, they dazzled the eyes.

The job was meant to be only temporary. That actually increased my stress over the whole affair, because I felt I didn't have that much time to figure out how to do things right. I'd spend a long time with the camera, framing the shot, then suddenly I'd feel everything was wrong, that I'd be leaving this family with nothing to remember their dead child by. So I'd compulsively start all over again adjusting, readjusting, my fingers shaking and sliding off the controls.

Invariably I'd take too long and the family's understandable nervousness would increase tenfold. They'd suddenly be anxious to let go of this child or they would slip over some invisible line and would act as if they might hold onto this child forever. The mothers, mostly. The fathers would usually just be irritated, but most of them started out irritated, angry. They were being asked or pressured into doing something they weren't really sure they could do.

Liz could see what was happening. She let me struggle a little at first, scoping out the boundaries of my difficulty, and then she finally stepped in, talking to these parents, letting them know what to expect, helping me set up, letting *me* know what to expect, by example teaching me what to say, what to look out for, how to pace things so the experience wasn't too much, wasn't too little.

Despite all my worries, I never took a bad picture for any of these people. Oh, some shots were better than others, certainly, but I don't think I ever took a really *bad* shot. As morbid as it sounds, I had found my subject.

And my subject had found me.

Taking pictures of dead children—well, as I've said the work generated the expected tension in both the families and the photographer. I'd spend so much time trying to get a pose that looked natural. Sometimes I'd be working so hard to make everything look just right I'd forget why these people were looking so sad and I'd catch myself hoping that the baby would wake up and look at the camera.

And when one of them finally did, I went on with what I was doing and took the shot without a thought about what had just occurred.

Then minutes later—I stood up and looked over the camera at the couple and their tiny, tiny baby. Dead baby—I could not have imagined a creature so small who looked so like a miniature human being could have survived our comparatively brutal, everyday air.

The couple looked at me uneasily. Finally the man said, "Are we done here? Something wrong?"

Everything's wrong, I wanted to say. *Your baby is dead. How much wronger could things possibly get?*

"No," I said. "No." And I looked closely at this child, hoping to see that it was sleeping, but immediately knew it was not.

Dead children, at least the really small ones, have an unformed, stylized quality even though there may be nothing missing anatomically. Their tiny bodies recall some unusual piece of art, perhaps of an animal that's never been seen before, some part-human, part-bird thing, or some new breed of feral pig or rodent. They are like remnants of the long, involved dream you just had, mysteriously conveyed to our waking world. They are like hope petrified and now you have no idea where to put the thing.

That was what sat perched against the young mother's swollen breasts, a sad reminder of her fullness craving release.

Of course I decided almost immediately that what I was sure I had seen hadn't even happened at all. One of the things that occurs when you spend a great deal of time staring into a camera lens is that stationary things appear to move, moving things freeze, and a variety of other optical illusions may occur. Things appear, disappear, change colour and shape. Of course you don't have to use a camera to see this—stare at almost anything in the real world long enough and these kinds of phenomena occur. That's true enough, isn't it? I mean, it isn't just me, right?

The great photographers are great because they see things differently from the rest of us. So from our perspective they see things that aren't there. I've long had this notion, not quite a theory, that the world changes when a great photographer looks through the lens.

As I said before, I'm not a great photographer. But when I took those first rolls home and developed them I think I got just a glimpse of what the great photographer sees. In three of the shots the baby's eyes were open, looking at me.

I admit that upon occasion I do fall prey to a certain suggestibility. I'm wound pretty tightly at times. I get somewhat anxious in the darkroom. I'm interested in shadows in an aesthetic sense, but I'm also uncomfortable with them. Unexpected sounds can make me jump out of my skin. I don't care for scary movies. And I'll believe almost anything that comes out of the mouth of a well spoken man or woman.

So I wasn't about to let myself believe what the pictures were telling me. Not without a fight.

"Liz, did you ever notice the babies' eyes? How sometimes they're . . . open just a little?"

I don't know if I expected her to ask me if I'd been drinking, or suggest that I get more sleep, or maybe just stare at me with that evaluating look I'd seen her give some of the patients. But I didn't expect the calmness, the matter-of-factness. "Sometimes the eyes don't close all the way. When they get to the embalmer, sometimes he'll sew the lids down, or glue them maybe. Whatever seems necessary for the viewing. Occasionally I'll warn the parents, if I think it will upset them. Why, has it been bothering you, or is it just something you noticed?"

Relieved, I almost told her what I'd been thinking, what I'd been imagining, but I didn't. "I just noticed," I said.

So for a while I refocused myself on just taking the pictures, trying to relax the couples (or in some cases, single moms, and in one very complicated case, a single dad, who seemed angry about the whole thing, and frowned during the picture, but still insisted that the picture with his son was something he *had* to have. Liz was obviously nervous about that one, and hung around outside the room while I hurried the session.) My composition got better; the pictures improved.

Sometimes there would be something different about a baby: a certain slant to the shoulders, a small hand frozen in a gesture, an ambiguous expressiveness in the face that tugged at my imagination, but I withheld any response. I knew that if I brought any of these details to Liz's attention she would give me some simple, calm, rational answer, and I would feel that I was only making myself suspect in her eyes.

Yet I felt almost guilty not to be paying more notice to these small details, as if I were ignoring the appeals of some damaged or frightened child. And what did I know of these things? I'd never been a parent, never hoped to be a parent. I knew nothing, really, of children. I had learned a little about grieving parents: how they held their dead babies, how they looked at the camera, how they held themselves.

And I could see clearly, now, the way the eyelids sometimes loosened a bit, sliding up to expose crescent-shaped slivers of greyish eyeball. I'd seen this look in people who were napping—there was nothing unusual about it. But I still didn't like seeing this in the babies. For in the babies it didn't look like napping at all—it looked like additional evidence of their premature deaths.

I had become more relaxed in my volunteer work. I didn't expect any surprises and no surprises occurred. And yet still I would occasionally take those special pictures out of their folders and examine them. And it did not escape my notice that the babies in the pictures, the ones who appeared to be staring at me, had eyes which remained wide open, with an aspect of deliberate, and unmistakable intention.

This vocation of bereavement photography is hardly a new one. From the earliest days of photography you will find pictures of dead people staring at the camera, sometimes with the surgeon's or embalmer's stitches all too visible around the scalp or chest. The adults are in their best clothing, sometimes slouched in a chair, sometimes propped up in bed, a Bible underneath one hand. Sometimes the women are holding flowers.

Many, of course, appear to be sleeping, caught by the sneaky photographer as they nap the afternoon away. Others look terrified: eyes wide and impossibly white, the enlarged dots of their pupils fixing you in a mean, unforgiving gaze.

These gazes are artificial, of course: the eyes painted on to the closed, dead lids. They look, I think, like stills from some badly animated cartoon.

In those days portraiture was quite a bit more formal, and sittings a special occasion. Few families owned cameras of their own, and you might have only two or three photographs taken of yourself over the course of a lifetime. Sometimes a grieving relative's only chance for a photographic record of a beloved's life was after the beloved was dead.

This was particularly true in the case of children. Infant mortality in the days of our great-grandparents was so high that without the photographic proof people might not ever know you'd ever been a parent. You dressed them up as angels and paid the man good money to take their everlasting portraits, money you doubtless could not spare. You put those portraits up on the mantel or in an honoured place on the parlour wall, and you showed them to friends and neighbours, even salesmen come to call. And you alternately preened and choked with grief when they commented "how precious," "how handsome," and "how terribly, terribly sad."

The issue returned with the Wilson child.

Did I mention before that most of the children I photographed were stillborns? Of course that would make sense as there would be no opportunities for school pictures or family portraits or any of the other usual domestic photo opportunities. The need for my services was greater.

But occasionally an older child of one or two years would be signed up for the service, accompanied by parents who were always a bit ashamed for not having engaged in that normal, parental obsession of incessant snapshots and home movies.

I have to say I was glad this particular age group didn't come up too often. It was awful enough to take pictures of parents devastated by the loss of a dream—a child who might have been anything, whose likes and dislikes, the sound of the voice, were completely unknown. Worse was the child who had developed a personality, however roughly formed, who liked toy trucks and hated green beans, who smelled of a dozen different things, whose eyes had focus.

The Wilsons were older than the usual couples I saw. She was in her early forties; he had to be on the far side of fifty. They had a small chicken farm twenty miles outside the city. Mrs. Wilson smelled of flour and of makeup carelessly and too thickly applied. In fact I think make-up was a rare accessory for her. She had pupils like little dark peas, washed up in cup of milk. There was something wrong with her hip; she shuffled and bobbed across the room to the metal chair I'd set up for her. The nice chair was being cleaned, and the appointment had been hastily arranged. I felt bad about that. I knew nothing about her, but I would have liked to have photographed her in the finest hotel in the city.

This reaction was all silliness on my part, of course. She wouldn't have cared—she was barely aware of her surroundings. Her eyes were focused on another piece of furniture in the room: a gurney bearing a small swaddled bundle, an elderly nurse stationed nearby as if to prevent its theft or escape.

Mr. Wilson also came to me in layers. Floating above it all was the stink of chickens, of years of too much labour with too little reward. Under that was a face like sheared-off slabs of rock, and eyes scorched from too little crying, no matter what. Unlike Mrs. Wilson, there appeared to be nothing wrong with his body, but he shuffled across the floor just the same, a rising tide of anger impeding forward progress. He stopped dutifully by the rigid metal chair, gripping the back with narrow, grease-stained fingers, a little too tightly because he thought no one would notice. He watched as his wife made her way painfully over to the gurney and stood there patting and stroking—not the sunken little bundle, but the sheets surrounding it.

He didn't move another step. He knew his place.

The nurse asked if they'd like to "get situated," and then she'd bring them their son. I couldn't imagine what she meant—it sounded as if they were moving into a new place, or starting a new job. They appeared to understand her better, however. Mrs. Wilson dropped into the chair and held on to her knees. Mr. Wilson straightened up as if to verify the height listed on his driver's licence.

The nurse carried the package over, whispering comforting things into its open top. She unwrapped the child and fussed with him in mock-complaint, trying to position him in his mother's lap so that the large dent in the side of his head wouldn't show. She almost managed it by laying the dent against his mother's chest and twisting his pelvis a little. She pretended not to notice the mother's profound shudder.

Then the nurse quickly backed away from the house of cards she'd just constructed, holding her breath as if even that might trigger collapse. She retreated to the back of the room, with a gesture toward the family as if presenting some magic trick or religious tableau.

The couple stared straight ahead, slightly above me at the dark wall behind. I didn't bother telling them to look at or reposition the child. They were done with me and what I represented.

All that was left for me to do was to gaze at the child and snap the shutter.

Even slumped inwards like that, he was actually a pretty sturdy kid. Broad-faced with chubby arms and legs. The head a little large, and I wondered briefly if there had been a spreading due to impact and I shook slightly, a bit disgusted with myself. This couple's beautiful little boy.

But the head wasn't quite right, and the composition was made worse by the couple's hunched forward, intense stares. I moved the camera and tripod a little to the left, while gazing through the viewfinder, ready to stop moving when things looked right.

The little boy opened his eyes, the pupils following me.

I looked up from the viewfinder. The eyes remained closed.

Back with my eye to the lens and the boy's eyes were following me again, as I moved further left, than back right again. It was probably just the position of his head and the slump of the shoulders, but he looked angry. He looked furious.

Finally I stopped. The eyes closed. But as I started to press the button they opened again. Bore down on me. Impatient, waiting.

I took shot after shot that afternoon. Most of them were unusable. What was he so angry about? It was as if he didn't want his picture taken with these people and he was blaming me for it.

After that day the children opened their eyes for me now and then, although certainly not during the majority of these sessions. I don't believe I'd still be doing this work today if it had happened with every child. Most of the time my volunteer work consisted of calming the parents without actually counselling them—I don't have the temperament or training for it. Positioning them, feeling out what they would be comfortable with, and finally taking the shot. That's what it's all about really, taking the shot.

The children who opened their eyes to me hampered that work, since obviously I couldn't send those poor couples home with that kind of photograph. Increasingly they seemed angry with me, and increasingly I was irritated with them for the obstacle they had become.

"Okay . . . uh, could you move her to the left just a bit? There, that's good. That's perfect."

And she is. This child, this Amy, my flesh, my blood, my niece. Tom grips Janice's shoulders a little too firmly. I can see the small wince of discomfort playing with the corners of my sister's mouth. I look at Tom, he looks back at me, relaxes his hands. He looks so pale—I think if I don't take this family portrait soon he might faint. The twin boys stand to each side of him, beautiful and sullen, yet they pull in closer to his body for his support and theirs.

Janice looks up at me, her little brother, not sure what she should do. I offer her a smile; she takes it, attempts to make it her own, and almost succeeds.

Then I look through the lens. I look at Amy, and she's otherworldly, beautiful as her mother. And then she opens her eyes, giving me that stare I've seen a hundred times before, but it's different this time, because this is Amy, this is one of my own. I see the anger coming slowly into her eyes, but I smile at her anyway. I make a kiss with my mouth, and I hope she understands it is just for her. And I take the shot, this one for me, and she closes her eyes again, and I take the other shot for them.

FIRESTORM

"The flash that covered the city in morning mist was much like an instant dream."

—Kyoku Kaneyama

He was not very old, as gods go. He could still remember that brief instant of his creation, and would remember it for all time. But without the need for understanding.

The winds like silver and black hair for him, fire like speech, uncontrolled, the power giving him wings, filling the sky with flame as he rose into the air. Turning the ground below into fire and light, discolouring concrete to a reddish tint. Granite surfaces peeled like onion skin. A pedestrian incinerated, his shadow a bas relief on a stone wall. Wide cracks in buildings, upturned faces gone white, metallic . . .

. . . like his own face, he somehow knew, and the word they were thinking, the name they were giving him . . . the "flashboom." Pikadon. The new god.

September 14, 1965

Tom woke up in his hotel room, feverish, shaking. Again he had had the dream of burning up in the holocaust, only to rise phoenix-like and spread the destruction outward, back to his home in America. In the dream he tried to stop himself, but was completely out of control. He was surprised at the depth of his anger toward his country. He was beginning to understand how profoundly his father had been affected by the war, the division in loyalties. And, uncomfortably, he was seeing in himself signs of his father's obsessions.

Tom had come to Japan to do a story on the "New Religions," the numerous sects which had sprung up since the defeat. He knew a major reason he had been selected was his Japanese-American ancestry. There had been another, more experienced, Religion reporter on his paper. This bothered him, but he thought the trip to Japan might help him understand some things. It was a religious quest, really. A search for context, for meaning.

Even though his family had been in the States almost a hundred years, he felt some ambivalence about America's role in the war. He dreamed about Hiroshima regularly. More than once he had screamed himself awake, feeling his skin burning from his body. The most disturbing aspect of those dreams, however, was that he was also the pilot of the plane carrying the bomb.

In the dream he prayed before dropping the bomb. The bomb was an offering, a gift to his god. A sacrifice. A return home. He wasn't sure, the dream kept changing.

During the last months of the war Tom, just a boy, had seen a dramatic deterioration in his father's mental condition. He could not understand how his father could change so quickly. It seemed magical, evil. He sometimes imagined his father had been kidnapped and that the FBI had put this impostor in his place to spy on them.

It was a crazy time. There were rumours of hostile warships cruising off the California coast.

His father had been a religious man. But toward the end he was cursing the "white" god, and wouldn't allow his children to go to white churches. He imagined he was under surveillance. Tom remembered his father's shock and outrage when Japanese products and art objects were burned or buried by angry neighbours.

His father clipped pieces out of the newspaper, hateful things, and read them to the family at dinner. "This one says we should be deported! This one that we are liars, barbarians, not to be trusted!" Later Tom heard a violent argument between his parents, and discovered by eavesdropping that his father was taping these articles above his bed.

> *A Jap's a Jap . . . no way to determine their loyalty. You*
> *can't change him by giving him a piece of paper.*
> —*Lt. General John L. DeWitt, 1943*

California was zoned, the Japanese-Americans barred completely from Category A zones: San Francisco's waterfront, the area around the LA municipal airport, dams, power plants, pumping stations, military posts.

> *Earl Warren, California's Attorney General, said that*
> *the fact that there had been no sabotage on the Pacific*
> *Coast was "a sign that the blow is well organized and that*
> *it is held back until it can be struck with maximum effect."*
> *He contended that the fact that Issei and Nisei had not*
> *committed sabotage was a sign of their disloyalty.*
> —*Dec. 7, 1941 Pearl Harbor. Executive Order 9066*

Germans and Italians were considered separately. It was believed their loyalties could be better judged.

> *They are cowardly . . . they are different from Americans*
> *in every conceivable way, and no Japanese . . . should have*
> *the right to claim American citizenry.*
> —*Sen. Tom Stuart, Tennessee*

The rumours of sabotage setting flaming arrows in sugarcane fields to direct the Japanese planes, blocking traffic to delay rescue efforts, arson committed by the Japanese during the attack on Pearl Harbor proved to be totally untrue. FCC investigations discovered no illicit radio signals guiding Japanese submarines off the California coast. But their white California neighbours apparently did not hear of these refutations.

An old Japanese man, a survivor, had promised to lead Tom to the strangest religious group of all, a sect which practiced its rites in secret, so afraid were they of public reaction. The old man claimed he had actually seen this new deity, "a young wind with flaming hair."

"You are here . . . seeking this god," the old Japanese man had said to Tom that afternoon, with such certainty it disturbed him.

"Yes," Tom had said distractedly. Then unaccountably had added, "I guess I need a new god."

On September 14, 1965, Nagasawa Shino stood in front of her bedroom mirror, brushing her hair. She planned to visit her cousin Takashi Fujii. He had been a patient in the A-Bomb Hospital, Sendamachi, Hiroshima City, for three months suffering from leukemia. The early morning sun flashed through the blinds, filling her mirror with a white light. *Kyokujitsu shoten*, a gorgeous ascent of the morning sun.

She pulled long black hair away from her forehead, revealing a narrow, bright red, keloid scar. Her hair slipped loose of the brush, fell to her shoulders. Then one by one the strands eased from her scalp and fell like dark streamers to the floor. White patches were spreading on her bald pate. Tiny spots of red, green, and yellow bled like an exotic makeup into the skin of her face. Raised, puffy skin.

She reached frantically for a glass of water on the edge of the basin and it broke under her hand. Her hand rose slowly in front of her face, bleeding from the base of the thumb. It kept bleeding, the blood soon covering her hand, her forearm, creeping up the white silk sleeve of her robe. She knew the bleeding would not stop until her body had been completely emptied.

The spots on her face blended into a brilliant rainbow that flowed down her neck, across her breasts, staining the length of her body.

She remained silent, stared into the mirror growing muddy with her colours, searched out the young, unfocused features of her face hidden within the mirror. Thirty-four, but everyone always said she looked twenty: they often wondered aloud if the bomb had done that to her, kept her young.

Always so many silly rumours, tales of magic. She had always kept the scar hidden under her hair.

Too much light. Too much to be said. The mirror burned, looking rich and jeweled, much like Japan's imperial mirror, the mirror the sun goddess Amaterasu had seen when she was lured out of the cave. Shino even looked like Amaterasu, under the swirling colours, the light of the *flashboom*, the Atomic bomb. A goddess; she smiled despite herself. Shamefully. She imagined that thousands of people had just disappeared from the streets of the city.

The immense cellar stank of fish and stale grain. Tom leaned back against an old crate in the back of the chamber, breathing in the smell as deeply as he could, thinking of it as the atmosphere breathed by his ancestors, wondering if any of them might have known this cellar. It seemed so familiar, some space from a remembered past, perhaps from before even his father's birth.

He could see now that there had been no reason to hide. The hundred or so Japanese crowded into the room were intent on the service before them, or lost in trance. Many were dressed in his own western style garb. An older man stood before them, head bowed, apparently praying. There was an altar behind him: a metal bowl on a table surrounded by flowers, and above that a stylized painting of a mushroom cloud.

Tom stared at the painting, mesmerized by the vibrant colours, the boldness and energy of the brush strokes. He could imagine ground zero, the leveled field that had once been city, the souls suddenly liberated in the flaming wind.

The bomb had been the climax of a series of humiliations visited upon his father, the memories of which would eventually unhinge him, leaving him saddened and diminished until his death in 1960. They'd taken away his small hardware business. The country he'd loved took him away from the house he'd spent much of his life building, and threw him and his family into a concentration camp in Colorado. Then they'd given him a new name. Nisei.

His god had forsaken him, and sealed this dishonour with a hell on earth.

His father could not believe the bomb; the first reports left him shaking in angry disbelief. Then as the truth became clear the old man fell into a depression from which he would never recover. He could not believe what his own country had done, what God had allowed, what evil power they had created and unleashed upon the world.

As an adolescent Tom had at first been confused and frightened by the changes in his father. Then frustrated, later angry. His father had been weak and silent when he had most needed him. He had let the American government defeat him as devastatingly as the Japanese homeland had been defeated. Tom was ashamed of his father and all the others who had let themselves be humiliated. He made a decision then that he would always be American, American in every way. They had the power. They had the bomb.

The old man was speaking to the congregation. "Pikadon brought a change all over the world; life will never be the same. One can gain power over the everyday problems of life by emulating the power of the great god Pikadon!"

The message was clear and simple. Tom could understand it even with his rough skills in the language. The theme, like that of most of the newer religions, was one of practicality. "Man built the bomb and brought a powerful new deity into being. This only confirms the great power latent in every man. If you meditate on the image of Pikadon, visualize the god within yourself, then you may utilize this power within your everyday life!"

Tom left the gathering secretly during the *zadankai*, a get-together after the ceremony for discussing specific problems and firsthand encounters with Pikadon. The old man who had told him about the group was speaking when Tom left. "The light, so brilliant. . . ."

Tom knew that soon he would have to visit the hospital.

Takashi Fujii tossed restlessly in his bed in the Atomic Bomb Hospital. The flash of light had moved east to west, as he remembered it, a curtain of pure white fire. It was August 6, 1945. He had been thirty-six, a journeyman welder at the time. His eyes had been giving him trouble, his lungs were congested, so he took the day off from his repair work at the Fukoku Seimei Building and stayed in bed. After the flash there was a burning heat, then a violent rush of air that flattened his wooden home and buried him under planks, clothing, and heavy roof tile. He could not understand; the "all clear" sirens had sounded but minutes ago. At the time his thoughts had returned to his biggest job: work on the domed Industrial Promotion Hall. Welder and rod had worked out of his padded arms like a cripple's hooks; but these were no handicaps. They spewed fire. And in the gathering darkness his fingers, arms, entire body became fire, welding metal and burning the superfluous to ash. Unseen people applauded; his children were proud. In his vision he could see his young cousin Nagasawa Shino approaching his bedside. She was fourteen, beautiful; he was very attracted to her. A bouquet of goosefoot and morning glories rose from her hand and floated down over the bedspread. Only a few flowers, but they covered the entire bed.

This is a race war . . . The white man's civilization has come into conflict with Japanese . . . Damn them! Let us get rid of them now!
　　　　　　　　　　　　　　—*Rep. John Rankin of Mississippi*

Religious men, all of them, Tom remembered.

Tom's family was given a week to pay bills, sell or store belongings, say goodbye, close up the house, get rid of the car, and assemble at a nearby centre with other frightened, confused Japanese-Americans. He could still recall the intense anger he felt. An old man died while they were waiting. Someone said he had a weak heart, but young Tom knew better.

At first they lived in a converted horse stall at the racetrack. Whitewashed, manure speckled walls. Spider webs and horsehair carelessly painted over. April 28 to Oct. 13.

Folded spring cots, boiled potatoes, canned Vienna sausage and two slices of bread. A bag of ticking to be stuffed with straw for a mattress. Hot. The grounds a mud pit in the rain.

Then they were forced to move again. Colorado, they were told. Some place out in the plains. Young Tom dreamed of tornadoes lifting him and his family up, casting them away. He dreamed that the Japanese-Americans had committed some terrible, secret sin, and that a great white god was punishing them. The Japanese nation had better watch out, he had thought, else this god would send tornadoes against them too.

"No Japs wanted here," the signs had said as they evacuated east.

The old man followed Tom out of the meeting hall. Tom watched as he gestured excitedly with both hands, his grey eyes feverish, rheumy. He motioned toward the alley and the dark, unmarked door in the shadows.

"Everything changed . . . so quickly!" the man said. "I had been sleeping, and in the dream, or after waking from the dream, I cannot be sure, I felt such a *power*, such a brilliant light consuming all the world! I'd been dreaming of defeat, defeat I was sure must happen, when this wonderful thing happened! You may think I'm crazy, *addled*, to call such a happening wonderful. But all had to be burned away, all had to be changed, before this new thing could come to be. Flashing eyes, bronze skin I could *see* him! I've worshipped him since, always!"

Tom held him upright, the old man so overcome by religious fervor his legs had collapsed beneath him. Tom looked again into the alley's dark shadows, and around at the drabness of the neighbourhood. It seemed an unlikely setting for a god.

Tom's family was sent to Granada in southeastern Colorado. Eight thousand Nisei there. The family lived in a 16' by 20' room, wood sheathing covered with black tarpaper. Furnished by a stove, droplight, steel grey cots and mattresses. Three hundred people packed into the mess hall. Soft alkaline dirt and sagebrush.

His father grew steadily worse. Crazy, said the other boys. Tom got into many fights.

Dust under the loose fitting window sash, dust under the doors, gritty floors, dusty bedding. People weren't meant to live in such desert. It reminded him of the Jews, when they had been cast out of Egypt. Why should the great white god punish them so? He could not understand. And where was their god? Didn't the Japanese have a god?

> *Earl Warren said that the release of the Nisei from WRA camps would lead to a situation in which "no one will be able to tell a saboteur from any other Jap."*

Tom remembered his father bending over backwards not to offend. Bowing and apologizing to the sadistic young white soldier who had tripped him on the way back from the mess hall.

The American Legion wanted them deported. Tom could still

see the windshield stickers: "Remember a Jap is a Jap." The *Denver Post* demanded a 24-hour curfew on "all Japs in Denver." There were rumours of bloodshed at the Tule Lake camp the papers said it was full of disloyals.

His father was never the same. Tom couldn't really think of his father as a human being anymore. Almost as if he had never existed . . . wiped away in the conflagration . . . gone instantly from the face of the earth.

Shino's brown suit fit perfectly. Months of exercise had brought her down to her old figure. The spots of seconds ago had disappeared from her face; the mirror had flowed back to normal. She was startled to find a slight smile on her lips, as if the smile belonged to someone else, another woman hiding under her skin.

There was no pleasure in her anticipation of her visit with her cousin; she did not enjoy associating with other *hibakusha*, the survivors of the bomb. But her cousin was a nice man, and she had no other family left.

She kept her hair combed over the scar and pretended to know little of the bomb horror stories; she didn't want to talk about it. She didn't want people connecting her with the Hiroshima outcasts, those living dead. The bomb people, they all die, some people would say. She wasn't sure this was true, but why argue with common opinion? A dying woman was not meant to be loved; love belonged only to the living. She was *hibakusha*, and those people, they never recovered.

She had never married. Her body remained fallow; there had been no children, although she knew it was medically possible. At twenty-five she had loved a young man named Keisuke, a lawyer. But his old mother had objected to their marriage, said that she bore the A-bomb disease, that the babies would surely be deformed. After years alone Shino too had this fear, that she might give birth to something other, something never before seen on earth. Males gave birth to strange things through their extremities; she found it difficult now, even to have a man touch her.

She hurried out of the house. She would be late.

As the morning sun rose high over the treetops of Asano Park
she remembered the park as it had been that day: the huddling

corpses, the silent stares of the living dead, the fire raging in the distance, flame and dark smoke floating over the trees. Everything she had known had suddenly become nothing.

Shino opened her eyes and stared at the two old women huddled over her. She had fainted, and one lady was offering her water from a pink paper cup. The sky was clear again; the smoke had been long ago. It is 1965, she reminded herself. That was so long ago.

The other lady had brushed back Shino's hair and seen the scar; Shino saw her pass a knowing look to her friend.

One evening Tom went to a double feature of old Japanese science fiction films. *Gojira no Gyakushu,* Godzilla's Counterattack, and *Uchujin Tokyo ni Arawaru,* Space Men Appear in Tokyo. He had seen them both as a kid but he found himself reacting to them quite differently this time. They had been fun then, although a little scary, and he hadn't seen all that much difference between Americans and the Japanese based on the evidence of those two films.

Now he had to wonder what the reaction of the young Japanese must be to these two films. What must they think, watching the enormous Godzilla, a deliverer of monstrous and bizarre death and destruction, and who is described as a creature born of nuclear tests? Surely he must be something from their own childhood nightmares, completely visualized and made concrete.

At least the *Space Men* movie seemed a bit more positive. In this invaders come to Japan for advice concerning all the nuclear tests being done on earth. The aliens are worried about them. Japan's unique knowledge of the bomb becomes a positive thing. And yet the aliens possess awesome power; Tom wondered if this was still another example of the Japanese feeling that they had all been guinea pigs, and that Hiroshima was an "experimental city."

The movies made the bombing seem even larger than before, mythic. Tom couldn't help thinking they were the stuff of which religions were made.

The water the women gave her was cool and reminded Shino of how different it had been twenty years before. There had been rumours that people were not to give water to the injured, or it would aggravate their sickness. Such a denial had been difficult to maintain; it was natural for the victims to request water. Water was thought to restore life by returning the soul to the body. The injured had been so polite: "*Tasukete kure!*" they had said, *Help, if you please!*

She could not forgive herself for ignoring them so, but she herself had been injured. She had walked as one in a dream, ignoring their pain. She had passed by the curtains of skin hanging off their bodies, her hands clasped over her own slashed breasts. She had been half naked and cowered in shame. Even knowing what they were, she had walked upon human bowels and brains.

She would be late for her visit with Fujii, but she needed some time to rest. Across the street, they were performing a shinto rite at the grand opening of a new department store. They had done the same when she was a girl. But the military had fooled them into blind support with *shinto*, the religion and the country become one. How could it ever be the same again? How might she trust either?

She was *hibakusha*, a person of the bomb. A new deity had been born into the world, a deity born of the loins of little, petty men. But he was greater than they. Man had brought him from the sun at the centre of the world for slaughter. He turned and faced her from the street in front of the department store, a slight smile on his lips. Amused by their petty nationalism. Appeared from the crowd, as if he had stepped out of their massed bodies. Flash off his teeth of metal and lightning and suns. He did not speak, but his loud breathing hurt her ears. Bright eyes and dark hair: very handsome.

She thought it strange that he looked only vaguely American; his face seemed to blur in and out of focus. Shaven eyebrows, almond skin. Sometimes he looked like her cousin Fujii.

The god thrilled her; how very handsome he was. *Isamashii*, brave. With him standing there, the breeze from the ocean lifting his long silver and black hair and laying it back against his shoulder, it seemed as if they were the only people really alive: she, the other *hibakusha*, and this new god. He spoke inside her head, and the power in his voice made her aware of the great responsibility they had; she could feel bombs exploding, giant mushroom clouds of red, yellow, blue and white, like flowers over the globe. People burned with an incandescent flame, then disintegrated into their basic elements, back into the earth to become trees, flowers, the very materials from which the bombs themselves had come. They would all be united; there would be no separation.

The dark-haired god smiled and this movement in his face seemed to harden his features, set lines firmly around his hawk nose, his black steel eyes. A square, mechanical jaw. Lines of sweat down the sides of his face.

A Coca Cola truck passed, spraying dust in its wake. She realized the opening ceremonies were completed; the people had all left. That day . . . sometimes it seemed like yesterday. She had stayed home that day; she had told her mother she was too ill to go to school, but she had lied. Her class of girls had been assigned to clear fire lanes in case the American B-29s dropped incendiary bombs. She admired the way the people had accepted this; many tore down their homes and buildings because they were in the path of a designated fire lane. But all this destruction saddened her; she couldn't bear to help. Her mother left her at home with her sister, who knew she was faking but kept silent. It was just after breakfast, the hibachi stove was still smouldering. At 7:45 her mother left to catch a train downtown. The bomb must have struck when she was still on the train. Shino knew her mother had almost expected it, some disaster like this had worried her for a week, the way the American planes had flown over every day.

The dark-haired god smiled out in the street, people walking by. Shino couldn't remember what year it really was; she breathed noisily. Everything silent, all she could hear was her breathing, the god's breathing. What year was it? She imagined herself a girl again, at the side of the dark-haired god. He smiled and embraced her, searing her breasts with his flaming hands. She did not cry out in pain.

Tom thought that Hiroshima looked much like any busy port city, although perhaps the setting was lovelier than most; the seven fingers of the Ohta river supported it, and it was ringed by low mountains. There still seemed to be much of the small, provincial town here in the people and their life styles. Certainly nothing to suggest the dramatic event which had once occurred here. But the castle, shipyards, and municipal buildings had been rebuilt. The Aioi Bridge, target site of the *Enola Gay*, once more spanned the

Ohta river. So many Tom talked to still expressed surprise that things could get better so soon.

The new downtown seemed western with its wide streets and attractive storefronts, arcaded shopping areas. The new pride of the city was their baseball stadium and their team the Hiroshima Carps.

But he was aware of something else here, whose presence betrayed itself in an accumulation of small clues: a bit of fused metal, a warped post. Imprinted in the steps of Sumitomo Bank was the shadow of a man who had sought refuge that day twenty years before.

The god drifted in the pollution staining the rooftops, the pollution defiling the wind, the sea. All the old gods of sea and air, defeated so easily by people.

By people's creations, which they themselves could not even control.

The god sensed without thinking the great stupidity of people, their lack of control.

The god disdained the attempts of the followers of his own religion to influence him, seek his favours.

The new god Pikadon knowing something like incompleteness even in his instincts of stone. . . .

Anger.

Tom spent the day in the Peace Park. The skeleton of the Industrial Exhibition Hall dome made an eerie backdrop. The park was full of children, and Tom thought how all that he had become obsessed with had happened long before any of them were born. He wondered what their parents must tell them.

He wandered around the Cenotaph, the official Atomic Bomb monument, where the names of those who perished, and continue to perish, are inscribed. Some had told him that the souls of the dead reside there. Tom stared at the sculpture, feeling like a survivor himself, drawn in to their horror, guilty. Many *hibakusha*, he knew, resented the nine story office building which had been built behind the park, as they thought it profaned this sacred place. There were conservatives in Hiroshima, however, who even wanted to tear the "Atomic Dome" down. Times change. People forget.

There is another statue in the Peace Park, an oval granite pedestal, symbolizing Mt. Horis, the fabled mountain of paradise. Atop this stands the image of Sedaho, a child who died. She holds a golden crane in her outstretched arms. Beneath her are tangles of colourful paper leis that people have left her, each lei consisting of a thousand paper cranes.

A crane can live a thousand years. If you fold a thousand paper cranes they will protect you from illness. At the base of her statue— "This is our cry, this is our prayer: peace in the world."

Tom spent a long time in the Peace Memorial Museum. A regular art gallery, he thought. First the "Atomic Sculptures," twisted metal, tile, warped stones, fused coins and convoluted bottles, a bicycle wrenched into a tangled snarl, a shattered clock stopped at 8:10, a middle school boy's uniform that had turned to rags from the gamma rays of the bomb, rows of life sized dummies modelling the remnants of clothing, a face black with ash, skin hanging from swollen faces.

The paintings, the photos: victims packing the barracks and warehouses all that death in a moment eyeballs melted across a cheek, peeling skin, gutted torsos.

There was a mechanical fountain in front of the peace museum. The Fountain of Prayers, offering fresh water to those who had died begging for it so long ago. Too late.

A few hundred yards downstream from the dome Tom discovered the Kanawa floating restaurant whose specialty was fine Hiroshima oysters. But he could not eat. He kept seeing the restaurant patrons as corpses, the people in the street as corpses, their stiffened forms accusing him, their eyes singling him out.

Tom looked into the stream and saw himself: his hair burned away, his skin melting like tallow, and he began to weep. Even his own eyes accused him.

And the all seeing eyes of an unknown deity, whose face Tom saw a moment in the water, but which disappeared with a passing ripple.

———————

Shino had this fantasy. At last she has a baby, her own. A miracle! But the umbilical cord is rotten, and the skin peels off the face like decayed cloth.

For a long time Tom was reluctant to visit the A Bomb hospital itself. He knew that most members of the cult visited there, seeking recruits. It was an essential part of the story. But he was afraid.

So he spent much of his time researching the hospital before making his first appointment there, with one Takashi Fujii. In the meantime Tom made many notes:

The A-Bomb Hospital

A-Bomb hospital completed 1956, 120 beds. Each admission disturbs the survivor community. Each death creates a new wave of hysteria. Local newspapers keep a faithful obituary list.

People suddenly dying, a bomb ticking within them. Severe anemia, need periodic blood transfusions. Depressed areas of the city often called Atomic Slums.

A reporter found all these abnormal children, all micro cephalic with small heads and mental retardation. Mothers three or four months pregnant and within two miles of the hypocentre. Others, twenty-four years old, mental age of three, size of a ten-year-old. The Mushroom Club first the cloud, then they're all growing like mushrooms in the shade.

176 leukemia victims since the hospital's founding in 1956. Coming down suddenly with leukemia twenty years after, with no previous signs.

Failure to marry many of those who are still living cannot find happiness.

Tom had made a long list of questions for Takashi Fujii, yet still he did not know what he could say to the man.

The young reporter ... Tom ... that was his name ... had come to visit. He was a young American, but with a Japanese face. His curiosity irritated Fujii. He did not like to be thought of as someone odd. He was just a man, a strong man, like many others. But he admired Americans as a whole; he had to admit that. They had brought the bomb, and the bomb was a big thing. It had been like a new beauty in the world, a terrifying beauty that had changed everything. And he really did enjoy talking about the bomb; he had little else to do.

The young American turned on his tape recorder, and, after some fidgeting with his bed covers, Fujii began to speak:

"I was in the midst of a well deserved vacation. There had been some repair work needed on the steel substructure of the Fukoku Seimei Building, and the owners knew I was the man for the job. But I did need a rest, so I told them they would have to wait. Of course, they held up the work just for me. They knew I was the right man. Unfortunate that I didn't get a chance to finish the job." Fujii twisted in the bed, a wide smile stretching his nose.

"I had been lying in bed, drinking some fine Suntory whiskey. Then I was buried under my home. Much later I woke up, blood running from my nose. Much as it did recently, when I first discovered I had been stricken with leukemia. Ah, the bomb gets us all in the end. It hides in your body for years sometimes before it strikes. But I am a brave man; I don't complain.

"When I got out from under the house I saw many terrible things. The city, it was gone, smashed like a nest of insects. People ran about like beetles, pulling possessions, their fellows, out of the wreckage. The great atomic bomb had done this; Hiroshima was a great religious experiment for man.

"The great dome of the Industrial Promotion Hall was but a skeleton. Hiroshima Castle had been flattened. The entire western sector was a desert. A reddish brown powder over everything. The Fukoku Seimei Building had only been 380 metres from the centre of the blast; I certainly would have died if I had gone there.

"I saw many beautiful women naked, running around with skin hanging from their limbs. *Sabishii!* Sad! I helped bandage many of the half-clothed women. There was much shame; they would crouch and try to hide themselves, but they were in so much pain; they needed my help. The bomb had left terrible burns they call them keloid on their bodies. One old lady's face had grown together so that with the puffy red tissue I could not tell if she was facing me, or if her back was turned. There were many young girls from the secondary schools who had been out clearing fire lanes, most naked and terribly scarred and frightened. They reminded me of my young cousin Shino. I felt very sorry for them; I helped them with much affection. It was a terrible time.

"But sometimes, I would think that the bomb had left them with beautiful—perhaps that isn't the word—fascinating, yes fascinating, markings. Red, and yellow, and blue green, and black stars and circles. Some so beautiful. The scars were like ornaments. I try to remember them, the women, as beautiful. I forget the disfigurement.

"The bomb was so large; I feel it has made me somewhat larger, stronger. For the first time, man had made a god, a god not . . . limited, like himself, but something part of everything, the dream that fills . . . everything. If I try, I can see him as a man. Multicoloured flames in his scalp; a bronze, naked body. He sleeps curled inside us, in our hearts, just waiting to be released through our working hands, fingers, genitals. I was never confused as to what this new weapon truly was. I knew it immediately. It was of man's interior, the Atomic Bomb."

Tom shut off the tape recorder and stared at Fujii's beaming, almost gleeful face.

"Everything collapsed," Fujii said. "My Buddhist neighbours, they thought that they were really in hell. They fell to their knees in prayer. Imagine! They really thought the world was ending . . . that it had become hell!"

He paused, and looked at Tom sadly. "I sometimes think it does no good for people to believe in a religion. If these Buddhists had not believed . . . they would not have been so mortally terrified. They would have seen this as an occurrence of war, not a sudden arrival of hell. Ours was an experimental city, nothing more.

"I could have done more. I must tell you, I know that now," Fujii said with tears in his eyes. Tom looked down, suddenly embarrassed. "Most of us, we acted selfishly. We were too frightened, our minds too full of this flash, this fire, to help each other. So we left people alone . . . left them to die. We shamed ourselves before whatever god there might be. I too, I admit it, feel a great shame. I did a terrible thing."

The dark-haired god of the gleaming skin, Pikadon, rested within a silver layer in the clouds covering the islands of Japan. He had just exhaled 1945, and breathing in 1965 left 1985 and beyond a mere exhalation away.

Hurricane force winds gathered in his hair indistinguishable from whiffs of cloud. Fire settled into the corners of his imagined mouth like small red droplets of spit. He looked into the heads of his followers and imagined himself with silver and black hair flowing out into the horizon line, scarlet wings lifting him up into the sun, his bronze form scintillating with hot vapour.

The god snatched a bird from the air and blackened it, swallowed it, cast it back through his anus. Concrete is discoloured. Human souls turn to flaming wind. He is enraged, frustrated.

Below, the Japanese islands appeared in the gaps of morning mist, divine children of the deities Izagagi and Izanami, along with the waterfalls, trees, and mountains. The fire god had been last, and killed his mother Izanami with burning fever.

A new fire god had come, and his rage could turn the islands back into the original oily ocean mass.

Takashi Fujii stared past his cousin, out the window to the parking lot. His cousin seemed strangely quiet. But of course she had said very little to him the last ten years, although they had lived in the same house.

Shino thought about some of her dreams of the night before. Dreams of white faces, keloid flowers on her body, the walking dead, undiscovered atomic bombs constantly overhead or imbedded deep inside her belly.

Shino remembered the way the red ashes rose out of the flattened rubble and took form as more survivors. Walking dead. No way to tell their fronts from their backs, arms dangling from elbows held out like wings. Ghosts wandering aimlessly. They couldn't bear to touch themselves. They walked very slowly, like ghosts. She had thought she had recognized an old friend. *Oh, my god,* she thought, *it is Okino!*

Shino had left her sister alone in the house. After a few hours, her sister had died. It made her feel very guilty: she had not stayed with her long. Shino's sister's wounds had oozed much pus and dark blood. She smelled so bad Shino couldn't stand to be near her.

She sometimes dreamed her sister would return some day from the realm of the dead to accuse her. She had failed her. She no longer found solace in the old religions; they had died when all those thousands of believers had died. They were religions for the dead. For memories. For ghosts.

It was a shame; he had never married. Neither had Shino; their family line would soon die out. Family was very important to Fujii; he didn't want the name to die. The family maintained one's immortality; this was man's central purpose in life.

Fujii thought much of religion these hours. Never particularly devout, but he was a strong patriot and nationalist. He believed in science, technology, little else. Shortly after the war he had become interested in various machine age cults, religions based on the glories of technology. But that had been long ago; Japan needed a new religion, an object to unite behind.

He glanced over at Shino. "I truly did not know what it was. Remember, I used to believe it had been a *Molotoffano banakago,* a Molotov Flower Basket? I did not know it could do these things."

"He is a god. He burns up the sky," she replied quietly.

Shino thought of how the day was much like an earlier September, when green had crept over the rubble and along what had been barren riverbanks. Spanish bayonets, clotbur, and sesame had covered the ruins. It had been beautiful, and even the tiny hemorrhages the size of rice grains on her face and hands did not bother her. Insects had filled the air, rising in clouds over the city.

Fujii thought of the bodies and their final cremations. The people had not been able to dispose of the bodies properly earlier, and many corpses were already rotting. They burned with a smell like frying sardines; blue phosphorescent flames rose into the air. As a child he had been told they were the spirits of the departing dead, fireballs, and he imagined he saw some of his neighbours' and friends' faces in the smoke.

Tom drove through the city streets lost in thought, the cyclic changes from skyscrapers and other technological monuments to slums and ancient architecture having a mesmerizing effect on him, almost convincing him that he was time travelling, surveying the lives of his ancestors and his progeny. A strange smell seemed to permeate the air, the smoke giving him a sense of great buoyancy. He decided to return to the church and talk to the old man about what he had seen, what the others had seen. He had a hundred questions.

First Street, Hell. That was what the survivors had called the city.

In the dream he had returned to Japan, land of his ancestors, to find god. No religion had ever answered his doubts before, none were identifiable within the context of the sometimes terrible and sometimes beautiful landscapes he saw inside himself. Every time, however the dream might begin, it always ended with the firestorm. With hell.

Violent inrushing winds . . . the air in his lungs seeming to combust spontaneously; he roared through the city like a part of the firestorm himself, aware of the moans of the burning, the asphyxiated in their shelters, but so caught up in his own fiery power he could not stop, for he was part of the flaming god himself, and the daily drama of frustration and loss undergone by people so similar to what he used to be . . . they were far removed from him . . .

. . . the glorious flames spreading, Tom leapt into the air with them, spreading the destruction back to America like a contagion . . .

. . . and the vengeance was a terrible one. Tom stood in his glorious cloak of flame, a few miles from each epicentre, one bombing after another, as eyelids ran, sealing the beautiful vision of himself forever within the eyes of all witnesses. Clothes melted into skin, bodies flew as if the law of gravity had been momentarily rescinded. The air filled with flames, brighter than any sun, brighter than anything an ancient god might concoct.

. . . as refugees wandered the streets in broken bodies wailing that God had forsaken them, but Tom was there, Tom in his God's form, welcoming all into his congregation.

. . . as stomach walls were ruptured, as eyeballs turned liquid and ran on cheeks like egg white . . .

. . . as metal ran into glass ran into cloth ran into flesh and bone and brain and the end of all desire and the end of all thought . . .

Tom smiled and took it all inside himself. The world had become truly one, flowing and intermingling, one within fire, one within God.

And all doubt, all loneliness was answered.

Fujii could almost smell the burning bodies of his friends and neighbours, the sweet perfume of their liberated souls, free of the body's gross control. He knew a man who talked of a new religion, a religion based on the bomb. Perhaps when he left the hospital. . . .

At last, Shino was seeing her lover again, the beautiful bronze face in the clouds, the endless streamers of silver and black hair reaching out toward the ends of the world. The god's beckoning wing. . . .

The smoke rose above the city of Hiroshima and spread to the surrounding islands, and out to cover the world. Tom watched the smoke mix into the clouds. The god Pikadon gathered the rising spirits within his scarlet wings. And his wings covered the world.

THE
MOUSE'S
BEDTIME
STORY

The boy always had trouble falling asleep. His mother, who could not bear to see her son asleep, would stand outside his bedroom for hours, making noises, then disappearing into another room when the weeping boy ran out to investigate. Not that she liked hearing her dear son cry—it was just something that had become part of the ritual.

Sometimes she would throw a small rubber ball inside the room, listen as it banged against walls and toys displayed delicately on shelves, wait for a whimper or groggy objection. Sometimes she would slip a bright red mask over her face, step just inside his room, then listen for his terrified breathing as he tried not to cry out. Sometimes she would crawl inside his room with a dark coat over her back, then rise beast-like and howling above the edge of the covers.

Sometimes she would simply stand to one side of the door, and in her hoarse whisper say, "Your parents are dead because you would not move. No more Mommy's sweet kisses. No more Daddy's funny tales. Now I have my knife and my claw and I'm coming into that room for you."

By morning his room would look as if a small animal had been trapped inside, covers torn to threads from his sleepless struggle.

Eventually she suggested to her son that milk and a bedtime story created the only path to sleep. And although the boy could no longer stand the sound of another person's voice after dark, he desperately agreed.

"Once there was a boy mouse as fierce and sleepless as you, my son, and though his elders insisted that mice never sleep—that their lives were in their nights wandering floors and the spaces between walls—sleep was all this little boy mouse ever thought of or desired.

"Finally one night one of these elder mice, tired of the little mouse's pleadings, told him to go see the oldest of them all, the ancient white who lay beneath the grandfather clock in the coldest room of the house. This was a room even the hugemans rarely visited, keeping it locked and alone. If any a mouse knew of a way to sleep, or recalled a single mouse who'd ever slumbered, the ancient white was he.

"So the boy mouse took to the walls and cavities and dry-rotted studs, made his way slowly but eagerly to the cold room and the large dry chamber beneath the base of the grandfather clock. And just as he had been told, there lay the ancient white, eyes closed and mouth open, too stingy to share a breath with the world.

"'Hey there,' the mouse said impetuously, 'Might you be asleep? Certainly there is slumber in the look of you! Tell me the secret, ancient white, for I will surely die if I never dream!'

"But the ancient white said nothing, and the boy mouse studied the dryness of him, the stiffness, and the way the spider webs travelled from ear to tail and back. If this was the only way a mouse might dream . . . In anger he turned, anxious to leave this cold place.

"'Only a mother can teach her brood the secrets of sleep, my child,' a dry voice scuttled up behind him.

"The boy mouse turned with excitement, but the ancient white looked no different from before. Its eyes were still closed, and not a strand of webbing had been misplaced.

"The boy mouse crept closer until he was nose to dusty nose with the ancient white. 'I never knew my mother,' he said, 'and no one would tell me her name or anything about her,' and waited.

"He didn't have to wait long, however, for after a moment the very dryness of the air around him began to speak. 'They are all ashamed, or frightened, boy mouse. For in this house there is a cat, and a cat is the mother of this boy mouse.'

"'But I don't understand,' the mouse began.

"'The cat is your mother, it was she who gave you life. And it is only your mother who may lead you to sleep.' Feathers of dust twirled in the dry, cold air.

"The mouse thought on this for a time, trying to sketch out its sense, but certainly there was no sense to be drawn. But he had doubted the ancient white, and yet the ancient white had spoken to him with a mouth frozen in age. He could not bring himself to doubt the ancient white again.

"And so it happened that the boy mouse went in search of his true mother the cat. The smell of her, of course, was everywhere. It always had been so. After a few hours of sniffing every particle of ash and moonbeam the mouse began to falter. A sudden collapse of the left front foot and he was rolling down an incline to the carpeted steps beyond.

"'Murem murum my son,' his mother sang sleepily from someplace far below.

"The mouse stopped rolling at the top of the stairs.

"'Murem murumm please come my tummy hurts iyum a rub rub rubbing from my lovely son murumm.'

"The boy mouse leapt the stairs two at a time, skated across sweet shiny floors until he came to the place where the hugemans gathered to watch their thoughts ride up the chimney in flames. And in the darkness at the far end of this room he spied the large eyes of his mother filling up with her love for him.

"'Murumm murumm,' she sang as she stepped quickly out of the dark to gaze down at him. The boy mouse could not move, so overcome he was with joy and terror.

"'Sleep, Mother. I need you to tell me of sleep!' the boy mouse cried.

"'Iyum,' she replied, with the most playful smile you can imagine, her front paw poised to stroke and play with her long lost child. 'Iyum,' again, as her mouth yawned wider with boredom or fatigue, and with that mouth proceeded to tell her son everything she knew of mice, everything she knew of sleep."

The boy was finally asleep. His mother held him close to her breast. He had shuddered violently once or twice during her telling of the tale, but now he slept so silently he hardly appeared to breathe. It was so unfair, she thought, how much young children sleep, sleeping their poor mothers' lives away, who only want a kiss, an occasional hug. Not all this sleeping, this sleeping so still, the air she breathed suddenly colder, and the dark as dry and old as death.

LAST DRAGON

Alec thrashed in bed. His muscles cramped. His right arm flapped and struck his chest. He had been dreaming that his wife's tongue was scraping at his eyes, his sons fingers clawing his shoulders. So real that his night's sweat was irritating the wounds.

His left fist tightened reflexively and made a painful knot under his lower back.

His body felt huge and unmanageable. It rocked and shook out of control.

His eyes sprang open and tried to focus. He coughed into his sheets and, terrified of choking, managed to turn his mouth to the side.

On Sunday mornings, he used to hide in bed until noon. His mother warned him about what happened to lazy boys who didn't go to church.

His father used to toss him into the air, too high. He'd kept his arms rigid and immobile at his sides in fright. This one thing had frightened him, this one thing. He'd never flown before, and it had scared him. No logical power could hold him up. It was magic.

"Daddy! Stop!"

"Fly, Alec! Fly! I won't drop you!"

Then one day his father did drop him. Alec had fallen slowly, trying to push his arms out to break the fall. But he had been immobile.

For just a few moments, he had been paralyzed.

Alec was fully awake now. The room was dark; heavy curtains covered most of the walls. "Light," he whispered. Nothing. Someday, as the sclerosis increasingly affected his throat, the house's computer would have to be reprogrammed to allow for a wider range in interpreting vocal commands. But this morning he knew it was just fatigue,

Just a lack of focus. He concentrated, and after a time again said, "Light." Curtains pulled back; ceiling panels began to glow dimly. "Light light light," he said, and the brightness increased almost to daytime intensity. He could feel Earth's sun beyond the sheer yellow gauze that covered the windows, and soothing familiarity chased away the night's last alien dreams.

Earth's sun. He had to remind himself. He saw so little of the Outside world that he could have just as easily been on Bennett, sleeping in the corporate headquarters there.

His throat burned from getting the lights on. And there was always this additional strain, not knowing if it was going to work anymore, if he was going to be left whispering in the dark, his throat aching, a headache blossoming from his attempts. He could have used the timer and saved his voice, but he never did. Each morning he wanted to make sure his larynx still worked.

Rick should have been up by now. Alec hated waiting; it made him feel helpless. But if he complained, the man might quit, and Alec wasn't up for another change.

The entire house could be equipped with personal care robotic handlers and controllers. It wouldn't cost him much; a few technicians from one of his plants could install the whole works. But he wanted humans around him, touching him, not a house full of metal arms. And robotic amplification wasn't anything like doing it on his own, anyway. At least he did have the choice. He was Alec Bennett. That name had control over people and things, even if the man behind the name did not.

Today, his wife and children were moving out of the house. He hadn't had the power to hold them, the words to convince them to stay. Most of the arguments had stopped this past year—he'd felt relieved. He'd thought things were going to be okay now. But they'd all just been avoiding him, not saying what they felt, not wanting to provoke an argument. They were hiding from him.

The last big argument had been a year ago with his older son Gene, fifteen at the time. It had been typical—unproductive, frustrating. And frightening, because now Gene was old enough to really hurt him if the argument went too far, if the volatile teenager were to lose control. That had become the peak of Alec's feelings of helplessness: to be frightened of his own son. It made him ashamed, and yet now he missed all the arguing—at least then his son was talking to him.

"You can't tell me what to do!" Gene had looked almost crazy in his anger, and as the boy continued to shout, Alec found himself wondering at what terrible thing he had brought home to them all.

"The aide quit, Gene. And my tube's popped. See, it runs down through the bedding and attaches to the pumps under the floor—"

"Jesus! You're messin' yourself, Dad!"

"Please, just get the tube back in."

But his son had just backed away from him, looking at the body of his origin wasted by the disease. His son's face was full of fear and loathing for the disease. Alec had spent hours explaining the nature of the disease, how no one was going to "catch" it. But now he could see that little of that must have sunk in. His son was seeing his own body lying there on the bed, spent and wasted.

"You're always asking me to touch you like that, and there's machines, Jesus. I mean, you can afford it."

"Gene, the tube!"

But Gene had already left the room. Alec could hear him debating with his brother and sister about whose turn it was to help, and arguing over the personal care machinery again. They hated him, or maybe they hated the disease, not that there was much difference anymore. And Marie was off at some club meeting again, so she couldn't talk to them.

"Get in here, *all* of you!" No one answered. He'd shouted for several minutes before giving it up. He'd lost them. He couldn't even tell them to do something as simple as throwing an empty milk carton away, and be sure they'd do it.

A hand was rocking his shoulder. His eyes blurred. Sometimes it seemed that, when he wasn't remembering the bad times, he couldn't recall their faces at all. The hand touched him again. "Rick?" he whispered.

"Yes, Mr. Bennett. Want a bath today?"

Alec looked down. Rick's arms were protected by membranous gloves, a little paler than white flesh, more the colour of cotton after it's been boiled. He'd thought the man had finally gotten over the fear of infection. "Afraid of catching a cold?" Rick didn't respond. "Talk to me, Rick."

Rick busied himself with the covers. "Just trying to be sanitary, Mr. Bennett. Now, how about that bath?"

Actually, Rick was braver than most; money could buy a little courage now and then when he really needed it. But it was getting harder every year, and Alec wondered how long Rick was going to last. They all thought they were going to catch the disease, and he honestly couldn't reassure them completely; no one knew enough about Bennett's Sclerosis.

Sometimes Alec imagined tiny cracks appearing in his skin. Sometimes he could swear he could see them, and they would spread onto Rick's arm, flaking the flesh away.

That first year after Alec came back from Bennett the media had been in a state of excitation that was almost sexual. The Bennett story had encompassed a number of topics sure to tantalize and entertain the public. The corporation-owned planet. The father's questionable business deals. And the rich, pampered son who was the first and only known victim of an extraterrestrial disease. Payoffs to regulating agencies. Aggressive exploitation of the strange new landscape. Rumours of safety violations. Rumours of dragons.

An insistent touch at his shoulder. "Mr. Bennett? Your bath?"

"No," he said, staring at the gloves covering Rick's arms and hands. "No, no thanks."

Rick didn't seem surprised. In the best of times Alec had an intense fear of the water. Even taking a bath, Alec would picture himself sinking beneath the surface, unable, even unwilling, to raise his arms to save himself. Whenever he and his assistants drove or flew over rivers or lakes, he'd have to turn from the window.

"Messages this morning?"

Rick pulled the recorder out of his back pocket and pushed the red button. After a squawk of interference Alec could hear the voice of Malcolm, nominal head of Bennett Corp. ". . . everything's ready. Not much chance of anybody catching on. Needless to say, I would still like to talk you out of this. We have an entire squadron of pilots ready to send up after this thing."

"Shut it off," Alec said.

"There's more . . ."

". . . don't need any more."

Alec looked at the wall. The polished mahogany beyond his feet stretched a good twenty feet left of his bed, another twenty feet right. Patterns of light and shade moved across the segments of bone that had been set into the wood planks.

The enormous skull had been taken apart; the three plates that had formed the cap of the skull had been spread and mounted here into a broad arch. A six-foot nasal ridge hung from the centre. Below these pieces, bolted to the wall a few inches from the floor, were the numerous broken sections of a long, thin jawbone. Alec could slice his hand open with just a careless touch along that bone, but he was far removed from that kind of danger.

Rick followed his gaze. "I don't know how you can stand to look at that thing. Makes my skin crawl just to be in the room with it."

"In fact, I don't think it's that skull making your skin crawl." It was hardly a skull, more like a collection of armoured plate, what had been left once the skin had burned away. Alec could picture where the creature's gas sacs had been—in both cheeks and temples, and suspended under the jaw. The eyes had been deeply set on either side of the nasal ridge. Dark red, glowing like the mahogany. The mouth so wide. That last time on Bennett he'd peered directly into that hunger, the jaws steadily expanding until he'd thought the mouth might swallow the ship whole.

It had been night, and his father had insisted that the pilot shield the exhaust so the creature's infrared wouldn't pick them up. His father had wanted to show Alec. He was always showing him things. The crash had been sudden, unexpected. An accident. No one had thought the dragon intended to attack. When the mouth had dropped open and they had stared at the night inside, it had seemed that the beast was showing surprise rather than hunger or rage.

Alec had been thrown out before the explosion. Soaked in the creature's vital fluids, he'd escaped with just a broken leg and a few scrapes. Or so they had all thought.

Watching the shadowed mahogany for movement, for the faintest flicker of light, he heard Rick say, "So they think that's the carrier. That *thing*."

The fire had been nightmarish in its speed and volume. With three to four percent more oxygen than Earth, the planet was a firetrap. The creature's sacs had exploded. It had roared, its head blazing, wings shrinking in the heat.

Rick's voice continued to intrude into Alec's thoughts. "Why don't you let them take care of it? You've got lots of pilots, and most of them better than you."

Either he had been delirious or the creature had turned its burning skull his way, looked at him, before falling ponderously into the flames.

"You're a rich man, but you're *ill.*"

Alec willed himself to move, but could not. He felt huge, impossibly heavy. He felt his skin burning, imagined catching the sheets on fire. Rick started to move toward him. "Don't . . ." Alec gasped. "Let it be."

Rick stepped away from the bed and stared out the open window. "Just tell me when you're ready, Mr. Bennett." A tiredness was evident in the young healthy voice.

Standing by that window, Alec had first felt the symptoms of Bennett's Sclerosis. He'd had his father buried on the planet.

Rick was pulling nervously at the arm coverings he wore, as if trying to protect a larger portion of his body. As if the sclerosis might reach out and penetrate his skin. As if Alec had brought back from Bennett something more than a viral disease—a native of that planet, an alien that thrived within the house of his body.

"My best people don't think it's contagious, Rick. I've told you that before." That was true—his top researchers thought there had to be actual contact of body fluids—but all the same Alec felt like a liar.

Rick just stood there, his back to Alec, watching the sun through the window. "Just being careful, Mr. Bennett." Rick scratched at his sleeves.

"I pay you enough, don't I?"

"You do that. And I have a family to support. But that's not the only reason I stay." He said the last part almost angrily.

"I had a family . . ." Alec stopped, embarrassed.

Alec had been back on Earth a month when he had felt the first signs of his illness. He'd been standing in this bedroom he'd shared with Marie and watching nothing in particular, still feeling a little disoriented because Bennett's sun was the same size and colour as Sol and because this time of year the climate was similar.

His arms and legs had begun to tingle, a low-grade burn deep under his skin that had made him think at first that he must have stepped onto an exposed wire. No matter where he had moved, the strange, vaguely disturbing sensation continued. He had begun to feel dizzy and had sat back down on the bed for a time.

When after an hour the sensation had passed, he had gone in to work. He'd thought it was odd, but since it went away, he'd chalked it up to a sleep disturbance, the flu, maybe something he'd eaten. Then a month later his vision had begun to blur. A month after that, he had lost control forever. The illness progressed like a brush fire.

The disease made him feel, simply, *older*. It resembled multiple sclerosis in many ways, but MS had been cured over fifty years before. And Bennett's Sclerosis, as it was soon to be labeled, worked more quickly, scar tissue grew more rapidly—like a fungus, some said—and there appeared to be no periods of remission. People wouldn't touch him, as if afraid something might burst through his skin.

It had been like a machine running down. The immune system backfiring. The alien virus replicating the body's nerve tissue. So his body had become alien to itself, the body had become a dragon, attacking itself. It couldn't help itself—the invader had to be repelled. Scavengers in the immune system ate away at the myelin. First, its layers were pried apart, then nerve transmission began to short circuit, then the myelin simply disappeared so that Alec became all exposed wires and loose electrical impulses. Scar tissue had crept over the nervous system the way ice sheathed the skeletal branches of a tree in winter.

His brain had been less seriously affected, his thoughts intact. Except sometimes thoughts arose that he did not recognize as his own.

"We're running a little late," Rick was saying, moving toward him. "Let me help you."

He tried to turn himself in bed. His arms flopped uselessly; he couldn't even feel them. He had the sudden, nonsensical fear that someone had cut them off when he wasn't looking.

A tremor began in his right leg. He tried to shut it off, but the mental plea had no effect.

"When are you leaving?" Rick asked.

"Next week."

"You know, I don't understand you. What if this just makes it worse?"

"I made *intimate* contact with the dragon. I was drenched in it. They think that's where the disease might have come from.

Somebody has to get one of those things, dead or alive, so they can study it. Maybe they can find a cure."

"Let them send a *professional* pilot. Or a full-time hero."

"I have to see one again, myself. There may not be any more. My people have sighted only one the past four years. They think it's the last dragon. I just can't risk waiting."

Rick kept his eyes on Alec. When he walked around the room, he moved awkwardly, his head turned toward the bed. It was obvious to Alec that he was trying to avoid looking at the dragon skull.

"Want to get ready for the day, now?"

"Sure, why not?"

Alec dozed as Rick began rubbing him down with a damp cloth. Rick used to carry him into the bathroom for this. Not anymore. Alec had felt too vulnerable, sitting slumped over the toilet. He used to fantasize Marie coming to him, taking off her clothes. They hadn't made love in a very long time.

Someone stepped into the bedroom. He could sense someone by the door, just beyond the limits of his vision. He saw Rick turn around.

"Machines and some special clothes can do this, too, you know," Marie said. Alec felt momentarily disoriented. Rick turned back toward the bed, looking irritated. He bent over, grunted, and pulled up Alec's pants a little too roughly.

Alec tried to clear his eyes. He felt on the verge of tears. "Rick, my eyes. . ." Rick dabbed at his eyes and cheeks with a towel. Marie swam suddenly into focus. Dark-haired, doe-eyed, beautiful. "Machines have their place. But not here, not like this." Rick was wiping at the metallic caps set into the back of Alec's skull. "Careful, there. I'm going to be needing those soon." He looked up at his wife. "So . . . when are you leaving?"

"An hour, maybe two. You forgot to give me the key to storage."

Alec found himself chuckling mirthlessly. "I haven't been too good with details of late."

"Well, that makes you the perfect pilot, now doesn't it?"

Rick sighed. "He's a good pilot, actually. Or so I hear." He worked so furiously at the clothes that Alec was afraid they were going to rip.

"It's not safe!" Marie snapped.

"I have to do this. If you really still cared, you'd know that."

"They're really going to let you do this, huh? Go back there, find the thing?"

"*They're* not going to *let* me do anything."

"Chasing dragons, like some kid."

"There are dragons everywhere, Marie." Alec chuckled again. "It's a dirty job, but somebody has to do it."

Marie's voice broke. "Stay here, Alec. We'll stay. I don't really want to leave—you must know that. But I can't sit still while you do this stupid thing. It's bad enough watching you die from something you can't help. But you don't *have* to go back to Bennett. Stay, Alec. I'll talk to the kids."

Alec tried to control his trembling, but could not. He was broken meat, flopping, ugly. "No."

Alec heard the sound of ripping cloth. Rick cursed and began removing the shirt.

The bedroom door slammed. Alec felt a need to say something, but the silence was suddenly intimidating.

"Mr. Bennett?"

"Yeah ?"

"Good luck." Rick gripped his hand, tightly enough that he eventually felt it.

Again he was seven years old. Again his father tossed him into the air. Again his father did not catch him. But he wasn't so afraid this time—he felt himself flying, despite his weight, despite his awkwardness, despite his doubt.

Alec dropped rapidly toward the enormous canyon bisecting the northern hemisphere of Bennett. He was fully plugged—adjusting the intensity of his more private thoughts against the almost subliminal babble of the computer medium. At last achieving some sort of balance, he felt the mental underpinnings of his ghostlike arms and legs reach out gradually and drift into the composite wings and weave-layered hull of his craft.

The illusion was that these actions were all conscious and deliberate on his part. In fact, the computer's controls had taken over and were leading him gently into the system, allowing him to

become part of the machinery with the least possible discomfort and disorientation. Before most of his impulses to act had even reached the conscious level, they had been recognized, evaluated, then accepted or rejected by the computer. Reaction times were crucial on Bennett—with a gravity slightly higher than Earth's, even a short fall could be fatal. The dragon had evolved under those conditions; no human could beat that.

Here, he was as light as a dream.

The compound's staff was down eighty percent since his father died, for Alec no longer saw the need for personnel largely involved in resource exploitation. They had been all set up for him, the plane fueled, checked and ready, and everyone seemed remarkably compliant to his wishes. Malcolm must have already explained to them that their novice employer was stubborn. But when they first carried him in, Alec did notice a few disgruntled-looking pilots standing around.

He spun the plane upside down, then dropped and rolled to the left. Up here, it was as if his muscles could do anything. The computerized controls made each arm seem to have numerous independently moving joints. At times he was afraid of folding up like a suitcase and plummeting to the ground.

The predominant colours on Bennett were grey, grey-green, and red. Some of the red came from rock formations in and around the numerous canyons and short mountains. Earthquakes brought bits of red up into the grey rock fields.

The other red came from a short, thick plant—a strange amalgam of moss, fern, and shrub—with a brilliant crimson centre. It grew everywhere on the planet. Many of these plants were spoiled by spots of black char.

A third of the plain south of Bennett Compound was now on fire, filling the thick air with carbon dioxide and tiny particles of black ash that attacked his windscreen like hyperactive gnats. Periodically, a cleansing spray washed through the microscopic V-grooves which tattooed the hull. Alec was aware of this spray as a vague, ghostlike dampness somewhere in his skin.

But even with the spray, particles occasionally burst into flame along the ship's fuselage. A sudden nimbus of white light or a rainbow blazed off the forward canard.

The constant fires were a nuisance, but they destroyed enough plants to keep the oxygen level down. A couple of percentage points more, and Bennett could have been an inferno.

Every few minutes the computer cycled through a systems check. He could eavesdrop when he was in the right state of mind. Electrical schematics overlapped microhydraulic graphic simulations on the undersides of his eyelids. Weaponry alignments multiplied across the mindscreen, then suddenly burst like bright, incendiary bombs.

He could visualize the wide telemetry shield, fielding impulses from his skull plugs and transmitting them to the computer controls then feeding it all back through his ethereal, yet perfect-looking arms and legs and the parts of the plane his arms and legs had become.

The plane dropped past red-brown walls dirty with grey-green and crimson growth. He didn't see any fires in the immediate vicinity, but they were raging only a few miles away, and he appeared to be dragging the ash down with him. It swarmed over him so thickly that at first he thought his eyes had suddenly grown worse.

Broad plateaus and massive chimney formations rose from a valley floor still miles below him. At times they came close enough together to form their own narrow passages. He was afraid to drop much farther. It would be like a labyrinth down there. And he would need the height when the dragon ventured out, if it did.

The bodies of the mountains were ponderous, spotted with red and green disease. Enormous, infested mounds of alien flesh. He felt sure that, if he broke into them, there'd be alien maggots: blue and green and brilliant silver, star- and cone-shaped heads.

The forward canard helped pull him out of the drop. The sides of the fuselage, his sides, rippled once, then set for better air flow.

Now he had another vista on the canyon: a series of flat places along an ever-broadening series of cliff sides, arranged like enormous steps, rich with the crimson-hearted plants. On some of these steps he could see short, broad grazers, a smaller and slightly hairy version of the hippopotamus. One looked up in a kind of slow motion startle, then lowered its head again. In the shadowed rock behind it, there appeared to be a wide tunnel opening.

Puff birds, their cheek sacs bloated comically, floated around the plane. If Alec looked carefully enough, he could see blotches of lizard colonies on the canyon walls, their jaws long and broad, crocodile-like.

Hand length insects with bloated wings and claw-like feet landed on the hull of his craft and were immediately washed away.

Wing, fin, and hull surfaces changed shape sixty times a second in a graceful, coordinated ballet.

He felt, to the core, lighter than air, with no care that his arms and legs were dead because he didn't need them anymore. He felt the rockets within his dead fingers, the fire inside his eyes straining behind the goggles. Darkness filled his chest.

Then he saw the dragon. At first it was a bit of black ash, turning the corner of the rock tower far below him. Fluttering and twisting in the wind, it seemed the remnant of some scorched field of alien, vegetable life. It changed shape as it rose, from time to time sending out projections first one way, then another, so that at times it resembled a black, funereal pinwheel.

Then it was a bat, flapping slowly upward out of the shadowed valley toward the heat-baked peaks and plateaus at the top.

Then it was a small black sail boat, floating unsupported in the valley air. A ghost ship. A Flying Dutchman.

And then it was a dragon, resembling everything and nothing.

It was hard to see the thing's wings clearly. They were three times the length of his plane. Vaguely bat-like, but with gas sacs lining the top and a doubling of the black-grey mottled skin where more gas might be trapped. The wing span appeared to be about eight times the height.

The dragon wrapped itself in its wings, then unwrapped, furled and unfurled, a dark lady teasing with her lingerie.

A wing dropped down, and Alec could see the dragon's head. The top of the skull was broad and pale, and Alec thought of the extinct condor. The eyes were large and opaque, seemingly without centres. The huge mouth dropped open, loose on its hinges, gulping air, as if hungry for anything that might cross it. He assumed that the large areas surrounding eyes and nose and mouth were gas-filled as well, since they appeared to change shape now and then, going from flat planes to gnarled ridges and swirls, giving the face as a whole an almost limitless expression.

The body was as dark as the wings, dull, and largely hidden.

The dragon lost altitude suddenly. For a moment it wrapped itself tightly for the drop, then unfurled its wings and let them drift up behind it. Alec watched as the dragon rapidly closed on one of the grazers on the steps below. Its wings spread, covering the step from view. Then it was rising rapidly, the grazer struggling in the dragon's jaws, a thin ribbon of yellow fluid trailing from a neck wound. When the dragon let go, the grazer smashed back onto the step and was still. The dragon settled slowly over it and began to gnaw.

The sheer physicality of the dragon was enough to take Alec's breath away. The plane rocked back and forth anxiously. Alec tried to stretch himself, but the wings would not budge. A warning light went off. He felt small and vulnerable, yet drawn to this physical massiveness, this beast of ancient health. Without thinking much about it, he felt the plane drifting down, the altitude readout racing past his eyes, blurring in a way that was almost soothing.

He was at nearly the same level as the dragon. It had finished its meal and winged itself gently off the cliff side. It hung in midair, watching the ship, watching Alec.

The creature's cheeks and neck billowed. Dust and ash shot up from it, as if caught in a thermal.

Alec let the plane ease closer, rocking slightly in the canyon updrafts.

The roaring thunder suddenly filled him, almost shaking the plane out of sync with him, a sensation he thought must be akin to out-of-body travel. A black cloud filled his field of vision at the same time that electrical charges worked at loosening his scalp.

The cloud fluttered and beat at his windscreen. Huge wing edges curled down at their tips. Then he was rocketing sideways, wings shifting, the rear thrust nozzles swiveling rapidly to direct him away from the looming blood-red rock walls.

Now the dragon was beneath him, massive devil's head coming up in front of the plane. The thing was flying upside down, blank eyes watching him, and Alec was suddenly bucking the plane ever so slightly, jabbing his belly fin at the dragon's exposed torso, then rolling out, climbing, banking, and settling back into his altitude once he saw that the dragon hadn't followed this time.

The dragon rose to a point distant and slightly beneath him, allowing him to circle. Its wings shuddered and rippled like a black paper kite. Only the head was immobile, held rigid in the turbulent air like an African mask. It drifted in the currents, watching.

Watching. One night when Marie had stood over him, thinking he was asleep, she'd lifted the covers, touching him hesitantly.

"Alec?" she'd whispered. "I'm . . . sorry. I just can't."

He had been surprised, and oddly touched.

The dragon revolved in midair, wings rising, dropping, paddling forward and back, darkness caught on a wheel.

The dragon was blowing air, or gas, out of cheeks, mouth, neck sacs. It began rising toward him. The instruments were in Alec's head, his eyes. The electronic goggles came up. Air speed, wind speed, and a half-dozen other functions read out along a muted silver band that ran across the bottom of the lens. Prepared to meet the dark, he aimed with the goggles and fired.

A cliff off to the dragon's left exploded into red debris. Alec trembled. A light flashed on his display. He looked out. The dragon was climbing above him.

From underneath, the creature's body blended in with its wings. Then the wings began to rotate, the head turned down, the dark mass hesitated, and the dragon was suddenly dropping. In seconds the mouth gaped grotesquely, the jaws unhinged, the gas sacs receding, expanding.

Alec pulled away and began to spin in an evasive maneuver. His sensation that the dragon was with him was confirmed by a ballet of graphic stick figures spinning at the bottom of his goggles. Black flaps slapped at his windscreen. He closed his eyes, felt his stomach drop as he cut the thrusters, tensed his shoulders, and prepared the surfaces for the drop. Swiveling the thrusters and cutting them back in, he roared toward the valley floor until he'd left the dragon behind him, then let his canards and altered surfaces bring him back up.

He stared at the dragon, feeling fire at the edge of his lips and at the tips of his fingers. The dragon stared down at him. It was terrible in its huge, limp fleshiness, but somehow Alec could not bring himself to imagine its destruction.

He saw the disease moving through his body, growing, reaching out to embrace his beautiful children and his wife. He saw their faces dissolve in slow motion, in blues and greens and reds.

Then he realized the dragon was descending farther toward the canyon floor, going away. And he was doing nothing to pursue it.

Alec watched until the dragon shrank back to a twist of black ash, then he dropped quickly, following the dragon around several twists in the narrowing canyon, past towers, chimneys, and spires. The surrounding cliffs loomed progressively closer, and at times Alec felt compelled to bring the wings in to reduce their span. Vegetation became sparser this far down, the lizards were in more abundance, and the grazers were nowhere to be seen.

Alec manoeuvred through a series of swirled rock formations, following the rocketing dragon that now looked eagle-sized as it threaded the bull's eyes, into dragon country.

Part of the wall began to curl overhead, and Alec could see that the canyon here was narrowing, gaining a partial roof. He hesitated, and the plane slowed down, but as the dragon drew farther away from him, escaping, he was seized by a sudden desperation and felt the plane shoot forward.

The wall curled more as he flew its length, forming more than a complete roof over him now, beginning to drop on the other side like a frozen wave. The space here was still hardly confined—a hundred such planes could have flown wingtip to wingtip and would still have room to spare. The walls danced with broken light.

He was enclosed in an almost seamless tunnel.

Alec suddenly experienced vertigo, imagined himself falling through miles of earth with no one there to catch him. He was too heavy, too awkward. Too ugly. He could not fly.

Bright warning lights tattooed his eyelids. He wondered that the plane had let him go this far, but knew proceeding was better than stalling out.

A message was up on his windscreen: THIS IS A HAZARDOUS FLIGHT AREA. ADVISE AGAINST PROCEEDING.

Alec wondered how long it had been there.

Amazingly, the plane flew on, faster and faster. He wished his wife and children could have seen it. Flying through the dark with no hands to hold him.

But it wasn't at all dark in the tunnel. He looked around. A yellowish growth covered the walls, broken here and there by a greyish, tendriled vegetation. But it was all blurred, blending together.

Up ahead the dragon revolved as if in slow motion, though Alec knew it was travelling faster than he was. Its wings were glistening panels of silver light that, when looked at, almost hurt the eyes. Rainbow light flowed over its head and down its back, trailed off into a tail of fiery dust, and travelled over the dark form, like hordes of migrating, fluorescent parasites in the dragon's skin.

The tunnel opened up periodically into a necklace of enormous chambers. The dragon slowed down, seeming to float, maneuvering coyly behind occasional spires and hanging lobes of stone. Coquettish.

Alec burned his thrusters lightly, wings tilted upward and the jets along his wing edges straining. So although there was forward progression, it was, like the dragon's, just short of a stall. An encounter between two winged insects.

Dark, concave ridges with sharp rock dividers, like the body impressions of a huge snake, ringed the chambers. Ribbed stone grew along the walls like roots or stiffened entrails.

His instruments detected activity in the recessed galleries, dark patterns of movement. Vague impressions of limbs and wings and unclassifiable appendages, nothing more.

The walls seemed closer, fecund and teeming. He suddenly imagined he could smell the stone.

Minute bits of material were bouncing off the skin of the plane, some of it darting off before it could be misted away.

Occasionally, something raked lightly along the underside of the ship, too close and too softly for stone.

Ahead of him the tunnel split, both branches far narrower than the one he had been in. The dragon floated at the juncture, its glowing wings and face drifting through highly stylized patterns of light, like a woman dancing in a kimono, her face painted a brilliant white.

He stared for what seemed to be a long time before following the dragon into the starboard tunnel.

The bright kimono began to wrap him. The plane revolved once rapidly on its axis, freeing itself. Alec imagined being wrapped within his own sheets, unable to get loose, paralyzed.

Ahead of him the dragon was imitating, making huge loops out of its pliant wings, twirling itself like a pinwheel.

Another tunnel was opening, even narrower. The dragon straightened and dove through it. Alec hesitated, the plane slowed, but there was nowhere else to go. He had to trust the dragon's expertise. He dropped his nose and entered.

The tunnel widened, then began to curve steadily upward, narrowing again. Tilting farther up, Alec could feel the strain. Soon they were almost vertical, facing a dimness ahead. Alec could now guess.

The dragon was racing up the hollow insides of a chimney formation. Alec shifted focus, gritted his teeth, and allowed his ship to follow as if towed. He felt sick to his stomach.

The ship gave him something for the nausea—he could feel the change beginning back in his throat. The centre of the chimney was a seamless grey, speckled red. The warning lights cooled, just in time for Alec to burst out of the chimney and into the dazzling sunlight.

As the plane floated out over the valley again, Alec scanned the sky frantically for some sign of the dragon. Nothing. He could see the gleam off the domes of Bennett Compound on the lip of the distant canyon wall. He'd come back to the departure point. Ground vehicles waited along the edge. He soared closer, into gathering shadow.

The shadow wrapped him up with a roar. Dark sheets wound around his chest until he couldn't breathe. A cry caught in his throat, his goggles blazed red, and with a high pitched whine he pitched over, dragging his mind screaming behind him.

He fired again and again, turning dirt and rock and sky into flame.

His eyes came open with the sense that the plane was folding back its wings. He looked out, straight down, at a fast-approaching ribbon of blue. He was a child falling out of bed, the bedclothes around him so tightly he could not move. He was a child tossed and dropped by his father. He was a dragon too large and much too dark to fly.

The water rose. The aide had left him in his bath too long. He could not move his arms. His legs were gone. And he was slipping fast beneath the waves.

Alec screamed as muscles seemed to tear from bone, as bones bent and snapped. But he was rising, pulling out of the dive, and the disfigurement was only illusory, he reminded himself, no matter how terrible.

He strained for the canyon rim, dragging the plane up behind him. Enough. He had no business here.

And then he slammed into darkness, and the darkness gave way around him, then came back fighting, eating his windscreen, folding wing and fuselage, crushing him.

The devil's head roared above him, blank eyes blazing. Flames coruscated down wings shrinking, turning to silver.

Crazily, the ship's computers began cycling through a systems check. Alec watched microhydraulics multiply and disappear, electrical systems blossom. His perfect cobalt-and-lime legs and arms jumbled, doubled, then faded away.

And on the top edge of the telemetry shield, the dragon's severed muscles and nerves danced madly. He'd speared it, pinned it. He could almost imagine reaching out and grasping it in his hand. It wasn't going to get away.

He could see the edge of the cliff only a few yards above him, in one unobscured corner of his windscreen. Personnel in red suits lined the lip. He'd never make it; he could feel the plane falling.

He reached with his mind, and the thrusters pushed.

He felt his stomach rise, the leap in his thighs.

And suddenly he was lifting both plane and shield-pinioned dragon up over the edge of the cliff to solid ground. Plane and dragon skidded over broken rock, crimson-hearted scrub, and cinnamon-coloured soil to a shuddering stop.

Alec thought of his body breaking, the disease spilling out, the disease murdering everyone around him, his beautiful, sleeping children, his wife. He heaved his useless body. He thrashed, palsied, cramping.

"Get him out of there!"

Technicians in black masks were pulling Alec out of his harness and trying to slip a mask over his face. He fought them. Smoke haloed their bulbous heads. He smelled something sharp. Ash began to fill his mouth.

He tried to turn. The dragon roared.

"Get him out!"

His head fell back when they lifted him. He could see the dragon rolling on its side, creasing a cindered wing. Huge blank eyes settled, stared.

Alec was exhilarated. It was like wrestling and pinning the nightmare, even as he was dreaming it.

Great cheeks blew clouds of gas that exploded into flame. Sacs ruptured, flames shot up, dark flesh blistered.

"Tether it!"

The techs carried metal claws to the dragon's trembling, black-grey mottled sides. The devil's head fell forward.

And Alec felt his own head fall forward. He looked down at his feet, caught by the twisted hull. His withered feet. Once grounded, he wasn't much of a bird, or dragon. His people were still trying to pull him out from under the telemetry shield. The dragon sprawled over the rest of the plane and beyond, sides heaving. Yellow liquid bubbled around the wound where the dragon had crashed into the plane, where the telemetry shield entered muscle and nerve, short-circuiting the dragon, becoming a part of the dragon. The dragon was part of his plane.

The dragon tried to rise, but kept jamming the plane wreckage farther into its wound as it struggled. The huge head faced Alec, still terrible, still beautifully dark.

This is wrong, he thought.

Alec was still in range of the telemetry shield—he could still control it, but his people almost had him loose, and then it would be too late.

Alec thought to lift his head. The dragon's head stirred.

Alec imagined his arms raised. Burnt wings fluttered.

Alec visualized the telemetry shield, the dragon pinned there. He tried to make the dragon rise, but it fell back, the wings flapping involuntarily, muscles cramped, its body huge, unmanageable, useless, alien.

What am I doing? he thought.

The dragon might contain his cure. He just needed to allow his people to drag it away.

The dragon thrashed, wings and muscles powerless. Its huge head turned. Alec stared into dark and found something familiar there.

They might be able to reverse the sclerosis. He'd walk. Marie and the children would come back. They'd all welcome him because he'd be clean again.

Who needs it? He'd changed, and if they'd loved him, they'd have accepted his changing.

The dragon's body flapped and rolled. Oddly lovely, moth-like. The last of its kind, tossed high and dropped, helpless. But still so strong; if it got back to its lair, it might be able to pick the pieces out. It might be able to heal. Again the eyes enveloped Alec, so dark they left him gasping.

He watched as the technicians struggled to attach the grappling claws. The thing bellowed hideously, leathery skin flapping. The beast had poisoned him, changed his life, infected him with its darkness.

The beast had changed him. The beast had brought out a life different from the one Alec had intended.

A darkness ran in his own veins, dragon's breath in his lungs. Another world lay under the bridges between neural synapses, a place where dreamers and their nightmares were the same, where only dragons and their hunters might fly.

The dragon had made him fly through the dark.

I have a choice, he thought.

Alec pushed with his mind just as his people pulled him loose of the plane, almost out of range of the telemetry link with the dragon. And the dragon rose with the crumpled plane clinging to its belly.

It staggered to the cliff's edge and went over while Alec watched, the technicians holding him back from the lip.

And under the shouts, the frantic scramble, Alec had a brief moment inside the dragon's head as it slipped over the cliff's edge, the wind filling broken wings, the darkness filling enormous eyes, heedless of the fire crisping its back as it dived once more into its alien world.

THE MONSTER IN THE FIELD

The monster had lived in the field for as long as anyone could remember. For much of that time he chose to lie there, exposed, gazing at the sky. Sometimes he wore a kind of rough tunic, sometimes he did not. He took what little he could find in the almost-barren field and shoved it into his mouth—roots, grass, small animals, trash. He ate with such evident displeasure the townspeople were embarrassed to watch. Every few years they tried feeding him something better, and he gnawed with a terrible aggression on what they threw out on the field, staring at them so furiously they were afraid to stay. He relieved himself, which wasn't often, without self-consciousness. He fell into sleep with the greatest reluctance, making snoring sounds so loud, repulsive, and full of such suggestive content the people living nearby sold their houses and moved away. Sometimes those houses remained unoccupied for years, unfit for any purpose save storage.

Sometimes the monster lived in a hut smeared together out of sticks and mud. Sometimes he destroyed that poor construction in paroxysms of rage, hurling the bits of it as far as he could, which was very far indeed.

Sometimes he rebuilt this structure slowly and lovingly, placing each stick and plane as if making art. The hut was of limited practicality, its regular destruction compelling evidence that the monster did not require it for either privacy or survival.

The townspeople rarely visited the field where the monster lived. It was not because he frightened them, although most would have professed varying degrees of discomfort in his presence. Their absence appeared to have more to do with the fact that he was the local landmark, the one the natives seldom patronized.

One day a university student from a distant county was traveling through this town where the monster lived. He had not heard of the monster before; in fact he hadn't even heard of the town. Some weekends he simply had an irresistible impulse to drive, and so traveled wherever the roads took him.

The student had driven through the town and was almost to its outer edge when he saw the naked creature lying out in the field. Being of a morbid inclination, he supposed it was a dead body and so pulled over to sit and watch. Eventually he climbed out of his car and stood leaning against it. He felt some disappointment when a blurry outline of hand reached up from the body and waved away a cloud of insects.

The student saw a young girl walking nearby. He strolled over to her casually, smiled and asked, "Who is that lying out in that field?"

"Him? Looking up at the sky? He's—That's our monster."

The student smiled down at the girl. "Thank you. You've been very helpful."

Possessing a studied lack of superstition, the student walked across the field until he was only a few feet from the monster. "Hello," he said. "May I speak to you?"

The monster's head resembled a great stone rolling over as he turned to look at the student. "At least you ask, politely enough."

The student thought carefully about what his next words should be. Although he did not find this figure to be terribly frightening, the monster was still one of the least attractive creatures he had ever seen. The monster's head was far too large for his body and a thin thatch of orangeish hair covered but a small area of his scalp in an elliptical tangle. His chest was lopsided, as was his belly. His smell was decidedly unpleasant, yet the student could not have explained in what way, as nothing came to mind that he might compare it to. The monster had surprisingly thin arms and legs, and both finger- and toe-nails resembled ragged, bitten-off shingles of shale.

"But your good manners do not earn you staring rights," the monster said.

"I was... composing my thoughts."

"That is all you humans appear to do, either composing or blurting."

"I am a student. They have tried to teach me to think before I speak."

The monster grunted.

"They have treated you shabbily, haven't they?"

The monster sat up, and was taller than the student expected. His huge head swiveled. "What do you know? You know nothing about me. I did not summon you, did I? You are but some random— person. The people here—" The monster tried to make a gesture then, but he apparently failed, for his misshapen arm stuttered and fell, trembling. He spat. "They have *not* treated me shabbily. Like people everywhere, they have not treated me—at all."

"I don't understand," the student said.

"For the most part, they ignore me. At best I am a tourist attraction, at worst, an eyesore. Even when they run away, it is as if they run away from a phantom, from nothing. They do not *deal* with me."

"How does it feel, to be alone?"

The monster swiveled his head. A piece of rough flesh like a peel of bark curled open. The eyeball was grey, like a spoiled egg. But the iris (or pupil, for they were one) was as dazzling and multifaceted as a jewel. "Are you saying this is something you have never experienced?"

"Well, no," the student admitted. "Sometimes I study by myself, in my room late at night away from the others. And most nights, I sleep by myself. I have a roommate, but he is seldom there."

"And do you enjoy these times alone?"

"Well, yes, many times I do. But I know I have a choice. Sometimes I find I must leave my room and find others."

"Others of your kind?"

"I'm not really sure what my kind is."

"You understand me, student. Do not pretend stupidity. I will tell you what your *kind* is—it is the kind that often feigns stupidity, without understanding what stupidity truly means."

"And what does it mean?"

"It means to be asleep to the world. And before you insult me again I want you to know that I am not stupid. I, unfortunately, have never been asleep to the world. It presses against me on all sides, and because I have not the company of others of my kind to soothe me, I feel the solitary brunt of it, the decay of it in all its unholy purity, the stinking rag and the fleshless bone of it. That, my friend, is my unasked-for wisdom, my untrammeled knowledge of the world."

"I apologize."

"Do not apologize when you are not sorry. I saw you with that female. Tell me, how does *that* feel?"

"I don't understand."

"To have a companion."

"We're hardly companions. I have never seen her before. I simply asked, well, I asked who you were."

The monster raised both his arms, and the student stepped back. The monster made a noise deep inside his throat, and it might have been a laugh, but it sounded as if something were trapped there, attempting to eat its way out.

The monster tilted his head back. "I would not mind," he said, his arms and hands contorting in a stretch, his legs splaying as if broken, "knowing the answer to that question."

The student thought he should leave, but discovered he could not. He watched as the monster ran around the field, grunting, now and then reaching down to claw at the ground to tear out clumps of grass and buried stones, the occasional bit of bone and other scattered debris from past meals. There was nothing remotely graceful about the monster's movements, but there was an unexpected eagerness that reminded the student of the enthusiasms of children: giddy, uncontrolled, vaguely desperate.

The student wondered if all this might be for his benefit, because he could not believe this morose-looking creature made a habit of such play. The possibility that even this small bit of company might bring out some quality of celebratory silliness in the monster made the student sad.

"Look!" The monster stopped a few feet away and lifted his head to the darkening sky. "Can you feel them coming?"

"Them? The town?" And the student felt anxious again, perceiving some form of danger he could not understand.

"No, of course you cannot," the monster said. "But if you will pardon my braggadocio I will confess I can *smell* them!"

"Them?"

"The stars!"

The monster reached up and peeled off the small patch of orange hair covering his scalp. The student could not see exactly how it was attached, but was alarmed to see bits of skin and a spray of blood come away with the sweep of the monster's arm. "Wait!" the student shouted, his hands pressed out in horror, feeling silly, sensing that to beg a stop from such a being was like crying halt to the wind and moon.

The monster dipped his head slightly, a bow to the approaching night, allowing the student to see the rough and bloody baldness of his pate. There in the centre were three wide grooves flowing blood, as if the great veins in the monster's brain had risen to the top and opened for direct access to the night air.

The monster staggered, suddenly unable to raise his head, the huge weight of it swinging precariously at the end of his neck. Then with a great crouch and heave he jerked his massive skull up toward a black dome rapidly filling with stars. The student was alarmed to see the tears streaming down the monster's face, for somehow the presence of tears made this creature even more repulsive than before.

"I suspect you find it monstrous that I weep," the monster began, and the student thought to deny it, even though of course it was true. "Yes, yes," the monster said, trembling. "It is monstrous that I weep. It is monstrous that I feel at all, that I breathe the air that generations have breathed, that I walk ground once trodden by thousands, who stood here and lived and sang and loved and then were no more, were bone and mineral and scattered chemical, one last vapor expelled into an atmosphere that winds the world like its death shroud. Monstrous, monstrous that I understand myself so poorly, monstrous that I know nothing of the hearts of those who pass through a town so close to me and yet an endless distance away. The despair I feel is monstrous, such a bitter, vile taste lapping these lips that have not kissed. And how repulsive, not to have kissed, how malformed the unrequited desire to be part of those who ignore you, whose gaze finds nothing when they look at you. How grotesque, that life, any and all life, will some day be extinct—I can see it! With this loathsome eye of mine! The end of life, the end of this world—in my dreams it has already happened! You call yourself a student, and yet you know nothing of consequence, while I, and all those around me, call me Monster, and I anguish over the things I know." The monster staggered drunkenly, leaning over the frightened student. "So, yes, child, I weep. I, Monster, weep."

And the monster toppled forward onto the student, who experienced a great shifting of the world, land, sky, and time converging in his skull.

When the student awakened he imagined himself back in his dormitory room in that life miles away. He seemed to be all head, but often a night of drinking accomplished that: the world a landslide that enveloped you, trapping limbs and all intention of movement. He shook his head—the weight of it threatened to pull him to the ground. Static fell out of his eyes and powdered the ground with stars. He gazed out over the field at the small crowd gathered at its edge, the ancient brick and stone walls of the town glowing hazily beyond as if smeared with a film of dirty oil.

His eyes seemed surprisingly acute this morning—he could see the faces of the crowd even though they were many yards away. He thought he saw the girl he had asked directions from, and it occurred to him now how pretty she was. A few older people stood behind her, talking, gesturing in his direction. Several men on one end of the crowd had bottles of liquor in their hands, and appeared to be toasting him. He concentrated on them, and it was as if he were gazing through a telescope: their images flew rapidly his way, filling his vision.

They were drunk and laughing as men will laugh, pointing as men will point, foolish and stupid companions. The one in the middle was the most repulsive, rough face and scaly forehead, and the student was alarmed to see that under one drunken lid peeked that clearly recognizable, dazzling jewel of an eye.

The student looked down and examined his poor nakedness: his stick-like legs, his distorted arms and poorly-defined hands, the dark broken nails. He touched the sides of his enormous head. He ran his hands down his swollen and lopsided chest. He looked up and saw the ugly man with the beautiful jewel eye grinning, his chin wet with drink and drool.

The weeping would come later, he knew, the rages and the useless complaints. But for now he settled himself down in the field and waited for the stars to come, tenderly probing the contours and crevices of his hideous flesh, gingerly acquainting himself with this new knowledge that he was monstrous of limb and monstrous of head, but most of all monstrous in his heart.

THE
HIGH
CHAIR

He woke up numb, as he did so many mornings these days, his lower legs, lower arms like unappealing cuts of meat he'd forgotten to stick into the freezer. He was forgetting too many things—names, favourite places, words with specific and useful meanings—but he wasn't too distressed about it. Perhaps he had simply forgotten to be distressed. People had far too many names, places, and words in their lives. They so crowded out what was important that importance was forgotten, filling life rapidly with trivia.

Swinging out of the covers, he planted his feet on the floor, where they remained. They tingled painfully, the tingling spreading into an ache that flowed up his legs. He stared at his misshapen toenails. He thought perhaps he had forgotten something he should be doing about sleeping, some trick his doctor may have told him about. *Don't sleep with your ankles crossed—your feet will be dead in the morning.* Something like that. His doctor was full of tips. But he couldn't remember half of them. Pat would remember that sort of thing—she always made notes about those "life tips," whatever you called them. Of course he couldn't remember the precise word. But he had the gist of it, didn't he? *Gist.* Now there was a mighty good word. It summed him up perfectly. He wasn't Byron Wembley anymore. He was the *gist* of Byron Wembley. But hell, what more did he need?

Out of the bathroom his legs felt better going down the hall. Blood was pumping, the internal furnace was coming on. Outdated and inefficient, but good enough for the job at hand. Soon enough there'd be colour in his cheeks and Pat wouldn't have to say, "What's wrong? You look like a ghost." Every day, practically, as if it were some new discovery. She didn't hear herself.

But he ran into her sooner than expected. The back of her. In the spare room off the hallway, her head buried in the big storage closet. She suddenly emerged, backwards, dragging the highchair out with her.

"What are you doing?" he asked.

"Mrs. Stevens' daughter needs a highchair for her little girl. They can't afford hardly anything, and this is still in great condition."

"Well, it's never been used."

She turned around. "I know that."

He scratched his face nervously. A little too hard perhaps (Was he bleeding? He'd never hear the end if he was.) "Well, of course you do. Are you selling it to her?"

"Of course not. They need it, we never did. I'm trying to help out. Why? You didn't want to keep it, did you?"

He didn't know what else to say. "I didn't realize we still had it."

"What are you getting at?"

He didn't know. Sometimes you said things out of a feeling and you didn't realize what you were saying. Like praying, maybe, like speaking in tongues. Now he'd have to come up with some kind of explanation for her, even though he had no idea himself.

He looked around. "I never come in here, so I didn't know we still had it."

"It's been in this closet the whole time. Twenty-five years. You just forgot."

"I told you, I never come in here."

She stared at him. "Are you saying there's a room in this little house of ours you haven't entered in twenty-five years?"

Of course he'd never thought about it that way. He'd never thought about it at all. He'd never thought about the unused chair. He'd never thought about why they hadn't tried again. But now that he did think about it, he thought it was all a strange and sad way to be in the world.

He went for his daily walk. Just because he'd realized this thing about himself (and actually, Pat had realized it for him) didn't mean he should change his daily routine. What was he supposed to do? Run off and find a therapist? He didn't know if men his age even went to therapists. Hadn't therapy been a fad? A lot of people went a few times, and he remembered some made-for-TV movies, but he didn't know anyone personally who still did.

Besides, what did he want to change about his situation? Not a damn thing. He had a right to. Whatever.

He was actually feeling pretty energetic, and thought he might be able to stay out walking longer than normal. Pat should be pleased with that, whether she actually would be or not. The walks had been her idea—after his retirement she'd complained how drowsy he seemed during the day, that obviously he needed a reason to move. She'd nagged him in that way she had of inserting phrases like *of course, if you were walking every day* into completely unrelated threads of conversation.

Not that there was actually anything wrong with that. She was probably the only person in the world who cared if he was anywhere.

He tried to let it all go—his mind was buzzing. He really didn't think you moved as well when your mind was buzzing. There was a hitch in the step, as if your foot was distracted by the inner dialog. The feet wanted to know what was going on, just like the eyes, just like the hands.

Usually he took his walk along the storefronts between the house and the new municipal centre. He'd never told Pat that he took that route—he knew what she'd say. She'd say he was probably spending most of his time window shopping. It wouldn't be an argument, either—she'd just say that was probably what he was doing, just putting it up in the air like that, and then she'd be about her business. She wouldn't wait to hear what he had to say about it. So then it was out there. Was it truth or was it just an unanswered accusation? She'd left some of these statements lying around the house for years. The aging changed them—some became irrelevant and forgotten. Some would age five or six years and then they'd be fact and it would be too late to refute them.

He and Pat almost never argued. But that meant different things to different people.

Of course, in this case, it would have been true fact. Pat was right

most of the time, which was both his safety and his aggravation.

He couldn't walk ten feet without stopping to window gaze. That was why his walks always took so long. That was why she worried.

But today he had this surprising gift of energy. Or was it just the heat from worrying over this high chair thing? He walked when he fretted—he'd always been like that. But it didn't make any difference. He was moving along pretty good—he was going to check out the park. They lived only five blocks from that big spread of trees, grass, and flowers, but he hadn't actually been inside in years.

There were a lot more kids than he expected. Running and shoving, they made him nervous. Didn't that prove he would never have been a good father, that it had been a bad idea in the first place? Pat always said it was different when they were your own kids. But how did she know? She'd never had any.

A couple of boys, nine or ten maybe, ran past him and jumped up on a low wall, teetering in exaggerated fashion, then falling off purposely, arms flailing. One of them complained that he'd banged his elbow. The other boy punched the kid on the sore arm and ran away. The injured kid ran after screaming like a banshee. It was a high pitched, unnatural sound, which Byron assumed was pretense, but how could you ever know for sure? Boys that age were one jump and a decibel away from psychosis. Perhaps he had been the same—he wasn't sure—that period of his life remained a sugar-smeared blur.

Several young girls came toward him pushing doll-filled strollers, smiling, their combined laughter a pleasant contrast to the earlier boy's screech. But as they came closer Byron pulled up short, startled to see that their passengers were in fact real, comatose, drooling babies. He stared at the mothers who stopped laughing and stared back, as if he were some sort of threat.

They were about as old as the high chair. The day he bought it there had been snow on the ground, the air smelling of wood burning stoves and fireplaces. He hadn't gone to one of the big discount department stores, but to a local specialty baby shop run by an elderly couple who seemed to know all there was to know about matters *infantile*. He wasn't sure if that was a good word as far as the rest of the world was concerned, but it worked for him. The endless beginnings of things, repeated in neighbourhoods and small homes around the planet, young families stepping up on time's wheel, without a clue as to their final destinations, but being brave about it just the same.

He and Pat and their unborn child had been one of those brave young families, until the child (Byron still could not bring himself to say "she") decided at the last minute to back out of the deal. "She decided to stay up with the angels," is the way his mother had put it at the time, and at the time Byron had felt betrayed. He didn't think he even believed in heaven, but he'd felt betrayed just the same. Somehow his daughter had decided he wasn't going to be a good father for her, and so had elected not to participate.

She would have been about the age of these young mothers. She would have some sort of career, her own thoughts and fantasies about the world, relationships, perhaps a baby, his grandchild, in a stroller similar to these. She would have made of his life a very different destination.

He trudged on down the path, picking up speed. What was he doing? He wasn't some marathon man in training. Practicing for a heart attack, more like it. It seemed an ironically healthy way to commit suicide.

As if on cue (*it heard me speak its name*), he felt an invisible hand squeezing his heart, fingers long and narrow like a young girl's. Suddenly dizzy, he was afraid he might fall, which for some reason seemed suddenly worse than death. He moved his swimmy eyes slowly and found a bench, staggered there, sat down and collapsed backwards against the wooden slats. Dizziness prevented him from holding his head up, so he let the weight of it fall into his chin, which he rested onto his chest, eyes closed.

The crowd roared in his ears. He was glad someone was having fun.

When he opened his eyes babies had hold of his knees, trying to climb up but slipping on the shiny worn material of his pants. He was surprisingly calm about it, perhaps. He blinked his eyes a few times and sighed in contemplation.

One of the babies had succeeded in reaching his upper leg, straddling him, compressing its chunky thighs vise-like to hold on. Remarkable strength, really, enough to make him wince. He looked around to see who was watching. A middle-aged woman strode by, glanced over, grinning. Whether she could see the babies or if she was just being friendly he had no way to tell.

He was trying to think, to remember, but the babies made it difficult. Now there were two up on his leg, and another two yanking at his other pants leg, crying. Another one had somehow scaled the back of the park bench, and now straddled the back of his neck, drooling into his ear as it released an endless babbled whisper.

He had seen the babies before, although it had been many years. They used to come to him when he was working out in the back yard, or sometimes late at night when he was in the living room by himself, reading. An ordinary person would have been alarmed, he supposed. But then they had stopped coming, and he actually had forgotten about them, which seemed like impossible behavior, now that he thought about it. Who could forget such apparitions? Who could avoid a bedroom in their own home for over twenty-five years?

He supposed the babies would make at least some sense if he had started seeing them after the unhappy event. When he and Pat no longer needed the high chair. An understandable reaction. But Byron had been seeing the babies for years before he'd even known Pat.

"You're back," he said to them softly, not wanting to be overheard. "Exactly why is that?"

The babies chattered nonsense words and crapped their diapers. Byron gagged on the stench, thick as bad gravy. He stood desperately, dumping the squalling infants, and stumbled away.

The babies had never come alone before, but had been simply the vanguard of . . . what was the word? Not exactly an army. "Plague" came closer. He glanced at the edges of the path. A viscous smear here and there like vomit. An indication of eyes and mouths. Not exactly hideous, but disturbing. The fecundity of the world. Creating life at its most inconvenient.

All the babies were crying now, and he wept for them. But there was nothing he could do. Let one of them tell him what he could do about this, this fertility of the void, and he would do it, or try. But they couldn't tell him. They were just babies.

He ran from the park, his chest working its way apart.

Perhaps he could forget about the pain. With a little effort, he was sure, he could be dumb again.

Byron waited in the living room while Pat finished preparing dinner. She was angry at his lateness, although she would not tell him directly. The way she banged pans was expressive, and almost musical. In fact he almost enjoyed the sound.

The living room had always been a quiet, elegant place to sit in. To Byron it suggested life in an English manor, the rich lord, the women kept away in their part of the house, which in contrast was a place full of the loudness, the messiness of life.

This room, however, was a place of safety, where emotions rarely raised a temperature, where the babies slept in the corners, in the shadows behind chairs, only a pink sliver here and there to betray the presence of a tiny bald head, where their soft snores might be mistaken for the breeze from the window or the steady groan of the grandfather clock.

He and Pat had done all right without children. They had travelled extensively and eaten in the best restaurants, and they had bought fine things, and in the evenings they had had their quiet, uninterrupted conversations, and the days had passed one into the other, and the hours had crept steadily from meal to meal and into their bed with little notice.

They did not need children to remind them how precarious life could be, how fragile, how momentary. They did not need children to remind them of how things change, day by day, how feelings are hurt, how limbs are broken, how disappointment waits to pounce, how lives entwine, then separate into distant houses, occasional phone calls, and increasingly remote connections. They did not need. They did not require children to teach them these things.

But tonight he did not forget about any of this. He did not forget about the babies, or the drama and magic of what did or did not happen in his brain. Even through dinner, and the companionable reading they shared after dinner, and the snuggle in bed, the spooning of their lives one against the other, he did not forget, and so just before they both fell asleep he asked her, "When you give Mrs. Stevens the high chair, would you ask her if we could have it back when they're done with it?"

She didn't reply at first, and after a time he decided she must be asleep, when she said, "of course."

DINOSAUR

Where did the dinosaurs go? The children looked down at their desks. A change of climate, ice age, caterpillars eating their food, disease, mammals eating their eggs. Freddy Barnhill was thinking these answers but was too self conscious to raise his hand. The teacher waited. But nobody's really sure, Freddy thought. Nobody knows.

Sometimes he thought they might be lost somewhere. They couldn't find their way. They couldn't keep up with the others, the way the world was changing so. So they got left behind. They got abandoned.

Twenty years later, Freddy drove the fifty-nine miles between Meeker and Rangely twice each day thinking about his father and thinking about dinosaurs. Only occasionally were there changes in subject matter, although he would have expected both topics to be exhausted by now. People might call him obsessed; hell, people would call him crazy.

Along Colorado Highway 64, endless streams of yellow-blooming rabbit grass whipped by, each scrub-dotted washout and arroyo threatening to draw his eye up its channel and send him into the ditch. Almost as soon as he turned the pickup onto the road, he would start to see his father's enormous hands pressing down at him from above the bar. He'd feel himself suddenly afraid of his father's instability and scurry under the table to hide. Then he'd hear the sudden crash of his father's huge head on the table as he passed out. An endless crash; his father's head slammed the hard wood again and again the fifty-nine miles between Meeker and Rangely.

There seemed to be little life in the gullies and low hills. Harsh land which had to be struggled with, which swallowed any failed attempts. Early settlers had named this land with their complaints: Devil's Grave, Bitter Creek, Camp Misery, Bugtown, Poverty Gulch. Rotted houses around clumps of tumbleweed leaned from the hillsides like aged throats, their swollen walls collapsing. The broken fingers of ancient windmills reached toward an empty sky.

Once he reached Rangely, the sense of lifelessness was even more pronounced—grey, lunar sandstone in ridges and flatlands as far as the eye could see. Wind-blasted landscape alive with sagebrush, little else. The oil companies' reservation: new and old riggings, abandoned shacks. His father had spent most of his adult life here, working for one outfit or another.

Mel Barnhill had originally been a cowboy. A drifter. Then when things had begun to change with the oil wells coming in, he'd changed, too. He'd been a mechanic, construction worker, jack-of-all-trades. Freddy remembered seeing him work on some of the early crude equipment, even some of the steam operated earthmovers. Enormous brown hands working with rough-made wrenches. Smiling, singing—he always had been happy working with machinery. Freddy had helped him, sort of, as much as any very small boy might help his father in his work. But that time had passed. As had the life of the cowboy.

His father liked thinking of himself as an outlaw. "Don't need no laws, no woman to tie me down. Like to do as I please."

Freddy remembered following his father up the street after one of the man's long drinking bouts. The swagger in the walk, he thought now, had been reminiscent of Butch Cassidy or professional killer Tom Horn, who used to hide out not far from there. Cattle were still being rustled at the time, and Freddy could recall more than once his father hinting that he had had a part in some of it. He'd wink at Freddy sometimes when he said this, but Freddy never could tell if that meant he was just joking, or that he really had done those things, and Freddy was supposed to be extra proud. The first time Freddy'd seen a John Wayne movie, he'd thought that was his father up on the screen. The walk was the same. After a time he began to wonder if his father practiced it.

Dramatic gestures seemed to be a lot of what the old-timers in the area were about. Gestures for a fading way of life. When he thought about it now, Freddy believed his father had known the life was rapidly becoming obsolete, the cowboy and rancher becoming extinct. It was the end of an era. Not long after his father's time, they built that new power plant at Craig, and the old timers suddenly didn't know every face when they came into town. People had to lock their doors.

"Dumb cowboys! Stupid sodbusters!" Freddy's father had been drunk, screaming hoarsely in a corral outside a Rangely bar. Freddy remembered the incident vaguely; he'd seen only part of it through the bar window. But every time he ran into one of his father's old friends, it was recalled.

His father had been drinking with some of his cowboy friends; there'd been an argument. They'd accused Mel of turning his back on them, becoming a city boy, because he worked for the oil companies.

Little Freddy had shuddered behind the window. His father was dragging a cow out of the barn. Before anyone could do anything, he shot it. The big brown animal collapsed as if in slow motion, its head making a sick thud on the hard ground. One of the waitresses had held Freddy so tightly it scared him, but it had calmed him down.

This was the landscape Mel Barnhill had willed to his son. It provided the backdrop for most of Freddy's dreams. And yet it was at the *outskirts* of Rangely that, every day, Freddy started thinking about dinosaurs.

Fourteen miles north of Rangely was the little town of Dinosaur. And twenty-seven miles west of there, just across the Utah border and above Jensen, was the big Dinosaur Quarry of the Dinosaur National Monument. One of the largest sources of dinosaur fossils in the world. Primitive land, or the way the earth might look after some catastrophe. Freddy didn't go any more. Standing up there looking out over the canyons, where the Colorado Plateau had crashed up against the Uinta range, it was as if his whole life might disappear out there someday, pulled into the emptiness.

Over each street sign in the town of Dinosaur was a little red cutout of a stegosaurus. The streets had names like Brontosaurus, Pterodactyl, Tyrannosaurus Rex. The town looked old, almost as old as the surrounding land, with tar paper shacks here and there and rough board houses. It used to be called Artesia before the Interior Department set up the park.

But most of the tourists went over to Utah, to Jensen and Vernal. Dinosaur was just a place people passed through on their way to somewhere else; there was no restaurant, not even a half-decent service station. Only a few hundred in population—there hadn't been many people in the first place, and most of them had gone a long time ago. The red on the dinosaur cutouts looked a lot like rust.

Freddy worked in Rangely, just as his dad had, but he lived in Meeker. He liked Meeker, although most of the other men his age complained that there was nothing to do. It was a quiet town; there weren't too many cowboys, and it lacked Rangely's construction and oil workers. Freddy was relieved.

The pickup slid in gravel, and Freddy fought to right it. You had to be careful driving the roads out here; they lulled you, made you careless. The truck seemed so easy to drive, it had so much power, that you sometimes forgot how dangerous one slip might be. One of the drawbacks to advanced technology, and to evolution. It made you reckless; it became too easy to lose control over the power. And that power could leave you upside down off an embankment.

Again, his father's enormous head crashed into the table. The glasses fell in a rain of glistening shards. His father's shapeless mouth opened to expose rough, broken teeth.

Dinosaurs used to walk the hills here, but it had been different then. Freddy thought about that a lot, how things used to be so different. And how they might be different again, with new monsters walking the barren land: giant rats and scavenging rabbits, but maybe rabbits like no one's ever seen before—long claws and hind legs strong enough to tear another animal apart. Just before the dinosaurs came, low lying desert then, the early Jurassic Period. No animals. Great restless sand dunes towering seven hundred feet, snaking and drifting like primeval dreams. Fading, dying away in the distance.

The earliest home Freddy could remember was an old boarding house a few hundred yards from one of the early oil rigs. A whitewashed shack, really, several crate-like rooms strung together. He and his father had shared one. He couldn't remember his mother, except as a gauzy presence, more like a ghost, something dead and not dead. He didn't think she had ever lived with them in the rooming house, but he couldn't be sure. It bothered him that he could remember so little about her—a hint of light, a smell, that was all. She had vanished. *She left us. She left me,* he corrected himself. His father had always told him that, but it was still hard to believe.

The land sank. An arctic sea reached in. Millions of years passed, and in the late Jurassic it all rose again. The dinosaurs were coming; the land was readying itself.

He sometimes wondered if he had ever known his mother at all. Maybe his memories were false. Maybe she had died when he was born. Maybe she'd gone away to die, her time done once she'd given him life.

The land just come from the sea was much more humid. Flat plains. Marshy. Great slow streams loaded with silt flowed out of the highlands to the west to feed the marshes and lakes. Dust floated down from the volcanoes beyond the highlands. Araucaria pines towered 150 feet above the forest floor, the tops of ginkgos, tree ferns, and cycads below them. Giant bat-like pterosaurs flapped scaly wings against the sky, maintaining balance with their long, flat-tipped tails. Crocodiles sunned themselves by the marsh.

And yet he did remember his father complaining about her. How she never cleaned, never helped them at all. He held a mental image of his father throwing her out. Her screaming, crying, reaching. "I want my baby, my baby!" Freddy couldn't be sure.

Apatosaurus raises its great head above the plants. Forty tons, plant eater. Cold eyes. Its head comes crashing.

Freddy loved a woman in Rangely. Because of her he allowed himself to stay overnight there on Fridays. But it scared him, loving someone like that. She might leave. She might vanish. And he didn't like waking up in Rangely; the first thing you saw were those barren white sandstone hills.

He loved her. He was sure of that. His love filled him, and formed one of the three anchors of his life, along with the memories of his father and the thoughts of dinosaurs. But lately something felt lacking. Some crisis, some drama. Loving her didn't feel like quite enough.

He wasn't sure why they'd never gotten married. The time had never seemed right for either of them, but after a time he realized that the time would never seem right. One time she was going to have his baby, but she miscarried. No one else had known about it.

Wasn't time for it, he supposed; its time had passed. He didn't believe in God or heaven, but sometimes he wondered if the baby might *be* somewhere. Hiding from him. Or waiting for him.

It was the same all over. They had friends—lovers and married couples—and all of them seemed to be breaking up. Still loving each other, but unable to stay together.

Sometimes his drives from Meeker to Rangely were specifically to see Melinda, but he almost never thought about her during the trip.

He thought about his father, and dinosaurs.

Freddy looked out the side window of the pickup. Sagebrush flats, rising sandstone buttes, creek beds turned to sand. Old wrecks out in the fields. Before the oil men there had been cowboys, a few farmers. Before them, the outlaws hiding out. Before the outlaws, fur traders maneuvering through the canyons.

Before that, Indians trading along the Green and Yampa rivers. Before that, dinosaurs roaming the hot, wet lowlands.

Freddy had watched his father slowly become obsolete, running out of things he could do, running out of places to live. The drinking had grown steadily worse, his father had gone from job to job, they had moved from shack to shack . . .

His father's great head, his enormous body falling, crashing into wood, Freddy scrambling to get out of the way of the rapidly descending bulk . . .

And then his father had left, vanished. Freddy had been seventeen. He had a vague memory of his father walking away, across the flat into dust-filled air. It had been early morning— Freddy had been trying to wake up, but couldn't quite manage it, and had fallen back into the covers. He'd been abandoned.

Freddy did minor legal work for one of the oil companies. Easy assignments, dealing with the local landowners on rights-of-way, leasing, sometimes the complaints of an especially disgruntled employee. Most of the time he sat behind his desk in Rangely reading a book, or daydreaming. In the office he had a full library on dinosaurs and other mysteriously vanished races and species. Many days he saw no one, and he ate his lunch at his desk.

Today was Friday, and he would be staying over at Melinda's place. Melinda taught school some distance from Rangely— rancher's kids, mostly—and Freddy often wondered why she didn't live closer to her work. But she said she liked Rangely. Over the weekend they would be visiting her father's grave on Douglas

Mountain. Her father had faded after a long, consuming illness. She'd been at his bed most of that time, waiting for him to leave her, but still not quite believing it when he finally abandoned her, his eyes going away into grey.

Freddy felt a bit guilty, but he had to admit he looked forward to it. The wild horses they called "broomies" roamed Douglas Mountain, one of the last such herds in the west. A dry and rocky highland there, over 450 square miles. The herd had been there for more than a hundred years, beginning with horses which had wandered off from the farms and ranches and gone wild. They were beautiful to see, wild and alive. Melinda's father used to catch a few, work with them. Then he'd died.

Melinda's old Dodge was already at her house. Something was wrong; she usually came in an hour after him. He walked inside; she was standing at the old fashioned sink, her back to him.

"They're closing the school," she said quietly, not bothering to turn around.

"Why?"

Now she turned, looking slightly surprised. "What do you mean *why*? It could have happened anytime; you know that. Enough of the ranchers have moved away . . . there aren't enough to support it now. One of the ranchers bought it; I hear he's going to turn it into a barn."

He felt stupid. "When is all this supposed to happen?"

"End of the term. Three weeks." She looked up at him. "I'll be moving away, Fred. I've spent too much time here; I've exhausted all the possibilities. I . . ." She looked at him sadly. "I can't get what I need here anymore."

He couldn't meet her gaze. He walked around the kitchen slowly, looking at things. He knew it was a habit which infuriated her, but he couldn't seem to help it.

"I . . . don't want you to go," he said finally. Then he tried to look at her directly, to show that he really meant what he was saying. He couldn't quite manage it, but he thought he was at least close. Maybe she wouldn't perceive any difference. "Don't leave me," he said in her general direction. "I love you."

"I love you, too, Fred. I really do. But that isn't enough these days, is it?"

"It should be, but it isn't. I'm not sure why."

"I don't know either; things are changing. Everywhere."

He held her for a time, but he knew it was simply a gesture. A last, not-so-dramatic gesture for some kind of end.

They went to see her father's gravesite anyway. It was a rough haul over broken land, and try as he might Freddy found it impossible to think about Melinda, the loss of her. As much as he cared, he found himself again thinking of dinosaurs, imagining serpentine necks rising up over the hills. Again he recounted the ways they all might have died.

Some thought the mountain-forming upheavals at the close of Cretaceous time must have killed them off. But why weren't the other animals destroyed? A favourite theory used to be that disease, a series of plagues, wiped them out. Or racial old age. Some people claimed it was the wrath of God.

The most popular theory held that they were exterminated because the world became a colder place, maybe when a giant meteorite struck the earth, the resultant dust cloud obscuring the sun.

But no theory seemed quite adequate to explain such a complete, worldwide extinction.

Perhaps they had known it was their time. Perhaps something within their bodies or within their reptilian, primeval dream had told them that their era had come to an end. They had had no choice but to accept. The others had left them behind. He imagined them going off somewhere to die, their great bodies piling up. And the world had gone on without them.

His father's massive head striking the floor, his great weight shaking little Freddy where he hid beneath the table. The large eyes rolling, the mouth loose and shapeless, groaning . . .

They went to her father's gravesite holding hands, not saying anything. Douglas Mountain was beautiful, the broken land made to seem purposeful, aesthetically pleasing in its shape by means of the fields of grey-green sage. There was no one to disturb them; this was real back country. Tooley-wads, the old-timers called it.

The grave was well kept; they had spent a good deal of time during their courtship on the mountain, and frequently they puttered around the grave and its monument. An old tree crooked its branches above the plain stone, and hanging from it were her dad's stirrups, lariat, a few of his leather-working tools, and a branding iron from his first job as a hand. Like a small museum. Artefacts already ancient-seeming and near-forgotten.

The wind picked up and lifted Melinda's sandy hair off her shoulders. "Sow coon," she whispered, and laughed softly. "Sow coon" was cowboy talk for a bad storm. Freddy thought he'd heard a horse, several, whinnying and pawing at the dirt behind them. He looked nervously around and saw nothing but a grey dust cloud spinning up with the breeze. His father used to say that the "signs" were always here if you just knew how to read them. Nature's secret messages. You could tell what was coming if you just knew what to look for. Freddy imagined his father out there in the dusk with the long lost horses, dinosaurs all, hiding, watching him.

"Where's the broomies?" he asked her.

"Here somewhere. They're a bit shy these days."

Freddy shivered and pulled closer to her. He looked back over his shoulder. A small column of the dust was settling, but for a moment it had looked like a horse's leg, bending, then slamming into the dirt. He could hear fiery air being forced through large nostrils. Ghost sounds, he thought. Then all was silent again, the air cleared, and Freddy could see for miles around. No dust, no disturbance of the slopes or barren, windswept flats to be seen. No life.

"I think they're gone," he said to her, staring out over the bare slopes. "My God, I think they're all finally gone."

She looked up at him, but did not reply.

"Love won't save us," he said.

Again the enormous head crashed into unconsciousness.

Hours later, Freddy was ordering another beer, staring at the sleeping cowboy at the table next to him. He hadn't been inside a Rangely bar since his father had disappeared. He hadn't been drunk in years.

The bar was lit by a few yellow lights. Cowboys and oil workers shifted in the dimness, each becoming the other, losing resolution. The darkness of the bar absorbed most of their vague individual shadows, but those Freddy could see seemed much too bulky. They shouted, almost howling, their mouths wide, cavernous, and it hurt his ears.

He found himself examining the tabletop. Ever more closely the more he drank. What he saw there, finally, scratched into the surface, seemed to be some sort of pictograph. Picture writing. Kokopelli, the flute player. The Fremont Indians, what was it . . .

AD. 1000? Freddy glanced up into the shadows, trying to find someone who might have carved it. He thought he saw a face darker than the others, a painted face, but then the area seemed to soot over again, two cowboys moving into the space. He fingered the carving gently . . . old, worn. Down around the Cub Creek area Freddy had seen a number of them. As teenagers, he and some of the guys used to camp out there, shooting at the pictures. He felt hot shame now, just thinking about it, and even at the time he had felt as if he'd done something dirty. The Fremonts had gone away around AD. 1150. Vanished into the hills. No one knew why.

"It was their time," he whispered to no one. "Their hearts weren't in it any more."

The shadows in the bar were moving, dancing up the walls. Horses thundering in the dark. Fremont Indians. The cowboys and oil workers seeming to dance with them. And behind them all, the awesome bulk of an ancient, thundering reptile, tilting, falling . . .

"Hey, boy, you look rode hard an' put away wet." A tall cowboy was slapping Freddy on the back. He blinked, and looked at him. The cowboy grinned back. "Buy you a drink?"

"Sure, sure," Freddy said blearily. It was hard to keep the old fellow in focus.

The cowboy sat down. "Been huntin' coyote up on the White River, thought I'd come into town an' stay out with the dry cattle." Freddy stared at him blankly. "Have a night on the town, don't you know." The cowboy looked around. "Been up too long, I reckon. Last night I was sufferin' the mill tails o'Hell, boy, drunk too much I 'aspect, and all the she stuff was just them old sisters . . . made me so swole had to pick a fight with one o'those riggers, just a youngun, put 'em down till he hauled out callin' me to the street. Beat 'em fine, rimfired the kid, but Lord! Stove up today!" He looked at Freddy and winked.

"You . . . trap coyotes? You can make a living doing that?"

"Middlin', for what she's worth," he said. "Hell, it's a life."

"A life . . ." Freddy said sadly, guzzling the beer. "Not much left . . ."

"Now that's a fact! Cobbled up way to live, but it was a livin'. After I'm gone won't nobody know what happened, won't nobody know how I lived!"

Freddy stared into the tobacco-stained teeth. The smile growing wider, expanding, growing lopsided, the rugged, enormous face falling, falling . . .

But it was Freddy's face falling, crashing into the wooden tabletop.

Freddy woke up on Monday with the sun burning his face. He rubbed his dry skin, afraid to open his eyes, certain someone had just dragged him out of the Rangely bar and left him lying in the desert. Then the ground seemed to soften a bit beneath him, he opened one eye, and found himself in his own bed in Meeker, with all his clothes on. "How . . ." he mumbled, then realized the old cowboy must have driven him home.

Freddy stumbled out of the bed and looked around the house, but the man was nowhere to be seen. Freddy's pickup was parked in the front yard. The cowboy must have hitched back into Rangely. Or gone out into the mountains or the prairie, back into hiding. Vanishing. Dying.

He sat down on the edge of the bed and rubbed his neck. The bed table clock said two. Hardly worth going into work now, but he supposed he should. He didn't have any appointments today, so he doubted they had missed him.

The house seemed unusually quiet. A light breeze ruffled the curtains over the open window, and there were no sounds from outside. No car engines, no children playing. He felt vaguely agitated. A sudden ripple of anxiety washed over his upper body. The hair on the back of his neck prickled. Strange feeling.

His coal black cat walked into the room. She stopped suddenly, turned her head, and stared at him. He saw her tensing, her back rising. She pinned him with her eyes, unmoving. He started to approach her, but she raced away with a sharp cry. Freddy couldn't understand it. It was almost as if she hadn't expected to see him.

The wind coming through the window seemed to rise, the temperature to drop, so that suddenly he was feeling sharp and cold gusts penetrating the room in an almost rhythmical pattern. He walked to the window to shut it, but stopped and stuck his head outside. The position was too awkward to see very much, but no matter how much he strained his head this way or that, he could see no one, hear no one. A few dogs moved quietly through the streets. Cars were parked, empty.

It took him only a few minutes to slap some water onto his face and get ready for work. He didn't bother with a shower. He slid into the pickup, started the engine, and pulled out onto Meeker's main street, waiting for the images of his father to come once again.

He stopped after two blocks. He got out of his truck.

Cars and trucks were parked awkwardly on both sides of the street, straddling alleys, parked in the wrong direction, pulled up on the curb, stopped too far out in the street. The engines had been turned off, the doors shut firmly, but it seemed as if the drivers hadn't really cared where they left them. Maybe it hadn't mattered where they had left them.

There was no one in sight. He walked around the main part of town; two dogs raced away when they saw him. The doors to the stores and cafes were wide open. Food still on the tables, but the grills and coffee pots had been turned off. Someone had left the radio on, but there was only static. On all channels. "Where are you hiding now?" he whispered softly.

Freddy ran out to the pickup and spun the wheels. He stopped, took a deep breath, then headed out toward Rangely. Off in the distance, a tall figure in battered hat and faded jeans was walking toward the mountains.

"Hey! Hey!" Freddy shouted, but the figure did not turn.

The wheels took the curves on edge, the arroyos drew him, the washouts beckoned him. He flashed on his broken body, twisted under the wreck down in one of the deeper gulleys, but still he pressed down on the accelerator, spinning the steering wheel.

But the receding figure was always too far away, and the road did not lead there.

"Hey! Cowboy!" Freddy shouted.

The cowboy did not turn, but continued to go away, to vanish.

He passed other vehicles abandoned at the side of the road. He saw no one on the hillsides but an occasional rabbit.

For the first time he could remember, the image of his father did not come to him.

Miles later—he had not kept track of the time—he stopped just within the city limits of Rangely, unable to drive on. A cold wind filled the streets with dust. There were no lights in the buildings, even with the overcast skies. A door banged repeatedly. At the periphery of his vision he was aware of the oil wells pumping on, unattended, unwatched.

He would not go to her house only to find her gone. He would not look at her things, the relics left behind.

It was well past dark by the time Freddy reached the top of Douglas Mountain. He had seen no human beings along the way.

He hadn't expected to.

Where did the dinosaurs go? the teacher asked again. Most of the standard answers were covered. The cute little girl in front of Freddy, the one he had such a desperate crush on, said that God had done it, and several in the class agreed. Freddy gave the answer about the plague of caterpillars. He liked caterpillars.

He stood above the old horse breaker's grave. Her father's grave. She wouldn't have a grave. None of them would. There wouldn't be anyone left to bury them. But maybe there'd be a quarry full of bones, and whatever might be there in the times ahead would dig them up and arrange them in display cases and dioramas.

The metal relics in the tree clanged together in the high wind. It was dark below, but Freddy thought he could see shadows moving there. Reflections of himself, maybe, inverse shadows. He was sure he could hear the wild horses thundering, the Fremont Indians calling to them, the trappers, the outlaws—or maybe that was his father's face in the darkness? Maybe that's where he went . . . all those years . . .

"I'm really the most ignorant of dinosaurs," he whispered to the shadows. "We're already extinct, and here I am talking to the dark. Here I am, again the one they've left."

He crouched down and leaned forward, straining his eyes.

Nothing.

"Don't leave me behind!" he shouted. "Don't *abandon* me!" He touched his head softly, then scratched at his cheeks. He had not heard an echo. "I love you . . ." he whispered, but he had lost the names.

The wind seemed to rise, colder, but then he knew it was a wind inside him, and he imagined it starting somewhere near the base of his spine, sweeping up over the intestines, the liver, the heart, picking up odd cells of flesh and bone as it went, taking old memories to the brain . . .

"Take me along," he whispered.

And he felt his head beginning to fall, as if from a great height. Pulling him somewhere.

GIANT
KILLERS

His name was Walt, but he much preferred Dad, also Daddy, when there was way too much fun to be had. Had with his two little boys, James and Terry, age six and seven, more or less. Every afternoon he was their giant, also mountain, also dragon, also cloud of delicious tickle.

"I . . . can't . . . stop . . . tickling!" he cried, and his sons died in laughter.

He came from a long line of giants, his father, his grandfather, big men who filled a room, big men in control of things, although they didn't necessarily want to be. Big men who remembered they had once been little boys, but were not too sure of all the details. Little boys who had swollen with time and ripened into giants, and who no longer knew how to fit the tiny spaces they'd been crammed into.

There was a great deal of responsibility in being a giant. Little people were everywhere, crawling over your shoes, getting into spaces you hadn't even noticed were there, chattering away in their secret languages, singing of their tiny joys. A distracted little person might easily be crushed because of your one misstep.

The giant Walt loved the little people in his house. In fact he had no words gigantic enough to express the size of his adoration. He was prouder of their small accomplishments than of the largest things he had ever done. At the same time they made him feel lonely in his isolated mental room high in the clouds. They had magically given uncertainty a physical form. They held it mysteriously in their fragile little bodies and in the regular but unpredictable pace of their hearts. He hated that they were so delicate, so ephemeral. Like fairies. Like dreams. Their impermanence horrified.

Now and then during the long afternoons of play he became almost convinced they were imaginary creatures, the results of some enchantment, some befuddlement of the senses. If he could only turn around quickly enough he might witness their transparency, their wings, their horns. But a giant's body is a slow, deliberate thing, hobbled by syrupy circulation and glacial reaction. So sometimes he was too rough with them, hoping to shake them free of spell and charm. He always felt terrible afterwards, and they always giggled.

When they climbed across his gigantic shoulders or balanced on his enormous knees, he had to restrain his movements in case one might fall. Some days his fears for their safety kept him locked behind the great door to his room, silent and frozen even as they wailed and beat dramatically on the other side.

"Come out and play with us!" they cried. "We're so bored!" they insisted. He'd rather lose an eye than wound their feelings, but all he could manage in response was some helpless growl.

But these minions, these Lilliputians, were not to be dissuaded. These little people were insane—he supposed it was their smallness that made them so. They maintained that chatter and dance until bed and after. Their lives were so much bigger than they could contain, and they did not know what to do with themselves.

Unable to tolerate their high pitched whining, he would periodically leave his bed and settle on the rug in the great hall, holding himself still as they climbed and hung from his neck and arms. They screamed gleefully as they beat on his massive chest and head. Sometimes he snarled, but only because they wanted him to. Most of the time he simply sat there, measuring out his patience.

Then in a moment of possibly feigned mania he threw off his children, laid them side by side on the battered floor and hovering over them shouted "I'm going to eat you! I'm going to eat you!" over and over again, putting his lips to their necks, their arms, their bellies, pausing to breathe in their dusty little-boy smells, then considered, considered, before opening his mouth and carefully pretending to bite.

They screamed, horrified, and laughed until they made themselves dizzy.

They were clever, these boys, and always got him back: a box of trash tipped from the top of a door, a rug full of marbles, jacks, and tiny, slippery cars. He fell more than once, he fell more than twice, and yet all he could think was how reassuring it was, because this is the way you survive in a world full of giants.

Today he's a mountain they can climb. He crouches to make it easier. The first one to the top plants a flag in his eye. He knows he is every impossible job they will ever have, every unreasonable boss. He is the hole that opens in the road, the dark cavern that has no ending, the terrible disappointment at the end of the day.

He knows that sometimes it is the giant in him that makes them feel so out of control. If they go too far he grabs and bear hugs the madness out of them. His enormous sad eyes see everything. He glares down at their pale, translucent faces from his so-different weather.

This morning he is their origin and their desire. This afternoon he is the seemingly unyielding shape of their destiny. At evening he is their demise.

Out of his body came everything they are, and yet to kill him would make them successful beyond their wildest dreams. Of course they should outlast him—giants are too big for their own good. In the final analysis, he is a dysfunction of disproportion.

When sleep finally comes the giant-killers dream of the giant who lives in these mountains. They can see his legs and arms sprawled into ridges, his enormous head in that peculiar stand of trees. In his sleep and theirs they are safe to live another night inside him. But they all know that other day will come. They pack their bags with crackers and Kool-Aid for the journey. He washes himself until every thread of dead skin has vanished into the drain. They gather their bats and rackets, sharpen the tiny nails at the ends of their skinny fingers. He sits quietly on his great landscape of rug, patiently awaiting the arrival of his beautiful sons.

THE COMPANY YOU KEEP

Richard lived alone in an apartment above a decrepit carriage house off an alley in the oldest part of the city. He believed that once upon a time rich people had occupied the neighbourhood— that's why there were so many large houses (now divided and re-divided) and oversize utility buildings, like his carriage house. These had been people whose faces and reputations were known, even written about. People who might sneak out in disguise from time to time for a brief vacation in anonymity, that place where he—and most people he knew—lived all their lives.

Of course, the rich all picked up and drifted away at the first smell of shabbiness, not even waiting until that shabbiness made its actual appearance. Now he survived as best he could, the end recipient of a progression of hand-me-downs.

He'd been in the carriage house at least twenty years. When he attempted to recollect his move-in day more precisely, he became irretrievably lost in the lies and self deceptions of memory. Surely, it couldn't have been that long ago. Surely, it had. Surrounded as it was by taller buildings with thicker walls, and a shadowing backdrop of huge trees preserved through some rich woman's personal campaign, it was quieter here than a room so close to the heart of the city's commerce had any right to be.

"People will judge you by your companions," Richard's father once said, responding to one of the countless confessions Richard had made concerning some trouble he and various friends had gotten themselves into. "You become known by the company you keep."

Good advice, he thought now. Very perceptive. But unbeknown to his father, somewhat off the point, as all of Richard's confessions had been lies. There had been no trouble. No legal entanglements due to bad influences, no youthful misadventures with peers less conscientious than he, despite dozens of such tales told and retold.

Richard would much rather have his father think he chose his companions poorly than know that Richard had no companions at all.

Not that he lied out of shame. He simply didn't want to have to explain himself to his father. Although he'd always desired friends, he wasn't sure what friendship might mean for him. He'd imagined the state of friendship as one in which your friend understood you, supporting your dreams, empathizing with your failures and imperfections. Someone always on your side. But he'd seldom seen such friendship in the relationships of others. And over the years his idea of a friend seemed increasingly improbable, a creature more at home among unicorns and banshees. Loneliness, on the other hand, was something he could always bank on, a predictable destination at the end of every workday when solitude became total, but more than that, an attitude he might carry with him into the office, out to restaurants, even into one of the increasingly rare social gatherings he might feel duty-bound to attend. He had come to carry that loneliness around with him much the way a monk carried bliss.

It would be difficult to say precisely when he discovered that his particular brand of solitude might not be as simple as all that. But certainly it solidified the day he met the pale man on the corner by the library.

Richard had been returning some long-overdue travel guides. He'd been in a hurry—he didn't like to linger in or near the library. Something about the enforced quiet, and all that wealth of information at your disposal if you knew the right questions to ask. But of course Richard never knew the right questions to ask.

Although there'd been no particular reason to isolate this one man among the many who gathered there that day, there had been something about the posture—something vaguely anticipatory about the man's stance—that filled Richard with a sudden, peculiarly overwhelming, and inexplicable empathy for this lone figure awash in the torrents of flesh, bone, leather, and cloth that flooded the sidewalks of this inhospitable concrete sprawl.

For a brief moment the man had turned to face him, and Richard had been struck immediately by the paleness of the face; then a look as of recognition vaguely distorted the sheet-white features, and the man turned away with a kind of desperate speed, stumbled, and almost fell.

Richard might have forgotten all about the incident, despite the strong impression of the man's seemingly bloodless complexion, when several other people in that vicinity made the same stumbling move.

Nothing remarkable or similar about these individuals in any way, both men and women, a variety of races, dress, and facial types— and yet for some reason they had stumbled almost identically.

But stranger still had been Richard's reaction. He felt as if he knew them, although surely he'd never seen them before. They were like him. They were meant for greater things they did not understand. They possessed capacities unrecognized, even to themselves. They had lived their lives as solitary warriors, and now at last their army had begun to form.

He had no idea why he should think such things. His life had not altered appreciably in years. He had seen no signs of change, had heard no call. No one approached him in the street, and at work he was still known by his last name and the relative coordinates of his cubicle walls.

When he was a boy he'd imagined himself imbued with superpowers. The drawback had always been that he didn't know what those powers might entail. But he had faith that they would reveal themselves at the appropriate time: A child would fall from a window and he would suddenly find himself flying up to catch her. Some disaster would occur—a factory explosion, a collapsed parking garage, a hospital on fire—requiring his unusual strength and courage. Everyone would be surprised by his transformation, but no one more so than he.

Richard was due for a two o'clock appointment up on the sixth floor. He found himself at the elevator in the lobby at a quarter till. He'd developed this habit of referring to himself in the third person. Found himself was a deliberate choice of words—often lately he would catch himself that way, find himself in some location or situation with no clear memory of what came immediately before. 253

It was a small group gathered before the elevator, staring at the downward progress of numbers over the doors as if in suspense over the outcome. Normally he would fix his own eyes on that fascinating numeric display, but in recent weeks his habit had become to examine the members of any group he might find himself in, looking for some vague confirmation of questions he had no language for, seeking some signal or sign, some indication that he had at last landed in the right place and time.

There was nothing remarkable about any of these people: four men and three women dressed in grey, black, and brown business attire. The one Hispanic woman who'd attempted to add colour with an orange scarf looked uncomfortable in it, as if the attempt might strangle her. One of the men was taller than the others by a few inches. He appeared to stoop further the longer they waited, as if attempting to reduce himself before anyone noticed.

They barely left room for the exiting passengers as they rushed into the opening doors, but those they jostled betrayed no discomfort at this, nor did Richard's group appear aware that they might have created some discomfort.

Once inside, they fit closely together. The elevator seemed to ascend slowly, as if hauling weight well beyond its posted limits. Richard watched as the man in front of him placed a hand on his right hip, sending a narrow elbow against the Hispanic woman, who in return leaned away and placed her own right hand on her own right hip.

The man beside her did the same. And the man beside him, all around to Richard, who, so embarrassed he found it difficult to breathe, did the same.

The man ahead of him put one foot forward and the others, including Richard, did the same.

A very slight shuffle to the right and a step back. Richard struggled to maintain his composure, did the step just the same, feeling as if he'd been kidnapped. By the time they reached the sixth floor, he felt barely capable of exiting. He turned quickly to see what might be in their faces, but they'd fallen back into their still, stuffed positions. He entered the offices of the insurance company sweaty and disheveled. And sorry to have left the elevator behind.

He was told he was ten minutes late and would have to wait an hour for the next appointment. The clock above the receptionist's desk pointed to two o'clock exactly, but he did not object. The reception area was full. He found a solitary chair against the wall, mostly hidden by a large potted plant. He had to remove a large pile of magazines from the seat in order to sit down. Not seeing any place to put these, he pulled them into his lap, hugging them and hunching over to keep them from falling.

A few feet away a fat man raised his right hand slowly and placed it on the front part of his head, immediately above the hairline, pressing down with obvious strain, as if trying to keep one particular train of thought from jumping track.

On the other side of the reception area, almost behind the desk, Richard saw another man—well-groomed, hair slicked back—do the same.

A younger man with his face buried in a financial magazine raised his hand slowly, palm up and wavering like a snake's head, then brought it over in a stretch-like motion, finally settling it somewhat surreptitiously onto the same region of his head.

Richard's vision filled with the nervous flapping of shadows like dozens of birds exhausted from their long journey. He closed his eyes, looking for his place of quiet solitude, and, unable to find it, opened them again. The men still held their heads in the same way, as if waiting.

Richard searched a last time for a place to put down the magazines, and, failing that, raised his hand high and slapped it over the same region of his head. The magazines crashed to the floor and spread in a wave over the shoes of the people sitting nearest him. Everyone in the room glanced his way except for the three men with hands on their heads, who now lowered their hands without a glance in his direction. He felt his face burning, got up, and left the office.

Out on the sidewalk and everyone appeared to be walking his way. As he pushed through them they raised arms and elbows, overlapping one against the other as if to prevent his flight. On the next street corner a small group stood off to themselves, wrists raised at exactly the same angle as they stared at watches that were missing, pale bands of skin left as evidence.

He felt only a whisper of guilt about stealing a car. Richard manoeuvred the stolen car through streets full of chatting, focused people, people with important appointments to go to, places to see, definite things to do, conversations to have, parties to attend, shadows to scatter, loneliness to bury in a cascade of forced laughter.

He at last felt the growing anxiety of someone with a destination. And he would not permit a crowd of other people, those people, the people whose full lives had always put the lie to the so-called life he had cobbled together on his own, to delay him in any way, make him late for the meeting he had waited for all his life.

It saddened him that the truth of it had never been clear to him before, that people like him, people who had endured a solitary desperation all their lives, required no words for their secret communications, that their private handshakes demanded no actual exchange of touch, that their meeting places were spontaneous and secret even unto themselves, that, like the early Christian churches in a world of persecution, they met wherever and whenever more than one of them came together in one place.

Richard looked out the driver's-side window into another car that had pulled alongside. He wagged his head to the left, veered the stolen car to the left, and that other driver did the same. And another car beside that one, as a result driving up onto the sidewalk, ploughing over the crowds there, striking the front wall of a department store, exploding into flame.

Richard grimly focused again on the road to his destination, hoping that none of the people he had recently recognized were out on the sidewalk just then, and sparing a good thought for the brave and devoted driver who had no doubt lost his life in service to the cause.

But of course we are legion, he thought. When one of us dies there is always another to take his or her place. We always thought we were alone, and our gratitude at discovering our belonging knows no bounds.

The building ahead of him looked little different from the rest, which was appropriate. No crowds pushed inside as if this were some concert hall or sporting event;, and that, too, was appropriate. Because no matter how many of them there might be they would never be a crowd, not in the way these successful and fulfilled unenlightened ones made a crowd.

Richard was pleased to see that no one lingered around the entrance to the building. No one paid it any particular attention, and that was as expected, and wonderfully, joyfully, appropriate.

He stopped the car a few feet from the entrance and abandoned it there. Going in he glanced at the sky, the way the roofline pierced it so nicely, demanding respect.

A few gathered before the elevators, joining him as he made his way through the doors, repeating his gesture of rubbing at his left eye (let it not offend), scratching at his neckline (let it bare itself before thee), pulling at his trousers (my legs belong to you).

They were on the rooftop, waiting, although they did not appear to be waiting. They did not appear even to be aware that others were up on this rooftop with them. They stared at the sky. They stared at the streets below and at the horizon of stone and steel containers stretching in all directions. His company. His associates. They did not look at each other.

But they were here together. Richard understood that the way of silence, the way of solitude, was their way. There was no plan or determination. None was needed.

Well after it began, Richard realized there were fewer of them. Then fewer still. Then he saw a few slip over the edges, like birds sucked one by one into a rising tide of wind.

He was proud that when his own urge arrived he did not hesitate, but floated across the border between gravity and release without a second thought.

They descended like huge, mad fowl, their mouths open in anger or weeping. There were a few hundred or more, and it was said that the way they twisted as they fell to their deaths, the way they swept their arms and legs out viciously in their final few feet of air, they seemed to be trying to kill as many in the crowds below them as they could.

CELESTIAL INVENTORY

DOORS

When he first moved into the apartment the number of doors in such small quarters seemed excessive and bothersome. He had never lived on his own before, and had never imagined that so many entrances and exits might be necessary.

Entering the front door he found himself thinking of his uncle Simon, whose death had made all this possible. Uncle Simon had lived on his own for over twenty years, seldom leaving his small house upstate, and seldom spending any money. In the will, he had explained that he was leaving his money to his nephew because "he is without a doubt the one who best understood my life style."

There was something vaguely disconcerting about such a judgment by a relative he hardly even knew, but he accepted the money. His annoyance with all the doors he had purchased was easily explained: in an ideal universe his preference would have been for one grand and enormous front door which he might enter once and never bother exiting again.

His new front door was far from grand, however. No stronger, really, than any of his interior doors, except for an additional lock. Still, he experienced a breathless moment of transition as he passed over the threshold, a stepping from theirs to his, from there to here, from exterior to interior. To open that door was to travel a long distance.

He realized that his actions would make many people regard him as a man who hated other human beings. But he simply had no talent for friendship, no aptitude for social interaction, and to people like him the agony of social contact eventually becomes unbearable. He had no hatred for people; quite the contrary—he loved even their eccentricities, and especially their weaknesses, which made him feel more a part of them, even at this self-imposed distance. But to watch them talking to each other one to one, laughing, embracing—this he could not stand, because he was quite incapable of participating.

Besides the front door he counted five more. The front door led him directly into an area that, depending on the furniture, could be either a living room or bedroom. Another door in this room fronted a closet (doors on closets had always seemed a fake to him, a deception as to the number of options one had). Two separate doors led to a combination kitchen and dining area. He supposed in larger quarters two doors would have eased traffic but in an apartment of this size they made no sense. He believed that at one time the apartment building had been a large private dwelling, so perhaps the long-ago subdivision into rooms had inadvertently created this anomaly. People didn't always adequately consider how their actions might affect people in the future—such short-sightedness was a basic human trait, he believed.

A fifth door led to a bathroom, although he did not know how useful a bathroom door would be, since he would be living here alone and could not imagine himself entertaining guests. But it was the sixth door which troubled him most: opening it, he discovered a bricked-in opening with an old calendar taped to this new wall. He despised such architectural trickery, and over this door hung a tattered quilt which he would never once remove.

The apartment also had two windows, which were like doors in that they were a kind of passage. But unlike proper doors which were practical, actual, and at times adventuresome, windows were for visionary pursuits, for dreaming, for planning trips the legs might or might not take.

After a few months in the apartment he began to see the doors differently. The front door became a hatch, a lid to protect his private activities here. The closet door still seemed to have little function, although it became the door used in most of his dreams. The privacy of the bathroom door achieved its purpose when he realized that sometimes he liked to be concealed from the presence even of his own things, the props which dressed his life. The covered door remained covered, too dangerous to tamper with.

But his attitude had changed most profoundly toward the two doors which separated the two halves of his apartment. These doors provided him with enough variety in movement and sufficient creativity in his transitions from space to space that he became confident for the first time that he might be able to remain in this apartment for the rest of his life, with only occasional ventures into the outside world for supplies. These doors encouraged his appreciation of an economical approach to living. They provided him with healthy exercise, recreation, and imaginative entertainments. If he passed through the doors in different ways they became metaphors for a variety of modes of travel, from boat to Ferris wheel. And after a time he became adept at imagining a different landscape thrown down before him each time he passed through one of the doors.

It was the wealth of association inherit in these doors, and his need to understand them all, which led him to the idea of the inventories.

The secret, he had discovered, was not how much you had, but how deeply you saw what you had.

And for the hermit, it was necessary to see very deeply indeed. The ordinary, he knew, could become extraordinary. His two rooms contained the stars. New universes grumbled in his belly. Through these doors lay the celestial. It would be essential to monitor his discards very carefully, else an enormous percentage of his life's significance might be lost.

COTTON BALLS

Along with steel wool, vinegar, and plastic wrap, his mother had depended on cotton balls. "A home isn't a home without cotton balls," she'd once declared in a near manic moment of dead seriousness. He'd been unable to suppress his laughter, and she'd treated him with contempt for almost two full days in consequence.

Over the years she'd developed hundreds of uses for the white puffs of near cloud: for applying makeup, for wiping noses, for reducing shoe sizes, for her endless craft projects, for miscellaneous padding. Once she'd tried to replace the left eyeball of his stuffed teddy bear with a cotton ball painted black in the middle to suggest a pupil. It frayed so badly that the bear's eyeball soon seemed to have exploded.

But most importantly, she used them to administer various sorts of medicinal aid. He could remember vividly the soft press of them against his skin as she cooed and sang to him, trying to soothe his hurts both real and imaginary. Eventually the touch of cotton balls came to represent for him the touch of her own gentle fingertips.

He had bought several boxes of cotton balls before he first moved into the apartment—keeping in mind his mother's definition of a "home"—but had never really found any use for them. Years later, they were scattered everywhere, like the corpses of tiny white mice, or like a purer, angelic variety of the "dust bugs" which now and then spontaneously generated among his inventory. He was always trying to think up some sort of practical use for them, feeling that his adulthood was somehow less than complete if cotton balls did not play a major role.

It was during a moment of half sleep one evening—his eyes shut down to slits, the air of the room gone grey with his weary brain cells—that he felt his mother's fingertips along his arm, urging him to stir.

He awakened to find a row of cotton balls pressed against his skin, their bodies spread slightly from the force of their labours. In the greyness of the room they were almost luminous. One by one they removed themselves from his arm, as if a hand tilting, the fingertips lifting in order, left to right. Then they drifted down into the darkness which blanketed his things on the floor.

He got up then, determined to search through his apartment until he had located all his cotton balls. He didn't turn on the overhead light, afraid of scaring them away, but carried a flashlight for sudden, surprising peeks into the darkness. He loved his mother, but now she was dead and he was on his own. He would not have her just suddenly dropping into his apartment this way.

He felt, rather than heard, the soft presence of the cotton balls as they gathered in the darkness to make a larger, even softer shape. He flashed the light past his empty closet as the cloud that was his mother's back turned from him and drifted into the shadows.

"Mother! You have no right!" he shouted, and pursued her with the flash, which refused to get a fix on her, always trailing her vague outline. Now he noticed the vagueness of the light from the flashlight itself, how it consisted of a series of pale concentric halos, and then he realized that the flashlight would be useless to him for it was in league with the spirit world.

He turned off the flash and groped for his mother in the near dark, counting on chance illumination from the city lights outside his window to guide him. He stumbled through the room, careless of the inventory crunching beneath his feet, paused, then turned back to the window. His mother stood against the light, a shimmering softness of cotton strands stretched near the point of dissolution.

"Mother! This is not a good time!" he shouted, scooping random objects from the floor and tossing them at the form that was forty years dead.

The stretched cotton tore with a whisper, then jerked back as if elastic, bits and pieces of her flying through the room.

He never found another cotton ball, but the cobwebs in the far corners of his room seemed much whiter after that, and hummed with any slight breeze. And scattered strands of white, like ancient hair or cloud, appeared now and then on his clothing, stuck to a dinner plate, or floated at the edge of his bathwater. Try as he might, even after years he could never get the cotton balls completely out of his life.

TOY

It was a piece of a toy, the whole of the thing long forgotten. But the piece was clear enough: a carved wooden bear in a soldier's blue uniform with a tall red hat, a drum in one paw. The figure might once have been mounted on a cart or a music box.

It didn't really matter what function this piece of toy had originally served. He had been one of those children whose toys had never lasted more than twenty-four hours intact. The question was always what long time purpose a thing might serve for him, not its original purpose when purchased. As a child he sometimes had intentionally broken a toy in order to end the suspense.

The figure was his one bit of toy remaining, emblematic of a sparse childhood, and he discovered that by dropping it strategically among the objects cluttering his floors he could recreate various points in his past, emulating these periods in the rooms of his childhood.

Dropped among bottles and tissues, it was a day spent sick in bed, waiting for visitors who never came. Resting amid piles of unanswered correspondence, it was the last reminder of long forgotten friends. Wedged among scattered tools and leftover materials, it was projects left unfinished.

Its importance to his life had become muted since he'd stopped working, when so many of the objects of his adulthood became nonessentials, focal points for play. Toys. He began to wonder if life itself might be a toy to a dying man.

Eventually it began to bother him that he didn't know which toy the fragment might have been part of. He had had a wooden train set, he remembered, brightly painted cars and, in each, the wooden figure of some animal in costume. The soldier bear could have come from it. Or there was the make believe theatre he'd had when he was six. There had been animals in that, too. Or from even further back, he had the vaguest memory of tiny animals staring down at him from a contraption which bridged the open top of his crib. He supposed the little bear could have come from that as well.

Sometimes he placed the toy on the top of his desk and stared at it for a time, meditating on all those things he had wanted as a child but had gone without. Back then, one old toy would be used to represent a new one, fantastic but unobtainable. So that an old wooden truck became Batman's marvellous Batmobile, an empty box the Batcave, and an oddly shaped piece of wood wrapped in dark cloth was the Batman himself. These substitutions became far more elaborate and arbitrary as time went on: a loose wheel was a flying saucer, an aspirin bottle became King Kong, a lone chess piece the Invisible Man.

If he had ever had a child of his own this broken off bit of toy would have been all he could have passed on. And even this bit of bear was slowly losing its definition: the face almost completely worn away, a piece of the drum missing, the left arm strangely warped.

He thought briefly of taking the thing to someone for repairs. He devised desperate, last-ditch plans for saving the integrity of the thing. He never carried out any of them.

One day he couldn't find the toy. It had warped itself so completely as to be indistinguishable from all the other shape changing debris which had filled his rooms. It was up to him, then, to find the form his childhood had warped into. Of course, there were several possibilities: the ornament from an old car his mother had owned, or a fancifully turned piece that had once topped a bedpost, or a bright red key whose indentations resembled the city skyline as seen from the upstairs bedroom window he'd had as a boy.

He picked up the key and put it on a chain he wore around his neck for the remainder of his life, touching it each night before bed to make sure it was still there. At night it was a locomotive with his hand at the throttle, churning away below his chin and laying tracks across his chest. Or it was the tiniest chainsaw removing his left hand. Or it was a red backed beetle with three eyes and tiny razor blades for teeth.

But most of the time it remained a key. Even in his sleep he could hear the locks coming undone before its greater presence.

PITCHER

He owned a pitcher with no bottom. He speculated that perhaps at some point the bottom had broken off. He bought it at a small junk shop down the street and did not notice its abnormality until he arrived home with it. He remembered trying to fill it with water at his sink, and being amazed at how much water it could contain. Now it sat atop his refrigerator, filling with air, in case he might someday require an emergency supply.

APPLE

Once, rather than eat an apple, he sliced it in half and set it on his small kitchen table. The apple still had a three-quarter inch stem. He came to understand that this was the sole bit of nature which had entered his apartment in years. If he had a magnifying glass, he supposed it would show the streams and valleys hidden within the white flesh of the apple. After a period of intense scrutiny he came to realize that at the centre of the apple was a woman's genitalia. And within that, the dark seed. He pulled out the seed and kept it in an aspirin bottle in his medicine cabinet, and felt it now and then when he went to the bottle to remedy a headache. After a few hours the apple browned and wrinkled. One morning it was mysteriously missing from his table.

BATTERIES

He'd never been able to throw away batteries, even the alkaline type which could not be recharged. He'd long suspected that all batteries were the same, that some were just provided different labels so that the shopkeepers might charge more, but he had no desire to risk "explosion, leak, or personal injury." The objects in his room were sprinkled with such dire warnings—domestic life was a dangerous adventure.

But even the alkaline batteries had always seemed too substantial somehow to simply throw away. Batteries had too much weight, and with their sleek lines, their designated positive and negative poles, they seemed too important somehow simply to discard. He'd always admired their clean self containment. There was something almost magical about the way they could be snapped into a calculator, tool, or toy, and then bring that device to life. It was a bit like having a plug-in heart, or a plug-in soul. A source of great, invisible energy.

Occasionally he would pick up a supposedly dead battery and put it into something like a radio. Now and then the radio would crackle suddenly, as if a ghost struggling back into some sort of consciousness. With some batteries he tried this experiment again and again until he was sure they were indeed dead.

Batteries came in a variety of sizes, but in a smaller variety of voltages. This bothered him, that the slim AA size contained within it the same 1.5 volts as the comparatively massive D cell. Even the smaller batteries were solid, self contained, full of life.

He thought about experiences he'd had with batteries in the past. Once as a boy he'd found an old flashlight at the back of his father's closet. When it wouldn't switch on he'd opened up the case and discovered a kind of dried milk corrosion on the inside. He'd been horrified, as if he'd cut open a human body and peeked inside.

With some friends of his he did cut open a battery once with a hacksaw. Inside the steel and cardboard outside there had been another, softer metal, and inside that a dark paste around a solid black rod. When he held the black rod it gave him a feeling of raw power, as if he were holding somebody's still beating heart in his hand, as if he had just reached into them while they were walking by and pulled the bloody thing out. The stuff around the rod made his fingers itch.

His health teacher once said that people were like batteries, and had to be recharged periodically by rest and food. That made more sense to him the older he got.

He collected all the batteries he could find in his apartment—including the ones inside radios and other things—and put them into a pile. They were of all different types, powers, and sizes. Triple A's and double A's, the flat, odd-looking 6-volt size J's (he couldn't guess what he might have owned that that would have come out of), watch batteries, and others with no code or brand designation. The reason for the variety of shape and size quite escaped him.

A more significant mystery, of course, was that of electricity itself, which bothered him as much as an adult as it had as a child. It ran through wires like veins, but the wires weren't hollow like veins—he'd cut several different kinds open just to see. Electricity was invisible, mostly, except when it was at its most dangerous, when it was loose outside a wire or wall plug or appliance. That was when it was sparks or fire or a sharp jagged line like lightning. Then it could fry you, roast you, turn your hair to ash.

Outlets had never made much sense to him, how they could work. Until he'd had a gall bladder operation. They'd run a tube into his arm and the other end went up inside a bottle of glucose. His arm took the glucose because it needed it. When an appliance was plugged into an outlet it took out the electricity because it needed it.

When he reached his teen years he began to worry that perhaps electricity actually consisted of the souls of the dead. His parents didn't consider this a very viable theory and to express their criticism they hospitalized him for a time. But by the time he was released he believed in the validity of his theory even more. In the hospital had been these great fluorescent lights and when they were turned on they buzzed somewhat grumpily and flickered unevenly, as if spirits jostled into consciousness. Sometimes he would spend hours staring at a bare, incandescent bulb, until he believed he could see the faces of the departed in the brilliant glow.

Sometimes the electrical roar of a vacuum cleaner, clothes dryer, or can opener sounded like the voiced disappointments of dead neighbours or relatives.

He had let go of these theories by the time he had moved into the apartment, but he still could not throw away the batteries, these little vessels of the dead, these miniature phone booths of the hereafter.

DIRT

For all his clutter, his apartment was remarkably devoid of dirt. Sometimes he would search for dirt with almost a desperation, anxious to find any traces of the larger world outside. The antiseptic quality of his clutter bothered him frequently. He sometimes believed that a mysterious force—the elves, the aliens, the government—was removing his belongings while he slept, charting their exact positions much as a movie director's assistant might, cleaning them before returning them to their previous locations in the morning. The purpose of this procedure was beyond him, but he'd decided a long time ago that purposes were well beyond the understanding of the ordinary human being. Purposes were available only to those with access to the "big picture," and the big picture was the province of those you never met, who worked behind the scenes.

What little dirt remained, he was convinced, must have been left there for a purpose, as a kind of clue or message. So inventorying this dirt became a task of some significance.

There was always some dust behind his dresser. He had trouble classifying this furry substance—it had the greasiness, the cohesiveness of dirt, but it also seemed light and air filled, as is the nature of dust. The fact that some of this substance remained after the mysterious renewal of his room led him to believe that this was a message: perhaps a reminder of the transitory nature of matter, or the prospect of his imminent death.

A thick layer of dry, feathery dust had been left on the north side of one of his lamps. He was particularly impressed by the uniformity and thoroughness of this layer.

For a time he believed that the dirt had been left to mark the location where a death had occurred, where flesh had jelled and bone had flaked and crumbled, until eventually a residue of earth was all that remained, He'd read about how many bits of dead insect and animal existed in the average ounce of dirt—a nearly incalculable amount—but was more interested in how many bits of human form were to be found in the soil. He suspected this was a taboo statistic. Still, it would be good to know how many of the dead the average child carried in on his or her shoes every afternoon.

CLOSET

The closet was a strange area. He thought most people must think of the closet as a storage place, for keeping items out of sight of guests. But since he had chosen a lifestyle in which items remained in plain view, his closet seemed of little utility. Some closets, he supposed, might be doorways to other realities, but his seemed content to remain an appendage of space.

During inventory the closet did become handy as a waiting area. Items were moved there as they were counted, then moved out again. The closet was very useful at this, and helped him keep track of what he had counted.

Once, quite by accident, he stepped into his empty closet during inventory. He found himself standing there, gazing out of its doorway, into his apartment beyond. Suddenly it was as if the apartment was no longer his. He had stepped out of the everyday world, a child again, and now gazed into the life of his future self.

He waited for some time for his older self to re-enter the room so that he might see exactly how he had turned out. After a few hours it was obvious that this event would not occur. Disappointed, he stepped back into his apartment, back into his old self, back into the seemingly endless task of inventory.

BOX

For all the objects which filled his room, he knew of only the one empty, unfulfilled container. Not that there were no objects which might contain other objects—there were far too many of those to count. And there were also the jars and tubes and pill bottles containing all his medicines, but he kept these always full. In the city, emergencies waited around virtually every corner. One had to be prepared. Although he'd never, in fact, used any of these medicines. Medicines had an almost desperate quality about them, and he'd always believed that desperate measures were to be avoided until absolutely necessary. This small metal box resembled something a magician might own, its sides brightly painted with black enamel and a finely detailed cloud of white, silver, red, and yellow dots which might have been a piece of star map, but which he would never be able to identify with any certainty. He'd bought the box in a little junk store on Colfax thinking it would be useful for containing something of particular importance, but he had never been able to find the right thing to put into it. Now its emptiness was an irritant—he wished he'd never acquired it in the first place—but it was too attractive to toss into the trash.

It might have made a good box for paperclips but he always lost the paperclips before he could get them into the box.

Boxes were meant to keep things in. Perhaps at this late stage in his life he had nothing left to keep.

Half-heartedly he walked around the apartment with the box in his left hand—lid sprung open as if to pay homage to the ceiling, the shiny emptiness of it like a sterile wound begging for infection—now and then stopping, stooping to sort with his right hand through the objects covering his floor, fingers spread into a rake, a fan. Occasionally he would stop and pick up something, measure it with his eyes, try to set it into the box, looking for the perfect fit. A small Buddha figure, its belly too large to fit. A limited collection of baseball cards—the '64 Yankees, his favourite team when he was in the eighth grade—too wide by a sixteenth of an inch. An assortment of cuff links from his college years, back when he favoured French cuffs, but whose blended rattle inside the metal box was too much to bear.

If he ever severed a thumb and had it wrapped carefully in cotton, it would fit perfectly inside the box. If he had been aborted at age two to three months, all three inches of his fetus would fit neatly within the box, his fingers and toes newly formed, his tiny body resting on a bed of green plastic Easter grass within the smart metal container.

Once again he stared into the clean, shining emptiness of the metal box. Its vacancy left him impoverished. He had nothing to put inside but his imagination.

Just under the edge of the bed a small furry head peeked out. This angered him so that he thought of catching the rodent, jamming its head into the box and then closing the lid with a snap. Then he realized that it wasn't a rat at all but a small, battered dog he'd had since he was a kid. One glass eye hung by a frayed string from a tattered socket. The other had been pushed in so far that greyish stuffing oozed out around its circumference. Both discs of dark glass stared up at him, silent witnesses to his childhood.

He pulled the knife out of his pocket and severed the glass eyes from the dog. They made a satisfying clink when he dropped them into the box. He held the open box beneath the overhead light and shook it. Light bounced off the metal in brilliant shards. He closed his eyes and his eyes filled with light. He rattled the box and vertigo opened up his head and brought a sick taste to his mouth. He clamped his eyes more tightly and held the box out in front of him, permitting the light to lead him out of the room.

FASTENERS

The fasteners were attached firmly to the card. He had no idea what they had been designed to fasten: he'd completely forgotten buying them, and the package simply said: ONE DOZEN FASTENERS.

They looked too large, and too strong for clothing. He imagined their function on camping equipment, or perhaps some industrial use. They looked strong enough to button the night up, leaving the day fastened safely inside.

He tried to pull them apart by hand but couldn't quite manage it, scraping his fingers raw in the process. Finally he picked up a screwdriver off the cluttered desk and pried them off the card. Each fastener fell apart into two large, shiny buttons, a male half with a broad, smooth, mushroom shaped head, a female half with a wide receiving collar.

Again he puzzled over why he would have bought such things. The world depended on fasteners, that much was true. Tacks and glue and rivets and laces. Even the human body had a seam, running from anus to genitalia, fastened with a ridge of hidden, mysterious skin. Most fasteners were intended to remain hidden, blending in with what they fastened, invisible and yet essential. Remove the fasteners from the human body and everything spilled out, everything we liked to pretend didn't exist.

As for himself, he'd always believed that it was the fasteners themselves that were all-important. He liked large, brightly coloured buttons, oversized day glow zippers. The first thing he looked for on any new and unfamiliar object were the fasteners that held it together.

He spent hours attaching fasteners to his furniture, his ceiling, walls. At one point he had to go out and buy a lot more fasteners. Fasteners had a way of multiplying their necessity. Put a few of them where none had existed before, and many more were now required.

Finally he attached fasteners to the front of his torso. It took a while to find a way to attach them firmly to his flesh. He tried all kinds of glues. Eventually he had to make use of the many small holes about the rims of the fasteners, and he sewed them into his skin, periodically wiping the blood away. Blood coagulated around the rims. After a few days firm circles of scab were in place around each.

When the right night arrived he went about his apartment unsnapping the fasteners. The walls split open revealing rusted plumbing and frayed, antique wiring. Long tongues of dust spilled out of the ceiling. Rats and insects stared out of the opened cases of his furniture. Deep behind the lips formed by the unfastened bits of his world, ancient songs issued from unseen mouths.

He pulled apart the fasteners in his torso one by one. He was surprised by the lack of blood or any other fluid. He reached in and emptied himself: pulling out the skeletons of his mother and father, the heart of a woman he'd once dreamed of marrying, miles of colon stinking with his rotted ambitions.

BREAD

There was always the one loaf, wrapped neatly in its own package and resting in the middle of the table. It was his favourite food, but still he could eat only one loaf at a time. One third gone, it always resembled a baby stamped with a brand name on its diaper. One child, he would have had. He'd never thought himself capable, and the woman had been one of his rare ones—they'd both been drunk. He'd agreed with her that there had to be an abortion; he was never cut out for marriage or children. But still there had been that one possibility, that single, remarkable, fully-imagined child. Now sitting on his table wrapped neatly in plastic, his favourite food. A brown heel for the tight curls capping the baby's head. Flesh soft, white, spongy. He tore into the baby every day, spreading it with mayonnaise and mustard, singing softly to it as he bit into it with a grin. The crumbs powdered his face, his lap. He devoured it hungrily. For it was his favourite food, this baby. It was a meal unto itself.

NUMBERS

The idea that he might inventory the digits of his life, that he might count, that he might find a number for the numbers, both fascinated and appalled him. He avoided the task as long as possible, and had no faith at all in a satisfactory conclusion to such an effort, but he felt compelled, at least for the sake of completeness, to attempt it.

He thought that he might have been more relaxed if he'd done better in math at school. But working calculations had always intimidated him. There seemed to be secret rules to the workings of the world, rules which the other students appeared to know. For years he would blame his failures, especially his failures to understand, on his ignorance of these special rules.

And yet despite these experiences he had a deep appreciation for numbers, in particular the physical look of them. The combination of elegance and simplicity in these figures could only have been arrived at after numerous centuries of evolution.

He had one each of a number of items, hundreds of ones actually, and yet ultimately this solitary mark, a single upraised finger, stood for himself and his aloneness, futile and without meaning by itself.

Whenever there were two of a thing it seemed an illusion, an accident waiting to happen. The second was always set aside in case the one broke or was lost. Any sort of relationship between the two was doomed.

Three seemed to be the oddest quantity; one could rest assured that the third would never be used. Most often it was stored, and from storage it was lost or might be given away as a present when adequate funds were unavailable for the obligatory gifts for birthdays, marriage, Christmas, and graduation (at least that had been his plan; in fact, he never knew anyone to give these gifts to).

Past this point one entered the realm of "few" and "several." He had four light bulbs, five dictionaries, eight pens, thirteen key rings which had never been used. After thirteen, things were measured according to the containers they filled—a box of paperclips, a vase of flowers, an old shoe full of marbles.

He'd discovered at an early age the power of simple mathematics. Two plus three plus four, takeaway five. He was fascinated by the pure rhythm of it, describing the movement of people in and out of a town square, the life and death of a hive of bees, the growth of communism, the decline of the family farm. Looked at in terms of an individual life, numbers measured the steady process of growth and development, the geometric acceleration of mental complexity, and the infinitely additive quality of even the simplest human life. Of all his inventories, this inventory of numbers seemed truly celestial.

But when during his schooling they entered the realm of square roots and algebraic functions, he found himself frightened. In these mysterious formulae he began to see hints of the secret workings of the universe, where an error in math might very well result in the wholesale destruction of planets. He put his books away, then. Eventually he dropped out of school entirely.

Now, decades after his last math class, numbers continued to haunt him. The tiles in the ceiling had a number, if he was brave enough to pursue it. So did the fibres of his carpet, the hair of his head. He had heard once that if you counted all the hairs on your head you would use up your allotted time and die.

One morning he would swear that there were microscopic numerals etched into the whiter portions of his fingernails. Another afternoon a shoe scuff across linoleum resembled the numeral 6.

These figures could be combined and calculated. They might be plugged into formulae. Things would be made to happen, but all the resulting events might not be particularly desirable.

Somehow he knew that if he could only escape this weight of numbers, he might truly be happy.

FLOORS

In the year of his thirty-fifth birthday paranoia held sway. He became obsessively concerned over the strength and composition of his floors.

It distressed him that, until now, he had never thought much about his floors. All this time they had been merely a repository for what had dropped out of his life during the transitions from one moment to the next. Those dropped items now seemed to be of the most importance in defining who he was and what he had become, the most essential items for him to inventory.

But now, in his thirties, he had come to realize that there was a platform, a stage, a foundation underneath this strata of his belongings. Not the rug, which had worn so thin that he could virtually feel the nail heads in the boards beneath, but the boards themselves, and the subfloor, and the timbers which supported the subflooring. These were the essentials, what a life was based on.

It became necessary to inspect the floor beneath the rug and his things, to see if there was more than one floor, if the floor varied from room to room (he'd never seen beneath this rug—it had been there when he'd first moved in and he had been a very foolish young man at the time). There was no telling what sort of disasters lay dormant in the mysterious floor boards under his feet.

To facilitate this inspection he spent two days picking his belongings up off the floor and putting them into boxes, bags, baskets. Then he moved all his furniture into one of his two rooms.

Peeling the rug off the floor was difficult in spots because past spills had resulted in the rug sticking firmly to the old boards. A firm tug usually pulled the rug loose, but often with a loss of fibre and backing. Tiny insects he did not recognize scattered and slipped—their group movement like a kind of crazed liquid— through the narrow cracks between the boards, perhaps into the apartment below him. He did not know the tenant there so this did not concern him.

Throughout much of the main living room the floor was made up of staggered planks three and a half inches in width. Two-thirds of the way across this room, however, these boards ended and faint lines and dark discolourations in the floor indicated that another wall had once been there. He could not imagine the purpose of such a wall, unless to conceal something at some point in the past. This made him anxious—there were limitless possibilities here.

Past this point the floor was made up of wooden squares a foot on a side. He thought they might be oak.

In his kitchen area he discovered the first real possibilities of a weakness in the floor. A steady leak from the mysterious plumbing (coming to surface under the sink, briefly, in a hard-to-interpret knot of pipe) had spread through the boards, leaving white mineral deposit and granular brown rot the length of their edges. A number of these boards were still damp.

He used a knife blade to pry up several for a deeper inspection. One split into two soggy strips in his hands. The subflooring had almost completely rotted away in one spot. Dark veins showed where the damp had ventured into the beams.

His fears had been justified, then, but no remedy seemed immediately available. He didn't quite know what to do. He was well aware of the building superintendent's attitude toward such things: he'd be blamed, told that he should have noticed the leaks. An excuse to raise his rent (which he could not afford), or move him out entirely (which he could not bear). And certainly he could not afford to hire a repair person on his own.

Finally he wiped up the moisture as best he could and stuffed the rotted cavity with rags, bits of junk, whatever he could find to bolster the weakened boards in hopes of keeping them from sagging. Then he put back the rug and scattered his things from the basket, seemingly at random but in truth not randomly at all. Even in such a scattering everything had its place.

For the rest of his life he would step lightly, waiting for the entire floor to buckle and collapse beneath him at any moment. Such anxiety did not seem unusual or in any way remarkable to him: he considered this about par for a man in middle age.

GLOVES

Gloves were what hands wanted to be, he thought, stylish and coveted by the poor, especially in cold weather.

He had nine gloves in his possession: three matched pairs and three solitary orphans. The matched pairs were worn and threadbare, but the orphans appeared virtually brand new, showing almost no wear at all. The other thing peculiar about these orphans was that he could not recall either purchasing them or receiving them as gifts (in which case they would have been from his mother). Moreover, their patterns and colours—checked, polka dotted, bright orange—were definitely not to his taste. The only other explanation he could think of was that they had been left in his drawers as a prank.

Wearing gloves had always felt strange, and he avoided it as much as possible. But he found himself wearing them more frequently than he had when he'd been younger. In fact, some days the rough weather in this part of the country made gloves almost a necessity.

Gloves had never felt comfortable to him, not even when he was a child. His mother had bought pair after pair in different styles and sizes, but it always felt as if he was wearing someone else's skin. Even when they fit they didn't fit, not really. He kept expecting to see blood seeping out of the cuff.

Now the gloves he wore most of the time were old and tattered, the fingers stained and faded as if they had handled something corrosive. They looked like his discarded hands, as if he had finally grown tired of their inadequacies.

They might have been a sculptor's gloves, or a gardener's. Now they were empty and flaccid, as if disappointed in him.

At night he worried about how they slept. In the light of early morning, when he first saw them, he was suddenly afraid that he had murdered someone in his sleep.

Because of these misgivings he tried to go without gloves for a time, even in the coldest weather. But as he grew older the skin of his hands became loose and wrinkled, and stains from what he had handled eventually became permanent. By the time he was forty, he realized, his hands would appear to be ill-fitting gloves he might have borrowed or stolen.

He would never again feel that his fingers were experiencing direct contact with anything. Touch became a distant sort of sense, and open to interpretation. After a time he realized he didn't even recognize the feel of his own skin, except from the inside.

RAZOR

He had only the one, but then he shaved only once or twice a month, when he had to go out in public. He maintained a full beard, but there were always these patches, on cheeks and at the base of the neck, where the beard grew a five-o'clock shadow and stopped. These he shaved as a bow to good grooming.

Shaving had always made him feel clean, and yet it also possessed the ability to unnerve him. He'd read somewhere that, besides cutting the beard, shaving removed infinitesimal layers of skin from the face. Thinking of this made him reconsider even his twice monthly shaves. A quick perusal of past photographs proved inconclusive, as most of these images of him were either too small or slightly out of focus. The few good portraits did give him pause, however: subtle differences in the contouring of cheeks and jaw, and apparent changes in the skin bordering the nostrils, which now made his nose seem more prominent. Looking at himself in the mirror now, he saw a stranger. He wondered absently if more or less shaving might make a man look younger. He supposed it depended on the particular face hiding under those thin layers of skin.

If a man wasn't careful, he thought, he might be awfully tempted to attack his face with a knife some morning, just to see who might say hello.

CHAIRS

He'd read in a book one time (sold in the quaint used bookshop downstairs that always carried such odd little books) that in the peculiar individual stresses of a chair were recorded the ghosts of everyone who had ever sat on it.

He thought this complete nonsense of course, although he could not shake this fantastic conceit from his imagination. If it were true, then he had had intimate contact with hundreds. All his chairs were secondhand, and relatively old. He started looking for body oils in the wooden finishes, vague impressions of trauma in the padded parts. With each day the chairs seemed more and more uncomfortable, as if preadapted to previous owners, the contours of countless corpses memorized by the fibres that pressed against him when he sat down.

He had five chairs in the apartment, only one of which was comfortable, and that one broken beyond repair. It sat by his bed, the sides splayed out and cushions fallen and fraying, like the abandoned nest of some huge, exotic bird.

This had become his chair, and he had given up all hope of finding anything comparable. Broken or not, it was the last thing he sat in each day before climbing into bed. His mother had always said that there was something of the lowlife in anyone who would slide directly into bed at the end of the day without the proper sedentary transition. He didn't really agree, but he had made the sitting a necessary part of his evening ritual just the same.

He would sit in this chair and read, or drink some juice, or listen to the radio, until the vaguest impression of fatigue stole over him, at which exact time he would climb into his bed. The chair fit him so perfectly, he suspected, because no one else had enjoyed it much. Any other ghosts had abandoned it once it began to lose its shape, and the chair's ensuing amnesia had led to a complete collapse.

He attempted now and then to discover what made the other chairs in his apartment so uncomfortable. Some were simply too stiff, like refugees from a military school, demanding a firm and upright posture from any occupant. Others were ill proportioned for his body, the seats too narrow or the legs slightly too short, as if they had been developed for some altered design of humanoid.

He began to wonder which came first: the chair or the being who sat in it. Which moulded which?

So always he was forced to fall back into his decrepit chair, which he seemed to resemble more each year. His flesh took on the same frayed, lumpy consistency. His hair the same stiff spray of fibres, his slouch the same broken collapse of back. It was only when the tiny, black backed beetles began their infestation of his sitting place, followed by the narrow white worms who moved back and forth on one end as if in trance, like some form of intelligent cancer, that he tossed the old chair in the alley where it sprawled in battered pieces like the mutilated corpse of a derelict.

He was never able to find another comfortable chair like that, and was often reduced to sitting cross legged on the floor—like some heathen, his mother would have said.

It felt good to have the beetles and the worms out of his apartment. But he would always feel that from then on he lived on borrowed time.

ASHES

Although he'd never had a fireplace, although he didn't smoke, sometimes he found ashes in his apartment. A blend of white, grey, and silver, sometimes vague trails crisscrossed the room, as if someone had been pacing with cigarette in hand.

Sometimes there was a small pile of ash by his bed, as if that same someone had been standing there watching him sleep.

During the worst heat of summer he sometimes imagined that his tired thoughts burned up in the night heat of the room, making the fine dusting of ash he found on the sheets every morning.

Sometimes in the dead of winter the presence of ash on his cold floors was almost comforting, reminding him of warm, rich earth, and all the possibilities that suggested. He would lie on his floor for hours and, using a pencil as probe, turn the bits of ash over and over. Sometimes he would position his high intensity reading lamp on the floor over the ashes so that he could make out more detail. He would churn the grey and white and silver flakes over again and again trying to determine what sort of objects had been burnt to make this ash, until he'd reduced the flakes to powder and less. He stared at the bare traces of them disappearing into the carpet, and thought he could see newspapers, trees, small houses, old women in rocking chairs.

One night he was aware of a stronger scent in the smoke: of perfume and shampoo and powder recently applied. He sat on the edge of his bed and let these smells drift over him and cling to his bare flesh. The dead woman who might have had his child was there in the room with him, and the baby two years old. He felt the fine powder of their passage all over his body, creeping into the crevices, slipping under his eyelids to make his vision blurred and gritty. He wanted to wrap himself in a sheet and rub the ash of them into his skin, and then he wanted to dive under a shower, wash it all off screaming. The taste of the ash on his tongue was bitter, like poison. He saw sudden rents in the walls, and then the dark air swam with red.

After several years the continuing presence of the ash in his apartment, its constant renewal, began to disturb him greatly. He lay on his bed staring out the open window, until one night he thought he could detect the barest trace of smoke entering there, and then he knew the answer. He spent the next few weeks scouring the nearby streets searching for a silent and secret crematorium.

Although he thought he might have come close at times, he never found it. He might, then, have doubted its existence, but there were all the stories in the papers about missing people from the downtown area, and now and then during his searches he would pass through faint clouds of powdery smoke, even though there was no apparent source.

Back in his rooms each night he would gaze through the veils of smoke that entered the window. The powdered ash which littered his floor was no longer an irritant or a comfort. It was crowds of people, speaking and gesturing; it was lives cut short; it was shadows and memory.

During the days he began to see his own flesh differently. He'd never had any luck with a tan—he just reddened quickly, then burned. He was practically the palest, whitest person he knew, except for an albino kid he'd spent half the eighth grade with. His limbs were a uniform shade of cream, with pink highlights over the joints and where he figured the muscles to be. Looking closer, he could see that his skin was a patchwork, irregular lines dividing up the surface. Its pallor gave it the appearance of glowing. In the midday light his body appeared filled to the brim with light, his dark hair a cap and an abrupt end.

He imagined his skin granulating, bits and pieces of it falling away as the inner fire that was his life consumed him, the flesh flaking off, turning into bits of ash. Each night, he knew he lay down to sleep a bit dimmer, a bit less defined.

Some day soon he knew he would wake up with ash filling his throat, ash on his tongue. He realized now that he needn't search out crematoria. The consuming fires were right here.

He breathed the ash in and breathed it out. He said a sudden prayer for his flesh.

LAMP

He owned one lamp, with a very long extension cord. He liked to move it around his apartment, several times each day, in order to achieve a variety of lighting effects. By his bed, he felt as if he were in the tropics. With the lamp in the other room he was an arctic dweller. Positioning the lamp in his closet put him out on a distant planet, centuries away in the bottomless dark. Sometimes he'd balance it awkwardly on his chest, and the sun rose and set across his belly. His mother sent him another lamp for Christmas one time (tall, blue, art deco), but because of possible confusion he never plugged it in. That particular lamp sat in one corner now. He pretended it was a statue of Venus.

MAIL

Mail was irrelevant. Sometimes he received advertising circulars, and he would wonder for a long time how they had acquired his name and address. He finally decided that some unfriendly neighbour was selling not only his name but his address as well, probably for an inflated fee. Rather than count his mail, he would ink out his name and address, then wander the hall randomly slipping the letters and circulars under his neighbours' doors. Some weeks he might make a hundred such trips. The mail stopped coming after a final postcard which read:

please stop

HAIR

There were a number of things he had never been able to understand about hair. He'd always lost it in prodigious amounts—every week he found mats of it in his bed clothes, scattered across his carpet, great gobs of it trapped in his drains and between the teeth of his combs. And yet when he looked in his mirror, his hairline looked no different. He should have gone bald years ago.

The hair he found scattered about his apartment was greyer than the hair remaining on his head, as if once free of his scalp it aged at an accelerated rate. Or maybe it was someone else's hair, blown in by the wind. Or maybe the hair from his older scalp, transported here by dream. Dream hair. He'd read somewhere that hair was related to bones and fingernails, although he could see no family resemblance. He tried to imagine bones like hair, snaking and fibrous through the vacancies of the body, a strong and flexible armature that would permit human beings to move in a way somewhere between the locomotion patterns of a snake and a lizard. Then he thought he could feel the hair growing throughout him, spreading its roots through his organs, webbing them and wrapping them so intimately his interior might soon be completely furry.

These meditations upon hair continued for several days. Each morning he discovered still more hair when he awakened: filling his shoes, layering his bedclothes, brushed into corners, swept up into his cupboards. It occurred to him that the more he thought about hair, the more hair materialized, as if these narrow, fibrous wisps of thought had solidified into the chains of protein hair.

He considered whether flesh or hair decayed faster and concluded that flesh was the probable answer. He'd heard stories that your hair continued to grow after you died but didn't think them true. Still, he liked to imagine the hair of all the dead growing beyond the grave, breaking out of coffins, spreading throughout ground and rock, entangling fibre by fibre until one day all the dead were linked by this massive hairy network. If your hair continued to grow long after you were dead then perhaps a kind of immortality was possible. If your hair continued to grow then perhaps it became a repository for all your final thoughts, your last dreams and unrealized aspirations. Your hair was the ghost of you.

With such obsessive speculations it wasn't surprising to him when the morning's supply of new hair began to appear accompanied by new stray thoughts of no apparent context, and discrete, distinctive voices—sometimes so low as to be inaudible, sometimes loud enough that they distracted him from his own thoughts. These ideas and voices gathered in every available corner along with the scattered hair.

It was with great reluctance that he eventually decided to clear the hair out of his apartment. Although he had a great tolerance for litter, the press of voices and foreign ideas began to grate. He was gradually being pre-empted in his own home by the ghosts of strangers and of his past and future selves. Besides which, hair was not properly an object for inventory but a part of the very fabric of the universe itself.

He gathered up dust mops, feather dusters, and lint brushes he had not used in years. He went through his apartment carefully, picking up objects one at a time and removing the hair from them. He worked his way through every square inch of carpet, into every corner and recess, across every level surface. As he usually kept his closet empty it was an easy matter to remove the bar and line the closet with trash bags he'd split and taped together, to make one, huge trash bag, a slit near the top for an opening.

Each day he added more hair to this closet/bag—long or short, dark or red or blonde, curly or kinky or straight, pubic or chest or head—until he had filled it, until the hair pressed out the front of his bag so that the bag looked like a huge, black belly.

He closed his closet door and searched the apartment. Finding no more hair, he locked the closet door. He left it that way several days.

The voices protested loudly at first. Once in the middle of the night he opened the closet door and peered down the slit with a flashlight. The mass of hair moved in rolls of lips, great ridges of gums, and yet out of synch with the voices he heard.

After a few days the voices faded to a whisper. After a few weeks it was not even that.

One summer morning he hauled the giant bag of hair out of his closet and slipped it carefully down the stairs, afraid that it might break at any moment to spill hair and voices everywhere. He wrestled it to the alley behind his apartment building and set it beside the dumpster.

By afternoon someone had scavenged it, before the garbage collectors could arrive.

PLUMBING

Plumbing was secretive, hiding in the walls. Sometimes it betrayed its presence by the noises which escaped it. He thought it might be embarrassed because of all the secret, seldom-talked-about bodily fluids it transported throughout the building. He did not know how to count it, so he entered it onto his list, simply, as: PLUMBING.

ICE

Ice was only an occasional visitor to his apartment, but a disturbing one when it came. Most often it indicated a leaky window or a furnace gone bad: the ice would fill the corners of the windows, sometimes layering itself so thickly it seemed to have penetrated the glass itself, so that it had all become cold, become ice, right down to the molecular level.

Ice reminded him how poor he was. Ice let him know that there was death in the air. "You'll catch your death!" his mother used to say to him. Sometimes it seemed this apartment was the trap he would use. He inventoried the ice according to the number of patches he found and their relative size. Then he described their shape, their consistency, and how they felt against his skin. The ice was a numbness in his reactions, a gap in his defenses. Ice was what happened when life no longer surprised you.

During the winter of his thirty-ninth year he could not keep his gaze away from the ice, the way it crept across the panes, the way it burned when the sun was high. If company came for Christmas he'd have to thaw it out somehow, get rid of it, so people wouldn't think him poor or otherwise deprived.

But he recognized that company was not likely. He'd be left to admire the beauty of the ice alone. If he left his holiday eggnog on the windowsill it would freeze. If he slept too close to the window, he would freeze as well. He would catch his death.

Ice was a death travelling through the veins, a numbness spreading through the skin until everything else was squeezed out. Ice killed the dinosaurs. Ice in the major organs started the Dark Ages. Ice killed forty-two inventions still brewing inside Tom Edison's aging brain. Ice put an end to the career of Charlie "Bird" Parker, and ice would effectively terminate him as well. He would freeze like the pipes in the worst winter, then melt down like a Popsicle in August heat. He would rot like spring ice on the river. He would turn into steam.

On the eve of his fortieth birthday the furnace went out again. Both of his windows cracked. Every ghost in his apartment—those he had known as family, lovers, and friends, and those he had never met before—froze solid into visibility. He walked from ghost to ghost, touching his tongue to their glassy surfaces as if they were a form of frozen dessert.

He remembers that taste even today: potentially sweet, but familiarity had made it bland.

NAILS

In his apartment nails were used to hang pictures. He hadn't the skill to use them for any other purpose. Nor the courage, for nails were sharp and capable of penetrating human flesh. Not that this is their intention. Nails possess a certain directness, he thought, but no intention.

A pile of spilled nails made him think of houses falling apart. After the war, after all the houses have dissolved in the brilliance of atomic ideas, will only the nails be left?

Nails were used to crucify the Christ, at least in the version of the story he knew. He wondered if blood had made the nails rust.

He discovered a number of stray nails on his rug during the inventory. He could not remember purchasing them. For several nights after counting them he waited for the walls of his apartment to fall down, or for Christ to appear at his front door, His hands and feet trailing rust.

At night he stared at the sky, searching for the nails the moon and stars were hung on.

One morning he awakened with an odd pain in his belly. Blood had soaked through his T-shirt. Stripping it off, he discovered blood welling up from inside his belly button. With great care he fished his right little finger into the bloody cavity and came out with a long, thin nail of shiny silver.

Over the next few days other nails appeared—out of his armpits, from behind his knees, under his chin. One especially long nail slipped out of his ear one morning as he first awakened.

He put these nails in his small black metal box with the clouds of multicoloured dots, and labeled the box clearly with the number, size, and probable composition of the nails.

He waited for an arm or leg to fall off during his sleep but this never occurred.

One evening at midnight there was a knock on his apartment door. Since he rarely had visitors, and never one so late as this, he was filled with trepidation.

The man at the door wore dark blue overalls and a bright, silver coloured construction helmet. His hammer, dangling somewhat lewdly from the front of his belt, appeared never to have been used. "Do you have any nails I could borrow?" the man asked.

He went immediately to his metal box full of nails and gave it to the man. The man opened the box and examined the nails. "These are exactly what I was looking for," he said. The man thanked him and left.

All night long there were the sounds of construction all around him. All the next day the halls of the apartment building rang with laughter and song.

But he had decided a long time ago he would never leave his apartment again. He kept that promise to himself.

FORKS

There were six forks, each of a different pattern. If he flashed a bright light on them, their silhouettes resembled the hands of cartoon demons. He enjoyed using his cartoon demon hands to spear potatoes and tear pot roast into shreds. Sometimes at night he would sit by the window, holding his demon hands up high as his sharp eyes kept a constant search of the dark city streets below.

CLOCKS

There were at least a dozen clocks in the apartment, but only half of them worked at any one time. Clocks were an odd sort of thing, ticking away in their dusty corners, achieving importance only when noticed. He wasn't sure what importance clocks were for him anymore—he hadn't had a regular job in years; he seldom went out; he watched whatever was on the television when he first turned it on; and whenever he was hungry, he ate.

Of the six clocks that still worked, four of these gave the wrong time. Three were within acceptable limits, if one were working or otherwise had to get to places on time. Moving around the apartment to inventory their faces (one was on his bed stand, one on the wall above the stove, the other standing awkwardly atop his small black and white TV), he recorded them as showing five to one, eight to one, and ten to one. The actual time, according to the telephone and the two digital time pieces on his battered coffee table, was one o'clock. He'd never called time on the telephone before, but thought it important for inventory purposes.

The sixth clock he kept hidden, inside a cupboard near the stove. Inside this cupboard it was currently eight thirty-two. He didn't know if this was AM or PM; the clock was a simple dial with no such indicators. He'd lost track of whether the clock was slow or fast—since it was kept from view most of the time he had no relative reference point, the clock keeping its own time. Every day he wound this clock, but without resetting it.

Six more clocks in his apartment did not run at all, at least not to his knowledge. Sometimes he suspected they might run, but so slowly as to be undetectable. Perhaps they were on some other, older time system: insect time, shadow time, or dust time. One of these clocks lay face up under his bed, infested with dust bugs and spotted brown by some unknown liquid. Under his bed it was always twelve. Another clock formed one bookend on the short bookshelf hanging on the wall: three fifteen. Three of them sat faceless in a tattered shoebox under a window—he'd taken the faces off for some forgotten project, and now even when wound and the gears churning they were apparently timeless, like the other side of the sky, or reality's backstage. But just because he couldn't see the time, did that mean the time did not exist? Or perhaps he could put a different sort of face on the clocks, using different numbers in a different arrangement, different colours? Would that create a different kind of time? The last of his twelve clocks was lost, but often he could hear its broken ticking, and sometimes in the middle of a dark dream it chimed the wrong hour.

Occasionally he would grow apprehensive about his timeless existence and determined to put his life under the clocks' measure once again. But for years he wasn't sure he could do this; he wasn't even sure he knew how. Finally, because of a sense of age (time running out), or internal confusion (time slipping away), he decided to reintroduce this idea of time into his life. He attempted to keep at least four of the clocks in good repair, wound and set to the correct time. The rest of his clocks he would studiously ignore, knowing that to be distracted by their erroneous times would return him instantly to his previous timeless condition.

But this new attempt at living according to the clock was an awkward one for him. He'd find himself watching their faces counting off the seconds to his next planned activity, betraying him as they smugly sped his life away. He began to worry about eating his meals too early or too late, afraid his sleep might be disrupted by hunger pains. He worried over the proper time for his bedtime, unable to ascertain the best hour for the maximum rest and renewal. At night, before he closed his eyes, he could hear the broken rhythm of his lost clock, reminding him of his shortcomings, failures and losses. The fact that his clocks all sounded differently worried him also; they ranged from electrical buzz through mechanical whirr through tinny ticks. In a safe and predictable world, all time would sound the same.

And then he woke up in the middle of the night convinced that all his carefully tended time pieces had stopped. Even the broken ticking of his lost clock had drowned in the dark silence. He sat up in bed, almost distraught that his attempt to live according to time had failed.

Despite the sudden silence he sensed rhythm in the room. He crawled out of bed, got down on his hands and knees, and felt a rhythm in the floor. He began picking up objects: shoes and batteries, marbles and buttons, a half eaten apple, and discovered a rhythm in all those things. The shoes felt like a slow movement through loose sand, the batteries a heated yawn, the marbles a jittery but cold pulse, the buttons a series of small explosions in water, and the apple had the rhythm of an ant hill after being stepped on. Everything wound down at its own speed with its own dance. If he stared into the darkness long enough, he knew he'd discover that even the night itself had a pulse.

When he realized he'd been holding his breath he released it with a soft quake. The characteristic broken ticking of his lost clock began again. He held his naked chest and could feel the broken rhythm there. He waited for the clock to stop. From a vague distance, as if the intervening space had been filled with thick liquid, he heard the growing alarm.

WALLS

Walls were essential. They made his apartment possible. They kept other people out. They were highly efficient at what they did. Like machines, he thought. Machines of containment.

But in his fiftieth year it was exactly this idea of containment which bothered him. The walls contained him. They prevented him from doing things. They kept other people out.

Although the walls possessed continuity, corners and variations in paint and wallpaper permitted an accounting. One: the wall containing his front door. Two: the living room wall with its northern window. Three: the blank living room wall where he kept his bed. Four through six: the walls of his closet which hardly seemed like walls at all, since he had never thought of the closet as a part of his apartment. Seven: the wall that divided his apartment, kitchen from living space, with its two doors of passage. Eight (?): the other side of seven, but which looked so different with its tile and stucco, so that he didn't know whether to count it separately or not. Nine: the wall with his dining table. Ten: the wall with his other northern window, and a plant box containing grey dirt but no plants. Eleven: the wall containing stove, cabinet, ice box, and rusted sink. Twelve through fourteen: the walls of his bathroom, slightly askew and with warped wall coverings from years of moisture damage.

Finally, he thought of the fifteenth wall, the invisible one which had been removed, the only remaining indication of which he had found vaguely traced on the floorboards when he lifted up the rug. It was this wall which had become the most significant as he entered his fifties. It appeared in his dreams: a shiny, silvered thing which lowered itself slowly and made everything look new again, refreshed in its mirrored surface. It was the wall with a purpose, the wall with a fresh look, the wall that made all the difference.

That, finally, was what kept him in the apartment and made it impossible for him to move. He had first to imagine all the possible ways he might have decorated that wall, and the effects of each on the total effect of his apartment.

SHOES

He wondered if other people never threw away their shoes. He did not, of course, but he had never owned many pairs. He wondered if rich people gave or tossed away their shoes. He supposed the conscientious ones gave theirs to tax-deductible, charitable organizations. But there were a great number of misers among the rich as well, and perhaps they recycled the shoe leather into belts or even fancy book bindings. Even he had twelve pairs cluttering up the place, and three more singles with no apparent mates. The two pairs he wore the most—the beat-up tennis shoes and the dull black, leather pair—sat at the ready by his bed. Now he wore the bright red loafers with the holes in the top. Why there should be such holes he did not know—these shoes seemed too loose to have worn in such a way.

He had never paid much attention to what people wore on their feet. He didn't understand why others noticed such things. Sometimes it made him uncomfortable, thinking that below eye level your feet might be doing almost anything. Feet could be completely detached from the rest of the body. Feet were the underworld, the low lying dark, the realm of subconscious impulse.

The rest of his shoes were scattered across the floor in a broken trail that led from bed to closet. There might be an odd shoe or two hidden under the dresser or his bed, dust filling them rather than feet, but he couldn't be sure.

Old shoes always seemed rather worse off than he remembered from the last time he'd worn them. His black canvas-tops were a good example of this phenomenon. When last he'd put them away—approximately five years ago—they'd been turning a little grey on top due to wear, and the stitching was beginning to come loose on the outer curve of the right shoe. He'd put them away in the corner by the radiator, and had never picked them up again.

Now when he looked at them they had collapsed, were almost

flat, as if someone with much larger feet had been wearing them and had stretched them quite out of shape. All the inner structural strength had disappeared. It then occurred to him that it was these same dark (but becoming grey) shoes he had been wearing in his dreams for years. In his dreams he had never taken them off. He had never replaced them. He had worn them through hot, burning sands and waded through the periodic dream floods.

It was not, he thought, because his dream self was more frugal than his waking self. There was just something peculiarly "right" about those particular shoes on his feet in his dreams. They seemed less like shoes than dark, mysterious, shadowfeet which took him into those realms his subconscious wanted to go. Sometimes in his dreams they even seemed to breathe on their own, to move independently, like dream animals, shadow beasts wrapped around the stubs of his ankles.

He realized that he must have been wearing these shoes in his dreams long before he actually owned the shoes. Purchasing the shoes had not been taking advantage of a bargain at the local discount store; it had been preordained.

He conceived a plan in which he would examine this old pair of shoes each morning for signs of change, signs of the previous evening's dream. He would put them back carefully each time, however, in their rather obscure resting place, because to do otherwise might adversely affect his dreams.

One morning the tops of both shoes were badly scuffed. He remembered dreaming the night before of a wild scramble down a steep slope, through a mass of sharp branches and rocky debris. Another day the shoes had darkened, almost charred, and he suddenly recalled racing through streets of fire, howling when the hot embers landed on his arms and back. Then there was the odd, hazy day when he had reached for the shoes and found them sodden, crumbling, and overgrown with moss. That night and many nights thereafter he dreamed nightmares of his own death.

As an old man he woke one morning and found the dark canvas shoes missing, and an exhaustive search of his apartment did not turn them up. Forever after that he would not remember his dreams. He lost his gift of prophecy. The subjunctive eluded him. He would also cease to use such words as "would," "will," and "shall."

PAPERS

His apartment always seemed to be filled with them. Originally, he had decided to inventory the papers according to a number of different categories—newspapers, letters, bills, magazines, advertising, general correspondence—but during one late evening of cataloguing he determined that they were all pretty much the same thing, whatever their physical forms. They were ephemeral display areas for words, words whose ultimate utility was dubious. So he stacked the papers in piles around his apartment according to size and weight. Then he restacked them according to their relative weights of sincerity. The "very sincere" stack was quite small, and controversial. He hadn't the temerity to create a "completely sincere" stack.

People spent an inordinate amount of time creating this vast volume of wordage. He wondered where they found the time, how they dredged up the energy and/or inclination. One could fill page after page over a lifetime and still not convince anyone to lend you money, change their opinion, or love you. Words were like dreams: the mind sweeping out its garbage. Here, all around him, were words. Possessions, words, dreams, garbage: they seemed little different to him.

If he took the stacks of papers—whatever the current scheme of classification—and dropped them from a height and permitted them to spread, interesting juxtapositions occurred where the papers overlapped. An old letter from his mother might blend in with an advertising flyer for men's underwear or cancer research and he might never notice the difference. At night he might dream of his childhood, and his mother putting cancer-causing agents in the front of his underwear while he slept.

Or old bills and overdue notices might become part of a page of poetry and he would feel a certain spiritual elevation because of the breadth and intensity of his debt. Words jammed into words and sentences ran and melded as his feet shuffled through the papers on repeated midnight journeys to the bathroom. Too many words produced nausea and lower abdominal distress. In the dark, the ragged piles of paper made him think of excrement experimentally processed for creative and elegant disposal. He thought there should be a statutory limit on the number of words a person might say or write. Some people could expand their limit by application for special licences. For others, there might even be a special lifetime limit court imposed as punishment.

Whenever possible, he tried to limit the amount of paper and accompanying wordage coming into his apartment. He removed all store receipts and flyers in the store parking lot. He cancelled all subscriptions and wrote mail order houses angry letters immediately upon suspicion that he'd been put on another mailing list. But still there was the necessary mail and other written information which slipped by almost unnoticed.

Feeling as he did, he might have removed all paper from his apartment, permitting the trash people at last to haul away his great store of it. But he came to see the act of creating these words, however inessential, to be as natural and incidental as breathing. He wondered whether copywriters had words appearing in sales pitches long after their deaths. And there was the issue of his mother's letters—how could he toss away the lost voice of her?

He thought the worst job must be that of the trash man charged with disposing of such paper. He wondered if he had to wear cotton in his ears to muffle the voices. He wondered how he kept his composure rifling through the casual or earnest utterings of the living and dead, the famous and the anonymous. He wondered how he handled the o's, the a's, the e's ground beneath the wheels of the bulldozers, pulping together in preparation for one last great garbled howl.

GRAVITY

It was everywhere, he'd been told, at least on this planet, and was therefore not to be counted, not even to be considered in day-to-day decision making. And so he chose to ignore it, to snub it, and was rewarded with a subtle lightening of his existence.

But now that he was old, such suppression seemed a waste not to be tolerated. During the course of these inventories he discovered that gravity existed within his apartment in great quantity and diversity.

There was the gravity that lined the inside of his shoes from a full year's travel, and another year of time spent standing in various lines, which added up to a gravity equal to one somewhat complicated relationship.

There, too, was the gravity of unopened letters, especially those he was afraid to open.

Cooking utensils had gravity, although less than that of the food which went into them.

He realized eventually that his mother had left her gravity behind when she'd last come to visit. He could feel its presence, although he couldn't quite locate it.

After months of searching he found a small depression in the rug next to his laundry hamper which he had not touched in months. He raised the rug to discover that the depression continued all the way into the floor boards.

He found that, if he put a wastebasket over his mother's gravity, thrown paper balls would always land inside. For several weeks at least this made him feel like a successful man.

CARDS

He once considered binding them with rubber bands or keeping them in a shoe box the way so many of his friends did. But that would have made them immediately all of a kind, with no special quality, a part of his past to be stored away and forgotten. At least with them scattered about the floor and piled carelessly on his dresser or bedside table, he could be surprised by these reminders that occasionally someone thought about him, even though it might simply be that he had never been removed from a Christmas card list.

The ones he liked best were vacation picture postcards from such exotic locales as St. Louis and Nashville. But he never quite understood why people felt the need to advise him of their recreational plans. He had, of course, a multitude of cards sent to him by his mother until she died. There was even one—a "thinking of you" card—which arrived in his mail box two days after her death, apparently mailed the afternoon she died.

He thought a prepackaged "thinking of you" card was a rather odd concept. Because what "thought" could be involved here? The card itself was rather nonspecific; surely his mother's thoughts of him weren't nonspecific as well? It was like saying to someone, "I'm thinking of you but I'm not going to tell you what I'm thinking." Such messages could lead to a rather paranoid view of the world.

Scattered about his apartment, the cards were voices, disconnected from time and physical bodies. They spoke eloquently of the futility of human attempts at communication.

Hope you feel better soon. Sorry I forgot your . . . Happy Holidays . . . Greetings from the tropics . . . Best wishes . . . Yours for a merry . . . Wish you were here.

SHEETS

He'd never quite understood the desirability of fresh, clean sheets. It was like sleeping in a manila envelope, waiting to be mailed to heaven or hell. He owned two at a time, a top and a bottom, and he used them until they had aged almost the colour of him. Sleeping in them was almost like sleeping in his mother's flesh, naked and ready to be born, not like some shroud, or ghostly manifestation of all the blank days ahead.

STONES

Following several passes across the rug he came up with sixteen stones of various sizes, all larger than what might have been inadvertently carried in within a shoe. He could not recall ever having brought them in. Were they part of some childhood rock collection? If so they seemed far less glorious now, a dull gathering of browns, greys, and blacks. But stones always seemed more glorious when beheld through sparkling water, and during his childhood his collection had always been gathered from the bottoms of streams.

One of the sixteen proved to be in fact a dried and hardened bit of apple, and yet that still left fifteen mysteries remaining in his collection.

TEETH

Teeth were one of those parts of the body which seemed a part of the room itself. Not only were they a form of interface to this room—chewing its food, articulating its air, gnashing together through its anxious energies—but objects which might deteriorate if left up on the shelf too long. They could never be completely his—he was far too aware of their separate existence.

He still had many of his teeth from childhood in his mother's old heart shaped jewelry box—she'd protected them religiously. It seemed that many parents put a great importance in their children's baby teeth, as if these were proof of their parentage, that the children hadn't been stolen and placed full-grown into their home.

His mother had gone a step further, collecting his teeth during his teen years, and even a few from his early adulthood up until the time she died. She was always calling him up, getting him to swear again and again to save any teeth he might lose in an accident, to retrieve any teeth a dentist might remove. "They're yours! He has no right to them!" she would say, although of course what she really meant was that they were hers.

Periodically she would travel the twenty miles by bus to his apartment to gather them for the jewelry box collection. She would examine each one carefully before adding it to the box, critical of flaws, speculating as to what terrible things he might have been eating which no doubt directly resulted in the loss of the tooth. These examinations always made him uncomfortable, as if he were witnessing his own autopsy.

He continued collecting his teeth for some time after his mother's death until the idea that he was now putting only permanent, irreplaceable teeth in the heart shaped box became oppressive to him. He became acutely aware of teeth as bone, and it seemed that he was storing away his corpse, one bit at a time. If he picked up the box and rattled it, he could imagine all those hard bits of himself calling for their brethren. He could almost feel the bones inside himself creaking, yearning for their place, yearning for death.

So now the teeth lay quietly in their box, collecting dust, the box shoved under the edge of his bed so that he couldn't kick it over accidentally. One of his teeth was missing from the collection— back when he used to take the teeth out periodically for examination, and hadn't been careful, he'd dropped it somewhere near the middle of the floor. It had been a tiny tooth from when he was five or six, and it had seemed to yellow by itself over the years, as if some trace of the food he'd eaten then had remained on it, candy or banana or perhaps a grape still working its discolouration after all these years.

It was slightly round, resembling an unpopped popcorn kernel or a yellowish seed, and he had picked up many such kernels and seeds in his searches over the years thinking he had found it. But the tooth had not been found. He did not vacuum, so he felt sure the tooth must still be there, but years of periodic searches had still not turned it up.

It seemed foolish to still be bothered by its loss, and yet if he had lost a finger or an ear, and he knew that it was lying about, hiding underfoot, then such a situation would of course seem intolerable. This wasn't the same, he knew a tooth wasn't the same, but where do you draw the line? He had never learned. Worse still was the fact that it was the tooth from a younger self, a part of a childhood self which was irreplaceable.

Sometimes he would awaken to the sound of a scratching somewhere in the room, and he would sense the presence of his childhood thoughts, but aimless now, detached from the body of his childhood self. Vague hungers and long forgotten yearnings floated through the room. All night and all day the scratching continued, as the tooth kept up its futile attempt to chew through his belongings—impossible without an opposing tooth to press against—as it hungered to eat its way through to his present life.

TRASH

The uninformed observer might conclude that his apartment was full of trash—a trash heap, a garbage pile. This wasn't true at all, of course, but the result of American cultural prejudice. Trash was worthless discard, refuse of no utility. Americans threw away basic utility all the time—containers for holding things, cans and plastics that could be cut into other shapes, and an immense variety of parts of things, knobs and hooks and protuberances of all sorts—much that could be called "spare parts." There were also all the recyclables, but that was a different argument.

Trash was anything left over: pieces too small to save, torn bits, non-reusables, organic debris. Anything which resisted inventory. The best trash showed clear evidence of its manipulation, or more often, destruction by human hands or teeth. He supposed this made this category, legitimately, "artefact" trash. He got rid of most such things after a brief study of the signs they displayed of human use, but there was always a bit he kept in a plastic container labeled "Trash" (and therefore capable of inventory)—a representative sample of all that he deemed permissible to throw away.

Non-artefact trash, trash which had been so thoroughly destroyed that it showed no signs of humanity, depressed him. It made him feel insignificant.

Some people were called "trash," although he had never used the expression in that way himself. He supposed this to be some sort of ultimate insult. And just like the trash he accumulated, there were also people who had been untouched by human hands.

Now and then he would take out his one container of TRASH and study it. Assorted debris filled his hands, fell between his fingers. With each new study the pieces became a bit less recognizable. Eventually, all the trash, human and nonhuman alike, would be so reduced as to be unrecognizable.

Then we would all be as one, he thought. All of it undifferentiated trash. There seemed no escaping it.

And all of it beyond the powers of inventory.

TOUCHES

After he'd lived in the apartment for so many years, not surprisingly his touches were everywhere. Certainly on every square inch of his furniture—except perhaps on backs or other obscure regions. Oil and dust with the trademark of his fingertips had layered until they had become almost a paste recording his arrivals and departures, his retrievals and his releasings.

Counting such touches was purely theoretical, of course. He finally determined a figure for the probable number of touches per square inch of surface, then assigned a multiplier figure for each surface based on his estimate of how many layers of touches had adhered to that particular place.

Some touches were more surreptitious, stealing through the air and kissing his belongings absentmindedly and leaving no mark to indicate that they'd been there. But he did not think he would have wanted to count such special, ephemeral events, even if an estimation had been possible.

Sometimes the shape of these prints, or the amount of oil they contained, seemed far removed from anything his fingers might have produced.

Sometimes he found prints on surfaces he could not possibly have touched, such as the bottoms of lamps.

Such anomalies disturbed him, and he might even spend a few nights awake attempting to catch in the act the source of these alien touches. A long time ago he'd decided he needed to know everything about his environment.

He liked to imagine sometimes that the objects were altered by his touches, at least in the most minute, chemical way.

He liked to think that, whatever happened to him, at least this much might remain: the ghosts of his fingertips searching, finding, soothing, departing, driven by his very human need to touch everything he saw, and thereby make it his own.

CANDLES

Old and yellow, the four candles had come to resemble his skin. He couldn't quite remember who had given them to him—although he should have, having received only a few presents in his lifetime—but he knew the giver could not have been a friend. The candles reminded him of the weaknesses of his own flesh, how the more he lived, the sooner his death might come.

And yet there were still events which inspired him to light the candles: the birth of a child to a friend or relative, the death of an acquaintance, some national or international event which he considered to have enormous impact upon a great number of people.

As life went on, the candles burned; they melted down to nothing.

Eventually he discovered, however, that many people weren't like candles at all. They were lumps of grey clay or they were splintered pieces of stone. They would not melt, whatever the heat or fuel applied.

His skin might be yellow, but at least during the night his head burned bright, so brightly his pillow had grown brittle as ash.

Melting was something you naturally did every day, if you were doing anything more than sleepwalking with your time. Age melted the youth from your face. Feelings melted, as well, and ideas. If you generated feelings and ideas of enough strength, you always left a residue behind on those you came into contact with.

At this point in his life he was mostly brittle, blackened wick that sparked and sputtered but gave no steady flame. His skinny hands had an antique waxy sheen.

But at night, on the edge of sleep, the room still danced with molten light.

CEILING

So finally it all came down to this: an old man on his back in bed, staring at the ceiling. He could not move his head, could not turn to see his things scattered across the rug. But all his things did not matter anyway. His inventory at last complete, all that was important now was the ceiling.

Even in the dark the ceiling was soft and luminous, all one thing, all one ceiling. In fact it looked as if the walls were capped by the sky itself, a dim milk sky going on forever.

The old man chose one area of ceiling for study, then another, and another. There it was—it was all the same thing, the same patch of world, and yet it was everything.

At last all the clocks chimed, the fasteners fastened, hair and teeth returned to their heads, and ashes built back into flesh. The old man found a proper pair of shoes and chose some well-fitting gloves. He stood on his bed and raised his gloved hands to the ceiling, where they searched slowly for the edges of an opening.

At last finding the door in his ceiling, the old man opened it and pulled himself up and out of his apartment. He closed the door firmly behind him. He stood up in the darkness and waited for the lights to come on, for someone to arrive and guide him.

Waiting there he began counting all the things left in his head: the one hundred twelve things he might have done with his child, the fourteen secrets he'd never told his mother, the twenty-two good wishes he reserved for perfect strangers.

ABOUT THE AUTHOR

Steve Rasnic Tem was born in Lee County, Virginia in the heart of Appalachia. He currently lives in Centennial, Colorado with his wife, the writer Melanie Tem. His novels include *Excavation*, *The Book of Days*, the recent *Deadfall Hotel* and, co-written with wife Melanie Tem, *Daughters* and *The Man On the Ceiling*. He is the author of over 350 published short stories, and is a past winner of the Bram Stoker, International Horror Guild, British Fantasy, and World Fantasy Awards. He was also a finalist for the Philip K. Dick, Shirley Jackson, and Theodore Sturgeon awards. His other story collections include *City Fishing*, *The Far Side of the Lake*, *In Concert* (collaborations with Melanie Tem), *Ugly Behavior*, and *Onion Songs*.

You may visit the Tem home on the web at *www.m-s-tem.com*.

PUBLICATION HISTORY

"The World Recalled" originally published as a chapbook by Wormhole Books, 2004

"The Disease Artist" originally appeared in *Dark Arts*, John Pelan editor, IHG nominee, 2006

"Halloween Street" originally appeared in *F&SF*, nominated for IHG and the Bram Stoker (reprinted *Year's Best Fantasy & Horror* and *Best New Horror*), 1999

"When We Moved On" originally appeared in *Clockwork Phoenix 2*, Mike Allen editor, 2009

"The Woodcarver's Son" originally appeared in *Offworld*, Winter 1993

"Invisible" originally appeared in *Sci Fiction*, IHG and Bram Stoker nominee (reprinted *Best Fantasy of the Year*, Rich Horton) 2005

"Head Explosions" originally appeared in *Bust Down the Door and Eat All the Chickens* #5, 2007

"Chain Reaction" originally appeared in *Black Static* #19, 2010

"The Secret Flesh" originally appeared in *Pulphouse: The Hardback Magazine* Issue 11, Kristine Kathryn Rusch editor, 1991

"Origami Bird" originally published as an Independence Day greeting card by Wormhole Books, 2002

"In These Final Days of Sales" originally appeared as a chapbook from Wormhole Books, winner of the Bram Stoker Award (reprinted *Year's Best Fantasy & Horror*), 2001

"Little Poucet" originally appeared in *Snow White, Blood Red*, Ellen Datlow & Terri Windling editors, 1993

"The Bereavement Photographer" originally appeared in *13 Horrors*, Brian A. Hopkins editor, IHG nominee, 2003

"Firestorm" originally appeared in *Perpetual Light*, Alan Ryan editor, World Fantasy Award nominee, 1982

"The Mouse's Bedtime Story" originally appeared in *Bedtime Stories to Darken Your Dreams*, Bruce Holland Rogers editor, 1999

"Last Dragon" originally appeared in *Amazing Stories*, Sept. 1987

"The Monster in the Field" is original to this volume

"The High Chair" originally appeared in *Flytrap* #6, 2006

"Dinosaur" originally appeared in *Asimov's*, May 1987

"Giant Killers" originally appeared in *The Pedestal Magazine* (online), issue #61

"The Company You Keep" originally appeared in *Outsiders*, Nancy Holder & Nancy Kilpatrick editors, 2005

"Celestial Inventory" originally appeared as a chapbook from Chris Drumm Books, 1991

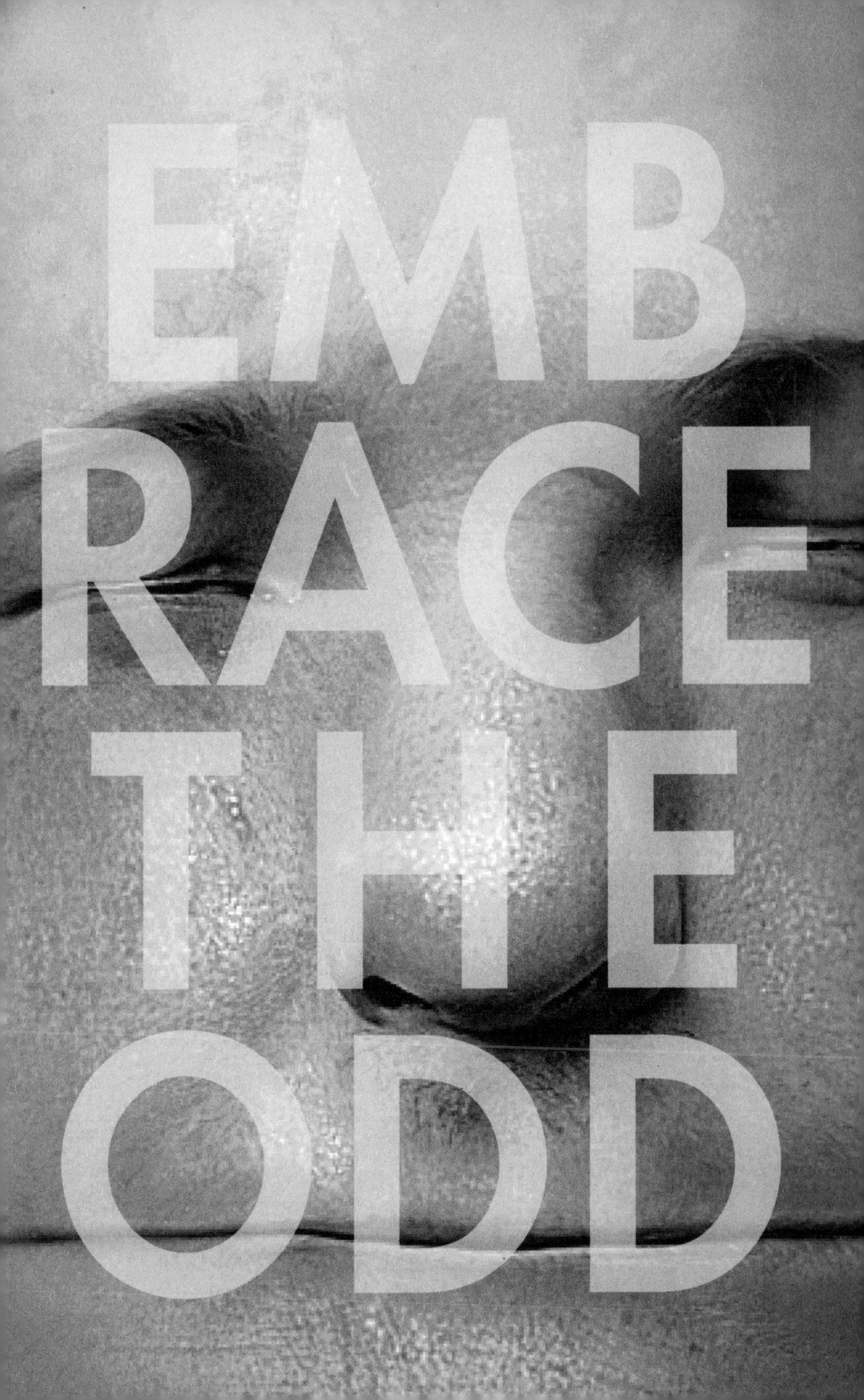
EMB
RACE
THE
ODD

THE INNER CITY
KAREN HEULER

Anything is possible: people breed dogs with humans to create a servant class; beneath one great city lies another city, running it surreptitiously; an employee finds that her hair has been stolen by someone intent on getting her job; strange fish fall from trees and birds talk too much; a boy tries to figure out what he can get when the Rapture leaves good stuff behind. Everything is familiar; everything is different. Behind it all, is there some strange kind of design or merely just the chance to adapt? In Karen Heuler's stories, characters cope with the strange without thinking it's strange, sometimes invested in what's going on, sometimes trapped by it, but always finding their own way in.

AVAILABLE NOW
978-1-927469-33-0

GOLDENLAND PAST DARK

CHANDLER KLANG SMITH

A hostile stranger is hunting Dr. Show's ramshackle travelling circus across 1960s America. His target: the ringmaster himself. The troupe's unravelling hopes fall on their latest and most promising recruit, Webern Bell, a sixteen-year-old hunchbacked midget devoted obsessively to perfecting the surreal clown performances that come to him in his dreams. But as they travel through a landscape of abandoned amusement parks and rural ghost towns, Webern's bizarre past starts to pursue him, as well.

AVAILABLE NOW
978-1-927469-35-4

THE WARRIOR WHO CARRIED LIFE
GEOFF RYMAN

Only men are allowed into the wells of vision. But Cara's mother defies this edict and is killed, but not before returning with a vision of terrible and wonderful things that are to come . . . and all because of five-year-old Cara. Years later, evil destroys the rest of Cara's family. In a rage, Cara uses magic to transform herself into a male warrior. But she finds that to defeat her enemies, she must break the cycle of violence, not continue it. As Cara's mother's vision of destiny is fulfilled, the wonderful follows the terrible, and a quest for revenge becomes a quest for eternal life.

AVAILABLE NOW
978-1-927469-38-5

ZOMBIE VERSUS FAIRY FEATURING ALBINOS

JAMES MARSHALL

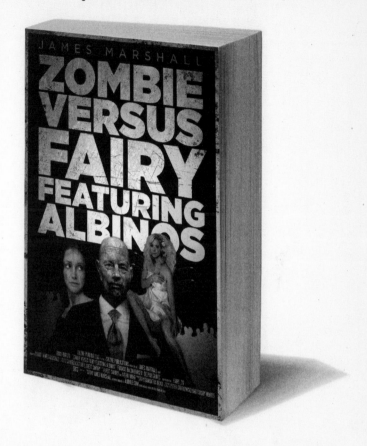

In a PERFECT world where everyone DESTROYS everything and eats HUMAN FLESH, one ZOMBIE has had enough: BUCK BURGER. When he rebels at the natural DISORDER, his marriage starts DETERIORATING and a doctor prescribes him an ANTI-DEPRESSANT. Buck meets a beautiful GREEN-HAIRED pharmacist fairy named FAIRY_26 and quickly becomes a pawn in a COLD WAR between zombies and SUPERNATURAL CREATURES. Does sixteen-year-old SPIRITUAL LEADER and pirate GUY BOY MAN make an appearance? Of course! Are there MIND-CONTROLLING ALBINOS? Obviously! Is there hot ZOMBIE-ON-FAIRY action? Maybe! WHY AREN'T YOU READING THIS YET?

AVAILABLE NOW

978-1-77148-141-0

THE MONA LISA SACRIFICE
BOOK ONE OF THE BOOK OF CROSS
PETER ROMAN

For thousands of years, Cross has wandered the earth, a mortal soul trapped in the undying body left behind by Christ. But now he must play the part of reluctant hero, as an angel comes to him for help finding the Mona Lisa—the real Mona Lisa that inspired the painting. Cross's quest takes him into a secret world within our own, populated by characters just as strange and wondrous as he is. He's haunted by memories of Penelope, the only woman he truly loved, and he wants to avenge her death at the hands of his ancient enemy, Judas. The angel promises to deliver Judas to Cross, but nothing is ever what it seems, and when a group of renegade angels looking for a new holy war show up, things truly go to hell.

AVAILABLE NOW
978-1-77148-145-8

THE 'GEISTERS
DAVID NICKLE

When Ann LeSage was a little girl, she had an invisible friend—a poltergeist, that spoke to her with flying knives and howling winds. She called it the Insect. And with a little professional help, she contained it. But the nightmare never truly ended. As Ann grew from girl into young woman, the Insect grew with her, becoming a thing of murder. Now, as she embarks on a new life married to successful young lawyer Michael Voors, Ann believes that she finally has the Insect under control. But there are others vying to take that control away from her. They may not know exactly what they're dealing with, but they know they want it. They are the 'Geisters. And in pursuing their own perverse dream, they risk spawning the most terrible nightmare of all.

AVAILABLE JUNE 2013
978-1-77148-143-4

IMAGINARIUM 2013
THE BEST CANADIAN SPECULATIVE WRITING

EDITED BY SANDRA KASTURI & SAMANTHA BEIKO

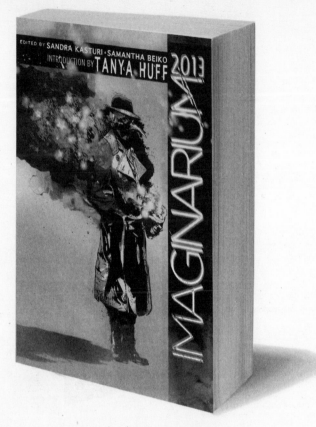

INTRODUCTION BY TANYA HUFF
COVER ART BY GMB CHOMICHUK

A yearly anthology from ChiZine Publications, gathering the best Canadian fiction and poetry in the speculative genres (SF, fantasy, horror, magic realism) published in the previous year. *Imaginarium 2012* (edited by Sandra Kasturi and Halli Villegas, with a provocative introduction by Steven Erikson) was nominated for a Prix Aurora Award.

AVAILABLE JULY 2013
978-1-77148-145-8

THE SUMMER IS ENDED
AND WE ARE NOT YET SAVED

JOEY COMEAU

Martin is going to Bible Camp for the summer. He's going to learn archery and swimming, and he's going to make new friends. He's pretty excited, but that's probably because nobody told him that this is a horror novel.

AVAILABLE JULY 2013
978-1-77148-147-2

CHIZINEPUB.COM CZP

TELL MY SORROWS TO THE STONES
CHRISTOPHER GOLDEN

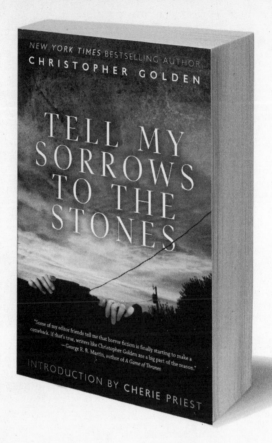

A circus clown willing to give anything to be funny. A spectral gunslinger who must teach a young boy to defend the ones he loves. A lonely widower making a farewell tour of the places that meant the world to his late wife. A faded Hollywood actress out to deprive her ex-husband of his prize possession. A grieving mother who will wait by the railroad tracks for a ghostly train that always has room for one more. A young West Virginia miner whose only hope of survival is a bedtime story. These are just some of the characters to be found in *Tell My Sorrows to the Stones*.

AVAILABLE AUGUST 2013
978-1-77148-153-3

MORE FROM CHIZINE

MONSTROUS AFFECTIONS DAVID NICKLE [978-0-9812978-3-5]

EUTOPIA DAVID NICKLE [978-1-926851-11-2]

RASPUTIN'S BASTARDS DAVID NICKLE [978-1-926851-59-4]

CITIES OF NIGHT PHILIP NUTMAN [978-0-9812978-8-0]

JANUS JOHN PARK [978-1-927469-10-1]

EVERY SHALLOW CUT TOM PICCIRILLI [978-1-926851-10-5]

BRIARPATCH TIM PRATT [978-1-926851-44-0]

THE CHOIR BOATS DANIEL A. RABUZZI [978-1-926851-06-8]

THE INDIGO PHEASANT DANIEL A. RABUZZI [978-1-927469-09-5]

EVERY HOUSE IS HAUNTED IAN ROGERS [978-1-927469-16-3]

ENTER, NIGHT MICHAEL ROWE [978-1-926851-02-0]

REMEMBER WHY YOU FEAR ME ROBERT SHEARMAN [978-1-927469-7]

CHIMERASCOPE DOUGLAS SMITH [978-0-9812978-5-9]

THE PATTERN SCARS CAITLIN SWEET [978-1-926851-43-3]

THE TEL AVIV DOSSIER LAVIE TIDHAR AND NIR YANIV [978-0-9809410-5-0]

IN THE MEAN TIME PAUL TREMBLAY [978-1-926851-06-8]

SWALLOWING A DONKEY'S EYE PAUL TREMBLAY [978-1-926851-69-3]

THE HAIR WREATH AND OTHER STORIES HALLI VILLEGAS [978-1-926851-02-0]

THE WORLD MORE FULL OF WEEPING ROBERT J. WIERSEMA [978-0-9809410-9-8]

WESTLAKE SOUL RIO YOUERS [978-1-926851-55-6]

MAJOR KARNAGE GORD ZAJAC [978-0-9813746-6-6]

"IF YOUR TASTE IN FICTION RUNS TO THE DISTURBING, DARK, AND AT LEAST PARTIALLY WEIRD, CHANCES ARE YOU'VE HEARD OF CHIZINE PUBLICATIONS—CZP—A YOUNG IMPRINT THAT IS NONETHELESS PRODUCING STARTLINGLY BEAUTIFUL BOOKS OF STARKLY, DARKLY LITERARY QUALITY."

—DAVID MIDDLETON, *JANUARY MAGAZINE*

ALSO AVAILABLE FROM CHIZINE PUBLICATIONS